THEY COULD HAVE NAMED HER ANYTHING

ADVANCE PRAISE FOR *THEY COULD HAVE NAMED HER ANYTHING*

"Stephanie Jimenez's characters want to know, desperately, sincerely, where they might belong. In pursuit of this question, they cross borders and expectations—of class and race, of their roles as women, daughters, fathers, lovers—barreling through their mistakes with clear-eyed hope that it will pay off. *They Could Have Named Her Anything* is a powerful reminder that moving between worlds is rarely free, and that the most valuable educations take place outside the classroom."

—Danielle Lazarin, author of *Back Talk: Stories*

"*They Could Have Named Her Anything* is a profound exploration of desire: the desire to fit in, the desire to understand ourselves, the desire to be accepted for exactly who we are. As our characters reckon with their own yearnings in a New York City full of dichotomies, this novel pulls us thrillingly between the Hamptons and Queens Boulevard, the private school system and working-class life. Stephanie Jimenez comes to her debut with rare insight and extraordinary empathy, bringing us characters so real they feel like family."

—Danya Kukafka, author of *Girl in Snow*

"This gorgeous debut from Stephanie Jimenez brims with visceral details. *They Could Have Named Her Anything* captures all of the aggressive beauty and tension of growing up, the complexity of families, and what it's like to come of age in a city among millions. I was immediately drawn in by Maria, Jimenez's sharp and observant protagonist, and her vivid, urgent journey."

—Natalka Burian, author of *Welcome to the Slipstream* and *A Woman's Drink*

"*They Could Have Named Her Anything* is surprising, explosive, charged with suspense and drama as it travels from Queens to the Upper East Side to Las Vegas. And yet, it's also contemplative and introspective, an intimate portrait of one young woman, stuck between secrets and lies, her responsibility to her family, and her own dreams. This book kept me guessing, intrigued, and revisiting my own adolescence, as I read to see how far Maria Rosario would go in her pursuit of her own life."
—Naima Coster, author of *Halsey Street*, finalist for the 2018 Kirkus Prize

"Lyrical, sophisticated, and oh-so-real, *They Could Have Named Her Anything* will take your breath away. Full of powerful, no-nonsense girls who know what they want and who'll do anything to get it, *They Could Have Named Her Anything* is a timely love letter to womanhood, the messiness of friendship, and the city of New York."
—Ashley Woodfolk, author of *The Beauty That Remains*

"In *They Could Have Named Her Anything*, Stephanie Jimenez has constructed a beautiful, unflinching narrative about the time in one's life when we go from being defined by what others think of us to unapologetically embracing our complicated and fluid selves."
—Natalia Sylvester, author of *Everyone Knows You Go Home* and *Chasing the Sun*

"Stephanie Jimenez uses ultra-fine brushstrokes to paint a portrait of two families intertwined by fate and desire, wanting and becoming. With flawless eye for detail, we see just how differently the same city can look, even from the eyes of friends. Tightly drawn characters and beautifully woven plotting reveal the simple truth that coming of age for young women in the modern era is never simple at all. As Maria navigates a tightrope walk as a scholarship student from Queens in the world of elite private education, she learns the adult world is not what it seems and that bitter often comes with sweet. A haunting, unsparing tale of girlhood from an important new voice in literature."

—Meghann Foye, author of *Meternity*

THEY COULD HAVE NAMED HER ANYTHING

A NOVEL

STEPHANIE JIMENEZ

Little
a

Excerpt from THE HOUSE ON MANGO STREET. Copyright © 1984 by Sandra Cisneros. Published by Vintage Books, a division of Penguin Random House, and in hardcover by Alfred A. Knopf in 1994. By permission of Susan Bergholz Literary Services, New York, NY and Lamy, NM. All rights reserved.

Published by Little A, New York

www.apub.com

Amazon, the Amazon logo, and Little A are trademarks of Amazon.com, Inc., or its affiliates.

ISBN-13: 9781542003742 (hardcover)
ISBN-10: 1542003741 (hardcover)
ISBN-13: 9781542003759 (paperback)
ISBN-10: 154200375X (paperback)

Cover design by Faceout Studio, Spencer Fuller

Cover illustrated by Ronald Wimberly

Printed in the United States of America

First edition

For Xiomara Useche Jimenez, my closest friend

All you wanted, Sally, was to love and to love and to love and to love, and no one could call that crazy.

—*The House on Mango Street*, Sandra Cisneros

QUEENS, NEW YORK

MAY 2006

CHAPTER 1

In the Rosario household, where four people lived on the first floor of a two-family home in Queens, where the tenants upstairs were always changing but the names on the mailbox never did, where instead of a backyard there was a long stretch of cement behind a row of attached shingle houses, and where there was no full-length mirror before the front door, Maria was never alone. Even in her bedroom, the sound soaked into and right through the walls. She was never alone when she was at home, which was why today was a special day.

"Virgins always suffer the most," Andres said. He reached into his black Nike drawstring bag, which he carried with him everywhere. It was what he used to transport his textbooks and money and weed. That morning, on his walk to Maria's house, he had packed it with something new. She was explicit about her instructions to stop at the pharmacy, because she knew what he kept inside his drawers at home, and she wanted a fresh one, one that wouldn't break. She smiled now when he pulled out a condom, and with it, fell out a receipt.

Andres's fingers were slender and long. Looking at them filled Maria with yearning. She knew Andres was concerned about physically hurting her, but this—like everything else they'd done together— would likely be fine. Above her, Maria could see the beige of the ceiling, where a fat water mark was laid over another, making an impression like

Saturn's rings. She was getting uncomfortable lying there, as if she were wearing a wet bathing suit she was itching to get out of. She helped him by rolling off her underwear and weaving her ankles out of each hole.

"Open," Andres said, pressing onto her legs.

He pushed, and Maria felt his reach in her mind. It was as if a thousand new neurons in her brain had been activated, and her voice dimmed to make space for the others that arose. It started with her father and brother, warning her about the evils of men. *Don't trust us,* they were saying. *We're rotten. We're liars.* But those voices quickly grew tiring.

Maria looked at Andres. She wanted him to glance at her, but he seemed in deep concentration. She mimicked his solemn intensity, trying to approximate whatever he was feeling. She concentrated until she heard a different voice.

But the unit of the visit, / The encounter of the wise,— / Say, what other metre is it / Than the meeting of the eyes?

Finally, Maria laid her head back. Not her family. Not Andres.

Emerson.

Maria's eyes were still closed when he pulled his boxers on. She thought today would be special, but now that it was over, it seemed so mundane. Sex could be happening on every school night, or in the mornings before she got on the train, and as long as nobody was around to hear it, nobody would ever know. This was an exhilarating fact as much as it was dreadful. It hadn't been good enough to want to repeat over and over again.

"Should we go get food?" Maria asked.

Andres said nothing. He still hadn't picked up his shirt off the floor. The morning light streaked his abdomen. He was seventeen, like her, but unlike her, he worked out every day at the gym. Every time she looked at him, she appreciated his beauty. His shoulders were like a yoke. His lower stomach narrowed into an arrow that always pointed downward.

"You move like a corpse," he said. "And you sure you're a virgin? You didn't even bleed."

Maria flinched. He was right—virgins always suffered the most. From her endless religion classes at Bell Seminary, she knew that much was true. Mary, most obviously, who watched her only son undergo the most gruesome public death. St. Agatha, whose wealthy family couldn't save her from having her breasts chopped off before languishing in prison. And St. Lucy, whose devotion to God was so singular that she gouged out her own eyes after a suitor told her they were the loveliest shade of brown he'd ever seen. All of these virgins had suffered, but none of them had even flinched. Not like Maria had just now at the thought of being a corpse.

"I didn't realize . . . ," Maria said. The bow of her lip was trembling. It was still so early that she didn't hear anyone outside. Her window faced the front of the house, and usually, on a nice Saturday in May, there was the song of children playing. By noon, the ice-cream truck would take over. But now, it was quiet. She could be noisier next time. Saints suffered in silence, but Andres didn't know that. He wanted to be able to hear it.

"Let's try again," she said. "Let's do it one more—"

The sound of a key turning ripped into Maria's bedroom, as if it were her own doorknob being pushed.

"Hide!"

She jumped up from the bed. Andres threw her forest-green beanbag toward the door and ducked at the foot of her twin mattress. Because they shared a front door and entry hall with the people upstairs, the house resembled an apartment unit, and her parents were already in the living room just as she switched off her light. They were talking outside her closed door. Andres and Maria held their breaths.

"She's asleep," her mother said.

Maria strained to listen. She heard her parents' feet make contact with the linoleum divider that separated the dining room from the living room. The kitchen was at the end of the house, and attached to it was a door that led out back. Once you were there, the hum of the refrigerator and the whir of the ceiling fan were so loud, you might not notice footsteps in the living room. They had an open floor plan, but the kitchen was in a nook to the left of the house, just behind her parents' bedroom, and back there, it was impossible to see the front door.

"Get up," Maria whispered.

But Andres didn't move. She peeked over her mattress, where he had sprawled out on her gradient floor rug, striped in pink and violet. He was holding her journal open. It was a gift from a second cousin whom Maria had only met once when she visited New York from Ecuador, and the cover image was made of gold leaf and depicted a magical forest with purple mushrooms. As a girl with three piercings in her upper cartilage, who just celebrated her seventeenth birthday that March, Maria knew she had long outgrown it. Secretly, though, she wrote poems in it every night with pens that alternated between red, blue, and green tubes of ink.

Andres was staring at the last page she'd written on. She'd used looping cursive.

If love his moment overstay,
Hatred's swift repulsions play.

"Maria, what the fuck is—"

Maria grabbed the journal out of his hands and slammed it shut. Now, she was just as angry as he must have been when he decided to call her a corpse. She thrust a finger over her lips, and he shut up. Slowly, she inched her bedroom door open. Outside, there was nobody in the living room, as she suspected, and quickly, as if she were crossing a busy street, she ushered him out of the door. When she closed it and replaced the tiny door chain, she stood there, counting. The house was at the end of the block, and by the count of ten, Andres would have descended the steps onto the curb and disappeared, anonymous, onto another street, and far out of the sight of the Rosario parents.

In the living room, she could barely hear their voices.

"It's not an option," her father said. "She needs to work."

Maria moved closer. She brought down her feet toe by toe. When she had crossed the carpet into the dining room, she leaned forward and held on to the wall, making sure not to unhinge the baby photos of her and her brother, Ricky, hanging in white plastic squares. The photos were peeling away from the corners, revealing glimpses of the sample images that had come packaged with the frames. Under the dog-eared image of Maria measuring her height against an orange traffic cone was the black-and-white snout of a golden retriever.

"I agree with you," Maria's mother said.

"Then why don't you take her to work with you?"

"Are you crazy? You know she would never clean."

"She has to!"

"Shh! She's still sleeping!" Her mother's voice quieted so Maria could barely hear. "She doesn't need to clean houses with me, Miguel. She can apply anywhere. She just needs her working papers."

"Where does she get those?"

"Bell Seminary."

It was confirmed. They were talking about Maria. Her dad had lost his job a month ago, and that same week, he had sat her down and told her to readjust her expectations about college. He suggested taking a year off to work. As if someone had taken a branding iron to her skin, Maria had started screaming.

"You know she's going to freak out," her mother said.

"Don't tell her right now."

"What are you waiting for?"

She fled to her bedroom. If she hadn't heard him suggest it himself, she would have never believed it. Maria was supposed to be the special one—the exempted one. She'd been awarded a full scholarship at Bell

Seminary, a school so elite it once was the abode of the richest man in the state of New York. She'd never told anyone about how her mother had been a maid who cleaned apartments in the same Upper East Side buildings her classmates lived in. How, recently, her mother had been forced to return to that work, and if her parents had their way, they would force Maria into it, too. She slammed the door, hoping they'd hear her. She had cried when they told her that they couldn't afford college tuition, boulders and rivers and typhoons of tears, and now she was crying again, in just the same way.

Outside her bedroom door, Maria heard footsteps race over the linoleum. But they stopped in the living room, just short of her bedroom. They never knew what to do when Maria was having an episode of despair. In the Rosario household, where Maria always felt her parents nearby, where someone would sing a song and minutes later, Maria wouldn't remember whose voice she was listening to, where her parents loved her so much they never quite knew how to make her understand it, Maria felt so alone.

In algebra class, they were given assigned seats early in the year. Maria, who got her worst grades in math, was assigned to the front of the room. Usually, she didn't mind sitting in the front because that's where Karen, who was the only other girl who lived in Queens, passed her perfect origami cranes made of notebook paper during class. But Maria, whose eyes were puffy and whose head felt clogged up with water, didn't feel like sitting in the front of the room today.

"I'm sitting there," Maria said, pointing her finger at the desk where Amanda Combs sat. Amanda was a girl who was wiry and had blond hair all over her, hair in places where it shouldn't be. She looked like an overgrown infant. By that point, Maria knew that certain girls at Bell Seminary were intimidated by her, though she didn't know exactly why. Sometimes, it was isolating. Other times, it was useful.

"You can't," Amanda said. "We're not allowed."

Maria clicked her tongue. It sounded the way Velcro does when it rips. It was the way her mother did it at home whenever she was annoyed. But Maria knew that girls at Bell Seminary didn't grow up with that noise, because whenever she did it, they frowned. To them, it was a foreign sound. It gave Maria her power.

"Get up," Maria said. "I'm giving you permission."

Amanda stood. She went to the front and sat in the seat Maria abandoned. When class started, Mr. Willoughby noticed Maria had traded seats.

"Maria," Mr. Willoughby said. "That's not where I put you."

Girls made Mr. Willoughby nervous. Maria knew this, and so did lots of her classmates. At the time he was hired, the class above Maria's had replaced all the dry-erase markers. He went to write the "Do Now" on the board and pressed down on the whiteboard with a tampon. When the girls at Bell Seminary told this story, they always said the next part with disgust. He dropped it as if it were a severed finger. As if the tampon he was holding were used. As if he'd been holding something squirming—alive. *Idiot,* they'd all say, when they got to that part.

"I know, Mr. Willoughby," Maria said, leaning over her desk. She uncrossed her legs, parted them slightly. She felt her purple bra strap fall off her shoulder. "But I'm comfortable here. See?"

Mr. Willoughby inhaled like something smelled really good.

"Whatever, Maria," he said.

Maria felt a firm tap on her shoulder. Rocky was sitting behind her wearing a pair of dark sunglasses. An extralarge cup of coffee made a brown ring on the desk. Rocky was a chocolate brunette who had such heavily bleached golden highlights that they sometimes looked white, giving her the appearance of a comic book superhero. A pack of cigarettes peeked out of the breast pocket of her black denim jacket.

Maria had always known Rocky was different from the other popular girls in the grade. The rest of them all wore matching ballet flats and

Tiffany hearts. Rocky had a Planned Parenthood sticker on her laptop, and she rubbed black eyeliner under her eyes. Rocky had never paid any attention to her before, so Maria tried not to, either.

"Nicely done," Rocky said. "That was professional."

Maria smiled. "You either got it or you don't."

"Rocky," Mr. Willoughby said, interrupting them. "Your sunglasses, please."

The whole class turned around in their seats. Rocky lifted her head and looked around, as if regarding her audience.

"Rocky," he repeated. "Now."

Rocky straightened her jacket. She brought her fingers up to her face so they framed her right lens. Slowly, seductively, like a French movie star, she looked at Mr. Willoughby and pulled the sunglasses off her face. All the girls in the room started giggling, including Maria.

"Let's talk later," Rocky whispered, leaning over her desk. Her breath was hot on Maria's neck. "We can learn from each other."

Maria nodded and turned to face the front of the room, trying to contain her surprise. Near the whiteboard, Karen was staring, puzzled. Maria shrugged with her face, then took out a pencil. For the rest of the class, she looked at the clock every couple of minutes. Rocky had never spoken to her before. Maria wondered what they would learn.

By the end of the day, Rocky had renamed her.

"Tell me about yourself," Rocky commanded. She leaned against the lockers with her arms crossed. It was late, and the sound of lockers slamming reverberated down the hallway. "Where do you live? What music do you like? What do you like better—chocolate or vanilla?"

"Strawberry," Maria replied, which made Rocky laugh.

Although Rocky was just now learning about Maria, Maria had always known about Rocky. She was an outlandish presence at the school. Rocky wasn't like other girls—defined by a rigid and particular sense of elitism, by opera and theater at Lincoln Center and weekly copies of the *New Yorker*. Instead, she used her wealth to circumvent rules; on one day she might wear Dior flats, on others she stomped into class in combat boots paired with a J.Crew V-neck, and on still others, she'd look just like Maria—in Chuck Taylors with hearts drawn all over the rubber sides. Nobody ever thought any less of Rocky for all her flamboyant multitudes. Rocky laughed at other people's goals, and she often told her classmates that greed is good. Maria had long been fascinated by all of these things about Rocky, who was really only a girl named Rachelle who had gotten every one of her teachers to call her by what sounded like a stage name.

Maria, who had spent three years at Bell Seminary studying and observing her peers, already knew all of these things about Rocky. Rocky hadn't seemed to know anything about Maria, though. Now, she was playing catch-up.

"I have a friend crush on you," Rocky confessed. "But it's your turn. Ask me anything."

"What's your favorite food?"

"Oysters," Rocky said. "But I can't even eat them. I'm allergic to shellfish."

"Shellfish? I've never eaten that fish."

Rocky burst into laughter. "You've never eaten that fish?" She looked at Maria doubtfully. "It's long and white. It tastes like tuna. Fillet of shellfish? You sure?"

"No," Maria said. "Haven't had it."

Rocky bent over at the waist in laughter. When she finally got up, she clapped Maria on the shoulder. "That's it. From now on, you're Shelly. That's perfect because it's like Rachelle, like my name. Shelly never suited me."

Maria wasn't sure it suited her, either, but because Rocky made it seem like a wonderful gift, Maria accepted.

"Shelly, why don't you come over? I'm meeting my math tutor now." Before Maria could answer, Rocky rolled her eyes. "I know," she said. "So lame. It's only because he's helping me get through these finals."

Maria could use a math tutor. She had always been jealous of the girls who could afford them. Her grades in math hovered between a C and B minus, which always made her anxious. To keep her scholarship, she needed to keep her grade average at least at a B.

Maria rolled her eyes, too. "Fuck math."

They walked away from the lockers. Rocky took Maria's arm in her own. Maria had seen how the girls at Bell Seminary often linked arms, and usually, she didn't like when people touched her, but at the feeling of Rocky hanging off her elbow, she tried her best not to tense up.

On the first step of the spiral marble staircase, a twenty-dollar bill was transformed into a small bird. Maria stooped to pick it up and undid its edges so that the panels came apart in multiple origami folds. She had never seen a piece of currency so beautiful; her heart fluttered in her chest.

"Nice spot!" Rocky said.

Maria looked around. The hallway had already emptied.

"We're running late," Rocky said. "Keep it."

Maria fingered the bill. She could stretch it so it lasted four or five days on afternoon pizza and soda. Or she could use it tomorrow morning on cupcakes with stabilized frosting and specialty coffees with whipped cream and cinnamon pearls, the way other Bell Seminary girls did before coming to school.

"Greed is good," Rocky said. "Let's go, Maria."

Maria felt the tube in her inner ear constrict once, then again at the sound of her proper name. The paper cranes that Karen gave her were always made out of notebook or printer paper, and she'd never seen Karen fold money before. But the wings fit perfectly into the lines of her palm, and Maria recognized Karen's handiwork. Maria could put it near the windowsill in her bedroom, along with all the others that Karen had made her. Or she could take it apart, unfold it and spend it, and no one would know the difference.

"It's Karen's," Maria said, leaving Rocky behind on the stairwell as she darted back down the hall.

Maria hadn't taken longer than a minute to tuck the bill into Karen's locker, but when she returned, Rocky's face was twisted. Maria pushed past her onto the staircase.

"Don't act like that," Rocky said, taking the flight two steps at a time before she caught up. "How was I supposed to know it was hers?"

Rocky's parents weren't home. The girls had only needed to walk six blocks from Bell Seminary before reaching Rocky's apartment. Leading up to the building was a long velvet red carpet, as if they were entering a movie premiere. The lobby had been enormous, too, and the doorman had followed them to the elevator to press the button up to the fifteenth floor. When Maria finally stepped into the unit that Rocky lived in, her jaw dropped. From the massive sunlit living room overlooking Fifth Avenue, Central Park shrank like an overgrown hedge outside of a two-family house, like the hedge outside Maria's home. Rocky's apartment was dead quiet, which was different from where Maria lived, where silence was rare among the sounds of pans clinking, the shower running, her mother yelling her brother's name from the next room—the space always clean but so cramped you could feel the air like a body, huffing over your shoulder and reading the words from your book.

Rocky went around each room, switching on lights. When she returned, she placed three tiny bottles of sparkling water on the table. They sat there, alone, waiting for the tutor. Rocky explained that the doorman would let him upstairs.

"Where are your parents?" Maria asked.

"Not here," Rocky said. "My parents can't stand each other."

"Are they divorced?"

"They want to wait until I graduate."

"That's stupid," Maria said.

"Fifty percent of marriages end in divorce. Are your parents divorced?"

"No," Maria said. She felt her cell phone in her back pocket. On the walk to Rocky's apartment, she had texted her mother that she would be home late. Her parents didn't like when she got on the train past dark, but they wouldn't give her that hard of a time if the reason had to do with school.

"So what's your deal?" Rocky said. "Do you have a boyfriend?"

"Yes," Maria said.

"Have you had sex?"

Maria's eyes widened. How did Rocky know she'd had sex just that week? Maria hadn't told anyone yet, and she didn't know how to tell Rocky that sex with Andres didn't seem worth recounting. Maria's family had made sex seem monumental, and in Sunday school they'd told her to wait until marriage, but Maria couldn't understand why. That week, her mother continued washing the dishes, Ricky kept playing video games in his room, and nobody seemed to notice Maria, or that she was now, supposedly, irrevocably changed.

"Only once."

"What's his name?"

"Andres."

"Oh my God," Rocky said. "Was it amazing?"

Ever since she'd been called a corpse, she'd been yearning to ask someone for advice. But Rocky, who wore red lipstick to her classes, had definitely never been called a corpse before. What if Rocky laughed at her now? She chewed on her lip, deliberating.

Rocky seemed to understand Maria's silence—that she was wrong, and nothing about sex with Andres was amazing.

"Oh no," she said. "That's a shame. But aren't Hispanics supposed to make the best lovers?"

Maria's face crinkled up like a ball of paper.

"It's Latino. Latino lovers."

Rocky giggled. "The phrase is *Latin lover*, Shell. And what do you mean, anyway? I'm not supposed to say Hispanic? I'm supposed to say Latino? Why? What's the difference?"

"I don't . . . It just sounds better."

Rocky cocked a doubtful eyebrow. Suddenly, Maria felt completely frivolous, as if she were trying to separate a kidney bean from a pinto bean.

Someone knocked on the door.

"That's him," Rocky said, jumping up from her seat. "We'll talk more later about . . . Andres." She giggled again and darted out of the room.

To Maria's surprise, Rocky had rolled the *r* in his name perfectly. Maria reached for her backpack under the table. When she pulled out her algebra notebook, the crumpled working papers fell out, too. Everyone knew what those looked like. They were rectangular and bright yellow. She quickly stuffed them back into her bag.

The tutor's face was paler than Rocky's. Peering behind his glasses and beard, Maria couldn't put an age to him. He seemed to her a person who spent time in libraries, and Maria wasn't usually shy around strangers—only people she thought might be smarter than her. It was the same when the school dean came down the hall and glared at her Sharpie-stained school skirt. Whenever that happened, Maria worried about arriving home to parents who sobbed as they told her that the school realized their mistake, after all, and decided Maria wasn't a good fit for Bell Seminary.

"Hi," the tutor said, extending his hand. Maria took it and shook—firmly, like her teachers always told her.

"Hi," she said, willing herself to look into his eyes. They were brown and wet, and Maria thought they must look like hers. She was heartened. "I'm Maria," she said, a bit loudly.

"I call her Shell," Rocky said.

Maria's shoulders stiffened.

"Thank you," the tutor mumbled as Rocky pushed the seltzer toward him. They waited for Rocky to fish a pencil whose tip wasn't broken out of her bag. Only after the tutoring session started did Maria's shoulders finally loosen, because it was then, as the tutor pointed at Rocky's textbook with his eraser, that Maria saw he had no interest in knowing how she had earned her nickname.

There was only one unopened bottle of seltzer left on the table, motionless among the textbooks and pens, after the tutor was gone. Rocky reached for the cigarette carton she had laid on the table at the beginning of the session, alongside her algebra textbook. Again, the girls were alone.

"It's late," Rocky said. "Why don't you stay over? I can give you clothes to sleep in."

Maria looked at the time. It was already past eight, and it would take over an hour to get home on the train. She hadn't been expecting Rocky Albrecht, of all people, to invite her over, much less to stay the night. Maria was flattered. Rocky had this whole apartment to herself, it seemed, and Maria could be sure that she also had things like cable TV and pay-per-view. She probably even had a whole collection of music that wasn't even downloaded illegally—Rocky Albrecht probably purchased it all, on iTunes. Maria texted her mom again. Her mother didn't like when she walked down Queens Boulevard alone at night, anyway.

"Where's your mom?" Maria asked as they walked down the hallway to Rocky's bedroom. At the bedroom, Rocky stopped and pointed down at Maria's shoes. Maria looked at her Nike sneakers, blunted at the toe, and white, if not for the occasional brownish spot. Maria kicked them off by the heels and saw her socks, one striped green and one yellowed white because she could never find a matching pair, and decided to take those off, too. Her toenails were flaked with stray pieces of nail polish, detritus of a home pedicure she'd done months ago, but now, with both sneakers and socks stripped off, there was nothing more Maria could do. Barefoot, she proceeded into Rocky's bedroom. The carpet was the softest she'd ever stepped on, but Rocky led her around the queen-size bed, past the walk-in closet, and ushered her into the bathroom.

The mirror cabinets were flung open. Inside, there were small armies of bronzer. Finally, Rocky took off her jacket, and Maria understood they'd reached their destination. Rocky leaned out of the open window, and the light from the street made her closed eyes look like two thinly veined petunia petals. There was something about Rocky that seemed to be flowering; when she spun her head, she smelled like gardenia and honeysuckle, and her arms were covered in soft woolen fuzz, the way that leaves of some plants are.

"My mom's staying at the country house this week," Rocky said, but by then, Maria had forgotten she'd asked.

"Do you have siblings?"

"A little brother. He's also hardly ever home."

Rocky repositioned herself on her enormous black granite sink so that she came into a low squat, and took a new cigarette out of her pack. She put the filtered side into her mouth, connected it to the glowing red end of the one she'd already started smoking, and then puffed incessantly. She then offered it to Maria.

"Thanks," Maria said. Because of Andres, she'd smoked a few cigarettes before.

From where they leaned out the window, Maria could see cars racing below. Three fire trucks sped by and Maria heard nothing. Rocky lived on the fifteenth floor, and the noise would never be strong enough to scale all those stories and climb into the window the way it did at Maria's house. Maria watched as Rocky flicked the ash off her cigarette into the newly set night sky, where it floated in place before descending. Maria's chest hurt, and she couldn't tell if it was the cigarette or something else. She thought of her mother cleaning apartments. She wondered if she'd ever been inside one as beautiful as this.

When she checked her cell phone, her mother had answered. OK. Did u get the working papers, she'd asked. Maria hastily typed.

"Shelly, you're not in love with Andres, are you?" Rocky asked, exhaling and speaking at the same time. "I think love is a sham."

"Not always," Maria said. She placed her hand over her belly. It felt more swollen than usual. At the thought of being pregnant, her soul shrank like a sundried grape. There was nothing that she needed more than to go to college. Even though her parents were asking her to take off the year, it didn't seem like something she could actually do. It was impossible to give up college after getting so close—just as impossible as becoming pregnant seemed. Both would be a death sentence—of the Maria she knew herself to be, anyway.

"Yes, always," Rocky said. "Don't you know you shouldn't trust anyone?"

They sat in silence. Rocky's cuticles were so neat they looked like the pressed edges of a laminated page. But when she hoisted her skinny arms over the ledge, Maria couldn't see her fingernails anymore.

Maria suddenly felt the enormity of the apartment, of those vast, empty rooms. She thought of Rocky sitting here on most nights, staring out her bathroom window with no way for anybody below to recognize her. She knew that Rocky couldn't mean what she was saying. For one, she'd trusted Maria. Showing a person your home was one of the deepest expressions of trust. There were very few people who had seen Maria's.

"I don't agree with you . . . ," Maria said, softly. "Emerson said, 'Give all to love . . . / Plans, credit and the Muse.'" Maria paused. "'*Nothing* refuse.'"

Saying the words made Maria's eyes water. She frantically blinked the tears away. Backlit against the harsh bathroom lights, Rocky's cheeks were faintly shadowed in tiny blond hairs. She stubbed her cigarette on the brick siding of the building.

"I used to like art, too," Rocky said.

She floated away into her bedroom, so that Maria was now alone. Maria threw her cigarette down the side of the building and followed Rocky out of the bathroom. From her closet, Rocky pulled out an air mattress, a big blue sausage, and hurled it to the ground at the foot of her bed. Then, Rocky turned off all the lights, just as Maria found the wall outlet, and the mattress began to inflate with a roar.

"I used to act," Rocky said, yelling over the sound. "In eighth grade, I was the star of *The Wizard of Oz*."

Maria tried to find Rocky's eyes in the darkness. "Dorothy? Can I see pictures?"

Rocky hadn't seemed to hear Maria's question.

"Now, the only plays the school puts on are Shakespeare," Rocky said. "Which is just as gay as whatever you just recited."

The roar of the mattress inflating stopped. *Gay* would be another battle—just like *Hispanic*—and Maria didn't know whether it would be worth trying to correct Rocky Albrecht. The more she thought about it, the more she came to think they weren't wrong in the same ways, either—what made *Hispanic* unsettling was its nonspecificity, and *gay* was only a bad one to use when it came out of the mouth like a slur. What Rocky meant to say is that she didn't like poetry, and she didn't memorize lines of it like Maria did. She should have known this. But Maria had expanded her vocabulary so drastically since attending Bell Seminary that maybe sharing the poem was an exercise in showing off what she'd just learned. Maybe it was only a gift she wanted to share with Rocky, the benefit of learning new words and understanding, more fully, how to use the ones she already knew.

"Still," Maria said, settling onto the air mattress. "You should be acting."

"Not at Bell Seminary," Rocky said. "Audrey Hepburn never played Juliet in high school."

"Who's that?"

Rocky laughed into the darkness, the sound taking on a weight of its own. "Audrey Hepburn? Who's Audrey Hepburn? Or did you mean Juliet?"

"I know her," Maria lied, and of course, she didn't mean Juliet. After *A Midsummer Night's Dream, Romeo and Juliet* was her favorite Shakespeare play.

But Rocky still hadn't stopped laughing, and the sound became heavy, unable to be ignored, like another body in the room. For the first time that day, Maria wondered what she might look like from Rocky's perspective. Maybe it looked like there was nothing inside that was bothering Maria. Or maybe it looked like Maria was only a shell of a person, and there was nothing inside her at all.

Maria was only asleep for a few minutes before she woke up to what she thought was the sound of someone whispering her name. "Rocky?" she asked, into the dark. But Rocky didn't answer. In her sleep, Maria had been adding up and dividing numbers in her calculator, the way the tutor had taught them only hours earlier. She woke up confused and exhausted, her brain jumbled from the arithmetic, and too revved up to fall back asleep. On her phone, a message was waiting. The room became bright. Maria pulled the screen close to her chest to mask the glare.

OK mami, her mother had written. TQM. I love you. Good night.

Maria was fully awake now, getting up noisily from the inflatable mattress and walking toward the living room to call Andres. He had seen Maria walk by one Tuesday night when she had come home late after school. Since then, Maria and Andres had been dating, but Maria always had the creeping suspicion that there was someone else in Andres's life, some public school girl that she'd never meet, who knew how to do all kinds of things that she didn't, like cook perfect pots of rice or dance a flawless bachata. At Maria's old middle school before Bell Seminary, she thought she could remember girls like that.

"Hey, baby," Maria said from Rocky's living room couch. "Did I wake you up?" She scratched at her weeks-old home manicure, scattering little red flecks on the ivory-colored carpet. From where she was contorted, she could see the front door to the apartment.

Andres sounded far away on the phone, as if he had the receiver partially covered. Maria thought she heard the sound of laughter in the background. "No. I was awake."

"What are you doing?" Maria heard a giggle again. She was sure she already knew the answer; he must be watching TV.

"Homework."

Maria laughed. "You never do homework!"

"Only you do, right?" Maria felt an insult coming on, and her fist balled up on the couch. Andres used to write letters to her that professed his love. She didn't know when things changed, only that his insults were usually iterations of the same nonfact: *You are such a white girl.*

"That's not what I'm saying," she said. "Is somebody with you?"

Andres laughed. "I'm just fucking with you. I was smoking a blunt."

Andres's voice became suddenly clear, and Maria had the impression she'd just been taken off speakerphone. He was probably at a friend's house, whichever one out of the dozens, and this friend had probably started laughing as soon as he'd heard Maria refer to Andres as *baby*.

"You know what's crazy?"

Maria grated her teeth. "What?"

21

"I wasn't smoking a blunt."

"How is that crazy?"

"Because you always think I am! I'm hanging up, Maria."

Maria was so mad when he hung up that she hurled the phone across the carpet so she wouldn't be tempted to call him again. Sometimes, she didn't understand why she bothered with Andres. Over spring break, and just after her father told her that she might need to hold off on college, the Bell Seminary juniors were taken to Vassar on a prospective-student trip. She had imagined college would be just like high school, but as she glanced around, in the classes, on the lawns, she realized that nobody looked like they'd come out of Bell Seminary. Hardly any of the girls were wearing makeup and some boys even had arm tattoos, and most shocking of all, they weren't even all white, and even the ones who weren't white were smiling. On the bus back to the city, Maria was melancholy, and every time they hit a pothole, she let her head bang on the window. She didn't want to go back to Bell Seminary, she didn't want to go back to her bedroom in Queens, and she didn't want to stay trapped with Andres forever. Maria feared that something horrible would happen if she couldn't manage to escape.

Recalling that trip now filled her with a longing so acute it made her gasp. She sat upright, and once she was sure it had passed, she lay on her back again. *Love is a sham,* Rocky said. Maria placed her hands on her stomach and folded them this time as if saying grace, as if praying to whatever was out there that nothing, not love and not anything like it, had taken root inside of her.

All at once the room came into focus: the starchy fabric couch, the oil painting on the wall of two girls playing piano, the built-in bookcase with so few books they were like teeth in the mouth of a baby—and she recognized Rocky's living room. At first she didn't know where she was when she heard the front door slam, much less how long she'd been lying there, but now she clearly saw his shape at the door. He looked at her from the entryway, not moving any closer, as if he'd just stumbled upon a rare bird that could be easily frightened away.

"That doesn't seem like the most comfortable place to sleep."

"Sorry," Maria blurted out. She scrambled to an upright position, not knowing if she should stand. Earlier that night, she had changed into a collared pajama shirt that Rocky had handed to her to sleep in. At home, she only slept in extralarge T-shirts with various logos splattered across the chest, and when she saw herself in the mirror earlier, she'd loved how she looked in the soft button-down. But now, she realized she wasn't wearing a bra. She crossed her arms tightly over her chest.

It wasn't her chest he was looking at, though. His eyes were resting upon her face, as if the most wonderful poem were written there.

"'Beauty is God's handwriting,'" he said, slowly. His voice was soft and sweet, a dish of caramel flan. "Someone smarter than me said that."

Maria covered her mouth, then uncovered it.

"That's Emerson . . . isn't it?"

He started to take off his jacket. Even from across the room, Maria could tell it was beautifully made. She knew her father would go to his grave never having tried on a jacket like that. He draped it across a chair upholstered in a smoother fabric than anything in her mother's closet. "Emerson," he said, nodding slowly. He brought his fingers to the bridge of his nose and squeezed, as if he had a headache. When he brought them away, his face was smooth again.

"How young are you?"

"Seventeen."

"I'm Charlie. What's your name, Seventeen?"

"I'm Maria," she said, and no sooner had she said it than she remembered watching *West Side Story*, the one and only time that she did. She could never forget how horrified she was, the singing and lunging and terrible hair, and worst of all, the accented English. Not English the way she learned it in school—the English of all the classic poets and great novelists. Remembering now the *Ah-meh-dikas*, Maria spoke with haste. She didn't usually tell anyone she was Maria Anís, the Anís coming from her mother, Ana Lisette, who changed her name to Analise once she got her citizenship, and then shortened it further for Maria's sake. People already tripped over saying Maria the way she wanted it said—even with white people, she sometimes had to insist that the English pronunciation was what she preferred.

"You can call me Annie, mister."

He fanned his hand in the air, correcting her. "Charlie," he said. "Your brain must be an interesting place. What else is in there? Got any more poetry for me?"

Maria stammered. No one had talked to her like this—ever. All she could think of was the mantra that had one day popped into her head when she first started attending Bell Seminary.

"Strange is the place / all strangers begin / Through darkness and light / like planets they spin."

"It's settled, Seventeen. You can stay. But from now on, you sleep in a bed." He smiled. "Pick a bed, any bed. We have six or seven bedrooms. Eight? I don't know. I lost count years ago."

Maria's eyes finally adjusted. She saw he was due for a shave, but with his tie, he looked important—as glamorous as Rocky did in her pastel nail polish. In his suit, he looked like someone she'd try to make room for if they were both walking down the same side of the street. The slight bags under his eyes, she saw, made him look sophisticated. Rocky's dad was fascinating, and somehow Maria had impressed him, and she wanted to continue impressing him. She found herself trying with her whole body, her back straightened so tall that it hurt.

When he turned away, Maria stood and followed. His bedroom wasn't far down the hall. He walked through the open door, but she stalled, not crossing into the heart of the bedroom, where only a slightly larger bed than Rocky's hid in the shadows. She leaned against the dresser at the entrance of the room.

"The best view of the city is here," he said, gesturing at the window. He began taking off his cuff links.

Outside, there were clouded lights everywhere, and rivers that saddled the island on either side. It was Emerson, too—Emerson gawking at the skies, gawking like Rocky's father did now at the buildings below—who said: *we are made immortal through the contemplation of beauty.* On some nights, right before the breaking of dawn, she and Andres and his gaggle of friends would wait on the elevated train platform in Queens, and as she looked across the river at the skyscrapers, at the moment before everyone would wake up and go about their everyday lives, she would fill up with a very strange feeling and know she'd beheld the sublime. Something about those moments really did feel immortal, even though they were gone as soon as the next train arrived and Andres and his group clambered on board, loud and stomping, hooting and howling like animals.

Now, Maria was silent. The man she had followed was the reason the Albrechts appeared every year in the school's donor catalog. She stole a glance at him, imagining the gold lining on the pages, and as if he had sensed she had taken something from him, he looked at her with such a look that Maria instantly recognized it. It was the same look Andres had given her the day she first walked by him on the boulevard, the pleats of her skirt dancing around the back of her bare legs. It was a look she knew because her mother taught her to be wary of it: *See how that boy looks at you?* Rocky's father's wasn't a boy, but the look was identical.

"Emerson said—" Again, Maria stammered. She knew the exact lines, why wasn't she getting it right? But Charlie didn't rush her, so Maria cleared her throat. "He said we're made immortal through contemplating beauty."

"Of course," he said, smiling. "I could live forever just by looking at you."

A window flew open, exposing her chest. It floated up her throat like a hiccup, involuntary. It came out unthinkably: her giggle.

She had been complimented before—but only by the brawny twentysomething-year-olds outside of mechanic shops, guys that made her anticipate growing up. It was one thing to hear those things on the street, where she knew she was to never make eye contact and walk on. Neither her uncle nor brother—men who had repeatedly warned her about the evils of other men—had ever instructed her on what to do if she found herself in a dimly lit bedroom, on the fifteenth floor of a high-rise apartment, with a compliment so wonderful, so real, it felt as if she could hold it in her palms.

"You're so smart," Charlie said, coming toward her. He took her hand, gently parting her fingers. Into her palm he dropped his cuff links, smooth and golden. "I can see you being a professor, one day."

Maria had never seen anything like them before. She bounced them in her hand. She wanted to ask if she could keep them.

Suddenly, her phone started buzzing frantically.

"Go ahead," he said. "But next time I see you, I hope you'll recite me something else."

Maria bent at the knees, her head lowered, and spread her fingers out as if positioning for a handstand. Onto the floor, the cuff links fell, making the sound of two heavy marbles hitting each other head-on. She dashed out of the room, but when she picked up the phone, she didn't hear anything. "Hello," she kept saying, over and over again, but Andres must've only called her by accident.

She looked down the hall where she came from, her heart racing. It only took a moment for her to decide. She couldn't go back, at least not yet. First, she would need to decide on a poem.

In the room, Maria was startled to see that Rocky was awake in her bed. The light in the bathroom was on.

"What'd you find?" Rocky said. She was lying on her side, with her head propped up on two pillows.

"What?"

"You were wandering." Her voice was monotonous, cool. Maria tried searching Rocky's face, but she didn't know which signs to look for. No one person, she suddenly realized, looks exactly the same when they're angry.

"I was on the phone with Andres," Maria said, cautiously.

"You sure it wasn't your mom?"

Maria was silent.

"I'm kidding, Shelly. I'm teasing you."

The comforter rustled as Rocky pulled it up to her chin. Outside, it was dark, but there were already signs of morning. Violet spilled over the horizon like a shade of watercolor paint.

"Poor thing." Rocky yawned. "On the phone with Andres. Remind me tomorrow to teach you about sex, okay?"

As if to dismiss her, Rocky closed her eyes.

CHAPTER 2

Charlie could never recall hearing coughing or sniffling, so he never anticipated the days when Khil would call in sick. He wouldn't know until after he'd step out of the elevator, until he avoided looking at the mirror that hung above two Tuscan urns overflowing with a delicate lace of green leaves, until he was close enough to see if his hair was standing up. From there to the lobby, he had to descend a flight of stairs, walk past a few tables, more planters, more flowers, a marble tube that housed a fleet of tall, black umbrellas, and then past a less forgiving mirror where he would forget to look down, and in which he would see, framed between curly gold spirals, just how exhausted he looked. The doorman would open the front door, then walk quickly ahead of him to open the door of the idling black car, and only then would Charlie know that Khil was sick, that the company had sent a substitute to drive him the half-hour ride to the office.

In the elevator, Charlie held on to his briefcase and watched as the numbers dinged. When he first bought the apartment, Veronica hadn't been able to stop telling her parents, who still lived in their old neighborhood in Westchester, about how odd it was, how when she first walked in, she thought they had walked past the gates of El Dorado because everything was lined in different shades of gold, and as they went down the hallway, each shade became deeper than the last. That was when Rachelle was still only two years old, and Nick not even a prospect, and Charlie had laughed and said she ought to stop saying that, that there really was another building in the city called Eldorado and that it wasn't to be confused with their building, which was newer, less stuffy, and better located, anyway, and if she could believe it, even pricier.

She had rolled her eyes, but later, on the first night in their new apartment, Veronica confessed how excited she was. She said she felt like a teenager who had snuck out of her bedroom and made it to the front road, the smell of grass all around her. He knew in that moment how lucky he was to have married someone who understood his life so completely. The two of them were from the same hometown, so it made sense that they'd shared similar experiences. The earthy smell of the ground beneath his feet, his adolescent heart pumping with adrenaline—it was as if she had plucked the memory directly from his heart.

That was then, years ago. Charlie couldn't remember the last time his wife said anything that made him feel like a teenager.

As the doorman held the door open for Charlie to step into the black Crown Victoria, Charlie was surprised to learn Khil was sick. He heard Alan before he saw him.

"Hey, Mr. Albrecht!"

Charlie shuddered. He deeply disliked Alan. Alan was loud and boisterous and was incessant with questions. Khil, on the other hand, always seemed to be in perfect sync with Charlie's moods—some mornings, feeling jubilant, they talked the entire way to Charlie's office in the financial district, and on others they sat in silence as they kept their pensive gazes out the window. Khil also liked art and literature, and he put on the most wonderful jazz, music that bubbled and soothed like champagne. He introduced Charlie to a tabla player named Zakir Hussain, who had apparently once toured with Bob Dylan and the Los Angeles Philharmonic. Khil even told Charlie when Hussain was playing in New York City at Lincoln Center. Charlie was out of town that weekend, but he appreciated the gesture. Alan, on the other hand, didn't have taste like Khil did. He was lardy and rough, all working-class bravado. Charlie found it hard not to roll his eyes whenever Alan said something.

"So, happy Thursday, right? We made it past the damn hump day."

"Where's Khil?"

"Sick! Sick as a dog! Almost summer and people are still getting sick as *dogs*."

Charlie brought his hand to his forehead.

"Not you, though, Mr. Albrecht. You're looking like a picture of perfect health. Like always."

It was enough to be so obnoxiously loud at seven in the morning, but now the man was mocking him. Charlie was sensitive about the bags growing under his eyes. His senior year superlative in high school was "most likely to get ID'd at forty." He was aware of the fact that he had started to look old.

"I have something to read before I get in." Charlie goofily lifted a pile of papers, a useless set of notes assembled by an assistant from last week's status meeting, so that Alan could see them through the front mirror. Alan wouldn't be able to discern what they were.

"I'll drive nice and easy," Alan said. "Don't get carsick on me."

As Alan drove, Charlie relaxed his head back. He could see his thoughts as if peering through droplets on a windshield—everything was obscured. Suddenly, Alan coughed, and it was as if a wiper ran over Charlie's mind. He saw her again. *Seventeen.*

He held her image in his mind like a still snapshot until finally it became a reel: him lifting the hem of her shirt.

With this fantasy in focus, Charlie felt his face flush. Sometimes Charlie talked about women with Khil, only because Khil always shook his head in compassion, like a priest willing to offer absolution. *I know we're married men,* Charlie would say, *but how about her?* In front of them, a young woman, no doubt somebody's intern, would be crossing in a too-tight pencil skirt. And Khil would chuckle, the slow flicker of his eyes looking into the rearview mirror as he changed lanes down Fifth Avenue. *Oh boy,* Khil would say, and he sounded so earnest, Charlie would go on and on. Khil's measured chuckles reassured him his bad behavior only made him a man, not a monster.

Charlie wouldn't dare bring Seventeen up with Alan, whose mannerisms were tasteless and depraved. Charlie was sure that Alan would stick out his tongue or lick his lips or do something even more ludicrous and disgusting that would only mortify Charlie. She was his own daughter's age, after all. But his daughter was moody and difficult and mean—whereas the girl wasn't anything like that. She'd quoted Emerson to him for God's sake. He didn't know that second poem she recited, the one about planets and strangers, but it was adorable how much she wanted to impress him. If he hadn't dismissed her, if he hadn't sent her away, she would've followed him like a puppy to bed.

When they pulled off the highway, Charlie folded up the papers he was no longer even pretending to read. He stuffed them back into his briefcase.

"Tell Akhil I hope he gets well soon," Charlie said, reaching for the door handle.

Alan laughed uproariously. "Akhil! Who's that?"

Charlie's eyes incised the mirror through which he could see Alan's fatuous grin.

"No, no, I know what you mean, boss," Alan said, who only now, after a half-hour drive, seemed to care that Charlie was irritated. "Akhil will be back tomorrow."

Charlie opened the door and stepped out, anxious to light his cigarette. He was still a block away from his building because there was a cobblestone pathway that led to the entrance and that, for historical preservation reasons that the firm's staff cursed whenever it rained, couldn't be driven on. He thought of how many days Khil had picked him up over the past nine years, when he decided to hire a permanent driver, rather than rely on vomit-soaked yellow cabs. He thought of the number of tips he had given him over the years, like for Christmas, when he slipped him hundred-dollar bills for most of the month. Khil always asked him how work was going, and Charlie went into long tangents about deals that would or wouldn't come through, numbers and derivatives and terms that he knew Khil couldn't possibly understand, but that he would listen attentively to, anyway. In addition to Charlie's tall cup of coffee and the occasional shot—very occasional shot—of gin, Khil was an integral part of Charlie's mornings, a part that Charlie missed when it was gone. So he had his name wrong, but so what? He had been close enough.

As Charlie approached the blue turnstile doors of his building, a sharp breeze reached him from the river, nearly knocking him over. The wind spooled around him like a thousand threads and yanked him back at the joints like a puppet. Fighting, he stumbled forward into the lobby. He skipped steps on the escalator and looked down at his BlackBerry. Instantly, Khil was forgotten, replaced by meetings, reminders, phone calls, calendar invites, more phone calls, and a few meals. Seventeen blew out of his mind, too, like a mandala blown into oblivion, though later that day, it did make him smile again. Out of all the people to woo a teenage girl. He chuckled. Emerson.

Rocky woke up smearing the saliva off her face with the back of her hand. It was no use—whether she fell asleep on her side or her back, a steady stream would find its way from her mouth to the center of her pillow, blooming like a hydrangea head alongside her face.

Maria was still asleep. She had seemed wide awake when the tutor left the night before, but now she looked unshakable. When she'd come back to the room, she looked wide eyed and scared. Maybe she'd been arguing with that boyfriend, Andres. There was so much Rocky knew she could teach her about men, starting with her own mother's mantra: "They're dirt."

Rocky sat up and watched how the sun stretched long rectangles of light across the carpet. If she stared at the space just above the ground, she could see clouds of dust suspended in air. They seemed to be making their own tiny orbits as if circling some invisible planet. She sat like that for a while, watching the dust float in space, and thought about her mother. Her parents usually slept on different sides of the apartment, but recently, her mom hadn't been coming home at all. She'd been staying at their country house in Long Island for the past several weeks. Rocky liked having the apartment to herself, but sometimes, she felt compelled to call her, just to say hello, just to talk. The last time she'd done that, her mom sounded annoyed. *Yes, Rachelle?* she'd answered. Rocky was put on the spot, so she whined about not having anything to wear. Veronica told her to call Isabel if she needed the laundry done, and Rocky said that she would, and Veronica promptly hung up.

Rocky's jaw clenched. Her chest became tight, as if she were wearing a corset. She didn't want to be sitting in bed anymore. She kicked out her legs from under her sheets and swung her feet to the ground. She didn't even feel how creamy and lush the fibers were under her toes.

She went to the kitchen, wanting coffee, but once she was standing by the refrigerator, she noticed the hunger instead. She opened the fridge and found an entire loaf of bread, unopened. She pushed aside a jar of mayonnaise, past a tub of margarine, but didn't see any eggs. She located a jar of blueberry jam instead. With a big, suction kiss, the top came apart from the bottom. The lid was crusted over in blue, and her fingers were now stuck together with jam.

Rocky knew it'd been a long time since Veronica had been home just by looking around the kitchen. On the stand where there were usually paper towels, there was only a cardboard cylinder. They'd been out of napkins for weeks.

But two nights ago, Rocky had ordered chicken wings for dinner and stuffed what was left of them into the garbage can. She opened the lid now and dug. Inside, a safe distance away from the greasy bones, was an unused plastic knife as well as a stack of square napkins. They looked clean enough. With her arm still plunged into the trash, she wiped her fingers clean of blueberry jam.

"Breakfast?"

Maria had changed out of Rocky's pajamas and into her uniform. She was wearing the polo she'd worn yesterday and the Bell Seminary blue kilted skirt. Rocky dropped the napkin and pulled her arm out of the trash.

"Help yourself," Rocky said, just as the toaster's bell rang.

Two slices of bread leaned out of the mouth of the toaster oven. Maria grabbed one and hurried to the table. Rocky watched as she smeared the jam on in thick slabs. Suddenly, Maria let go of the bread.

"Ah!" Maria screamed, pointing.

Right at the edge of a lumpy streak of jam, Rocky saw it—an aquamarine lump, textured like a piece of gum flattened on concrete. Rocky stared but didn't understand what she was looking at. She had an idea, but still, she wasn't sure.

"How did you not notice?" Maria got up from the table and went to the toaster. With both hands, Maria yanked.

"This one, too," she said, her voice harsh. "They're all bad. It's disgusting!"

Rocky stomped over to the refrigerator and opened the door for the third time. Again, she pushed past the mayonnaise and margarine, and finally looked at the bread. Each slice was a unique shade of blossoming green. She tried to think of the last time her mother had been home but couldn't remember. The last person who'd stopped by that week was Isabel, the cleaning lady whom the doorman knew to let upstairs. Isabel should have found the bread first. Isabel should've been stopping by more often. Rocky remembered her last conversation with her mother. Why should Rocky be in charge of the chores? Why couldn't Veronica do that?

She pulled the green loaf out of the fridge and put it on the counter. "Aren't you going to throw it out?" Maria asked.

"No," Rocky said. "The cleaning lady will."

As they rode down the elevator, Rocky saw a look on Maria's face, a certain intonation she used when she commented that she was still hungry, that made Rocky angry. Before reaching the school, they stopped at the Dean & Deluca's near Rocky's apartment, and behind a set of see-through doors, Maria picked up a chocolate chip muffin and inspected it for excessively long, tilting it from various angles, as if Rocky couldn't see what she was doing. "This one looks okay," she finally said, and Rocky gritted her teeth. *After enough time,* she thought, *everything goes bad,* but still, she said nothing to Maria. As Rocky collected the change from the cashier, Maria wandered ahead of her, her mouth already full.

For the rest of the day, even when they went downstairs for lunch, the two girls hardly spoke. At three, Rocky saw Maria coming out of the bathroom and walked past her, toward her locker. Her face was pointed into her books when she heard Maria's voice.

"Hey, Rocky," Maria said. "I'm going home now. Thanks again for breakfast."

Rocky grimaced, but if Maria knew how annoyed Rocky was, there was nothing in her voice that showed it.

"You mean that muffin?" Rocky said, without looking away from her textbooks. "That was nothing. I'll see you tomorrow."

Only after she heard Maria's footsteps down the hall did she close her locker door. *Who does she think she is,* Rocky thought now, *judging me for just a bit of mold?*

On the train to Queens after school, there were too many people. There were always too many people on the ride home. Maria hated having to balance her book bag on her lap, hearing the grumbles of the people sitting next to her, their annoyance with her stinking like bad breath.

With its balustrades and bougainvillea, its carved, wooden doors and secret gardens, the Upper East Side existed as if caught under the thin glass of a snow globe, and it always took Maria a while to adjust after exiting this tiny terrarium to enter the jungle of regular city life, full of its wild inconveniences and unexpected smells and millions and millions of people. She could feel it, always slightly painful and jerky, like her body was changing gears. Something would have to click into place before she could go on being her usual self, pushing through crowds on the subway, walking as if she were in a footrace, operating in a constant state of low-level fear and frustration.

Her mother was outside the house, sweeping the porch. She stopped as soon as she saw Maria heaving toward the house, her backpack swinging so low Maria had to be careful it didn't lift up her skirt.

"Long time, no see!" Maria's mother called out into the street, raising her voice so that it cut through the sounds of everything else—a car blowing its horn, a teenager biking down the sidewalk, a dog barking from where it was imprisoned behind a window. She held the broom in one hand and posed the other on her hip. "Was the tutor any help?"

Maria climbed the two steps up to the porch. The Rosarios lived on the ground floor of a two-family home, and Maria's parents, as the property owners, saw fit to decorate the house however they liked. Aside from a multitude of tiny American flags stuck into the soil of a row of potted geraniums, there were various plaster statues painted and molded to resemble animals. On each step there was a plaster statue—the first was a puppy holding a daisy in its mouth, the second was a bespectacled frog holding up a sign that inexplicably read "Wellcome." When her mother first brought it home, Maria railed against it, demanding they get rid of it, and she may have even been successful had the tenant upstairs not told Maria's mother que el coquí era precioso, and after that, the little frog had officially cemented its position on the porch.

Every time Maria passed it, she still heard the questions in her head, like how many frogs had been shipped out to retailers before the manufacturer realized the mistake? How many women like Maria's mother had purchased the frog without even noticing? Why didn't anyone care as much as she did? She tried not to look at the frog today when she stood next to her mother and leaned into her face for a kiss.

"Yeah," Maria said. "The tutor helped."

Maria went into the hallway and walked past the staircase that led to her neighbor's floor. On the right was the door that led to the Rosarios' apartment. Nobody left their shoes in the hall because Maria's mother strictly forbade it. *The hallway is not a storage unit,* she told everyone. But once inside, there was nowhere to take off one's shoes, and not even a closet for coats. It was one source of her mother's seemingly unending frustration—how people walked right in, dragging in the mud, and everywhere they went things became dirty. It was also one of the reasons that Maria's mother was always cleaning. Maria walked into the living room with her sneakers still on, to the sound of a brass-horn love ballad. It was always love ballads when her mother was cleaning. It was always women's gravelly voices, horns like torrents of tears.

Even with the lights off, the heat coated everything, bubbling up the walls of the room like a pot of boiling water. Maria went straight for the corduroy futon, throwing herself onto the cushions. She poked her finger into the hole left by one of the uncles, sienna foam exposed from where he'd left his cigarette. Her mother had cried when she found it, but now it was part of the order of things, and she often passed the vacuum over the hole to gather up lint that collected there.

The couch sank under Maria's weight. Her legs and her arms relaxed. The couch was her charging dock; she could feel herself gaining power. She closed her eyes, absorbing heat from the sunbeams that peeked past the blinds until she no longer noticed the way they cast bright spots on her eyelids like fireworks in a July night sky.

In those explosions of light, she imagined Charlie.

She saw the worry lines creasing his forehead when he laughed. He smelled faintly like citrus, lemon or lime. He'd been wearing shoes of the richest leather she'd ever seen. But none of those things were even the best of it. The best was the way that he'd looked at her. Not the way Rocky did, who only saw a shell. Not even the way Andres looked at her, like she was made of pure sugar. Actually, it wasn't the way he looked at her at all.

It was the way she had been seen.

Suddenly the music changed, and Selena came on. Whereas everyone else liked the hits, the only song that Maria really loved was a manic song called "El Chico del Apartamento 512," which was about one woman's high-energy obsession with her forbidden neighbor. Maria sprung off the couch twirling. She cocked her hips to the left and the right. She thrust her hands up in the air and when they came down, first they went down the length of her neck, then her collarbone, then pushed on the flesh that curved there. She felt around her breasts. They seemed larger, and even though it hurt when she pressed, it was a pain that felt good. As she held her hands there, she sensed someone behind her. Her hands fell to her sides as if she'd been struck dead.

"So you still like my music," her mother said. "You know, that's the worst part about cleaning other people's homes. You never get to play your own songs."

Maria thought of Rocky's rotten bread. She could think of much worse things.

"Why wouldn't I like it? I love this song."

"You don't seem to like anything I do anymore."

Maria could feel a fight coming on. "I don't want to clean people's houses! Those people in those neighborhoods go to my school!"

"It's not that." She clicked her tongue, the way Maria always did when she wanted someone at Bell Seminary to shut up. "It's other things."

She left Maria to attend to a pot in the kitchen. Maria went to the bathroom, and on the toilet, she flushed away a burgundy wad of toilet paper. Maria had already said a little prayer that morning when she saw the coppery trail of her period in Rocky's toilet, but now, she brought her hands together and gazed up at the ceiling. Her mother had once warned her that she could get pregnant instantly, that *one second* was all the time it took. Maria had seemed to follow all the steps to prevent it from happening, but since first having sex with Andres, her paranoia that she was pregnant increased each day. From her squat on the toilet, Maria closed her eyes. *Thank you,* she said again.

Her father was sitting at the kitchen table when she came out of the bathroom. The music had been turned off, but she hadn't heard him come into the house. His elbows were resting on a place mat. Maria's mother fluttered around an assemblage of pots by the stove.

"Hi, Dad." She leaned in to kiss him, but only because she had to, or else. His face was oiled with sweat like a turpentine rag. On his place mat, there was only a knife and fork. There was a dense silence between them, and she wished the music were back on. Unlike the silence of freedom at Rocky's apartment, there was only the silence of tension at Maria's.

Her mother pounded a serving spoon on the kitchen sink to clear off the rice that had stuck. "How much do you want, Pa?" she asked.

"Hi, Maria." He looked at her face first and then her school skirt, so short that it hit the middle of her thighs. At school, even the teachers didn't bother reprimanding the students for rolling up their skirts. It was different in front of her father, though, and Maria moved her hand as if to smooth the pleats out and pulled down hard at the hem. She turned back toward her bedroom with her tailbone tucked.

"Pa," Maria's mother said.

Maria dragged her sneakers across the bare floor. They made the squeaking sound they sometimes did in gym class, and that made her feel more athletic than she was.

"Pa!" Maria's mother's voice was louder. "Do you hear me? One or two scoops of rice?"

Just as Maria opened the door to her bedroom, she heard her name. It was her father who called, but Maria looked at her mother instead.

"Come," her mother said.

"I'm not hungry."

"Sit," he said.

At the table, she slowly pulled out a chair. There were only four chairs, which meant that nobody was ever at the head of table, no matter which seat was picked. Her mother came around with a plate and set it down. It was swimming in orange liquid. Meals at her house were always some variation of rice and stew. At school, they served solids: toasted bagels, hard wedges of lettuce, wraps. They never served meals like her mother's—meals that were dripping, that had to be slurped from the small bowls of spoons, that called for endless napkins.

"Where's Ricky?" Maria asked. She hadn't seen Ricky in a long time. They weren't as close anymore as they were when they were younger because now all he did was play video games, and when he wasn't doing that, he was out playing basketball. Still, Maria liked when he was around. It took some attention off her.

"He's out," Maria's mother said.

"How was school?" Maria's father scraped his spoon against his bowl.

"Fine."

"Where were you last night?"

"At my friend Rocky's house. She let me come to her math tutoring session."

"Did you get your working papers?"

She pushed some rice to the corner of her plate.

"What jobs are you applying to?"

Maria picked at the white runner, stained and frayed at the ends. She hated this conversation because she knew what was being said. At

Bell Seminary, everyone lived on campus for college, and Maria wanted that for herself, too. Ideally, she wanted to be far from home—at least a few states away. In that distance, she would be able to actualize herself. She would study and write and do art every day. She would meet boys who would also be painters and poets who could teach her how to perfect her perspectives and arcs, so that her landscapes stopped coming out skewed and inflated, like a novel whose pages have dried after being drenched in the rain. The only image she used to have of college was from movies, but when Bell Seminary started taking her on trips to prospective campuses, Maria got to see for herself that there were other people, aside from her current, stifled self, that she could aspire to be. There were other landscapes that were still mysteries; they could incite in her the same thrill she once had with Andres from the train. She wanted to experience more of the sublime.

Her parents stared at her with the same expressions they wore early in the morning. She wondered if this was why they had turned the music off, so they could have this awful conversation again, so they could hear with no difficulty the sound of her dreams being crumpled. What if instead of asking what jobs she was applying to, he asked her what colleges? What if instead of asking, Where do you want to work, he asked her, Who do you want to be?

"Maria?"

"I don't know yet."

He looked into her face, and Maria didn't know what to do with her hands, so she drove them into her jaw. *What are you hiding?* his gaze seemed to ask. Maria thought of Charlie, and for the first time in her life, she wondered if she had an answer that would merit her father's reaction, which was always, unrelentingly, anger. The last time she was grounded, it was for coming home three hours after curfew because of Andres, and it had lasted an entire month. She took her hand away from her mouth, and when she swallowed, it tasted like kettle corn on her tongue.

"Ay, por Dios, Maria! Stop that already, you're ruining your lip!"

Maria's mother had come over to the table and was staring at Maria with disdain. Between her thumbnail and her forefinger was a piece of dead skin, flat and dehydrated like seaweed paper and translucent as a window.

"You see what she does to herself?" her mother said. "And what's the big deal if she took a year or two off before starting college? It's just for now. College can wait, but family can't, right, Papi?" She picked up Maria's plate. "It'll be a good lesson for you, Maria Anís. You'll know what it's like to have to make your own money."

The whole time that she spoke, she stared at Maria's father. He had slowed down since his first ravenous bites, and there was still plenty of food left. Now, he looked into his napkin, darkened with a blot of canola oil, as if he were trying to discern some message there.

"Look at Jonathan," Maria's mother continued as she dropped Maria's plate into the sink. "Jonathan got his associate's, and now he has an apartment with roommates and everything. And look at Ricky. Ricky isn't going to go away to some fancy school. He's starting his new job at Verizon next week. He's going to help out and stay right here in Queens."

On the wall, a second hand ticked.

"More rice, Papi?"

"No," he said.

"But there's still a lot left."

Maria got up from the table as discreetly as she could before her parents could tell her to sit down again. Going to college, as far as Maria understood, would determine *everything*. It was a matter of becoming a person like Rocky or having a sensible job in a sensible apartment in Elmhurst, like her uncle Jonathan. It was a matter of life, or something that came just short of it. Her mother was right in one sense, that Jonathan and Ricky hadn't done it, and Maria would be the first. She would be the first in her family to make something of herself. She'd be the first to really be free. Her mother's assessment was right when she walked in on Maria dancing to Selena—Maria *had* been in a good mood. Now that it was gone, Maria noticed.

"Maria," her father said. "When I'm done eating, I need you to help me type something up."

"Okay."

When she reached her bedroom, her lip was still bleeding, but he hadn't called after her again.

Behind her closed bedroom door, Maria collapsed into her computer chair. Finally, she unrolled her school skirt. In her backpack, crumpled among pens that exploded like overripe bananas squeezing out of their peels, were the books she'd checked out of the library earlier that day. She'd never read Emerson's essays before. She was starting with one called "Self-Reliance," and as she opened it up to page one, she thought of the way her father looked at her, as if searching for something terrible on her face.

It'd been worse ever since she'd been accepted to Bell Seminary. Maria, her father, and her mother had been among at least two hundred families in the auditorium of the community college, and all of them were anxious to know if their child had been accepted into the after-school program, the one that guaranteed a full scholarship to some of the city's best private schools. Any seat that could have been empty was occupied by the padded arms of winter coats, and Maria was squashed between her parents, her knit cap pulled down just above the eyelid, so that it neither fully obstructed nor fully allowed her a clear view of the stage. She knew that this was a decisive moment, and she preferred to be there, but also not there, and the cap seemed to understand that desire, and it became an accomplice to her indecision by only slightly obscuring her view.

There were nine whole syllables of it, a mouthful of a name. Maria Anís Rosario took a full 2.6 seconds for the woman hooked up to the microphone to stumble through, and Bell Seminary cost her another 1.2 seconds, and somewhere within the passing of those seconds, Maria's eyebrows stood up and shrugged the knit cap right off them, and Maria looked up at her father, whose face was going from the place where he usually held it to an expression that Maria had never seen before. It was like butter softening fast in the microwave—any longer like that, and he'd be rendered useless, a puddle of oily sweet on a plate. Maria couldn't understand why he was crying. *I'm so proud of you, Maria,* he told her when he had recovered, and it was the first time she'd heard him say that. Maria didn't know how to answer. All that she knew was that she never wanted to see her father, that man whom she drew in elementary school portraits with *V*'s for eyebrows, that close to melting away again.

Only months before she was accepted to Bell Seminary, that same year as a rising eighth grader, Maria had gotten her period. Her mother demonstrated just how she should curl the sticky wings inward, folded up in layers of toilet paper so that nobody would see the dark stains. She packaged Maria's pad into a white bundle the way she might tie up a Christmas tamal, unflinching, in steps. When she showed Maria how to bury it at the bottom of the trash can, Maria understood then that it was the men in the family from whom she was supposed to be hiding. It was the men for whom her body was doing something wrong. And it wasn't just her body—she soon learned that everything about her was wrong—her questions, her values, her dreams. By the time she was a student at Bell Seminary, there were countless things Maria struggled to hide, and she also knew that she would never succeed, that whatever was so upsetting about her was something she felt on a cellular level. On the day that Maria Rosario was accepted to Bell Seminary, on the day she made her father so proud, even then she foresaw in that terrible glimpse of emotion what a struggle it would be to be who she was when it came at the risk of someone else's disappointment.

In her bedroom, Maria could no longer concentrate. She put her book of Emerson essays down because she wasn't reading a word, only listening to herself think as her eyes scanned the page. She went to her purple notebook instead, and as she lay on her belly on the hardwood floor, avoiding the itchy striped carpet beneath her bed, she held her pen tentatively in the air, unsure of where to begin. She could start by describing the air mattress, how it had deflated so her elbows and knees were like bedposts on the ground when she awoke. She could write about how in Rocky's bathroom, she stared at her reflection, and felt that her breath was arid and her tongue was thick like the finger of an aloe vera plant, but still, miraculously, she looked beautiful. She could write about how she hadn't meant to be cruel to Rocky in the kitchen, but after she was, she liked it. Guilt, where it should have made Maria apologetic, made her defensive instead. It felt good to point out that the bread had gone bad. It felt good to put her down. Maria knew it could be useful to put a little distance between them because it was in this distance that Maria would be able to decide that *yes, of course,* she wanted to see Charlie again, Charlie who'd seen what was truly in her heart and told her it was not only good, but special. He'd only looked at her once, and he immediately understood that Maria was meant to be immortal.

Just as her pen met the paper, her father barged into the room, and her hand sprung from the page. She slammed the book shut and shoved it under her bed. Here at home, hiding was second nature. She didn't need to think about it. It'd become a reflex. She had written only a single letter—*I*—but even that seemed like more than enough to hide.

CHAPTER 3

"Ready?" he asked, his hand clenched around a sheet of loose-leaf. Without waiting for her to answer, Miguel dragged the wooden stool his daughter used to reach the top shelves of her closet and placed it behind the computer chair. He sat down close enough behind her where he could read the text on her screen. At the bottom of her browser, a little box flickered in orange.

When they first came to tell him he was being fired, he was sitting in the shop where they received the maintenance calls in the building. He had just finished eating, and the Tupperware container that his wife had packed him was still stained red from spaghetti sauce. A stranger appeared at the doorway and asked if he would step out. There'd been some complaints, the stranger had told him, once they settled down in a nearby conference room. Even then, he didn't know what was going on. As they continued to talk, as he sat face-to-face with this man in a suit and tie whom he'd never seen before, not in the lunchroom, not in the lobby, nowhere until right now, he realized he was listening to his own words read aloud, typed and pulled from a manila folder. Months before, they had hired two new guys, and one of them was his supervisor's nephew, an insolent boy who sucked his teeth and gave him long glances whenever Miguel gave him an order. *What's wrong with you?* Miguel had yelled more than once. *Hurry the hell up!* The commands had been empty, innocuous, the kinds of things he always said. Now, as he heard his own words from the mouth of a stranger who enunciated so clearly, without any affect or any identifiable accent, he remembered those scenes with a sinister edge, saw himself with face red, arms flexing together in anger, puffed up like a bear on hind legs. When the man in front of him mouthed *harassment*, he was convinced so totally that he was a monster that he didn't dispute it, for fear his words might come out not as words at all, but something indecipherable, a roar.

He left the building early that day, took the train home as usual with only a few extra things in his backpack. They reassured him they'd mail the rest, and Miguel said nothing because at the time, he thought the union would help him. After all, there had been no warnings, and in the days that followed, he learned that the same supervisor's nephew who accused him of wrongful conduct had been promoted to fill his place. To Miguel, no evidence could be more damning that his firing was an injustice. But after countless phone calls, after dozens of times of being transferred and put on hold, of dizzying instructions involving acronyms he didn't know the meaning of, he understood that he'd been naive. He learned that the union had two hundred thousand members and only two union representatives who decided which grievances they would pursue—apparently, his was not one of them. For reasons they refused to disclose, they didn't think he was likely to win. When they emailed him with a list of open positions that were well below his paygrade, they signed the message "regards" and Miguel knew this was the last he would hear from them for a while, so he applied to them all.

Miguel was down to his very last option when he met with a private attorney that Saturday, who told him the first step was to write everything down. The lawyer was kind and explained to Miguel that he would represent him on a contingency basis so that he wouldn't have to pay anything other than the slight percentage of whatever Miguel won—in case he did in fact win. Miguel was used to asking his kids for things like making doctor's appointments for him or booking the occasional hotel room when they went on small vacations near the Jersey Shore, if not because they were better at it, then because he thought it was important they know how to do things themselves. But he had never asked for their help on something like this, and it was his wife, Analise, who knew even less about computers than he did, who finally convinced him. *The only difference asking this time,* Analise told him, *is that now you actually need it.*

Initially, he thought he'd ask Ricky because over the past year, Ricky had been coming in on weekends to clean desks and empty trash cans on the slowest day of the week. But when Miguel lost his job, Ricky quit the next morning in what Miguel had first thought was a touching act of solidarity. Racist Italians, Ricky had said, and at first Miguel agreed, but when Ricky started coming home complaining about their clouds of cologne whenever he went to get pizza in Astoria, Miguel thought it'd be better to not have Ricky involved in filing the grievance. He asked for Maria's help instead. And he asked a week later than he wanted to because when he came home from that first meeting with the attorney, Maria had overheard him talking about her to Analise, and stormed to her bedroom, crying. She refused to speak to them for the rest of the day. Analise advised him to give her time to cool off.

As Miguel said "wrongful termination," Maria typed it out.

"What are you writing? Read it to me."

"I think you should change this to 'notwithstanding,'" she said, highlighting a word with her cursor. But she continued typing before Miguel could focus, and more letters unfurled as her fingernails clicked and clacked against the keyboard. She was no longer typing what he'd been dictating to her from his paper, and he knew because there were at least twice as many words on the screen as there were on the page. He had started drafting this letter while commuting home, and the words glided and jumped like a train hurdling over debris, rising like bumps of brail, the topography of his journey home, mapped onto college-lined loose-leaf.

"I'll read it to you in a second," Maria said, pounding down on the plastic keys. "Let me finish this sentence."

Miguel didn't know how to type like Maria did, with both hands, without even glancing down at the keys, but the way she jabbed at the buttons with so much violence struck him as wholly unnecessary. When he first bought the house, Maria was still an infant and she had spent her formative years punctuated by summers spent sitting in inflatable pools and sandboxes constructed from recovered plywood. She collected scabs from the paved concrete yard as if they grew there in bushes like azaleas. They had cookouts and a clothesline. A perennial litter of kittens came back every summer with doubled abundance, like morning glories. It wasn't the suburbs, and there were tenants upstairs, but still, Miguel was proud. He treasured all of it, and he even liked when things went wrong, the endless spackle and varnish. As Maria pressed on the keys, he felt his back muscles tense. He could see how the loss of the job would engender further loss; it was already happening with sleep, with weight. If the letter worked and he had a case, he could at least collect thousands of dollars in damages. If the letter didn't work, he thought, and then he tried to stop thinking. He brought his hand to his temples and pressed. His head was pounding. Finally, Maria stopped typing.

> Notwithstanding, the actions that were taken against me were vindictive in nature and did not take into account the eleven plus years I have spent as a valuable member of the Jenison team. My performance throughout my time at the company has been consistently excellent, with no prior history of complaint, and as many of my peers and former supervisors can attest to, I was wrongfully dismissed. Not only have I suffered financially as a result, I have also suffered a loss of dignity due to the nature in which the termination was handled. I thus believe that I am entitled to damages and am requesting that I am reinstated into my position at Jenison Consulting LLC.

Maria's voice hastened as she reached the end of the letter, and Miguel saw how, once she was done, she dragged her hand over the flashing orange box. She hovered over it, sighed, and then returned to the keyboard.

"What else?" She tapped her fingernails, making a jittery noise against the plastic, like the feet of running mice.

Miguel sat with his palm across his mouth. There had been a mild lisp in the way she said "suffered." The letter sounded entirely like her. He tried to submerge the thought somewhere deep in his mind. He woke his wife up to go to church every week, but sometimes he still couldn't chase away the thought that faith is what you have when you have no other choice.

"Nothing." He pushed the stool back and stood. "Print it."

At her public school, Maria had been one of the only girls in her grade who didn't speak Spanish perfectly. She was embarrassed by the awkward way that she fumbled with the burring words. Her parents both spoke Spanish, but they spoke English, too, and neither of them had strategized around how to raise perfectly bilingual children. Her Ecuadorian mother spoke Spanish fluently, but her Puerto Rican father spoke a raggedy, macheteado form of Spanish that Maria found baffling, considering that her father's parents hated speaking in English. She had asked her mother once how it could be that his Spanish could be so poor when it was all his mother spoke at home. "Mija, please," Maria's mother had said. "You think when your father was young he spent time at home?"

So Maria didn't know how to switch from English to Spanish and from Spanish to English with the smart dexterity that the other girls in her school did, welding the melted Romantic with the molten Germanic in the span of a few hot breaths. She had grown up being one Maria out of many—Maria Torres, Maria Hernandez, and Maria

Daza all having been classmates of hers during one particularly bad year in middle school—and for a moment that was over so quickly that she hardly remembered it happening, she had begun to litter her sentences with "diques" and "peros" and "como asis" like the other girls in her classes did. Still, she sensed a difference between them. At Maria Torres's house, she only responded to her friend's mother in English even though all of the questions were delivered in Spanish. She had let her friend explain away the puzzled look on Mrs. Torres's face. "Entiendo pero no hablo," she had offered, and Maria silently conceded to Mrs. Torres's disappointed, if not censorious, frown.

Maria expected she would have been subjected to more encounters like these if she hadn't been accepted to Bell Seminary. At Bell, Maria never heard Spanish songs blaring from phones in the hallway. She didn't need to keep up on Spanish telenovelas to have after-school conversations. At Bell, she could finally converse with her schoolmates' parents without feeling ashamed at the fact that she hated speaking Spanish, was self-conscious about her dopey accent. Nowhere in their downcast eyes did she see the thoughts about how raro it was, how much of a pity, how great a pesar, that a girl named Maria only answered in English. And what a relief it was, what a mollifying effect it had on her to find that she no longer needed to explain away her Spanish name. The parents of the girls at Bell Seminary shook hands with Maria, they invited her to family brunches, they asked if she'd ever tried rhubarb before. They never asked Maria to invite her mother over for un cafecito or said that they wanted to conocer a tu mamá.

When Diana Benitez first started a club for students of color during Friday noon elective, Maria remembered those awkward interactions in public school and had no intention of going. Diana had invited Maria early in the school year with a handwritten note she had slipped into her locker, and when Maria found it, she crumpled it and threw it into the trash. She didn't know much about Diana besides the fact that she was very pretty and very big breasted and spoke Spanish with another senior named Adriana; Maria had heard them in the bathroom once, and they reminded her of public school girls. *Dígame, Adriana! En serio, gorda?* She waited to come out of the stall until she was sure they had left.

On Friday, like always, Maria hadn't planned to go to noon elective. She had planned to find Karen, so that the two could go to Cranky's, where she would order a plain coffee with three packets of sugar and a good pour of whole milk. Maria liked to hang out in Cranky's; it was quieter than the Starbucks, and somehow, homeless people always knew to stay out. As long as Maria was in her school skirt and paid for one item, the staff would leave her alone at a table for hours. The night before, as soon as she'd printed the letter and her father had left her alone in the room, Maria stood up to close the door. She opened Karen's messenger box. There were at least six messages waiting to be read, all of them ending in exclamation points and followed by numerous question marks. What do you mean it's bad?!?! the second to last one read. Maria and Karen had first become friends after discovering they took the same train home from school, and Maria liked her even more after finding out that she liked origami and art, and was half Chilean, too, and spoke even worse Spanish than Maria.

TELL ME!! Karen had begged.

You don't take Friday noon electives, right? Let's go to Cranky's. A minute had passed and Karen still hadn't answered. Maria insisted: I have to tell you in person.

Karen had agreed to meet Maria by the lockers on Friday, but now, Maria didn't see her anywhere. Instead, Maria saw Diana skipping down the hall, a big grin on her face. She hadn't thought about Diana since she'd first invited her to the club for students of color, and Diana hadn't ever commented on her absence, so Maria didn't think she had reason to avoid her. It was only once Diana grabbed and pulled her forearm that Maria realized the smile was for her.

"Maria!" Diana said, out of breath. "We're meeting right now—the last meeting of the year! You're coming, right?"

"Um," Maria said, too surprised to muster anything else.

"Come! There will be donuts."

There was something that made it hard for Maria to look at Diana in the face. *You're one of us, aren't you?* was what Diana's look seemed to say, but this question, if Maria replied in the affirmative, would only lead to more. *You know this song, don't you? You've heard this joke, haven't you?* If the answer was no, Maria would be revealed to be a fraud. After several years at the school, she'd already worked so hard to learn the vocabulary (rhubarb, quiche, even Lapsang Souchong, made popular by one classmate whose parents who grew up in England), and she didn't have any more space in her head for more. Maria avoided Diana's eyes and caught sight of Diana's neck instead. Something golden, an oval inscription, hung there. Was it some kind of religious pendant? Maria couldn't tell.

"You should come," Diana repeated before she walked away.

Karen still hadn't texted her back when Maria walked through the door into room 323. For such a small school, Diana had rallied a significant number of students—at least, more than what Maria expected. Maria counted five. At the desk where the teachers usually sat was an Entenmann's box filled with white powdered donuts. Maria had never seen anyone bring Entenmann's donuts to school before, so she went up to the desk and took two. Diana passed around an agenda that included a bullet about making T-shirts and hosting a dance workshop. All the girls laughed when they heard how Diana snorted between every few of her giggles, the golden pendant climbing up and down her chest each time she gasped for breath.

Hello? Where are you? Maria texted Karen, halfway through the meeting.

Sorry! Karen answered. In the art studio. Working on something good.

By the end of the period, Diana was outlining plans for the following year. When someone requested they switch to chocolate-covered donuts instead of sugared ones, Diana frowned. "You bring it then!" she shouted, and the room erupted again in giggles.

Maria watched in wonder as Diana's laughter finally fizzled out in its own time, like a bubbling soda coming to a hush. "We could go to the Entenmann's factory store," Maria said, quietly, and it was the first time that anyone in the room heard her voice. It was a suggestion she wouldn't give around Rocky, who told her she should never eat things packaged in plastic, and she felt her heart bang wildly in her chest. "There's one not too far from where I live in Queens. They sell every kind of donut and cake there. We could get one of everything."

"I've never been there." Diana's smile flattened. "Queens is far."

"No, it's not," Maria said, more confidently. "Well, only by train. But it's only like a thirty-minute drive." Maria cocked her head, but Diana didn't say anything. Her face was inexplicably blank, so Maria continued. "Don't you live in Brooklyn?" Maria asked. "You could take the BQE! Ask your parents! I bet they'll drive you!"

"Drive me!" Diana's voice was stormy, and it elicited a hush over the room. She stared at Maria for what seemed like too long, and Maria sank into her chair. Finally, in a quieter voice that signaled the end of the conversation, Diana said, almost under her breath, "Cars are expensive."

The girls gathered their things and stood. Maria followed their lead, making a wordless escape to the hall. There were five minutes left until their next period, and Maria hurried to her locker. If cars were expensive, that couldn't include the brown Oldsmobile that her parents drove everywhere, whose reverse gear was so battered it made a tiny shriek every time they backed into a parking spot. Maria was sure that like her, Diana had a full scholarship to Bell Seminary, but something had fissured when Maria mentioned the car, and Maria knew she couldn't piece it back together. She must've thought that Maria was just as privileged and spoiled as all the other Bell Seminary girls.

How could Maria prove herself different now? And why did she suddenly want to? It wasn't a secret that Maria attended the school on a scholarship, because those who didn't explicitly know likely assumed. But whenever the used-skirt sale was hosted at Bell Seminary in early September, Maria still became anxious about who was volunteering that day and would witness her and her mother browsing the racks. Maria's mother hadn't been trained like Maria had—what if Mrs. Lerner wanted to talk about rhubarb? What would Maria's mother do? The shame Maria felt just at the thought of it made her anxious and hostile, which often meant that she and her mother would leave the school that day on nonspeaking terms, with Maria, inexplicably to her mother, on the verge of tears.

Now, she felt compelled to assert that she was poor. She wanted to drag Diana all the way to Queens and show her the weathered, old futon. She wanted to point to the plastic bins in the living room filled with winter coats because they didn't have closets that could accommodate all the seasons. She wanted to show her the way they hung their shower towels to dry over the wooden rocking chair in the living room. But then the tour would stop because Diana didn't need to see Maria's fully stocked pantry or Ricky's new PlayStation console. Sometimes, when Andres came over, he huffed and called Maria rich, just because she didn't live in an apartment and there were so many flowers leading up to their door. But would Diana, who would be able to understand *rich* in the context of Bell Seminary, really see it the same way?

As she approached the lockers, she saw Laura and Rocky in front of her, their Longchamp bags buttoned and slung over their shoulders. They were huddled together, giggling. The pain in Maria's chest dampened a little when Rocky turned to her with arms outstretched.

"Little Ms. J. Lo!" Rocky laughed. "How was Minority Club? How does it feel to be an empowered woman?"

She beckoned to Maria as if summoning her for a hug, but Maria took two paces backward instead. She felt the burn spread from her heart to her face, turning her cheeks bright red.

"What did they talk about?" Laura said.

Laura had never spoken to Maria before, but Maria knew she was Rocky's friend. She'd seen them sneak out to smoke cigarettes together. Maria wanted to answer honestly, but all she could remember of the conversation was the way she had butchered its ending, with her comment about cars, her assumption that everyone had one, that everyone had been to the places she'd been to, even if, in Maria's mind, that place was nowhere.

"Maria?" Laura cocked her head. "What did you guys talk about?"

"I don't know," Maria said. Laura's face looked bony and gruesome, even though most girls in the grade called it gorgeous.

Rocky hadn't stopped laughing. She was bent over Laura's arm for support as her chest rose and fell in giggles. Blinking furiously, Maria looked up, then down, then sideways—anywhere to throw off the gravitational pull that kept trying to bring her to tears.

"Oh come on, Laura," Rocky said. "She's a strong woman now, so we shouldn't fuck with her. Her homies will come after us."

Maria blinked herself into a grin. Rocky was right; a strong woman wouldn't have eyes like a swollen lemon rind, so easy from which to draw liquid. But as Rocky and Laura smirked at each other and as the two of them moved in tandem from the lockers down the hall to their next class, it occurred to Maria that behind that dispassionate mask, the one that could reabsorb water like a pot of soil, the one that grinned and swallowed and calmed and quieted, there might not be a strong woman at all. She tried thinking of Diana flicking her hair. What would Diana want her to do?

"That's right," Maria called. Laura turned around. "Or I'll come after you myself."

Eso! She heard an imaginary Diana cheering her on.

"You hear that, Lore?" Rocky whooped. "She'll come after you herself!"

Maria smiled. Rocky's excitement was contagious. She felt herself getting giddy.

"You better watch out." Maria looked Laura up and down. *"Lore."*

"I told you, Laura! Shelly is the real thing!" Rocky let go of Laura's arm and linked into Maria's. "Stay on Shelly's good side. Or else."

Rocky escorted Maria to her next class, the two of them laughing loudly. But once Maria was inside the classroom, she started to feel funny, like a large rock had settled at the bottom of her stomach. She wasn't sorry about what she said to Laura. But it didn't feel right, this pretending to be tough. If she continued this way, maybe she'd eventually forget who she was. Maybe she'd eventually become a mirror, except instead of showing a perfect reflection, she'd appear distorted, a fun house of all the wrong ideas. It would be terrible. It would be a life sentence. And it wouldn't affect anyone else but Maria, who would always remain not a strong woman, but unseen, an alone-feeling girl.

For the rest of the school day, Maria was shuffled around by the moving tides of blue kilts at Bell Seminary. In that ocean of girls going to and from class, Maria eventually forgot about Laura. But when Rocky invited her to get food after school, Maria still hesitated, knowing that she only had a couple of bills in her backpack. "I'll get you," Rocky whispered, meaning to reassure her, but sounding like a bogeyman instead.

Maria had meant to find Karen, but by the time Maria went looking for her, Karen had already left to take the train to Queens alone. Karen never hung out with Rocky's friends, and she scrunched up her nose when Maria talked about them—and Maria could understand why. Rocky's friends were popular girls, mean girls who wore push-up bras and hiked up their skirts to show off the scars they'd cut into their own thighs. They bragged about knowing where to find cocaine, and they did shitty things to everyone not in their clique, like when one of them took Karen's textbook right out of her locker, and poor Karen, who was always so organized and responsible, nearly lost her mind looking for it. When Laura returned it at the end of the year, Karen almost cried in frustration. Maria, despite her performance this afternoon, was uneasy around them, too—especially when they fussed over each other, comparing how much their skirts lifted off their backsides. The bigger their butts, the more they said they hated themselves, even though they were, objectively, tiny girls. They said things like that and more all the time, things that convinced Maria that to them, she must seem like a horrible monster.

Patrick's was a sit-down place that everyone knew for its milkshakes and fries. Bell Seminary girls went to Patrick's during free periods, and then made a detour around the school, and when they came back, they smelled distinctly like teenagers: cheap tobacco and chocolate milk.

"Hey, how about we get pizza instead?" Maria said as they ran out onto the street. They were anxious from being cooped up all day and eager to fill up new spaces. She and Rocky trailed behind Danielle and Laura, who had coupled up, arms linked. Maria only had a five-dollar bill in her backpack, and at Patrick's, all she could get with that much money was a pickle and a side of fries. Even though Rocky had already promised to buy, Maria didn't like the idea of Rocky paying for Maria when everyone else would be paying for themselves.

Maria had both hands in her hoodie's front pocket, so there was hardly any room left between the two girls when Rocky looped her arm into Maria's elbow and left it there as they walked.

"It's fine, girl," Rocky said, her arm limp on Maria's. "I'll spot you."

Maria didn't like being touched without first being asked. The sudden presence of another body forced her into an awkward consciousness of her own, and she always felt a little ungracious once she tried to initiate disengagement. But now, as Rocky looped her arm into Maria's, Maria remembered how earlier, Rocky had left Laura's arm for Maria's, and she felt a peculiar tinge of pride. She carried Rocky along on the street, quickening her pace so they even passed Laura and Danielle. Inside, she and Rocky marched toward a table, the other girls following closely behind.

When the waiter came around, each of them asked for milkshakes with their food. When it was Maria's turn, she didn't even bother to glance at Rocky for approval. With her dad, she was used to ordering tap water with ice, but so was Ricky and so was her mom. If all the other girls were going to order a milkshake, she would order a milkshake, too. While the rest of the girls ordered chocolate, Maria asked for strawberry.

"I still can't believe it," Laura said once the waiter walked away. She was speaking with a vehemence that made her left eye shrink as the right eye grew bigger. "It's absolutely ridiculous!"

"It is pretty shitty," Rocky said. Maria looked at her from the corner of her eye, her other eye transfixed on the door. "I just bought this new Longchamp."

"Well, that'll be okay," Laura said matter-of-factly. "It's anything better that's banned."

Rocky broke into a toothy smile. "Lucky my Dior bag's too small for my books."

That afternoon, in the auditorium, the school had announced a new rule to go into effect starting next year: no more designer handbags. All textbooks were to be carried in one of two options: backpacks like Maria's, or plain oversize totes.

"It's just a denial of a basic right. Why should my freedom of expression be infringed upon just because of someone else's hurt feelings?" Laura's eyes darted to the window, then darted back to the table. For a split second, she looked right at Maria, taking Maria by surprise.

"It's not my fault if people are jealous of me," Laura said.

The waiter came back with plates lined with sesame buns scarred with grill marks, strips of chicken fingers, and french fries. As the girls all fell quiet around their platters, Maria thought of the glossy magazines that the Bell Seminary girls left lying around classrooms and the student lounge, the ones that warned about overindulging. She remembered that cravings were to be heeded; if not, you risked overindulging later. There were a couple of cravings Maria found herself fighting against: one was to finish her milkshake too quickly, but the more salient one was to resist grabbing Laura's veggie burger and slapping it against Laura's pallid face. Laura pushed a french fry around her plate, taking tiny nibbles off it just to put it back down and pick up a new one, until all the fries on her plate were three-quarters bitten. At school, on the slight chance that they ever found each other alone, Laura always took out her cell phone rather than speak to Maria. It irritated Maria to know that this was a person that Rocky called a friend, but now, the irritation felt stronger, less shakable, and not like irritation at all. It was while staring at one of Laura's browned fries, overcooked and nubby, that Maria realized that she hated her.

"I agree," Rocky said, wiping grease off her mouth with a napkin. "I mean, what's the big deal if I have a nice bag? I don't understand why that bothers people. And if you're jealous"—Rocky lifted two fingers to her mouth as she swallowed—"then that's your own problem."

A brief silence fell over the table. Maria licked her finger and began pressing it to her plate for crumbs. Of course, it didn't matter what bags they used. Everyone had already seen the pictures of Laura's family vacation to Paris and Rome last year, and Prague and Berlin the year before that. Anyone at school would be able to see the differences between the students, even if the annual donor catalog didn't spell it out for them. In the world of Bell Seminary, no school rule or regulation could trick Maria into feeling that she belonged.

"You know who really runs Bell Seminary?" Laura finally said. "A bunch of fucking communists."

Rocky looked at Maria and smiled. Her plate was full of detritus, shredded onions and a pockmarked bun from where she'd scooped out the bulk of the bread and rolled it into a ball at the edge of her plate— *empty carbs*, she had said, as if they didn't already know why. When the waiter came by, he pulled a notebook from his breast pocket, ripped out a piece of paper, and laid it facedown on the table. "Pay at the counter," he said.

"I'll pay."

"Rocky, no," Laura said, but Rocky was out of her seat, following the waiter's trail. Danielle yawned, and just as she did, Laura bent at the waist and disappeared under the table. When she came back up, she was dragging her bag onto her lap and unzipping its wide flap open. Maria looked at the label: Prada. Maria smiled to think it would be the last time she would ever see it.

"I just don't understand why she always tries to pay for everything," Laura said, frowning. "We each got a special and a milkshake. Each of us puts in fifteen. And a dollar or two for tip."

Maria picked up a napkin and started tearing its edge as Danielle reached for her own bag tucked under her chair. There was no use looking in her backpack; she knew exactly what she'd find there, the single bill crumpled somewhere in her front pocket, thin as a Post-it Note.

Laura now had both her and Danielle's contributions in hand. The bills were crisp and flat, as if they had just been pulled from between the pages of a book or from under a steaming iron. Maria looked away from the table. Even if Maria wanted to pay Rocky back, she'd have to go through her mother first, and Maria knew she'd never hear the end of it. *I make food every night!*—she could hear her mother yelling with her propensity for always rounding up—*And you spent twenty dollars on a cheeseburger?*

"You know you don't need to buy our friendship, don't you?" Laura said, just as Rocky returned to the table. Laura's smile was odd and her laugh inappropriate, as if she were recalling an unspeakable joke. Sometimes, Maria would burst into laughter on the train platform recalling something Andres had said, and everyone's angry eyes would find her, as if Maria had awoken them from a deep and luxurious sleep.

Laura was looking at Rocky as if they shared something like that, something they didn't want anyone else to know.

A sheepish smile scuttled across Rocky's face, as she looked at the wad of cash Laura held out to her. "That's too much."

"We actually owe you more."

"It's on me," Rocky said, ignoring the folded bills Laura held to her face. Maria watched in wonder as Rocky grabbed her bag from where it hung over her seat and led the way toward the exit. Outside the smudged windowpanes, it was raining. Rocky held the door for the rest of the girls, and Maria let everyone else walk ahead of her. When it was Maria's turn to pass Rocky, she leaned in to her ear.

"Thank you," Maria said, and without warning, her eyes became warm and filmy. Rocky could've taken the bills, but she didn't, and Maria knew she had done her this kindness. She was sure that Rocky understood what she meant, but Rocky seemed bewildered. "I mean," Maria began, unsure of how to explain.

"It's pouring!" Laura yelled as Maria and Rocky looked at one another under the canopy of the doorway. Their feet were getting splattered. Maria started to shiver.

"I'll see you Monday, okay, Shell?"

Laura, Danielle, and Rocky all went down the street in one direction, huddled beneath one enormous umbrella held high in the air by Laura, whose advantage was her willowy height. They'd be at their apartments in minutes. But Maria went in another direction, her sockless feet becoming numb with water. She zigzagged down the street. She would be soaked by the time she got to the station, soaked even further on her walk down Queens Boulevard, soaked as she climbed the stairs to her house. It was only after her mother opened the door, ushering her inside the house with several towels, wrapping them around Maria's hair until it was dry, that Maria would be home, and warm.

CHAPTER 4

Birthdays in Harlem called for Dominican cake. Whenever they went up to her grandmother's apartment, Maria could expect it. Technically, customers chose between an array of options for filling: guava paste, strawberry, dulce de leche. Maria's family never ordered anything other than dulce de leche—a thick layer of it smeared between two stacked yellow cakes coated with white sugar frosting. Everyone considered the frosting the worst part, never mind the unhealthiest, and they scraped it off their pieces in mounds. Maria, on the other hand, ate all of it, including what was left in heaps atop empty plates—*Hey, are you not gonna eat that?*—and when that was done, she'd go after what was left in the thin streaks under her fingernails, lapping it up with her teeth, made slightly more savory from the tart of her skin. When Maria saw the purple sugar flowers, she imagined them coming apart on her tongue.

"Mine!" She watched as her mother slid the knife down in a motion she couldn't take back. The knife came up and left broken petals in its place. Half the frosting had come off one side and fell to the paper cake board. Maria had asked to cut her own piece, for reasons that now were apparent. "I'll do it," Maria's mother had told her. "You don't know how to."

"You never let me do anything!" Maria said, turning away from her mother, who was offering Maria a mangled cake slice. Instead, Maria moved toward the counter and picked up the only plate that was there, a tiny sliver so small nobody had claimed it yet. She walked past everyone crowded around the table, past the dining room, and stood in the farthest corner of her grandmother's kitchen. She was pushing around the cake with her fork when she saw Jonathan close the refrigerator. When he looked up, he saw her and smiled. Maria was relieved. She was getting bored alone.

"What happened with your mom? She's over there saying you're a drama queen."

"What is that?"

Maria aimed her fork at Jonathan's glass and its hissing, dragon-red contents.

"Sprite. And cranberry juice."

"Why?" she asked.

Jonathan shrugged. "It's good. How's your boyfriend?"

"Um, he's fine." With the side of her fork, Maria carved out a baby-size bite. "We're going to a party tonight."

"Really? Where?"

"Um," she said, swallowing. "In Maspeth."

"With who?"

"Me and Andres. Karen's coming, too."

"La morenita?"

"Huh? No. Karen. She goes to Bell Seminary, but she lives in Queens, too."

"With the long hair?"

"Yeah," Maria answered. She was taking microscopic bites, rolling the frosting around from one cheek to the other until finally swallowing.

"That's the one that was over at the house the other day?" Jonathan asked. "Your rich friend, right?"

"They're all rich," she said, putting her fork down, and then immediately picking it back up. There was really no cake left on her plate, other than a tiny scrape of frosting. "But some are richer than others,"

Maria continued. "Karen's the one you met. She's the one with the straight, dark hair. She was just over at the house last weekend. Chilean."

"Yeah?" He looked up, as if he were scanning the skies of his mind, a file he might be able to drag down and open. "Maybe if you show me a picture." He looked back at Maria, and with a lowered voice he asked, "Are you gonna get drunk tonight?"

"I'm gonna try."

Jonathan laughed. He was Maria's youngest uncle and always asked about Maria's personal affairs, including Andres. When Jonathan told Maria that she should watch out, that it sometimes looked like she was taking the relationship too seriously, Maria would tell him that Andres wasn't long-term, and that even Andres knew it. *Are you going to leave me for one of those white guys you love?* Andres would ask her, and Maria would giggle and imagine a line of half-naked white boys at her beck and call like a harem. She didn't tell him about the school dances where she lingered too long in the bathroom, abandoned by all of her class-mates who had been pulled one by one to the dance floor. *I love you, Maria, and if you leave me, I'll kill you,* Andres would say, a thick piece of her leg in his hand. Maria had imagined a distraught Andres pacing the streets of the Upper East Side with the machete his father had brought from Peru and stored in their front-door closet next to the umbrellas. Would he really kill her because of how much he loved her? Of course, she didn't actually want to be murdered by him, but she liked what it might symbolize. A crime of passion, just like in the movies. She had taken him by the crown of his head to kiss him.

Yes, I'm going to leave you, Maria would tease as he slapped her thighs with so much force that she felt flecks of her heart become dis-lodged, like dust beaten out of a floor rug.

Now, there was nothing on Maria's plate. She was sucking the prong of her fork clean.

"You want more?" Jonathan asked.

"No," she lied, still angry at her mother, and by extension, every adult. Besides, Maria couldn't tell Jonathan everything. She had a suspicion that in the end he would be just like her brother, Ricky, who was probably just like her father; they all just wanted to control her. They all gave her the same disapproving looks whenever she wore tight dresses out of the house.

Jonathan followed Maria across the kitchen as she went to the garbage can and lifted the lid with the foot pedal.

"Hey," Jonathan said. "When are you gonna hook me up with one of your rich friends? Hook me up with one of them."

"No."

"Why not?"

"Because they'll probably think you're ugly," Maria lied, again. She knew what Rocky thought of Latino boys. Amazing lovers, she'd said.

Jonathan was indignant. "*Ugly?* I'm the most good-looking guy they'll ever see."

"Jonathan." Maria dropped her plate into the trash can. "I'm not hooking you up with my friends."

"Why not, though?"

"Why would you want to get with a white girl?" She asked the question aloud as if she hadn't fantasized about the day she could tell Andres that she was dating a boy who wore boat shoes. She imagined Rocky, Rocky with skin the color of soy milk, whose green veins shone so brightly under her skin it was as if they were permanently held under a flashlight. With the satisfaction a child derives from saying a word she has been instructed to never say aloud, she added, "She's not even that cute."

Just as she moved away from the garbage, Maria's older brother walked by, maneuvering around her with an empty plate.

"What do you think, Ricky?" Jonathan said. "Do you think Maria's blanquita friends are cute?"

"Nah." Ricky put his foot down on the pedal and threw his plate on top of Maria's.

"See!" Maria shot Jonathan a nasty look.

Jonathan sucked his teeth. "Oh come on! You would pipe! Show us a picture, Maria."

"No!" Maria shouted.

"I wouldn't pipe."

"You would!"

"Pipe?" Maria's voice was getting even louder trying to drown out the two men. "Do you really think I don't know what you're saying?"

Ricky and Jonathan looked at each other, then looked away.

"You're both gross." Maria drove her hands into her hips. "Neither of you are allowed to go anywhere near my friends." Maria thought of Rocky again, her straight hair, her paleness, the thinness she elongated and calcified with stilettos. "Especially not you, Jonathan. You're almost thirty!"

Jonathan scoffed. "As if you girls are so innocent." He went to the living room and Ricky followed, leaving Maria alone in the kitchen again, by the can overflowing with balls of crumpled trash, like flowers in full bloom.

Mostly due to how cluttered the apartment was and how much tinier it got when there were so many people inside, visits to her grandmother's apartment were always short. Before the sun had fully set, they were leaving. Maria's father went downstairs to get the car and pull up in front. "Take this for me," Maria's mother said, holding out a Key Food bag full of leftover forks and plates. Maria watched as her mother disappeared to say bye to her grandmother. She went back into the kitchen and glanced at the counter. There was still so much left when she took the knife out of the sink and carved out her second piece of cake. This time, she cut her own perfect slice. Nice and neat. This time, it was thick.

The Key Food bag was still looped around her elbow as she ate. When she looked up from a mouthful of simultaneous bites, she saw that her mother and her grandmother had come to the doorway, her mother's hand around her grandmother's wrist. Their faces were pointed at her as they whispered, and Maria couldn't tell if they were looking just past her at the window, where the sound of the block poured in despite the metal bars, or if they were staring at her. She only had one piece of cake—one very tiny piece of cake—and now she was on a second, more moderately sized—but she felt her jeans pressing up against the inner wings of her thighs, and she crossed her legs self-consciously, hoping that folding them over each other would help make them look smaller. Her mother and grandmother went on whispering, and if she could have, she would have crumpled into the floor, into the tiny crack of plaster that separated tile from tile. *Stop looking at me,* she would have shouted, but it was one thing to say that to her mother, and something else entirely to say it to her grandmother.

"Maria! Come say goodbye to Mamita."

Filled with dread, Maria put down her plate and crossed the kitchen to the doorway. Her grandmother brought her hands up to her shoulders and held them, forcefully, with a grasp so intent it startled Maria, as if Maria was the rail to a staircase her grandmother was climbing down.

"Parece a Miguel," her grandmother said. "Tiene la misma cara." Her hands were on Maria, but her face was angled toward Maria's mother, as if she weren't addressing Maria at all.

Her mother smiled. "Grandma says that you're starting to look like a woman."

"Okay."

Maria's mother cocked her head. "What's wrong with you? Don't you think you're beautiful?" She laughed, and with her open palm, she smacked Maria's butt.

Maria felt a wild emotion shoot through her arms and her legs, as if the blood that ran through her veins had turned to concrete, and suddenly, she couldn't breathe. It was like the Bell Seminary dances where she knew they were laughing at her, pointing at where her footsteps made the dance floor sink in the same places where Rocky floated, leaving behind clouds of glittering dust. They were making fun of her.

"Don't touch me," she hissed, without looking back at her grandmother. She pulled away from them and fled toward the living room, to the front door of the apartment.

"Malcriada," her mother said, lingering on the hard sound between the *c* and the *r*. It sounded like a pair of dice being rolled. She heard its echoing clatter even as she flew down the staircase, skipping several steps as she tried not to trip over her feet. *You are empowered,* she reminded herself. *You are a strong woman! Strong!* She hoped the lines of her face, creased in emotion, would be smoothed into place by the time she reached the first-floor landing. The last thing she wanted to explain to her father was why she had started to constantly oscillate from rage to despair, why she looked like she was always moments from breaking down. The truth was she could hardly explain it to herself.

CHAPTER 5

Maria liked art, but she wasn't a great visual artist like Karen. At Bell Seminary, they had enrolled in the same drawing class, and Maria could have learned a lot more about how to mix oil paints if she spent more time looking at her own canvas. Instead, Maria would abandon her easel to gawk over Karen's shoulder, at the underpainting that she'd yet to fill in. "How do you get it to look like that?"

"It's not done yet," Karen would say, but Maria would keep on lingering until the teacher coaxed her away. Maria hardly ever completed her own paintings. She left the apples in her still life half-formed, and she erased the mouths in her portraits so often that they always looked like they had five o'clock shadows. "Hey," Karen said one day as Maria went over the same stroke again and again, drawing an indefinitely blacker and blacker eyebrow over her charcoal self-portrait. "I've been taking art classes since I was like two. Your stuff really isn't bad." After that, Maria stopped looking over Karen's shoulder as much, and even though she knew Karen was so good that she accepted commissions from her parents' friends, Maria didn't feel as bad anymore.

"I'm getting on the train right now in Harlem," Maria said to Karen, into the phone. Karen had been waiting for Maria for an hour after her Saturday painting class had ended. "I'll be right there. Just wait for me at the train station," Maria said as she stepped onto the gum-splattered curb, still carrying the plastic bag filled with plastic forks from the supermarket where the rank was distinctly of plastic.

When Maria's parents appeared at the landing only a few moments later with Jonathan, they all walked over to the parked car. Aside from Jonathan, who lived in an apartment not far from Maria's house, nobody else in her father's family had left Harlem. Her father rarely complained about it, but sometimes, when he was around his cousins, he did like to joke. "A lot of Ecuadorians and Mexicans in the neighborhood, sure," he'd say, "but what do they know about New York City when they haven't even lived here long enough to run out of their first bag of rice?" Maria's mother, who was in fact Ecuadorian, rolled her eyes.

"You know what train you need to take?" Maria's mother had asked as she took the bag full of forks from Maria.

"Of course," Maria said, refusing to look at her mother. She tried to suppress the snarl in her voice. "I go to school around here, remember?"

Maria raced away from the car before her parents could think to call out with her curfew. As she crossed the avenue toward the train station, careful not to step onto the circulars and Chinese food menus that collected in potholes all over the street, Maria knew that what she'd said was untrue. Bell Seminary was near her grandmother's apartment, in that it was closer than her home in Queens was, but it was certainly not in the same neighborhood. Before going to private school, Maria would have never known the difference. She had taken for granted all the obvious clues, the catcalls, the smell of fish frying, the stomped lotto tickets all over the curb. She had taken for granted the skunky smell on the train that slid and wove through her head like a silk ribbon, and made her mother go, *fo!* She hadn't taken note of how dirty the streets were as she descended 125th Street and how much cleaner they were once she approached Eighty-Sixth. It was only after the day she told her friends at school that her grandmother lived on the Upper East Side, too, in a one-bedroom apartment off Fifth Avenue, that she was able to distinguish the differences.

That's not the Upper East Side, a classmate had said, gesturing with her wrist. *That's Harlem.*

I know, Maria said, and the immediacy of her response surprised even her. *I'm just kidding.*

But it hadn't been her first mistake. There was the time, when she was still just a freshman, when she went to Genevieve's house and didn't know what to do with the papery pouch on the table. She sipped and sipped at the hot water in her mug until halfway through biting into a croissant, Genevieve shrieked. *No way!* she said, her cheeks rising up to her eyes. *Do you not know what a tea bag is?* Genevieve's mother was born in London, and within hours, all of Maria's schoolmates had heard a variation of the story, a couple times told within earshot of Maria, and more often as she stood directly in front of them, nodding her head, nervous and laughing. *I knew what it was,* she protested. *I just didn't know what I was supposed to do with it.* At this, her classmates laughed more. At Maria's house, it was the coffee pot that was attended to first thing in the morning. Karen was the only one who'd listened silently and hadn't laughed.

When Maria saw Karen standing on the corner of Sixty-Sixth Street with her leather messenger bag slung over one shoulder, she went to her and gave her a hug, wrapping her arms around her whole back. From the way Karen stiffened, like the trunk of a tree, Maria could tell she was angry.

"Okay, I'm sorry I'm late! But I'm here now! Forgive me?"

"You need a hair tie," Karen answered, extending her hand. A pale-yellow hairband, now gray from endless use, was the only thing that circled her wrist. Maria tugged it off. It left a concave imprint on Karen's skin that suggested something essential was missing.

"It's that bad, huh?" She held Karen's hairband between her teeth as she pulled her hair back into a french braid. She knew that sometimes her hair was so frizzed and crazed, she gave the impression of a cartoon struck by lightning.

"It must be really bad," Maria said, tying the elastic into place.

Karen began leading the way down the subway stairs. A current of people stormed by, threatening to overtake them. Amidst all the noise and the chaos, Karen needed to shout over her shoulder to make sure she was heard. "It was pretty bad," she called out, honestly, like the good friend that she was. "But I forgive you."

On the train platform, Maria leaned against a white-tiled wall and kicked an empty bag of chips from beneath her. A man with no shoes on sulked past them, muttering aloud. Maria avoided looking him in the eye, and Karen picked at her cuticle. Andres had said that whole populations of people lived underground, that they had even gone blind and hairless, like babies born premature. What advantage being blind or hairless would give a person who lived in subway tunnels, Maria did not know.

"Um . . . ," Maria started to say, once the man was out of earshot. "So, can I tell you now?"

"Oh yeah." Karen laughed. "I forgot."

Maria leaned into Karen's face and moved a strand of hair away from her ear, as if they were a pair of school children. Karen laughed, jerking away, and looked at Maria with one eyebrow raised.

"Come on," Maria said. "It's important." They weren't far from Bell Seminary after all, and it was possible that someone would overhear them. With her hands cupped into a bowl against Karen's ear, Maria whispered. Immediately, Karen's face changed.

"Rocky's dad!" Karen shouted.

"Someone will hear you! Shh!" Maria brought both hands up to her face as if shielding herself from view. "Charlie," she whispered. "His name is Charlie."

"You've got to be shitting me. He's married," Karen whimpered.

"It's not like that." Maria wanted Karen to stop looking at her. It was making her nervous to see that much consternation on the face of a person who was usually unaffected by everything, who usually just blinked at Maria's antics. "They don't even sleep in the same room. Most of the time they're not even in the same apartment. Actually," Maria said, with the sly smile of a person who's confessing something that isn't hers to confess, "I don't think Rocky's mom lives there anymore."

"What would your parents say?"

"They won't find out unless you tell them."

Karen's eye roll was violent, the black pupils skyward. Maria noticed the red veins that crept around the whites of her eyeballs, like red vines of ivy.

"Maria," she said. "Think about what you're saying."

Maria knew that this rational Karen was a Karen she learned to be from talking to the school psychologist. Maria had seen her there countless times through the little window of the closed wooden door. Whenever she confronted her about it, Karen brushed it off, saying that she liked eating from the candy tray that the psychologist always kept there. Maria knew that wasn't the full truth. There's only so many Twizzlers you can eat before you'd rather not be divulging your life story to a person who only needed to walk down the hallway to the dean's office to have your parents' home and work numbers on speed dial.

"I'm not pursuing anything."

"And Andres?"

"As if he would care," Maria said, if only to indulge Karen's contempt for Andres. She knew how much Karen disapproved of their relationship, how many times Karen had asked what Maria saw in him. *He probably would care,* Maria thought, but Maria's response had incited in Karen the tiniest grin, almost imperceptible. Maria knew better, knew Karen, and saw it.

"But aren't you worried? What if Rocky finds out?"

"She won't," Maria said.

On the opposite side of the tracks, a train rumbled by, cutting their conversation short. The girls stared at the tonnage of weight flying past them, its roar so bestial and primitive, it was hard to believe there was a person inside it, controlling its trajectory down the platform. As soon as it passed, Maria spoke again. She spoke before Karen could.

"Andres says we should bring our own stuff to the party unless we want to drink rum."

But Karen hadn't looked away from where the train had been passing, and now, as if in a daze, she stared down the black tunnel. "Why do I always have to go with you to these things?" Her voice was airy and contemplative, as if she were posing the question to herself. Now, she turned to Maria, and her tone became heavier. "Why don't you ask your new best friend, Rocky?"

"Because! Queens isn't safe enough for her."

Karen looked hard at Maria. "She said that?"

Maria frowned. She couldn't remember now if it had been Rocky or someone else in the grade, or if the comment about safety was concerning something else entirely, like after Maria had inadvertently divulged that her grandmother lived in Harlem.

"No," she said. "I don't think so."

"So then?" Karen dipped one leg, and stood in a defiant contrapposto, like a Grecian sculpture. "Am I just gonna be your backup plan for whatever Rocky won't do?"

"You know it'll never be like that." Maria came closer to Karen and gently put her hand on Karen's elbow. "It's just, can you imagine Rocky at one of these parties? With all of Andres's friends? She'd lose her mind around all those *Latin lovers*. And that actually is something she said."

"Jesus, Maria."

In the distance there was a light approaching. The girls felt the breeze of an oncoming train. "Maybe we can get forties tonight," Karen said. "Use that ID you bought."

"There's this place I go to that never cards."

"What was the point of buying that ID if you were never going to use it?"

When Maria first tried to show off her new ID at school, one of her classmates pointed out the font was Calibri. Maria's ID wouldn't work at McFadden's, the joke went, but it would work at McDonald's. When she realized that the thirty dollars she had saved up to spend on the ID was as good as if it had been lost on the curb, Maria wouldn't stop beating herself up. *I am so stupid,* Maria kept saying over and over again, until Karen chided her. *Okay, Maria,* she said. *Stop that.*

"I'll use it in college. Nobody will know what a Florida ID looks like there."

Karen smirked. "Unless you go to college in Florida, right?"

The train whistled and screamed as it arrived. When the doors opened, nobody got off. Men and women were draped over each other, their limbs crossing their faces to hold on to the nearest pole. Maria and Karen each took a deep breath. Clutching their bags with both hands, they stepped into the mass and stood so close to each other that Maria could see straight through Karen's concealer to a pimple just between her two eyebrows.

"So," Karen said, cracking her gum again. Maria noticed the pause and deliberately said nothing. "Are you going to tell Andres?"

Maria grabbed at her lip. She imagined her mother swatting her hand away from her mouth, clicking her tongue.

"Tell him what?" Maria asked. A small sliver of skin came away from her mouth between her thumb and pointer finger.

"You know. About Rocky's dad."

"His name is Charlie," Maria said.

"I still can't believe you went to his bedroom."

"Wouldn't you have been curious?"

"No." Karen popped a gum bubble. "Isn't he gross and old?"

"Karen!" Maria saw a woman turn her head. She stopped just short of looking. "It's not like I'm having sex with him," Maria whispered. "We didn't do anything."

Karen cocked her head at Maria.

"But you have a crush on him."

Maria rolled her eyes. "Is it wrong that I find him interesting?"

Under their feet, the train rolled noisily forward.

"Well," Karen said, folding her arms over her chest and leaning on the door for balance. This was the clinical Karen—the Karen who strove to be objective. "Do you think anything good will come out of it?"

"Nothing is going to come out of this at all," Maria said, without hesitation. She wouldn't admit to Karen that she'd been fantasizing about him since then. She wouldn't show Karen the books of poetry she had highlighted and starred in search of the perfect quotation. The train rolled forward with a steady thump-thump that lulled the girls into silence.

"I guess," Karen said, after a while. "It wouldn't be the worst thing in the world. Rocky's family is so rich, maybe he'll fall in love with you and want to buy you a helicopter."

"Are you kidding? Of course he won't fall in love with me! I'm not that stupid, Karen!" Maria stopped peeling the skin off her lip. She made a face like she was angry, but in seconds, it had dissolved. Edging away from the woman who had glanced over at them, she flashed Karen a sidelong smile.

"But even if he did, I wouldn't ask for a helicopter," Maria whispered. "I can't live in a helicopter. I'd ask for a country house." The train lurched forward, and to the ire of everyone around them, the two girls fell over, bumping into countless bodies until they found each other again. They fell into each other's arms, laughing.

When they got to Brian's house, it was only half past nine and nobody was home. Karen and Maria were early. The streets were quiet save for the scraping noises that the heels of Karen's boots made against the sidewalk. A light breeze ruffled the saplings that lined Brian's block. Sparse and wobbly, their leaves waved like teeth in a very old or a very young person's mouth. The emergent summer weather was uncomfortable; the socks the girls wore made their feet sweat, and their denim jackets made pools under their armpits. They felt cooler as they took off their jackets and spread them to sit on Brian's doorstep.

Karen and Maria waited for what seemed a long time before Brian arrived with Andres. They were with several other boys whom Maria had never met before. Maria looked on giddily, confident from the forty-ounce bottle of beer that she had opened and already finished on Brian's front porch. She and Karen were like stray cats crouched under tires, pupils fierce and dilated and legs tucked underneath, ready to spring at the faintest sound. Maria was on her feet as soon as she saw the boys.

"We're celebrating!" she yelled. "School's almost out!"

"Private school sounds nice," Brian said, leading the pack of boys. He stopped on the porch to kiss Maria hello. "We won't get out for a month." He looked over at Karen and stooped toward her. Karen tried to hug him, even as Brian stuck his head out for a kiss. When he saw that she shirked from his cheek, he attempted to put his arm around her, but by then Karen had already lowered her own. Maria regarded the two with bemusement; together, they hadn't accomplished any sort of proper greeting.

"I love you guys!" Maria said as they walked up the steps into Brian's house. She pushed Karen into Brian with so much force that she nearly fell on top of him. Karen scowled, but when she sat down on the living room couch, Brian immediately took a seat beside her, and Maria sat on the other side.

"Andres?" Maria asked, when she saw him going up the stairs with the other boys.

"I'll be back," he called. Brian got up and turned on a speaker, and the room was flooded with music. Karen didn't touch her beer again, so Maria picked it up. The bell to the house started ringing, and Brian got up each time to let a new person in. Maria recognized no one, and as each minute went by, she took another sip of Karen's beer. When Andres finally came back, it felt like he'd been gone for an hour. It felt like every cell in Maria's body was drunk.

"Andres, where were you?" she said, getting to her feet, swaying.

"You're fucked up," he said.

"No. I'm just hungry."

"Well, that's what happens when you don't eat. Stop trying to be like those white girls at your school."

"Andres," Maria cried. "Do you even love me? No! Do you think I'm pretty?" Maria was slurring. *Pretty* took such a long time to come out, it took on an extra syllable. "I mean pretty," she said, loudly. She grabbed his hand.

"Fuck, Maria. You know the answer to that." He pulled away and her wrist fell to her side. "Stop asking stupid questions."

Suddenly, Karen was off the couch. Standing between Maria and Andres, Karen took Maria's hand in her own.

"I'm taking her home," Karen said.

"But you just got here. I mean—whatever. You'll be okay, right?" Andres asked. "I would go with you, but I should probably stay here."

"We'll be fine," she answered, leading Maria away.

Outside, blue slivers of light bubbled from the streetlamps and slipped like water into Maria's eyes. Looking into the glass storefronts was like looking into the surfaces of puddles and rivers, a glazed film through which Maria could see herself. Cars whooshed by. A diner hummed. The world looked like it was painted over in some sort of sheen. Maria lifted her hand like she could reach out and touch it. It was all so beautiful.

"Are you all right?" Karen asked.

"Yeah."

"I hate boys," Karen said. "They're idiots."

They continued to walk in the dark and didn't speak again until they crossed Queens Boulevard. Sometimes, when Maria walked down Queens Boulevard, she felt as if she were in front of an ocean. Twelve lanes wide and spanning far into the horizon, it provoked a similar sense of awe. In those rare moments when she had it to herself, when the sun had gone down and even the cars were sporadic, fleeting like flies, Maria was overcome with emotion. She felt so deeply her full humanity then. Some people had backyards, other people mountaintops, but Maria had Queens Boulevard to help her appreciate the ample beauty of existence.

"I think," Maria said now, dropping her head onto Karen's shoulder, "he likes me. He likes me more than Andres does."

"Who? Rocky's dad?"

"His name is Charlie," Maria whined.

"Sorry," Karen said. "Charlie."

"He called me beautiful, Karen."

"That's such a dad thing to say."

Maria frowned. It was true that her parents called her beautiful. But what Charlie felt toward her had to be more than just paternal affection.

"It's not just that," Maria said. "He—he knows my poetry. He knows I'm a poet."

"Maria, what are you talking about?"

Maria's body lurched forward, and Karen fell with her, and suddenly Maria was vomiting. In front of them was a three-family apartment that didn't have a walkway, just a front door that spilled right out to the curb. Karen got up from the ground in horror.

"Jesus, right in front of their house! What is your problem, Maria?"

Maria was having trouble getting up on her own, but Karen didn't move any closer, so she sat for a while on the concrete while Karen stood a few paces away. Finally, Karen offered her hand.

As they walked, Maria pulled Karen toward her and placed her head where it had been before, resting atop Karen's shoulder. Karen sighed, but she didn't shake her off.

"Do you really think I could do better than Andres?"

"Yes, Maria. Of course you can."

"Thank you," Maria said, just beneath Karen's earlobe. "I feel much better now."

CHAPTER 6

Miguel could hear his heart thrumming inside his head. His shoulders made a frame around his ears, deepening the shell of his collarbones until they became like an echo chamber, the sound growing tinny and loud. He had been thrashing in bed—the way he sometimes did after leg days at the gym, when he'd wake up with his quads stinging and begging to be stretched. But it'd been weeks since he'd last worked out, and his muscles, which were always so easy to feel, were starting to disappear, getting submerged under the skin, like a valuable coin sinking farther and farther into the ocean floor.

Miguel got up, out of bed, and paused in front of the fan. The house was scorching. He stood in front of the spinning blades, each pore of his skin wide open. Before he knew it, he was no longer hot, and the wet pieces of salt-sodden chest hair now were making him shiver. Even with the blinds down, a hazy mist of light filtered in from the streetlamps and made it so that the room was never so dark as to make things invisible. He found the knob to his bedroom door without fumbling and went into the living room.

He paused when he saw the futon mattress pulled out. He had not been expecting to see Maria and Karen huddled beneath a thin crumpled sheet, their arms outstretched to each other, like children. Maria was such a thing full of life—rivers of it coursed through her.

He had heard women's voices like hers described as gravelly, but Maria's was bigger than that—there were boulders in her voice. But asleep here, in her oversize pajamas, with her mouth parted in an underbite, Maria looked so young. She looked, shockingly, like the little girl they had put in special dresses for the holiday sermons at church. Miguel rubbed his eyes. It was an apparition, a mirage. In front of him was the daughter he once had, the one whom he couldn't reconcile with the young woman he knew that she was. There was the past and the present, and he knew they were two distinct things. But he had a hard time keeping them separate.

It was the other thing, the past thing, that worried him when he thought about her getting a job. She was seventeen and she needed to work, but still, it made him anxious. When he'd pressed her, she'd said she could apply online to Taco Bell, but it made him uncomfortable to think of her dressing in those two-button polos, her hair swept behind a greasy visor, staying well past midnight at the twenty-four-hour drive-through. He'd rather she stay in school. He'd rather she go straight to college. When Maria was accepted to Bell Seminary, the all-girls Catholic school, he thought he'd been blessed. He didn't want her behind a cashier counter, taking orders from boys who had barely just gotten their license, boys who'd invite her to get into their cars, boys, who in other contexts, under other lights—on government tax forms, as military recruits, in court proceedings—were not boys at all, but men.

Maria didn't want a job, either, no matter how much he tried to convince her it was a good idea.

"Don't you want money? It'll be good for you to have some money. We'll only take half. You can keep the rest."

She had pushed her plate away from her, where she'd left two pink vienna sausages uneaten. Like little life vests, they were buoyed by a pile of rice.

"I don't care about money! I'd rather go straight to college!"

"But I'm not saying you'll never go to college, Maria! You'll go to college! We'll send you to college! But now, you can get experience. Won't that school help you find something? Can't someone get you a job in an office, where you can start building your career?"

Maria puffed her face out, her cheeks big like water balloons. "Everyone graduates college now, Dad," she said. "The only thing I can get in an office is an internship. And those don't pay!"

Finally, Miguel lost his temper. "My house!" he thundered. "My rules!"

Now, as the blue light made ripples on his daughter's face, he felt a tinge of remorse. She still had the peculiar look of her eyes being too big for her face, of her rounded, curved forehead too prominent. It was undeniable: she resembled a baby. Before he'd lost his job, they had just finished paying off two rows of her braces. Her life was still full of promise and possibility. She deserved to study and become whatever she wanted. It made his heart sink that right now, he was asking her to act like an adult, and put her dreams on hold.

In the darkness, he wondered if everything in his life was really a Rorschach inkblot, a passing cloud, that maybe it was in his power to see one thing and not the other, to see Maria as either woman or child, and this thought made him cold, as if he were standing in front of the fan again, wet with sweat and shivering, all the pores of his skin tiny and stiffening.

Finally, he went into the bathroom. He switched on the light and caught himself in the mirror. All over his skin were indicators of age—new wrinkles appeared all the time. He knew Maria looked like him, but it was hard to believe he ever looked like Maria. He couldn't remember a time being so awash with innocence, you could see it just from the sight of his face. He sighed noisily. It jarred Miguel to see how sallow and sunken he looked. He feared his skin might tear from where it strained to hold up the sharp corners of his face. He imagined his skin flying open like a brown paper bag ripping from the weight of too many groceries. Age, he could see, was just the physical traces of pain, grief, sorrow traveling around the eyes in rivulets, in wrinkles as deep as the depth of experience. He had thought he looked older since he'd lost his job. Now, he could see it was true.

On his way back to bed, he tripped. He made a noise and put his hand out, and luckily, he caught the back of an armchair before he could really fall. Regaining his balance, he looked down and squinted at something hard and square at the foot of the futon. It was glittering purple, a prism of color and light like the back of an abalone shell. He had seen it tucked away in Maria's bedroom before and knew it was her journal. He knew Maria wrote in it all the time because she left her chewed-up pens everywhere, and he had wondered what she was writing about before. He wouldn't dare touch it when it was in her room, but now it was out in the open. He stooped to pick it up. He placed his fingers on the front cover. He had the book right side up in his hands when he creaked open the spine to look inside. On the first page, she had written her name and phone number. He turned it to look at the opposite side. The paper made an imperceptible swoosh through the air, and when he looked up, he saw Maria's friend, Karen, staring.

Miguel said nothing. He lowered himself, but his entire body had clenched, making it difficult to return the book to where he'd found it lying faceup on the floor. He opened his mouth, readying for an excuse. She had seen it, his moment of weakness, how in the dead of the night, he had tried to sneak up on Maria's secrets. He had to say something. He had to apologize. And then he saw Karen's chest falling into itself, and at the corner of her mouth, almost invisible, a tiny bead of saliva.

He hurried back to his room. When he got back into bed, he no longer noticed how hot it was. He no longer noticed how the fan spun. He no longer noticed the pain that had taken up residence in his body, making all his recent nights sleepless. He was too intent on trying to rid himself of Karen's face. If the look of a thing was merely a reflection of what was inside it, then what was inside the girl? What did she know that was so horrible that she had taken to sleeping with her eyes open? But it was something else that was making loops around his mind like a carousel. Miguel knew she'd been asleep; there was no other way to account for the drooling or that thickness of breath. What he didn't understand was how it was possible to have your eyes wide open, pupils dilated to full moons, and still not be able to see the thing standing in front of you.

At the grocery store near the school, Rocky purchased a midprice bottle of a California red blend to celebrate the end of finals week. School was officially over. Summer had begun. She poured two equal glasses and had just set them out on the table when she suggested they should also order some food. When the bell rang a half hour later, Rocky went to the door to receive the doorman, and Maria followed, carrying the bags inside, leaving Rocky alone to pay. In the kitchen, Maria separated Rocky's chocolate milkshake from her strawberry. She took her first bite of a cheeseburger just as Rocky stepped into the room.

"As always," Maria said. "Patrick's is so good."

Rocky grinned. At the table, she collected what was hers, and with one limp french fry in her mouth, she walked to the living room. There was a set of long wooden doors that separated the dining room table from the living room, and when the doors were flung wide open, their yellow-brass knobs in line with the yellow-brass hinges, you could see the living room TV. But instead of sitting next to Maria in the dining room, she sat on the couch and squeezed a mound of burgundy ketchup onto a napkin, despite the ivory-colored carpet just beneath her, that ran from wall to wall. She picked up the remote controller and started flipping through the TV guide. "What should I put on?"

"MTV," Maria said, gathering her burger and milkshake, and ambling to the couch. Once she had set them down, she hurried back to the kitchen for her glass of wine.

"What about *Grey's Anatomy?*"

"What's that?"

"You don't know *Grey's Anatomy?* God, Maria, how? What world do you possibly live in?"

Maria tasted salt in her mouth. She brought the glass of wine to her lips and imagined Andres. Whenever Andres surprised her by not having heard of a book or a song, he always said the same thing. *You are such a white girl.*

"Well," Maria said, gingerly placing the glass on the table. "It's probably just a white-person thing."

Rocky glanced at Maria's glass of wine, and then looked back up at Maria's face. She crossed one arm over the other, and then rearranged them so that her chin rested in one palm.

"A white-person thing?"

"Yeah. Like *Grease.* Or *Clueless.* Or scones. Or," she said, exaggerating a British accent, *"English Breakfast."*

"*Clueless* is a classic," Rocky said, the double *ss* in both words pronounced with fervent intent.

"I guess."

Maria brought the wineglass up to her mouth. The only other time she'd tasted wine was when Ricky turned eighteen and the whole family went to dinner. At an Italian restaurant in Corona, a few doors down from the famous Lemon Ice King, her mother had let her take a sip. Maria asked for more, but her father frowned, and by the end of the night, the corners of her mother's mouth were stained in a brown outline, like henna. It took a while for Maria to realize it was the alcohol, because when she rubbed it away with her napkin, it looked like clumps of dried food. Maria glanced at Rocky's lips now, but they were pink and pristine, so she smiled, in relief.

"Do you hate white people?"

"What?"

"Do you hate white people," Rocky repeated, flatly.

"Is that a serious question?"

"I just think that's a prejudiced thing to say. Not all white people like the same things. There aren't any *white*-person things."

"Okay, Rocky. It's a joke."

"It didn't sound like a joke."

Rocky inspected her nails. Her mouth was perfect, but her eyeliner was running. At the corners of her eyes, there were deep pockets of black, and it made Rocky look extremely sleepy. Maria wanted to get up and rub it off for her.

"Your makeup is running. Here." Maria got up and posed a finger tentatively toward Rocky's face. "Can I?"

Slowly, Rocky closed her eyes. Maria took great care to run the pad of her fingers as gently as she could under Rocky's eyes, until the black was all gone. She didn't want to hurt her.

"Thanks. You've got something right there." Rocky gestured to her own lips.

"Where?" Maria asked, but Rocky kept her hands to herself. Maria frantically wiped at each corner, and when she took her fingers away, there were purple clumps under her fingernails. Streaked in Rocky's eyeliner and with scoops of dried wine under the nails, her hands were a splatter of black and purple.

"Better?" Maria asked.

"Better," Rocky said.

Side by side, the girls walked over to the wine bottle on the kitchen table and filled their glasses again.

They lost count of how many episodes of *Real World* they'd watched by the time Rocky pulled a third bottle of wine from the cellar behind the pantry. In front of her, on the glass table that Rocky had pulled close to the couch, two wineglasses sat next to two milkshakes from Patrick's. Even though Maria had long finished her milkshake, she occasionally picked it back up, hoping that something sweeter than air would come out of the straw. Beside her, Rocky scrolled through Facebook on her laptop, looking for a new profile picture. Maria looked away from the television just as an old photograph appeared on the screen. It was Rocky and Laura in front of a stadium-size fountain, and Rocky's arms were draped around Laura's spaghetti-strapped shoulders. Rocky spent more time with Maria these days than she did with Laura, but still, Maria couldn't help it when her face screwed into an envious pout.

"Where's that?" she asked.

"That is Las Vegas."

"I've never been there before."

"It's kind of a white-person thing."

Maria pulled her straw out of her mouth, and Rocky erupted into laughter. "I'm just kidding," Rocky said. "God, you should've seen your face!"

She lowered the computer screen as she looked Maria in the eye. "How about we go together?"

Maria smiled. "Really?"

"We go every summer. I'll just tell my mom."

The two girls fell quiet. Maria picked up her wineglass again. The silence between them was interrupted only when a woman on the reality show suddenly bellowed. Even though Maria was looking directly at the TV, she wasn't able to tell whether the sound came from a place of pleasure or fear. The images and figures danced in front of her, but it was impossible to follow a story line, and it was only getting harder. Finally, she shifted her legs so that both feet lay flat on Rocky's carpet.

"So your whole family goes? Every year?"

"Me and my mom." Rocky stared at the TV. "Nick's too young to come."

The picture of Rocky and Laura was still open, but Maria could hardly see it now that the laptop was angled so that it was almost closed. She'd been jealous of Laura a moment ago, but now, there was another feeling: desire. It was alcohol soaked, and blurry, and heavy, and if she wasn't careful, it would become known. Maria would blurt it out.

What about your dad?

Maria stifled the question by putting down the wineglass, which squealed with a giddy clink. She took a sip of her strawberry milkshake instead, which made the sound of emptiness, of hot air.

Maria walked into the house on tiptoes. Her mother stood in the kitchen alone. Her father was napping in the living room. Asleep, he was oblivious to the way that Maria hummed around her mother like a fruit fly, buzzing about her excitedly as her mother worked her way around the kitchen, packing up the remains of dinner.

"Who's going to pay for that?" Maria's mother said, speaking in an uncharacteristically quiet voice. She shoved the lid of a Tupperware container into the grooves where it fit, and opened the fridge door, pushing the plastic container inside. Littered around it were other boxes and bins. Inside them, there were things to be eaten later. The fridge was always a jigsaw of edible objects that huddled together indiscriminately to try to withstand the cold. Maria had noticed more than once that at Rocky's apartment, aside from full bottles of ketchup and jars of blueberry jam, the fridge was always a carcass, empty.

"Rocky's mom said it was fine," Maria attested, not actually knowing what Rocky's mother would say, and knowing that Rocky had yet to ask. "We're going to go in July."

"In July! That's next month!"

"I know, Ma, but they go every summer. All they have to do is buy my ticket." Maria brought her hands together in a faux prayer. "Please, Ma? It's only three days. Not even! It's only two nights."

"Sheesh," her mother said. "I wish I could go to Vegas."

"So I can go?" Maria paced an inch away from her mother. She was so close she could smell the gel her mother had used in the morning to slicken and straighten her curls. "I can go?"

"Only if her parents are going with her."

Maria gave her mother a forceful kiss on the cheek.

"Maria, have you applied to a job already?"

"I did, Ma. I did. I applied to Taco Bell."

Maria fluttered away to call Rocky, her feet pounding on the floor. As soon as she crossed the linoleum patch that separated the kitchen from the dining room, she froze, remembering to lighten her steps. In the living room, in the faded summer light, her father was still asleep on the couch, impressions of corduroy like lanes of a racetrack running down the length of his face.

CHAPTER 7

As her departure date drew nearer, Maria realized there were many things she needed to do before leaving for Vegas. She unearthed her passport because even though Rocky said she wouldn't need it, she wanted to use it, anyway. She started packing and bought travel-size versions of shampoo and conditioner, despite her mother's reminder that they'd have them at the hotel. But there was something else now that she needed to do: she'd decided to get on birth control.

Maria didn't like doctors. Her suspicion of them was solidified recently, on the last day before finals week. Mr. Willoughby had finished writing the morning "Do Now" on the board. There was murmuring in the room, and Mr. Willoughby twitched his head like a cow, as if a fly had threatened his ear.

"Have you finished the assignment, Maria?" he had asked, a vicious rip in his voice. Ever since she had started sitting in the back, he'd become nasty to her. She was twisted around the back of her desk, speaking in loud, harried whispers to Rocky.

"Um," Maria said. "Not yet."

"Then you shouldn't be talking."

Maria glanced at the math problem on the board. When she was done reading, she read it a second time. She didn't have anything to consult; when she took notes—if she took notes—it was always on loose sheets of paper that either wound up in some unrecognizable form at the bottom of her bag or were lost somewhere incomprehensible, like in the folds of her living room couch. It was 8:20 a.m., just the start of the day, and Mr. Willoughby's eyes were incising her. Whether at school or home, everything felt like war. Everywhere she went, she was forced onto the defensive.

"I hate this," she said, and her classmates looked up now, their pencils still in their hands. She dropped her head to the desk and stayed that way until Mr. Willoughby asked another student to demonstrate the answer on the board. Maria looked up and watched the chalk move across the board. Whenever the student was unsure of her next step, she lowered her fist and smudged the numbers into baby-powder clouds. When Maria was younger, she had learned how to simulate a baby's footprint by pressing her paint-doused fist onto paper and drawing five dots with her fingertips. When the student was finished, Mr. Willoughby erased the "Do Now." Maria spent the remainder of class wondering what would be served for lunch.

That afternoon, the dean of students called Maria into her office.

"We want you to start talking to Dr. Beth," the dean said. "We're worried you're not meeting your full potential. We'd like to help you figure out why."

"But school ends next week!" Maria shouted. She wondered if they'd already called her parents.

"Exactly," the dean said. "It hasn't ended yet."

At lunch, Maria saw Karen. "It won't be bad," Karen said. "Dr. Beth's office has candy."

Maria imagined it not being bad. She knew she wasn't like those girls in her class who ate the lettuce and tomatoes off their sandwiches and left everything else untouched on their plates. She wasn't like the other ones who came to school with lines on their ankles that made crags like lightning bolts and were dark as prunes. There was no reason she needed to see the psychologist, and by the time she went into the office to meet her, she knew that Dr. Beth would chuckle at the misunderstanding and tell her she needn't come back. She hoped there'd be candy she liked.

"I can't say with certainty," Dr. Beth had said, during their first session, "but you could be depressed." Maria sat up in her seat. She was so shocked she became sullen, and later she told her mother what happened as they cleared the table after dinner. Her father had already gone to his room.

How? Maria's mother had turned off the faucet. Tears sprouted in her eyes. When she wiped them away with her dishwashing gloves, her whole face became lacquered with liquid. *What did I do to make you unhappy?*

Maria had to speak to Dr. Beth every day for the rest of the week. She didn't want to be reminded of her new diagnosis, so she decided she wouldn't tell the psychologist a single genuine thing. The silences weren't easy to create. Dr. Beth paused so deliberately after her questions that Maria always found herself saying more than she wanted to. At the beginning of their sessions, Dr. Beth asked, *Maria, how do you feel today?* Maria would try not to roll her eyes, and later, she would make her mind into a white slate on which she would write the same question over and over. *How do you feel? How do you feel?* Maria came up with snarky responses, ones that would give nothing away. *Fantastic! Just getting over a fever!* But it was only a fantasy—Maria's bad attitude was what landed her in Dr. Beth's office in the first place, and she knew she shouldn't push it.

On one of those days, the temptation to answer Dr. Beth honestly was too much to resist, and Maria felt herself slip into conversation the way she curled into a ball after getting out of a shower on a cold winter day. She mentioned Andres, and the fear that she had fallen in love. It felt so nice to say Andres's name aloud, and Maria wanted to go on and on about him, about identifying isosceles triangles not in her textbooks but in his abdomen, about being terrified of pregnancy but feeling her body expand like a thousand open mouths whenever he was near, about the time she'd run a comb through his hair and wished that she knew him in a different capacity, in a way that surprised her, like father to son. But then she remembered how Laura, whom they'd forced into rehab for refusing to eat, had spent a lot of time in Dr. Beth's office before they took her away for two months, and she suddenly became angry, her face tightened and sealed like the margins of a laminated page. Maria wished that talking to Dr. Beth hadn't constituted a betrayal, but it was clear that talking to her meant she had failed her mother, and now, telling the truth carried too much risk to herself—and was it really impossible to find any adult who would be on her side and her side alone? Maria flinched like she'd been called a bad name and stopped talking about Andres. She kicked her sneakers off Dr. Beth's candy table and reached for her backpack, unzipped it.

"Can you help me study?" She pulled out her Spanish workbook, and when Dr. Beth saw that Maria was serious, together they conjugated verbs.

Even though Maria gave all the right answers, inside, the sadness was careening. Her eyes stayed on Dr. Beth, but her attention was drawn to that space in her mind where she would attempt to escape. All of her classes were unbearable because any moment that wasn't hers to decide what to do with always felt like a complete waste of time. Judging from the way her father talked about it, adulthood seemed to be more of the same thing—waking up every morning with a resistance so stubborn she'd have to wrestle it to the ground just to get to the front door. And death didn't seem much better, either, because then her life would be reduced to a single grain of dust in God's mansion, and in no time she'd be wiped up and erased, the way Rocky's cleaning lady wiped up her moldy bread, the way her mother did the same for other families, too. Maria tried to return to the present perfect tense, and she stared at the candy bowl. It was filled with Snickers bars ever since Dr.

Beth asked what she liked to eat. There were still six minutes left of her session, practically an eternity.

What's the point of therapy? she wondered. It wasn't making her feel any better.

But despite her disdain for doctors, Maria couldn't avoid them entirely. She and Andres had been going at it again, and now Maria was equipped with Rocky's advice. Practice with a cucumber, Rocky had advised. Make sure you make lots of sound. Maria thought she'd been doing better, but Andres was still unsatisfied. He made his dissatisfaction even clearer when halfway through having sex, he rolled off the condom and threw it across the bed, where it hung off the side of the mattress like a used sock. When she called Rocky, distressed, Rocky told her what she needed to do. For that, Rocky said, you should go to the clinic.

In the waiting room at ten in the morning, Maria was given a form to fill out and there was a box that asked if it was okay to contact her at her home address. She made a giant *X* next to "NO" and went over it three times, and thinking of the stacks of letters they received every day at their door, Maria told the receptionist that she didn't think she had insurance.

"That's fine," the receptionist told her, "but can you find out for sure next time?"

They called her name and escorted her to a hallway where a young nurse with two french braids and a set of bright-pink scrubs weighed her and took her blood pressure. The nurse handed her a little blue cup, and after she peed, Maria was taken to another small room, where she was instructed to wait on the examining table. When the nurse left, she had kept the door open. On the wall was an illustrated poster of the fetal cycle. She took a picture of the watercolor image of a baby attached to an umbilical cord and tried to send it to Andres as a joke, but she didn't have any service. When Maria looked up from where she sat on the edge of the table, she saw a girl walking past her room, another patient. There'd been a boy slumped beside her when Maria first saw her, but now that she was alone, her smile was slack. The girl's eyes watered, and Maria was pinched with remorse. She deleted the photo, and just as she did, she heard a voice.

"Maria?"

The doctor said her name the Spanish way, and Maria's face quirked into a smile. What did this white doctor with her neat auburn bun know about saying her name? Even Maria's parents usually said it the English way unless they were furious. The doctor closed the door behind her. She was holding a clipboard and pen.

"You wrote that you've only had intercourse with one person?"

"Yes."

"Only one?"

"Yeah." Maria brought her hand to her chin. There had been a pimple forming there, but she had stalled its growth by scratching it until it became a wound. "He's my boyfriend."

"How many partners has he had?"

Again, Maria's smile twitched. Andres was more experienced than she was—she had heard about some of his escapades directly from him. As Maria continued to pick at her pimple, she stared at the floor to think.

The doctor clicked her pen against her clipboard so that Maria was startled into looking up.

"Do you know how many partners he's had?"

"No."

"Is he older than you? Your age?"

"Yes."

"Older?"

Maria tried to concentrate. She was still on the last question, trying to figure out how many girls Andres might've had sex with.

"No," she said. "We're the same age."

"What's your current method of protection?"

"Right now, we're pulling out," Maria said. "Sometimes condoms, but he hates wearing them."

The doctor jotted something down on the page, and Maria kicked her sneakers together. One of her laces was untied, the same one on the left foot that always came undone. It annoyed Maria how people on the street would always yell after her as if she couldn't feel the loose strings dancing around her foot. Maria looked at her fingers, where she'd pulled off her skin's latest attempt to scab over her pimple. What was the point of all of these questions, and why did they make her pee in a cup even though she had told them her period had just ended? She stared up at the walls, but there was no clock to be found. She felt its absence profoundly. She felt like she was taking a test she was failing.

"Maria," the doctor said. "What's your partner's name?"

Without anticipating the change, she became very hot, and the word came out scalding from the roof of her mouth. "Andres," she said. It burned like hot soup.

"Have you ever been intimate with Andres when you didn't want to?"

Maria heard a ringing in her left ear, a sound that she recognized from hearing tests every year at the nurse's office. She closed her eyes tight, but once it was gone, she heard the same ringing in her right ear. She saw her mother crying in the kitchen, and when she blinked, she saw how the makeup coursed down her cheeks like twin rivers, black and poisonous.

"Have you ever been intimate with Andres because you were afraid of what he might do or say?"

Maria thrust her arms against her chest. With both hands, she clung to her elbows. There was no reason to make her mother sob. There was no reason to be depressed, and there was no reason to talk to this white woman doctor, who pronounced her name as if she knew who she was, as if she'd wanted Maria to believe she'd grown up down the street, with Maria's aunts and uncles. There was no reason to trust this woman and no reason to tell her the truth.

"Are you crazy?" Maria said. "No. I'm not afraid of Andres."

The white paper on the examining table was darkened with sweat when Maria stood up to leave with a month's worth of birth control pills. The doctor said that the next time she came back, she would give her three times as many, but for now, she wanted her to try out a month and see how her body responded.

Outside the clinic, Maria's phone rang.

"Hello?" she said.

"This Maria Rosario?" A woman's voice boomed.

"Yeah."

"Can you come in today for an interview? This is the general manager at Taco Bell on Queens Boulevard."

It was still very early. Maria had nothing to do.

"What time?"

"I'm free now."

Maria wondered, with some embarrassment, if the manager would remember her. Taco Bell was where Maria and Andres had their first date, and now that they were both out of school, they had been spending their afternoons getting high and eating gorditas with extra sour cream. They both loved unwrapping those meals tightly packaged like candies, the tacos sweating inside. They would meet in the parking lot, where Maria would be forced to watch six thousand attempts at a kickflip or a heelkick or an ollie, or something. Then, they would take a hit from Andres's pipe that looked like a cigarette—which was one of the coolest things Maria had ever seen—and splurge on cinnamon twists with money they pooled together. Taco Bell was where Andres and Maria plotted their adventures. In the parking lot, they'd shared their first kiss. Maria didn't write any of that on her online application, but the truth was that she only wanted to work at the fast-food restaurant out of sentimental value, and now, as she approached the faux adobe walls of the building, she couldn't help but feel a little humiliated. She looked away from the black orb of the camera affixed to the front door, but that wouldn't change anything. They would recognize her as the girl who gets stoned in the parking lot and immediately turn her away.

Inside, she went to the counter as usual and asked for the manager.

She was wearing her hair back in a tight coiled bun. She was younger than what Maria expected. Maria had never seen this woman before.

"You're the first person I've called that has showed up today." She smiled. "That's good. I'll need to be able to rely on you."

Maria followed her through the kitchen. Back there, she looked around in awe. Everything was made of stainless steel, and despite the heat emanating from the stoves, it was surprisingly cool. She saw someone assemble a gordita with gloved hands, sprinkling lettuce that was shredded like confetti. From a pump that seemed to lead into the ground came out sour cream, like water from a well.

"What do you want? Do you want anything?"

Maria wanted a gordita, a quesadilla, but she also didn't want to be greedy.

"Cinnamon twists."

"You in school?" the manager asked.

"Not right now. I don't start until September."

The manager nodded. "That's fine."

On the walk home, the sun was high in the sky, relentless. Maria started sweating. She ate the cinnamon twists one by one, slowly and deliberately. She let each piece dissolve until it was a pool of sugar on her tongue. Then she swallowed and started all over again until the bag was empty.

"How much do they pay?" her mother asked in the living room. All the windows were wide open, but the house was sweltering. Every few seconds, Maria's mother spritzed herself with water from a handheld misting fan. Maria had never seen it before. The nozzle looked the same as the ones her mother used to spray cleaning product.

"Six seventy-five."

"Good. If they like you they'll give you a raise." She held the fan toward Maria. "Here," she said, spraying her.

Maria laughed. It felt better than she expected.

"I got it from the ninety-nine cents store. It's good, right?"

"Yeah."

"I'll get you one. So when do you start?"

"Next week. As soon as I get back from Vegas."

Maria's mother sprayed her again. She gave Maria a kiss on the cheek. Maria fell into the futon, and her mother leaned on the armrest. They stayed that way for a while, in silence, the two women reclining as if in a nineteenth-century painting. But respites were rare, even the brief ones. Maria's mother had been called for a shift at an apartment in Manhattan that same afternoon. Maria was supposed to help her get started on dinner. Very soon, they would need to get up.

CHAPTER 8

The letter Maria wrote for Miguel was only the latest in a series of many fraught communications, of phone calls and emails that did little to assuage his increasing sense of hopelessness. Initially, they had petitioned the union until the union finally told him that they wouldn't take his case to arbitration. It had been a devastating decision, one that ultimately led Miguel to seek his own lawyer, but in the meantime, as he waited for the case to be prepared, which he had been warned could take several months, the union had found him work in a different building, monitoring a freight elevator. For nine hours he stood in the same corner and pulled two doors open like the jaws of a mouth. From top to bottom he yanked them apart with a chain. Men lifting cardboard boxes entered, lines of tape creaking behind them. All day it was a variation of the same scene, daylong coffee smells on everyone's breath.

Along with the demotion came the pinstripe shirt. He had never worn a uniform to the workplace before, and the sight of the shirt, freshly ironed and hung from the corner of his bedroom, patched with only his first name, *Miguel*, made him want to scream. The blue and white stripes wrapped around him, curling like the painted grimace of a clown. The stiff collar itched and closed too tightly around the neck—like the knot of a balloon; he felt pressed for air.

Worse was how carefully Analise handled the shirt, smoothing out its creases and wrinkles atop her ironing board, the steam doubling over itself as it hit the low ceiling. *I hung up your shirt for tomorrow, Papi,* she would say sweetly, and he had to suppress the urge to slap her, this woman whom he had never come close to—never even considered—hitting before. It terrified him, how many firsts he'd been brushing up against recently.

Because it wasn't the only, or even salient, fantasy. All day the shirt went creaseless, unfettered by the gentle earthquake that rocked him, hour by hour, minute by minute, with each "good morning" and "good afternoon" and jerk of the handle that opened the door. In between breaks in the bathroom, he could feel the breath rise out of him like an impending warm rush of vomit. He began to fantasize about bringing the elevator up to the very top floor, climbing the staircase that led to the roof, and at the water tower—he was still in good shape—he'd hike to the very top point and hurtle himself into the gray sea of concrete below.

Of course, it never happened. He doubted he even had access to the roof. Either way, the worst part always came early. If he could manage the indignity of fastening all the buttons of that ridiculous shirt in the morning, he could also live through the rest of the day, and he did live through the days for several months. He woke up through them, even though they were long, waiting to be reinstated. In the meantime, he had trouble keeping track of Maria. He didn't lock her out of the house anymore. He didn't ground her for coming home past curfew. He had even stopped demanding that she sit with him to eat dinner. He was eating less dinner, anyway.

A week after he thought he saw Karen staring into the dark, he had consulted with Ricky. Ricky, who had always been close to Maria, was at first reluctant. But Ricky, who was only two years her senior, needed to know that he had a responsibility—and that responsibility was to his family. *What would you do if something happened to your sister?* Miguel said, and Miguel didn't even need to name any worst-case scenarios for Ricky to tear up and finally oblige. *Keep an eye on your sister* was all that he'd asked him. Analise was too good-natured to truly understand what he meant. After all, she had given Maria permission to go to Vegas alone, and now, it was too late to take it back, too late to tell her not to drive to the airport in the morning. Ricky nodded and told him he'd talk to Maria, and Miguel was proud and pleased with his son.

Miguel wasn't *born yesterday*. He knew he could read things by the glaze in a person's eyes. He knew he could divine things from the long naps before dinner. He could take a guess by the way she kept her door locked on weeknights and did her makeup behind closed doors. But much worse than any of that was that Maria was so sullen and quiet, so reticent, so moody. So sad. She'd been locking herself in her room for hours. She seemed to be acting—well—like him.

Even though Miguel was distracted now, distracted by this pending lawsuit, distracted by the anxiety that barreled down on him in the middle of the night, the same one that heightened whenever he checked his bank statements or saw the outstanding bills in the mail, Miguel wasn't distracted enough to stop caring about his daughter. Not distracted enough to stop thinking of her. Sometimes he didn't know how to understand Maria, and most of the time he had no idea what to say—and he had less time than ever to puzzle over it. Nowadays there were a million reasons for Miguel to be worried, but that didn't change the fact that stored away in some hidden compartment in his heart was a worry devoted to her.

Maria was sitting on her forest-green beanbag chair in her oversize school gym shorts, sorting through a pile of clothing, when Ricky walked into her room. Outside, it was drizzling, and Maria knew it was stopping soon, because through the *tin-tin* of the raindrops, she could hear a faint hum of crickets, as if they were waiting for the last song to be over so they could get their turn.

His face was puckered with attitude. Maria knew he'd just come from Alex's apartment, because he always had attitude whenever he came back from hanging with Alex. Maria didn't understand why— Alex was always nice to her when they'd run into each other, which led Maria to believe that it was her brother who must be doing something wrong. He was constantly on the phone, apologizing to her. Sometimes, Maria even heard him weeping in his room. Maria teased him whenever it happened, but Ricky was always so sensitive, and she had to be careful not to get him even more upset.

"Hey," he said now. "What are you doing?"

Maria tilted her head. Her brother's T-shirt was wet. His jeans looked heavy and uncomfortable. Instead of being slickened down to his head, his hair was so short that the tiny droplets of rain were scattered like jewelry beads balanced atop his head.

"What do you mean? I'm packing."

"Packing?"

Suddenly, Ricky coughed. Ricky's asthma was bad—so bad that the family kept a big box in the living room that he plugged in sometimes to help him breathe. When it was turned on, it made as much noise as a small power generator, but the fumes it gave off were nothing but magical. Maria had always wished she had asthma, too, so that she could have a taste of that healing white steam.

"Didn't Ma tell you already?" Maria got up from where she was sitting. She picked up a hoodie and started to fold it. "I'm going to Vegas with my friend Rachelle. We're leaving tomorrow morning." She pushed her suitcase against the wall. Underwear spilled out of it, along with pieces of bikini string. There was a tiny bottle of conditioner sealed in a ziplock bag.

Ricky shifted his weight, his shoes squelching with moisture. Like Maria, he wore Nike sneakers, but unlike her, he took great care that they never looked like they'd aged more than a day. As Ricky stood there, with his hard look, his unbudging stance in her doorway, Maria's eyebrows furrowed. He wanted something, but she couldn't decipher what. The two lines of her eyebrows joined in the middle, and together they stared back at Ricky.

"What's up, dude?" she said.

"We need to talk, Maria." Again, he coughed.

"About what?"

"You've been coming home late every weekend," he said. "Or sometimes you're not even here at all. And you reek of cigarette smoke. Don't you know that? Even now I can smell you. You know you shouldn't—you can't do that."

"That's not fair," Maria said. "That's not fair at all. I don't smoke cigarettes."

"Stop lying, Maria. It'll kill you for one. But also, it's really disgusting."

Maria's face became tight. One of the things that she liked about her relationship with her brother was that aside from a few passive tidbits of advice about boys, he never butted in on her personal life. Their relationship was built on movie references, inside jokes, and giving gag gifts to each other to the chagrin of their parents, who were always so solemn on Christmas Day. They didn't tell each other their darkest secrets, because they didn't need to. What they had instead was nice.

"You stay out late all the time," Maria retaliated. "And I never say anything about what you're doing wrong."

"Yeah, but it's different. I don't do what you do. You've been acting so . . . crazy."

"Crazy? What are you talking about?" Maria felt her anger take hold. It was one thing for Andres or Dr. Beth to think she was crazy. But no, she wouldn't take this from Ricky, too.

"What are you," she said. "My fucking father?"

"Don't fucking curse at me!" Ricky's wet sneakers squashed against the floor as he took a step toward her. "You go out every weekend with that idiot boyfriend of yours. I know he smokes weed. Everyone knows he smokes weed. I'm almost positive he sells it."

Maria was shocked. She'd only brought Andres to their house a few times, and she never even kissed him in front of anyone. She always hated that Andres and her brother both went to Newtown High School, but now that Ricky had graduated, she thought they'd never cross paths again. Andres told her when he saw Ricky around, even gave her status reports on the girls that he saw him with that day, as if Maria cared about whether Ricky was cheating or wasn't cheating on his girlfriend. It was inevitable that Ricky knew who Andres was—but how did Ricky know that Andres sometimes sold weed?

"How do you know about Andres?" Maria said.

"Oh come on, Maria. I'm not a complete idiot."

Ricky coughed so hard, he bent over. His wheezing was so bad he sounded like a videotape getting caught on rewind.

"God," Maria said. "Of course you know Andres sells weed. You hypocrite! You're smoking it, too."

Ricky snorted, his face even tighter, like he'd just licked a lime. His phone started to ring. He pulled it out of his pocket and stared at the screen. Maria looked on, the hairs on her arms standing up. *Pick it up,* she thought. *Leave me alone.*

He didn't. With a quick jab of a finger, he silenced the phone and jammed it into his pocket. He looked down at her suitcase, at the clothes spilling out. Maria looked, too. Her birth control packet wasn't hidden. Its green case seemed to shine like a neon sign. Maria reached for something to throw over it, but Ricky had already seen.

"Ms. Goody Two-Shoes, right?" he snarled, staring into her eyes. "You think you don't need to listen to anyone. You think you know better than anyone else. But the truth is that you're acting like a slut!"

For a moment, Maria thought she lost her vision. She blinked, and then, without knowing she was moving, she got up from the beanbag chair and stumbled past Ricky, half seeing the ground in front of her, half knowing from memory how to get out. She went into the living room, through the dining room and then the kitchen, and finally, opened the back door. She had always heard the way that Jonathan and Ricky talked about girls—it was from them that she divined the difference between first base and home, and then later between A and D, and then between the kind of girl you fuck and the kind you marry, which hadn't even taken Maria by surprise, because she tacitly understood what kind of girl she would be. But somewhere along the way, she must've crossed over. She'd gone from the good to the bad. Whenever it happened, it hadn't hurt at the time. After all, it could happen on any school night. But now, she heard it from Ricky, who'd once been her teacher. Now, it felt like it nearly killed her.

I hate him. As soon as she closed the screen behind her, she texted Karen, and bent her knees forward to sit on the pavement. She groaned, realizing it was wet. There was a half-inflated beach ball outside the neighbor's door, and from her perch on the ground, she tried to rename its colors as if they were Crayola: a white stripe that was less White than it was Puddle-Gray from having rolled through so many inky receipts; a green that was not Forest Green but Empty Beer Bottle Green; an SOS Red for how much it screamed desperation. All these sad bursts of color. They faded into the gray cement berm behind the long row of closed doors. Everything about this house was pathetic, she thought. Pathetic that this was the best her family could do. Pathetic that her family might not even be able to keep it.

Rocky's house in the Hamptons was so different. Maria knew because she'd seen pictures online, the same way she'd seen pictures of Vegas. Rocky's was a real house, the kind that could be featured in a movie, the kind that Maria's cousins abroad always imagined Maria's family owning. Between hedges and trees was a sprawling lawn that looked more like a golf course than a backyard. When Rocky first showed her, Maria announced her amazement and thought she was saying something profound. "This looks like something from a catalog," she said, and Rocky grinned. "Well, it's not a rental."

Maria turned her phone over in her hand, but Karen still hadn't answered. Maria already knew Rocky's country house well, but Rocky didn't know anything about Queens. It was still drizzling, unrecognizable from the thick orbs of rain that had fallen earlier in the day. She noticed her breathing; it was finally even. She heard a dog bark in the distance.

If Maria was a slut, what did that make Rocky?

The dog that barked once was now barking consistently, in intervals of silence that lasted no more than four seconds. Maria looked up from the pavement. She got up from the ground, unfolding her legs out in front of her. It smelled like wet concrete and garbage, and that was a different smell than what Rocky's country house might smell like, which was probably always like lavender and vanilla candles. She closed the back door and went to the dining room table, where a pile of mail teetered toward the floor. She paused when she spotted her mother's uneven cursive and an inky line running down two boxes of text. On one side of an envelope she had written: "Psalm 46:1 God is our refuge and strength, a very present help in trouble." Even though her parents went to church every Sunday, it was strange to find handwritten Bible verses lying around the dining room table. They were a "God-fearing family," as her father would put it, but their leather-bound Bibles went unopened during the week. Staring down at her mother's words, Maria knew they were prayers, but they read like omens instead.

At midnight, Karen still hadn't responded. That night, Maria had a dream, and in the morning, she reached for the purple poetry book she kept on her bookshelf. She scribbled down what she remembered before her mother could yell at her, with mossy teeth and sour breath, to hurry up. She had to be at the airport for her 10:00 a.m. flight to Las Vegas. When she clasped the book shut, she reached under her pillow for her phone and saw a message alert. First of all, ugh, that's a stupid insult—Karen had sent at 1:06 in the morning—Maybe he just had a bad night? But Maria's mind was still whirling from the dream that she had woken from, and she texted Andres instead.

I had a dream about you. You had an identical brother that I was going to marry, but I was in love with you. Before hitting send, she remembered how Andres was always so jealous. From the way he freaked out whenever she mentioned imaginary white boys who were smitten by her at Bell Seminary dances, she knew even hypothetical people weren't off-limits. But even though you were twins, I could tell that he wasn't you.

How's that?

His dick was smaller than yours.

Andres replied how he normally did, immediately, with a giant LMAO. Maria reached for the towel draped over her bedframe, and as she wedged her toes into her shower slippers, she remembered her brother. If it were things like this that made her a slut, it didn't seem fair—after all, she couldn't decide on the things that she dreamed. When Maria was still in preschool, she would have terrible dreams of meeting the devil behind rows upon rows of closed doors. Like a game show from hell, out he would pop, no matter which door she chose. If Maria was responsible for her dreams as much as she was for her actions and thoughts, how could she account for all those encounters with the devil during her Sunday school years?

"Maria!" Maria was startled to see her mother's face wedged in the tiny crack between the bedroom door and the doorframe. It made her uneasy to wonder how long she'd been standing there, watching, without saying a word.

"Jesus!" Maria said.

"Don't say that! And what are you doing? Come on! We have to go!" Her mother's eyes were poised like a pair of open scissors, ready to come down and cut through her.

"Get ready," she whispered, as if she hadn't already woken everyone up.

Maria got her things together, and when they were about to leave the house, she remembered her books. She dashed inside and picked the only one thin enough to fit into her bag, a collection of Emerson's essays.

The station wagon was the color of sand, and through its center ran a thick line the color of stained wood flooring. It was an old car, one that her family had driven for as long as Maria could remember. When they were younger, Ricky and Maria would sit in the back, their shaggy heads hanging out, and the two of them would wave like pageant queens to anyone who walked by.

As Maria brought down the trunk door with all of her weight, she thought of Diana. What was this car really worth?

"Mija, you don't have to close it so hard!" Maria's mother stared at her as she climbed into the passenger's seat. Maria avoided looking down, where her bare legs had ballooned out onto the leather, and when she closed the side door, this time, she did it slowly.

"So what, Ma? This car is so old."

"Old? What does that mean?" Maria's mother started to drive. "Don't you see how I take care of my things? This car will last me another ten years."

"Yeah."

"How could you even say that—*so what?* Don't you see how I always park away from the other cars? Don't you see how much I take care of it?"

"Okay, Ma. Sorry."

"You don't know how to take care of anything, that's why. Look at your room. When are you going to pick up all those books and those dirty clothes off your floor?"

Maria stared out the window. It was early in the morning, and the sun still hadn't risen completely. Outside, the city was a bleary blue, the color of muddled paint water. For being so early, it was already hot, so Maria leaned over and cranked the lever of the window down until the glass had fully retreated. She watched the signs on the highway whiz by. Her mother pushed a button on the dashboard and voices filled the car.

"Are you nervous?"

"For what?" Maria looked at her hands, where the cuticles of her fingers were ripped.

"To get on the plane. These terrorist attacks. It's just—you never know."

"I've been on a plane before."

"It's different these days. You were three years old."

Maria brought her nail to her mouth and bit down. "I survived that time. I'll survive again."

Her mother clicked her tongue. "Maria Anís, why do you think you know everything?"

A man's voice rose from the speakers. It was the news report that her mother always listened to in the morning, the one that operated on a loop. It replayed the same headlines after a terse twenty minutes. Maria hated listening to this program because it did more to create gaps in knowledge than fill them. It's where her mother got all her ideas about rapists who lurk inside parks after sunset and killers who massacre teenage girls.

"I'm not nervous," Maria said. "I'm excited to go somewhere new."

"I'm jealous."

"How come? You said you hate gambling."

"I just want to go on vacation."

According to the news, there was a mugging at four in the morning in the Bronx. Maria sucked on the sweet taste of blood on her finger.

"I'll bring you something back," she said.

The left turn signal started ticking as her mother merged onto the highway. The sound rocked Maria like a lullaby. She leaned back in her seat and closed her eyes.

"No, don't spend your money. I don't need no gift."

Maria opened her eyes. "I don't need *a* gift."

"What?"

"You said it wrong. It's 'I don't need *a* gift.'"

"That's what I said."

"You said you don't need no gift. You can't say that."

"What do you mean I can't say that? Why do you always try to prove me wrong?"

Maria couldn't help it—she was protecting her mother. She thought of the next time they'd be at Bell Seminary, going through the racks at the used-skirt sale.

"Did you tell Andres you were going to Vegas? What does he think about it?"

"He's jealous, too."

They pulled into the airport. On the long expanse of tarmac, Maria could see the airplanes from a distance, lined up in rows, unmoving. They looked slightly dusted, like a set of toy cars. Maria looked on with disbelief that in a couple of hours she'd be hurtling through the air in one of those funny planes that looked exactly like they did in movies.

"It's Delta," Maria said. Overhead, there were big blue signs. One after another they listed the names of different airlines, and some of them made Maria's heart flutter—Japan Airlines, Aerolíneas Argentinas, British Airways—there were so many places Maria had never been. She looked but didn't see Delta. "I think you need to go farther up."

"Maria, are things okay with Andres?"

Maria brought her finger to her mouth again and bit until the nail ripped off. She held the strip between her teeth. "Yeah. Why?"

They pulled up to the Delta terminal and stopped directly in front of the glass doors. There was nobody standing outside, and even inside, the place looked deserted, though the lights were pumped full of power and blaring. *Are they open?* Maria thought, just as the sound of a plane taking off flooded the car and rattled its old tinny insides so much that it trembled that way for a full minute until the sound of the radio surfaced again. There was a mugging at four in the morning in the Bronx.

"I heard you crying last night."

Maria felt herself sink as if the seat had given way beneath her. She hadn't thought that anyone was still awake once she came back into the house after her conversation with Ricky.

"It's fine," Maria forced herself to say. "It wasn't about Andres."

"Maria." Her mother took her hands off the wheel and turned her whole body. "I don't know what you're always crying about. What I really think is that you should save all those tears para cuando yo me muera." She sighed, and it took an eternity to come out. "But I know something's going on with you. You have to tell me what's going on."

Maria stared out the window, yearning to get out of the car. "Nothing is going on, Mom. I don't know what you think is going on."

"I just don't really think you know what you're getting into."

Maria's pulse quickened. "What are you talking about?"

"Maria, you're too young to even think about having sex—"

"Ma!"

"—but if that's what you're doing, then you need birth control."

Maria looked at her feet in horror. Ricky must've told her about what he saw last night in her room.

"I don't agree with it," Maria's mother continued, "I don't agree with it at all. But it'd be worse if you were to get pregnant. Just don't tell your father we talked about this. And make sure he never finds out that you're—"

But Maria wasn't listening. She was thinking of all of the times her mother had told her that she needed to wait until marriage. Of the women at church who told her that she should treat her body as a temple. Maria was sure her mother was setting her up, but Maria wouldn't confess, and she surveyed her mother now as she spoke: she was still in her pajamas, a waffled powder-blue long-sleeve shirt and a pair of basketball shorts. As if she'd only needed to adjust a stray wire to tap into the frequency, Maria could hear the crystalline voice of her own inner rage. *Why did they always tell me to not have sex? Was it because they didn't want me to end up like you?* Did they think Maria would end up a powerless woman, a woman who was constantly cleaning up after, who didn't graduate college, who got pregnant too young? A woman who didn't speak the truth to her daughter until the men were no longer in the room?

Maria's thoughts became aggregate, until they became heavy, a sodden mass in her mind. Her mother was a *housewife, a cleaning lady*, and Maria didn't need her mother's advice.

"Stop!" Maria had angled her body so far away that her shoulders were pressing against the side of her door. "I'm doing everything you want me to do! I got a job for you even though I didn't want it! Why can't you just leave me alone?"

Maria's mother squinted, as if she was trying to think of what to say next and couldn't come up with anything.

"Rocky's waiting for me." Maria opened the door of the car, and when she tried to lift off from her heels, the force of the seat belt holding her back by the waist was so strong that it made her gag. In her throat she tasted what she could only imagine was her raw stomach, and without waiting another second, she unbuckled the seat beat and bolted toward the back of the car. Her mother came out to meet her, but by then Maria had pulled her luggage out, and the two said goodbye hurriedly, just as a police officer strolled up to the car and a plane flew so close overhead that Maria almost lost her anger as she watched its frightening underbelly move past them, like a strange and horrible fish.

"I'm moving right now," Maria's mother said to the officer once they could all hear again. Regaining composure, Maria started toward the glass doors. "Maria," her mother called. "Be careful! Comportate bien! Okay, Maria? Be safe!" But Maria was moving away from her mother, from the policeman, the old station wagon, the highway back home, walking farther and farther until she was inside the airport, as safe, of course, as she always was, but now she was also alone.

CHAPTER 9

On a sweltering afternoon in late June, Charlie had been downstairs in the lobby of his office building, eating a peppered turkey and swiss sandwich, when he rolled his BlackBerry cursor over the envelope icon and opened an email from Veronica. For months, he had been unnerved at how transactional their relationship had become, but he was also keenly aware that there was only a certain extent to which she could ignore him. As a piece of mustard-streaked lettuce fell from his lip and onto the table's metallic surface, he saw a new message at the top of his in-box: *FW: Your Trip to Las Vegas (LAS).* Veronica's name skittered along the subject line, the letters in her message all lowercased, evasive like a row of bare toes avoiding the cold tiles of a public shower. The first line of the email read: "hope this works for you." He knew that Veronica had booked their rooms at opposite ends of the hotel, had even put them on separate flights, but it did seem nice of her to hope that something would turn out well for him.

Still, Charlie didn't understand this email. Hadn't she already forwarded him the flight details? Without double-checking, he was sure it would work. Years ago, he had granted her permission to view his calendar, and it was updated compulsively by his secretary, so Veronica would know if he needed to be in London on one weekend or if on the next, he'd be in Hong Kong. It was once he scrolled past her sentence that he realized that she hadn't been referring to the time of his flight at all, but to the fact that, without having consulted him, she had purchased a ticket for Nick, and not on her and Rocky's flight, but on Charlie's.

Charlie groaned. It was, from all angles, a terrible idea. Nick couldn't sit at the tables when Charlie went out to casinos, and Veronica would refuse to take him to her spas and shows, and even if it turned out that Isabel, their sometimes housekeeper, had a passport, even she wouldn't want to babysit Nick in Las Vegas. In fourth grade, Nick had been getting in trouble for riding the staff elevator at school until finally Charlie suggested they get him a doctor's note for something severe but not debilitating, so that the teachers would stop sentencing him to detention. When the doctor, after meeting Nick, mentioned Adderall instead, Veronica gave Charlie a knowing look that infuriated him. She had lately been of the mindset that Charlie had ADHD. Charlie said it was ridiculous to treat mental illness as if it were only a fad that would eventually go out of vogue, like Rocky's velour Juicy jumpsuits or Veronica's Atkins diet. He knew it was only her newest way of rationalizing his drinking, his working, the things that she'd told him she hated about him. He got even more annoyed when he googled *adult ADHD*, and was told, by the pop-up banner, that it was time to take charge of his life, as if he'd spent the past forty-six years flailing somewhere just behind it, as if he hadn't made his family millionaires before Rocky's first year on earth.

"Is this seat taken?" A young woman in a shapeless black dress was pulling at the chair opposite him, its heavy feet dragging so that it made an unbearable squeaking across the floor. The sound was awful, like his hair being pulled. *Lift it,* Charlie wanted to yell. Everywhere, there were people around him, and everywhere, they never failed to irritate him. He liked to eat in private, but unless he sat upstairs behind his closed office door, it was impossible to avoid the crowds. Upstairs, he liked to put on NPR and listen to the news. When he was younger, he hated the news, found it a bore. But now, the world they were talking about seemed so far away that it was more like listening to grim fairy tales, and fairy tales were something he'd always enjoyed.

But even upstairs, he was liable to someone's phone call or knock, and he would put his lunch on hiatus until it went cold. Anyway, how did this young woman know the seat wasn't taken? She hadn't waited for him to tell her no.

He looked at all the people standing by the deli counter, staring and typing helplessly into their phones. As he dislodged a compacted mass of bread that was stuck between his gums and back molars, he remembered how he had saved his son from a diagnosis that would have introduced him to uppers in early childhood, as if he didn't already have the rest of his professional life to become acquainted with them. Standing next to Veronica, he had felt superior to her as they descended the doctor's stairs onto Park Avenue, because for as much as she read and thought that she knew, there were just some things that she didn't.

He rolled the ball compulsively over the email. Where did Veronica get off doing something like this? If he wanted to, he could leave her, but she would never be able to leave him. All of her threats were empty. If he and Veronica were to get divorced, he would still be the one putting Rocky through college, and then Nick would follow. As long as they stayed together, he'd support Veronica, too.

"Are you getting up?" A man with an impossibly clean-shaven face hovered over the table. He looked like he mustn't have been a day older than twenty. Charlie sighed, balling up the parchment paper of his finished meal. Whereas everyone else left their trays on the table for the staff to clear, Charlie brought his with him to return at the counter. In the tip jar, he left a twenty-dollar bill and waited to make eye contact with the cashier so that he'd make sure to catch her smile. But when she looked up, her face was expressionless. Charlie looked away, a bit rankled. He opened the door to the lobby, and a flurry of sound overtook him. He wondered if next time he would leave a fifty. Then that bitch would smile.

She had remembered to wear deodorant, had applied it three times over, but Charlie was nowhere to be seen. When she saw Rocky and her mother standing outside the line to check bags, Maria's breath was taken away. Rocky's mother was more beautiful than she could have imagined. Maria tried not to stare as they passed through security, and when they finally arrived at the gate, Rocky's mother sat down at the café. Maria watched as she smoothed the creases of her long silken dress, which was patterned with abstract oblong shapes, before sitting with both feet firmly planted. She called for the waiter without opening her menu. Rocky yanked on Maria's arm.

"You seem so out of it," Rocky said, leading her to the newsstand.

They needed provisions: snacks, cigarettes, and reading materials. Maria leafed through copies of *Teen Vogue* and *Seventeen* and couldn't decide what would be more useful to learn: the Hottest Trends of the Summer or the Best Makeup for All Shades of Skin. Rocky was paging through *Cosmopolitan*, whose cover boasted a new and improved guide to the Kama Sutra.

"Impossible," Maria said, looking over Rocky's shoulder as they stood in line to check out. On the page beneath Rocky's finger, there was an image of a big ruby mouth frozen in tentative consideration of an apple. At the top of the page, in big black text, the headline read "How to Have an Orgasm (Every Single Time!)."

"You think it's impossible?"

"Don't you? I've never orgasmed with Andres."

Rocky glanced at Maria's hands. "Where's your magazine?"

"I didn't know which one to get."

"Get both. It's a four-hour plane ride, you know."

Rocky underestimated—the total flight time was five hours and fifteen minutes. On the plane, they hardly spent twenty minutes looking through the magazines before they resigned them to the pockets of the seats in front of them. Rocky had already read the most interesting article in *Cosmopolitan* while she was waiting in line to pay for the rest of the pages, which were mostly an assortment of glued-up folds of paper that, once opened, were stained yellow on the inside and smelled, to Maria, like less-pungent versions of the Bath & Body Works lotions that Maria's mother kept in a wicker basket in the bathroom.

"Let me try!" Maria yelled when she saw the perfumed sample pages, and Rocky watched in amusement as Maria reached over to grab the magazine from her hands and rub the paper all over her wrists and forearms.

"Try all of them," she suggested. "Here. This one is Marc Jacobs."

The stewardess offered them soda and complimentary snacks, and Maria accepted them all. "Let's play a game," Rocky said, caffeinated and jittery. "The favorite-thing game. Go." They compiled a list of favorite superheroes and villains, favorite toppings on pizza, favorite type of mixed drink (which they both admitted was orange juice and vodka, a drink they agreed could be enjoyed for breakfast), as well as favorite seasons and three reasons why. Maria was on a roll, and in the middle of proclaiming why autumn was better than summer, when Rocky suddenly interrupted with a stark whisper.

"So you haven't orgasmed with Andres?"

"No," Maria said, a little taken aback. She thought Rocky hadn't been paying attention when she'd mentioned it at the newsstand. "Well, maybe once? I don't know. The sex isn't good. I think I'm doing something wrong."

"Hmm." Rocky looked at the seat in front of her. The shiny yellow cover of *Cosmopolitan* peeked out of the sleeve like a child peeking into his parents' open door.

"Do you have any suggestions?" Maria had grown accustomed to Rocky playing the role of sex connoisseur. Rocky told Maria she'd had sex during the summer after eighth grade, before her first year at Bell Seminary. By the time she was sixteen, she said she'd already tried everything—at least, mostly everything, Maria suspected. Some things were a little too embarrassing to ask about and confirm.

"Well—are you able to do it yourself?"

"Like if I can make myself orgasm on my own?"

"Yes," Rocky said, not having blinked.

"Then yeah. I do every time with Bob."

Rocky uncrossed and recrossed her legs. Bob was Maria's nickname for the ivory lipstick-shaped vibrator that Rocky had bought her. Just like her birth control, it was a recent acquisition. Rocky had called Maria one morning and told her to meet her that day in the West Village. Maria had been intimidated when they paused outside the store with three descending steps leading to the entrance, but Rocky strode inside with confidence. She navigated expertly around the neon-blue dildos and handheld toys that looked like they were made of the same material as the jelly sandals Maria used to wear in elementary school. But when Rocky picked Bob up, an egg-shaped piece of plastic no bigger than a shot glass, Maria was disappointed. It didn't come with bunny ears or cat whiskers or a ribbed-for-maximum-pleasure shaft, and there weren't even exotic words printed on the box, labios mojados or el gordo—tantalizing with images of men in leather thongs. It wasn't an exciting color; it was colorless, really, bleak and miserable in comparison to the Sanrio cuteness of the Jack Rabbit, and so meager and small when held hand to hand with the waterproof, quadruple-speed Hulk.

"This is the one you want," Rocky promised, and Maria said nothing. She watched as Rocky placed the package on the counter and asked for a pack of double-A batteries.

But it was only because of Bob that Maria learned that sex had been holding out on her. It started as a peculiar tightness that surged from the insides of her thighs to the very top of her pelvis, and soon she was straining almost as much as she did in phys ed class whenever they were forced to lift weights. The discomfort stung, it burned down to the bone, and even though Maria couldn't register it as anything other than pain, it wasn't entirely unpleasant. So intense was the sensation that she switched the vibrator off a number of times before she decided she had finished, and even then, she hadn't been sure of what exactly had happened, only that the bathroom mat was drenched beneath her, and Maria no longer had to pee. For minutes she sat there, with Bob clasped in one hand, and hoped nobody had heard her. "Whoa," she mouthed audibly, and when nobody came out to knock on the bathroom door, Maria remained on the floor, scrubbing the mat with balled pieces of toilet paper, grateful that she had the sense to try out the toy when everyone was asleep and there were still hours until morning during which a wet thing could become dry. She never doubted Rocky again, at least not when it came to sex, and when Rocky told her to go to the clinic, Maria instantly obeyed.

"Why don't you use Bob with him?"

"Is that what you do with Matthew? Have Matthew and Maserati met?" Maria laughed as she imagined the buttoned-up boy from the all-boys Catholic high school whom Rocky sometimes invited over to her apartment. She imagined him examining Rocky's vibrator, his big blue eyes widening, and then turning into a terse little squint like they did the only time Maria had met him. He had frowned at their plates of french fries at Patrick's. He then taught Maria the phrases "refined carbohydrate" and "highly processed food." Sometimes those phrases rankled in her mind now, like charms from a wristlet, like the Tiffany hearts engraved in capital letters that were so popular at school.

"They have," Rocky said, breathily. "Anyway, if you're unsatisfied, I'd say to bring Bob into it. Keep going at it, even if he's already done. Remember," she said, and then paused to mouth the word *sex* before continuing in a normal voice. "It's for women, too."

"You're right," Maria said.

Rocky's face tore into a smile. The ends of her mouth reached up toward the lights of the cabin that instructed them to keep their seat belts on in preparation for landing.

"I know," Rocky said.

Moments later, Maria stood to pull her bag from the overhead compartment, but the flight attendant beat her to it. As the pilot and flight attendants muttered cheery goodbyes and the girls walked off the aircraft, she considered what Rocky said. Sex was to be enjoyed, sure, but it was Rocky's suggestion to give Andres a tutorial of Bob that gave her pause. She knew it'd be impossible to explain to Andres that she owned a vibrator, never mind tell him that she was sexually unsatisfied. Even that word—*unsatisfied*. He'd call her a slut, like Ricky had. Somehow Rocky was able to reconcile these things—namely, having sex and enjoying it—but Maria knew she couldn't, and her Bob would never meet her Andres. In all of her life, she was used to this separation of things, and it was at Bell Seminary where she first saw the wisdom in the fragmented whole, how two things were sometimes better off when they were kept at a distance: Rocky and Karen, Bell Seminary and Queens, now Andres and Bob. Andres had already told her the first time they had sex that he didn't believe she'd been a virgin. *You didn't even bleed,* he said.

"Rocky," Maria said as they raced down the hallway toward the gate, giddy from regaining their ability to run after so many hours trapped in their seats. It was good to be on land again, to take in air that was freshly circulated. Maria emptied her lungs with a long sigh, and when they stopped at the concourse, Maria stood close to Rocky and lowered her voice. "Do you think it's possible to tell when someone isn't a virgin? Like is there something about them—physically—that other people can see?" Maria brought her hand up to her lip and tore at the skin. "This morning, my mom asked if I've had sex yet."

"Your mom asked you that?" Rocky's eyes darted across Maria's face, like she was trying to look at all of her at once. Little wrinkles like stitches appeared between her eyebrows, as if she were trying to figure out a difficult math equation. "My mom would never ask me that."

"Yeah, I know," Maria said. "My mom isn't cool like yours."

Rocky didn't answer, but the look of concentration wasn't gone from her face. Maria wondered if she'd said something wrong. Rocky's lower lip quivered and her face was blanched.

"Rocky?"

Rocky leaned toward her conspiratorially.

"They say when a girl's legs get fat in the thighs, you can tell she's having sex," Rocky said. "But I think that's stupid. My thighs aren't fat!"

Maria resisted looking down at her own legs. There was no space between her thighs like Rocky's, and no matter how lightly she stepped on the ground, her legs always rippled like a seismic wave.

Beyond Rocky's shoulder, Rocky's mother came toward them, down the carpeted gate. In her long maxi dress, the pleats swayed as she brought one calf in front of the other, and Maria saw now that the pattern wasn't just oblong shapes, but a series of intricate white feathers. On her wrist was a single gold bangle, no wider than a spaghetti noodle. Rocky's mother was slightly dizzying to look at. She gave off an ethereal air that made her seem more like a cutout from a magazine than a real, breathing person. Her crêpe de Chine silk and chunky sunglasses made her impervious to categorization. Rocky's mother belonged in a genus of her own, and as Maria watched her approach, the wheels of her luggage pattering on the carpet so softly, Maria knew Rocky wouldn't notice.

"Your mom," Maria said.

Immediately, Rocky ceased speaking, but she didn't turn around. With a grin on her face that looked deadly, Rocky walked forward through the concourse, past the glittering newsstands, ignoring the moving walkways and barging toward ground transportation. Maria hurried to follow, listening for the footsteps of Rocky's mother, unsure if they'd lost her. As if she were only floating behind them, she didn't make a single noise.

CHAPTER 10

At the hotel reception desk, engulfed in a half dome of bronze ceiling carvings, Maria stared out the glass doors at the enormous fountain shooting spires of water into the desert sky. The trio was splitting up.

"One for me and one for you," Rocky's mom said, handing over a miniature envelope containing the room key card. "Just make sure you're back to the hotel by midnight."

Maria watched with awe as Rocky's mother went into the elevator with the bellhop, their bags stacked atop one another on the elegant brass-handled dolly. She wore her hair in a stylish bob. Even in the parched heat, Rocky's mother wore a jacket lined with faux fur. Maria wouldn't have known it was fake if Rocky hadn't already told her that her mother refused to wear anything made from real animals' skin. "Your mom is unreal," Maria said as the elevator doors closed. Maria and Rocky were alone now in the immense Vegas lobby. On the walls, they saw their images reflected back at them in a clean shade of gold.

"She's so cool."

"Stop fucking saying that," Rocky snapped. The pupils of her eyes had thinned. "I get it. You don't have to say it every five seconds."

"It was a compliment." Maria shrank. "I'm sorry."

"Well, it's annoying. So stop it." Rocky walked toward the enormous revolving glass doors. She pushed with her flat palm, and even though Maria could see they would both fit in one turn, Rocky had charged ahead. Maria waited for the next rotation to jump in.

Outside, Maria wasn't prepared for what she was seeing. Not only was the sun brighter than she'd ever seen it in New York, it also left so much more exposed. As she crossed the curb, past the hotel's winding esplanade, where cars kept dumping passengers and zooming off, her mouth hung open in awe. Women in pink feathers and elaborate head-dresses walked topsy-turvy around the curb with eyes that stayed fixed like porcelain dolls'. Outdoor casinos and their boozy patrons poured onto the street. Stands that looked like they should sell pretzels and hot dogs exclusively sold piña coladas. Everywhere, something was glitter-ing or lighting up, and people walked around with sixty-ounce plastic cups that looked like they should be filled with soda but were filled with alcohol. Strangest of all, hordes of men were gathered on street corners, slapping what looked like business cards on their wrists and whispering things that Maria didn't understand. When one of them handed her a card with a picture of Jean, a woman wearing a bra that was clearly three sizes too small for her, Maria understood.

Everything, Maria thought, was laid bare here. Everything screamed to be looked at. It was so different from New York, where people always looked away. When people got into fights, you kept moving. When people passed out on subway staircases, you stepped right over them. Here in Vegas, people took their time, stopped in the middle of the street to glance up at billboards, to banter with girls with airbrushed faces. The heat rose up as if she were standing directly on a rock, and Maria felt like she could see right through it, with none of New York's blurry humidity to obscure the view. She was dazzled by the grotesque facades, the semblances of places she had only seen in photos and knew existed elsewhere in the world—the Taj Mahal, the vast Greek coli-seum, and most endearing of all, the New York–style town house. Maria and Rocky looked one way and looked the other, over and over again, with nothing to discourage them except their own shyness. Eventually Maria's eyes started to burn.

"I brought an extra pair," Rocky finally said when she saw how Maria's face had folded into a million wrinkles, like the petaled layers of a rose. She handed Maria her sunglasses. They were circular and purple, a translucent violet, with delicate golden rims. With the sunglasses on, Maria's face opened up again, and she felt a tremendous relief. In one minute she was right in the furnace, and in the other, she was peering at it through the oven door. Even a minute later, when the oversize frames started to slide down her nose, Maria thought she would never take them off again.

Maria snapped photos as Rocky paraded in front of ivory sculptures, as she crossed the boulevard's elevated bridge. The sun made everything clear in the frame and made Rocky small in the glittering sky. How everything was so static and plastic was conveyed tenfold in the pictures she took, and later, when Maria would upload the files to her computer, Rocky would comment on how much it looked like she had been standing in front of a green screen—the contours were so strangely defined. But Maria also noticed something else in those photos, which was that they were all so flattering. She noticed how Rocky's hair always fell at the perfect angle, how she didn't have to bring her hand to her hip and jut out her elbow so that her arm wouldn't expand. There were so many things Rocky had—and now here was another thing. The simple luxury of knowing that no matter which way you looked at them, Rocky's arms looked great.

When they got back to the hotel room, it was only nine, well before Rocky's curfew, but the sun had made them exhausted, and after walking the Strip at least three full times, they didn't know what else to do. On the street, they had collected an impressive number of escort cards, and now Rocky held the whole stack in her right hand as they entered the suite.

"Where's your mom?" Maria kicked off her shoes, following Rocky's lead. Then she remembered how Rocky had reacted earlier in the lobby. "Actually, whatever."

"She said she was spending the rest of the day at the spa," Rocky said.

"Oh," Maria said, not wanting to interrogate further.

They went toward their side of the suite, across the hallway from Rocky's mother's bedroom. On one of the queen-size beds, Rocky arranged the stack of cards as if dealing a game of blackjack. But since both sides featured photos and prices, and sometimes a different girl on each side, Maria thought of it more like flipping coins than playing cards, both heads and tails equally as interesting to look at—and at fifty-fifty, just as likely to be played.

"Let's call one of them," Rocky said, looking down at the nude girls sticking up from beneath her knees.

"Yes," Maria said. "You do it."

Rocky dialed the number into her cell phone as Maria looked on nervously. If there was someone best positioned for breaking the rules, it was Rocky, who didn't have to worry about keeping her grades above a certain average in order to keep her scholarship money. She waited as the phone rang.

"Kara?"

"Hey there."

Rocky threw her phone down so violently that Maria was convinced she had broken it, and as she leaned over to pick it up from the corner of the mattress where it had landed, she looked at the screen to see if it was still intact. She pressed down on the red button with the telephone icon, just to make sure the call had ended.

"It was actually Kara!" Rocky could hardly get a word out, the laughter was bubbling out of her nose. "Seriously! It was actually her!"

Maria was nonplussed. "What else were you expecting?"

"What do you mean?" Rocky glared, the smile gone from her face. "As if you would've ever called her!"

Maria tried to suppress a giggle, but it was too late. Rocky saw her opening and took it.

"What were you expecting?" Rocky imitated Maria in falsetto. "You're an asshole, you know that, right?"

Maria was laughing now, her hand over her face to shield her eyes. She knew Rocky was right; it was a dare, one that Maria hadn't expected her to act on. Rocky was still shouting when a pillow smacked against Maria's raised elbow, and then, a few seconds later, another one against the side of her head.

"I would've called, too," Maria lied. Finally, she picked up the pillow that hit her last and hurled it as hard as she could in Rocky's direction. "But you're the one who wanted to talk to a literal whore."

The pillow flew about a foot above Rocky's head and crashed into the wall, where it grazed the bottom corner of a mounted painting that hung to the right of the bedpost. As the painting trembled on its axis, crawling up the wall from left to right in deliberate, furious movements, Rocky and Maria looked on like statues. When the painting finally stopped shivering, Rocky whipped around toward Maria. Her face— pretty, bare, her mouth open with words to come tumbling out—filled Maria with such an acute feeling of dread that she felt all her organs rise up to her ears, pushing themselves onto the lungs, which had tightened together like a set of balled fists.

"Lucky," Rocky said. "You would've owed me a thousand dollars." Maria kept her gaze on the painting that she nearly unhinged. It looked like a bad imitation of a Monet.

"There's no way that thing is worth a thousand dollars."

"You're right. More like five or ten."

Maria looked away from her friend, from the painting, and her gaze fell on the other side of the room. Outside the window she could see the glare of billboards from the fronts of hotels, black silhouettes of buildings against the purple night, rooms with curtains drawn. Maria tried to imagine Kara, her crotch spilling out of her G-string, answering Rocky's phone call with one hand while she shaved her ankle with the other.

"I'm sorry," Maria said, turning back to the room.

Rocky was sucking her hair. She had crawled over to the side of the bed to retrieve her cell phone again, and now she was enthralled by it, frantically pushing buttons.

"Just be more careful, okay? I'm not made out of money."

Maria felt the muscles in her face tense up. "I never said that, Rocky."

Rocky continued to stare into her phone's screen. Maria noticed how all over her arms, even down through her chest and knees, and even through her undeniable sunburn, there were tiny, faint cobwebs of blue veins. It looked as if, were a sheaf of paper to scrape against her a little too roughly, Rocky might never stop bleeding. There was no muscle anywhere on her body. She seemed so weak. Finally, she looked up at Maria. *She saw me,* Maria suddenly feared, but when Rocky spoke, the fear went away.

"My dad gets here tomorrow morning. You know what that means? I get the credit card!" She was brimming with a smile. "They've got good shopping here."

Maria lost her breath. Charlie was coming.

"Well, I don't have a credit card," she said. "So you shop, and I'll watch."

"Oh, come on, Maria. Don't be like that."

Maria tried to laugh, but the giggle stopped short in her throat. In the silence, she walked toward the bathroom. Behind the closed door, Maria kept her gaze on the floor. Cautiously, she looked up at the mirror, to brace herself for her reflection. But what she saw was not nearly as bad as what she'd expected. She looked severe, yes, with her hair flattened out by the lack of humidity, and her skin slightly dry from the sun, but she also looked suntanned, not burned. In her tight jean shorts, she didn't look skinny. She looked strong.

When Maria returned to the bedroom, Rocky was curled under the sheet, her phone still in her hand. "Can you turn the light off?" she asked in a small voice, and Maria stepped in between the two beds to twist the knob below the brittle lampshade until it switched off. She stood submerged in the hardly dark dark, enveloped in the purple that radiated from the window, the aura of light that filtered into the room and washed the walls in the colors of a sun-setting sky. In the glare, Maria didn't need to feel her way to the mattress. She went to her bag and fished for the book. When she'd found it, she brought it with her to bed.

"Hey, Maria," Rocky said, as soon as Maria had stopped moving beneath the sheets. "Let's skip the stores. They're probably white-people stores anyway."

But Maria wasn't paying attention to Rocky anymore. With her head on the pillow and her arms crossed over her book, she closed her eyes. She liked to look at the things that formed behind her eyelids, those squiggles of light that someone once told her were the walls of her mother's womb imprinted in her mind. But something new and unrecognizable was forming in that pixilated canvas of black. In that darkness, she saw a seat by a window and the view of a tiny skyline, like a Lego building set. She saw it emerge from behind a blanket of clouds. She saw the pocket in front to store magazines, the fold-out tray for water on ice. It was a journey she was watching unfold, and in an instant, as the Vegas Strip appeared and the overhead lights snapped on, she became aware of the thumping of her heart, so loudly and quickly against the duvet that she turned to the direction of the hallway, away from the window, away from Rocky's bed, where there was less of a chance Rocky would hear it.

CHAPTER 11

On the night before his flight left for Vegas, Charlie received a frantic phone call from Kenny. He was supposed to be meeting a client for a Rangers game at Madison Square Garden, but according to Kenny, the client had bailed, and wouldn't Charlie go with him? Kenny was his only friend from college who still worked in sales, who complained about how he seemed to be aging out of his department once he realized all his coworkers were twentysomething frat boys who had all graduated from the same cluster of mediocre upstate schools. Still, Kenny hadn't left his company, and Charlie suspected that for all his complaining, Kenny enjoyed letting brigades of stocky young men take him out for lunch, their emergent beer bellies all tucked into the same starchy button-ups and their toes curled in anticipation in their burnt sienna oxfords, hoping that among the fish flakes Kenny would throw them, there would be the prospect of a career.

But the fact that after all this time, he still got excited, *stoked,* like Kenny said, about unlimited chicken strips in the skybox, and that he still yelled whenever fights broke out between men armored with wooden sticks on ice, made Charlie very tired. It also made him a little regretful, because he could also remember having once enjoyed spending money on his company's tab, and he had once also called himself a hockey fanatic. Charlie had simply reached a point in his life where he wasn't enticed by free things anymore, and perhaps, in some perverse way, that was what going to Vegas was about: that he no longer sought out ways to enrich himself, but was willing to—got a thrill out of it even—gamble it away. He knew other men who swore by their bookies, but he liked sitting right there at the table. With a bookie's help, it was too easy to win.

"Charlie! Over here!" Kenny was sitting at the bar. Around him were men's faces, sprouting like garlic from their pinched, collared necks.

As Kenny patted him on the back, Charlie saw how Kenny was already red in the face, and it looked like another roll had been added to his midsection since Charlie had last seen him. When they were competitive college students, it would have brought Charlie joy to see Kenny so disfigured, but now, it only made him self-conscious. In school, while the rest of them rotated through girlfriends, Kenny was the only guy Charlie knew whose decision to never lie to women didn't adversely affect his ability to bring them home. At twenty years old, it had been impossible to imagine a way to bed women without leading them on. It still seemed that way at forty-six.

"I've started to play in a band," Kenny said, waving his hand to flag down the bartender.

"Get outta here," Charlie said. Whenever he saw his college friends, a different version of himself—a decidedly native New York one—had a habit of coming out.

They finished a couple of rounds and still had time to kill. Kenny raised his hand again to flag down the bartender. "I've been drinking way too much," Kenny said as two foaming pints of beer were placed down in front of them. Charlie hated how Kenny could just come out and say things like that. All the things that Charlie was secretly ashamed of, Kenny readily admitted to, and it was off-putting precisely because it was true. Maybe that's why all those girls in college chose Kenny over any of the other boys—even if they were depraved, at least they weren't deceived.

"Charlie, did I tell you?" Kenny punched Charlie on the arm. "I got hit by a car! A fire truck! I was suddenly on my back on the street, surrounded by a bunch of dudes with axes and hard hats. Oh my God, it was fucking hilarious, like a real life 'Y.M.C.A.' video!"

"A fire truck? Are you okay?"

Kenny leaned toward Charlie conspiratorially. With his chubby hand, he grabbed Charlie's forearm. "I walked away with not a single broken bone. You know why? Because I was loose!" Kenny threw his arms up in the air like a human field goal post. "You know why I was so loose? Because I was fucking *wasted!*"

Kenny's face was still red, gleaming like the shine of a polyester purse. Charlie felt he should feel sorry for him, but when he imagined a bumbling Kenny getting hit by a car—by a fire truck, no less—he found he couldn't stop laughing. It was, like Kenny said, hilarious. He kept laughing and laughing until he started to cry. Maybe they were rotting bodies after all, but did he really care? That night, when they realized the game had already started, but that neither wanted to get up from the bar, Charlie was immediately relieved. The bartender served them another round. Their chairs at the bar were suddenly so comfortable.

In the morning, Charlie felt his toes first. He curled them and stared up at the ceiling. He realized he couldn't remember how he got home, and that he hadn't heard the alarm go off. He didn't have to be at work today—but wasn't there something else? He sat there, at the edge of the bed, rubbing his knees.

As he watched the sun make gleaming panes on the carpet, he realized he would miss his flight.

The door to Nick's bedroom was open, but he wasn't in his room or his bathroom. Charlie cursed when Nick didn't pick up his call. Then, when he called a third time, and it still went to Nick's voice mail, Charlie yelled out loud. He paced around the apartment, waiting, his packed suitcase against the wall. Where was Nick? Didn't he know they were leaving that morning? He knew bringing the boy had been an awful idea, and he brought his fingers to the bridge of his nose. The dull throb of the headache he woke up with was now ringing like a school bell.

He called Veronica, but she didn't pick up. Charlie gripped his phone in his hand, wanting to throw it, but instead, he yanked the handle of his suitcase and rolled it out of the apartment door. He'd have to explain later why Nick hadn't come, and Veronica would be furious. Nick would be more than fine, and Charlie knew this because they left him alone in the apartment constantly, but that wouldn't stop Veronica from seizing on such a perfect opportunity to make Charlie feel like an asshole. He was slamming on the elevator button again with his fist, even though he'd already pushed it several times, when his phone rang.

"I'm at the Wendy's outside the gate." Nick paused. "Where you at? I don't see you."

Charlie said he'd be there soon. He hung up, and when his phone rang again, he dug his nails into his hand. "What does he want now!" Charlie shouted, and his voice echoed in the tiny pearlescent hallway.

"You called?"

Charlie saw the elevator, the lit-up button, the suitcase, the rage and embarrassment that had made the veins stand on his hands, shrink into miniature. He imagined folding everything up like a piece of origami paper.

"Yes, hi," he said. "We're on our way. Just wanted to make sure you checked in."

"We're all set." Veronica's voice was ardent and firm. "I'm at the hotel now with Rocky, and Rocky's friend."

"Great."

The elevator doors opened, and quickly, before he lost service, Charlie bid her goodbye and hung up the phone. Charlie was grateful that nobody else was in the elevator, because he was sure he reeked of raw alcohol. He could taste the way it had shriveled his tongue and made his teeth feel like ancient tusks.

He closed his eyes, listening as the elevator dinged on each floor. He hadn't known Rocky would bring a friend, though now that Veronica had mentioned it, he remembered she had brought one last year. He wondered if it was the same girl, or if it was another one—if it was Seventeen. He imagined Kenny, and Kenny's hearty laugh, and how his willingness to admit to his vices had the effect of making them mundane, unimportant. Maybe Charlie had an inflated ego to think that not everyone did sleazy things. The girl acted like she was in her twenties, and when she spoke, she was unashamed. Depraved, not deceived. Who said that? Thoreau? No, just idiot Kenny. Like an insolent child, he smirked. He had sixty-nine minutes to get to his flight. With no traffic, he was sure he would make it.

Rocky had failed to inform Maria that her brother, Nicholas, would accompany her father to Vegas. She also failed to inform her that the two of them would be saddled with looking after him for the remainder of the trip—which was already half over. Maria had never met Nick before, so she didn't know what to expect.

"Hopefully he won't be too annoying," Rocky had said casually as they exited the elevator to the lobby.

"I've been around thirteen-year-old boys before," Maria said, thinking of Ricky when he was that age. He was even fussier back then and spent hours fixing his hair in the mirror. Around that time, there had been a big argument between her parents when her father told Ricky to stop acting like a girl.

They met outside the hotel buffet, tendrils of clattering metal and voices just reaching them from where they stood at the entrance. Rocky's father seemed to be looking above their heads as they approached, like the men at the airport standing with signs, men who somehow knew that Maria wasn't whom they were looking for. He was wearing a suit again, but Maria didn't see the gold cuff links. Beside him was a reedy little boy with dark eyes. Maria was a ball of nerves. She had to restrain herself from picking her lip.

"Where's your mother?"

Rocky held out her arms to embrace him. He looked neat, and his hair was combed back, but his eyes were ringed in darkness like Rocky's were whenever she wore kohl eyeliner.

"She ordered room service. We thought we'd eat at the buffet with you."

"I think I'll go upstairs and get settled. But take Nick. I bet he's still hungry."

"You're not coming?" Rocky's eyebrows arched in surprise.

"I don't really have an appetite."

"I do," Nick said. He crossed his arms as he stared at his sister, as if wanting to challenge her.

Rocky hesitated. Maria wondered if it was obvious to anyone that Rocky was disappointed, or if she just had spent enough time with her recently to be able to tell. She watched as Rocky crossed her arms over each other and pinched the skin of her elbows. "Then we'll meet you for dinner later?"

"Yeah, that's possible. Coordinate with your mom. You know she manages the schedules." He reached into his back pocket and retrieved a small leather wallet. "And before I forget, you'd been asking for this?" He slid out a gold plastic card and held it out for Rocky to take.

"Thanks, Dad."

Suddenly, Rocky's father pulled her to him to hug her, and she hugged him back awkwardly. He turned from her, patted Nick on the shoulder, and stepped aside. All of it made Maria uncomfortable, and instead of wondering if her hair looked right or if Charlie had remembered her, Maria felt bad for her friend. Maria's father would never do something like this. He made her mother knock on her bedroom door every time she was home in time for dinner. He would never pass on an opportunity to share a meal with her, especially if it had been her suggestion.

"Bye," Nick said, walking toward the dining room.

"Bye," Charlie said. "Have fun."

And then just as Rocky followed after Nick, Maria saw Charlie wink. It was blurred, as if she'd been driving past it, like a highway traffic sign. But she'd been so timid, so unable to look at him straight in the face—it was likely that it hadn't happened. It was likely her imagination. But a doubt tugged at the faultless corners of Maria's explanation. Would she really imagine something like that?

"You know we won't see him again," Nick said as soon as Charlie was out of earshot. They approached a long buffet table, and Nick pulled a silver knife from out of a black caddy. "Good thing you got the credit card from him."

"You heard him." Rocky picked up a plate. "We're getting dinner later."

"Oh right, I forgot. Mom will jump for joy."

They moved toward the hot bins of scrambled eggs and croissants, and Maria would have been able to listen if she'd liked, if she'd kept close enough to try to hear them. But it was the wink that had her attention, the wink that was over so quickly she could hardly know for certain it happened. That's what she was debating then, not a choice between home fries or waffles, but if Charlie's wink had been real. It made Maria woozy to think they were sharing this secret. It made her heart leap. He had been brusque with Rocky, but was that really significant? Rocky already had so many things—Matthew adored her, she had the best clothes, she was rich, her arms always looked great . . . and all Maria wanted was this one thing.

Maria watched as Rocky clipped a pancake so tightly, it ripped down the center, and she lifted one half onto her plate. Maria picked up the tongs right after, and tossing aside what Rocky left, she picked up a whole pancake, round like a moon. Then, she picked up another. If Rocky had it all, Maria deserved some, too.

In the airplane bathroom, he had stared at his face and put a finger to the bags under his eyes. If he pressed hard enough, they looked like they would burst. At one point, when he was younger, there was one vein on his lower stomach that felt the same way, the blood coursing through it so healthily, he sometimes became afraid that if something scraped up against him, it would start gushing. He had no idea where to find that vein anymore. Quietly, he had tried not to despair.

So of course, he was delighted when he saw the girl again, standing in her jeans and black tank, a pair of purple sunglasses pushed atop her head, looking doleful and tan and clearly stricken. Of course, he had liked the way she kept furtively stealing glances at him. It even made him feel good to know he was financing her trip, that he was the reason she was standing across from him in Vegas, and something surged in him, made him feel powerful, capable. And as he handed over his credit card, of course, he forgot about the bags under his eyes, about what his daughter was saying, about why he had ever allowed Veronica to make him feel unimportant. If Kenny was right, if he was being honest, then he could admit that it felt good, and that after seeing her, he walked away grinning, tucking a little laugh into his breast pocket, and went straight to the bar from the lobby, to taste his first drink on land. He already had a faint spring in his step, and already, he felt like he was a little bit high, and it likely was a mix of the altitude and desert air that had him feeling this way, and then something else altogether.

By dinnertime, neither Rocky nor Nick had mentioned their father again. By then, they had posed in front of all the hotels and ridden on the New York roller coaster twice. On consensus, they went to Denny's to eat, and by eight o'clock, they were bored. Denny's had been Nick's suggestion, which had made Maria laugh. Apparently, there was no class difference wide enough in America to breach a liking to a chain diner. Rocky ordered a grilled cheese and chips, while Nick and Maria both ordered variations of a hamburger. By then, Maria had decided to stop hating Nick, and even convinced him to ask for onion rings over fries so they could share off each other's plates. She was sure that he was only tolerable because he was slightly afraid of her, his big sister's moody (if not slightly bitchy) friend, and she let herself enjoy this new revelation, and bossed him around gently enough that Rocky wouldn't take offense or fully notice. At the end of the meal, the waitress came around again with a three-page dessert menu. Maria's eyes watered.

"Oh! Look at that!" Her face was buried behind the foot-long menu. "Can I get a banana split, too?"

Rocky's dessert menu lay flat on the table. "How are you still hungry?"

"Nick and I can share it, right, Nick?" Maria laid down the menu and leaned over the table. "Come on! Get me one!"

Rocky gave her a funny look. The edge of her lip twitched. "Can you at least say please?"

Maria blinked before she smiled. She noticed Rocky's fingernails tapping against the table. Suddenly, Maria realized that the two had gone all day without smoking a cigarette. It was the first time Maria thought about it, but for Rocky, maybe it wasn't. The only thing she could think of was that Rocky didn't want to smoke in front of Nick, but even if Rocky was on edge now, at least her concern for her brother was endearing. "Ha," Maria said. "Sure. Please?"

When the waitress came around, Rocky ordered for the table. "Two spoons," she clarified, meeting the waitress's eyes. "I'm not eating any of it."

The ice cream came out, and Rocky looked on with disdain as Maria and Nick scooped big globs into their mouths. By the time there were five or six bites left on the plate, Maria glanced up to see Rocky staring. "Do you want," she said flatly, holding out her spoon.

"You ask me now? All that's left in there is a puddle of spit."

"But you told the waitress you didn't want a spoon."

"That didn't mean you couldn't offer," Rocky answered.

Maria looked at her in confusion. "Sorry, Rocky," she said, but Rocky was waving her hand, trying to flag down the waitress for the check.

When they stepped back out on the Strip, Maria was engorged. As she walked, she saw a giant illuminated ad for a rendering of *The Wizard of Oz*, starring a busty, blond-haired Dorothy. "Look at that," Maria said, pointing. "Hey, you never did show me your pictures as Dorothy!"

Nick looked up at the sign. He turned to his sister. "When were you ever Dorothy?"

"For a school play," Rocky said.

"I thought you were the scarecrow." Nick turned his whole body toward his sister.

Rocky stared at her brother. Her mouth seemed to be shrinking. "Shut up, Nick."

"You had triangles painted on your face!"

"Nick, will you just shut up? Seriously?"

Maria looked from Nick to Rocky, and then back again. Even in all that light, she couldn't tell if Rocky was joking.

"You weren't Dorothy?" Maria asked.

"When did I tell you that?" But even though Rocky was smiling now, it didn't sound like a question she wanted an answer to.

Nick laughed. He wasn't going to let up.

"You told her you were Dorothy? As if you'd be good enough to be picked as the lead actor!" Nick put his hand to his face in a mock burst of laughter. "You're not good at anything!"

"Thanks, Nick," Rocky said with a surprising degree of calm in her voice. Her mouth was full size again. "Neither are you. Neither is Maria. That's why we're friends."

Maria was taken aback. She would have stopped right there, but the light changed, and they were now crossing the sparkling boulevard. By the time they reached the other side of the curb, Nick had finally stopped laughing. Maria came up so she was standing side by side with Rocky, and even their steps were in line.

"Hey," she said, facing Rocky. "I thought we were friends because we liked each other."

"Obviously," Rocky said. "Isn't that a given?"

A line of black limousines came down the pathway as the three made their way up to the entrance of the hotel. With the enormous fountain roaring outside, Maria waited before answering Rocky's question, so that she wouldn't have to strain to hear. A group of women in tank tops and magenta lip gloss tapped Maria on the shoulder and asked if she'd take their picture. They posed over the ledge, some climbing up on their butts, others thrusting their legs and elbows out, all with their lips pouted, their long blond hair looking so bleached it became almost white against their leathery skin. Maria fumbled to find the viewfinder, which stayed black even though she kept holding down on the button. By the time the photo was taken and she was sure it wasn't awful, she had to sprint to catch up to Rocky and Nick. She entered the casino and found the siblings, but by then, there was no use in bringing up what already had passed.

At the hotel room, the lights were all off. On the couch, a cardstock brochure with leather binding was splayed open on its spine, where a variety of breakfast items were listed in looping cursive. Beside them, digits were listed without dollar signs, which had a disarming effect on Maria. The prices were made into numbers, the kind she and Rocky were used to plugging into their TI-83 calculators for math. It was so striking to Maria how something that usually put her on edge could be deweaponized so easily and made innocuous.

"Wanna watch TV?" Rocky asked as they walked into their side of the suite, the bedroom where two queen-size beds were arranged side by side.

"I wanna go back to Dad's room," Nick said at the same time that Maria said "Sure."

Rocky looked at him as she unlaced her sandals, one foot at a time. "That's fine by me. Do you know what room you're in?"

"Nineteen eighteen. What number is this?"

"Nineteen eighty-nine." Rocky collapsed into the bed by the window, the one she had claimed first.

"Does that mean I'm seventy doors down? That's so far!"

Rocky looked at Nick blankly and then turned to Maria with a sigh.

"Can you believe this kid, Shell?" Rocky said. Maria, who had been fishing for her phone charger, didn't look up from the suitcase to meet Rocky's gaze. Nick saw how Rocky had failed to co-opt her friend's approval. He snorted, narrowed his eyes at his sister. Rocky cleared her throat.

"Do you need me to come with you?"

"I can find it myself."

"Mom would get mad."

"Who cares?"

Maria plugged the charger into the wall, and her face glowed as the light on the screen turned on.

"Maria," Rocky said, requesting her attention for the second time.

"What?" Maria was standing with one hand on her hip, leaning against the dresser drawer. With her eyebrows furrowed on her face, she looked like she was ready to argue, and Rocky forgot why she had said her friend's name in the first place. Hadn't she only wanted to ask her a recommendation for something to watch on TV? Feeling Nick's gaze on her, and hearing the chortle under his breath, her hand twitched from under the cover.

"Go with Nick. Take my key card so you can get back into the room."

"Sure." A springiness returned to Maria's voice, and the furrowed look was gone.

Nick went to the door. He held it open for Maria to pass. Rocky scrolled through the pay-per-view menu.

"Be back soon," Maria said. She ignored Nick's gesture and motioned for him to go ahead of her, taking care that the door didn't slam.

The hallways were wider than any others Maria had ever seen, and they were so silent and empty that immediately, as if trying to fill a vacuum, Nick and Maria began to run. Glimmering chandeliers sped by, and they only ran faster, laughed harder, throttling and gasping, making as much noise as possible on the beige carpeting that did everything in its power to muffle their heavy footsteps. They stopped only after noticing they had come down the wrong way. Nick pointed it out first.

"I won't tell my sister," he laughed when he saw how Maria went silent.

Tremendo, Maria thought.

When they reached room 1918, Nick's key card swiped green. She peeked inside as Nick barged through the door. Aside from what looked like a set of house keys that rested atop the glass dining table, the suite looked identical to the one she and Rocky shared, and it was also identically empty. Maria felt her heart rate slow. Her giddiness split into two and was replaced by one part disenchantment and another part relief. Nick and Charlie shared a room, but Charlie was clearly not here. She hated the duality of what she was feeling, torn between going back to her hotel room and wanting to seek him out. Maybe, she thought, feeling conflicted like this was something particular to girls. Whenever

Maria went to her father with questions about politics or the things that she read in the news, he always answered without hesitation to tell her which side of the story was right.

When Nick said good night, Maria realized there was nothing to do but go back in the direction she came from. In the enormous hallway, so empty Maria could hear the hidden pipes and hardware thrumming inside the walls, Maria imagined what the people of Vegas were doing. Downstairs, they wouldn't be asleep. There would be international billionaires eating late dinners at restaurants that overlooked the Strip, clinking wineglasses and paying in cash, bills newly converted and still pressed flat from the machine. There would be midlevel businessmen picking up pieces of raw fish with chopsticks from the bodies of West Coast–born girls, sake dribbling out of their belly buttons and slurped up into stubbly mouths. Maria could go downstairs and try to find him, but she was sure Rocky's father couldn't be one of those guys. He had wrapped his arm around Rocky's back that morning, drawn his daughter in for a hug. He lingered even after Rocky pushed him away. He couldn't be the kind of man that collected those porny cards off the street. He knew literature.

Maria stood at the elevator and watched the buttons light up, trying to decide what to do. *Eleven eleven,* the clock above the elevator read. Maria pressed her eyes shut. When she opened them, the elevator doors opened and Charlie came barging out, and Maria's wish, before she was through even thinking it, abruptly came true.

"Well, hello!" As he approached, he seemed to be bouncing rather than walking. Maria didn't know if it was because he had seen her or from something he'd just finished up, but it was clear he was excited. "What are you doing over here? Did you come looking for me?"

Maria felt her face swell in embarrassment. It was obvious she'd been expecting him. She could imagine herself through his eyes, waiting outside his door with her eyes closed, picking split ends as if they were petals, blowing on them like dandelion hairs. She straightened her back as tall as she could in her little black flats with no heels.

"Of course you didn't. Ignore me. 'The miserable have no other medicine / But only hope.'" He smiled. "I bet you know who that is."

Maria blushed. "Emerson?"

"Almost. Shakespeare."

"Well," Maria said, trying to maintain her composure. She tilted her head to one side like she did whenever she was going to say something true. "I've definitely decided that my favorite poet is Emerson. I've been reading more of his work recently. I think he's wonderful."

He chuckled in one syllable. She had never heard her parents laugh like he did. Her mother still giggled, like a little kid. Maybe her mother didn't count as an adult at all, especially when she often bragged to strangers about being confused for Maria's older sister.

"Are you hungry?" he asked.

"We went to Denny's."

"That's too bad. A great mind like you deserves better than Denny's. I would've brought you to the best steak house in Nevada."

Maria blushed. She looked down at Charlie's shoes—still polished, the richest leather.

"I would have rather gone to the steak house with you."

Even she was surprised at how the words stirred her. She saw him hesitate. *Too much,* she thought, *too soon.* In fear, her heart held off on beating.

"I would have liked that," Charlie said.

"Take me next time."

"How about next summer?" He took a step backward, as if to appraise her. "'Beauty is God's handwriting'. . . have I told you that before?"

Maria giggled. Only now that she felt her jaw go slack did she realize she had been clenching it.

"You're leaving tomorrow, aren't you?"

"Yes. We only came for two nights. Our flight leaves at four thirty."

"Right, right. And have you seen the casino?"

"Not really. Well, we've walked through it." Maria was confused by the question. Of course she had seen the casino; it was massive, and there was no other way to get upstairs but to walk a solid five to eight minutes, depending on the crowds, past all the tables and slot machines that adorned the hotel's first two floors.

"'Cause I'm thinking," he said. "I can show you how to play."

"I don't know how to gamble."

"How about the pool, then?"

Maria smiled, baring all of her teeth. "I have a bathing suit in my room."

"No," he said, in a harsher voice than before. "We'll just sit by the water."

CHAPTER 12

Maria was disappointed. She had wanted to swim.

She didn't excel at any physical activity on land. Clumsy and a little soft, she ran pigeon-toed during relay races in the gym and gazed at the wall distractedly whenever they sat at machines in the weight room. When she signed up for the swim team during her first year at Bell Seminary, her gym class teachers discussed and discussed until they came to the conclusion that one of them ought to call Maria's home to speak with Mr. or Mrs. Rosario, with the intention of explaining that the swim team was one of the most competitive sports at the private all-girls school. None of them had seen Maria swim, but based on her performance in the weight room and how she always walked through the semestral one-mile test, they knew she'd never qualify. They'd never seen her swim, but they assumed she didn't know how to—most kids who grew up in the outer boroughs didn't. There weren't, they chortled among themselves during their planning periods, any events dedicated to the doggy paddle.

On one Wednesday night in October, the Bell Seminary seventh- and eighth-grade swim coach was on the phone with his landlord, threatening to call the New York City housing department for still not having sent someone to fix a leak that had created a bubble like a big plaster pimple that hung from his living room ceiling. At the end of the phone call, he was frazzled and distracted, but that same night, finally, someone did come. For no other reason did he neglect to call Maria's parents the night before the first practice of the season, and so when Maria showed up with her swim cap and one-piece and sank into the pool with a clap, he had nobody else to thank for the blessing than his negligent landlord. Within seconds of sinking into the water, she propelled herself forward with a force that only Grace—the swim team captain who, at only fourteen years old, had developed certain physical characteristics and vocal intonations that prompted mean rumors that she was a lesbian—could surpass, and even so, only marginally. As the swim coach looked on, he shook his head in disbelief. Maria Rosario, newest addition to Bell Seminary's eighth-grade class, could swim. And not just that—the coaches agreed that she'd be set to make varsity as soon as she entered upper school. And all because of those summer afternoons that her mother left her at the YMCA pool, where they fed her chocolate milk and chicken medley for lunch, free for any family who showed up willing to eat it.

But within three weeks, Maria had quit the team. She'd been genuinely sad to tell them it was because making a practice that started at 6:30 a.m. required her to wake up at 4:00 a.m. and get on a public train. But when the Bell Seminary coaches continued to approach her, stopping her in the hallway, going on about *dedication*, she traded her sadness for anger instead. What was the point of competition? What did they even care? She'd never swum on a team before; no one had ever cheered her on. If she'd ever continue, it'd be the same way she learned: in a pool by herself, with nobody watching. Nobody but the lifeguard—and even he was irrelevant. Maria knew she would never drown.

The hotel pool was lit up by fluorescent panels that beamed brightly from under the water. As Maria descended a wide flight of stairs, she gazed out at the long chairs that were arranged in careful formation around the pool edges. Some were empty and others were speckled with bodies. She noticed their clothing first, their midsections draped in slinky white garments that fell below the collarbone and bunched at the hip, and then noticed the glasses they waved as they spoke, coated with rims of salt or garnished with flowers and fruit, sticks of cinnamon twisted into art. Maria knew Karen would love all those details. Music thumped apologetically, low enough so that conversation could carry on, and as Charlie walked through the crowd, Maria felt awkward around so many women who towered above her in stiletto heels.

"Everyone's dressed up."

"Overdressed. You look great."

"I would've changed if I knew I were coming down here," Maria said, which was not wholly untrue. There was nothing she had packed in her suitcase that was appropriate to wear past 5:00 p.m. in Las Vegas. Her suitcase overflowed with tanks and blue jeans and a pair of sneakers, and the flats she was wearing now. Even so, she could have managed to look nightclub ready by means of Rocky's wardrobe, whose contents Maria felt as comfortable sorting through as the food in Rocky's family's fridge. Rocky would undoubtedly have a pair of leathery pumps to spare.

They walked past the swimming pool and the bodies that were posed around it like mannequins until they reached a platform, where the chairs made way for cabanas. Even though the sun was down and there were fewer lights here than there were by the pool, Maria felt that she could see everything very clearly as if it were still midday. This bothered her, not because she didn't want to look at Rocky's father, but because she worried about how she looked to him in such strong and transparent light. Didn't she have a pimple in the space right between her eyebrows, and hadn't she forgotten to shave her upper lip for days? She felt a hair sprout from one of her moles just then, like a sprig from the eye of a potato.

Rocky's father lit a cigarette and handed it to Maria.

"Thank you," she said, and she looked up, faults and all, to see he was smiling at her.

When Charlie started his second cigarette, Maria hadn't yet finished her first. He watched her inhale. The paper had burned down to the double gold lines that mark the start of the foamy white filter, but Maria still hadn't thrown it to the ground. They were sitting at the far edge of the pool in two separate cloth-draped seats.

"It's nice here."

"Oh, yeah. It's nice."

He grinned. He liked how her comments were void of pretensions—she didn't know to overuse words like *gorgeous* and *beautiful. Nice* was good enough for her. Maybe if she knew the costs associated with their hotel rooms, she would start to sound like the women who had sat at the table next to him at dinner and told the sommelier that the wine was superb. Imagining Maria interact with a sommelier—he could see it now—a Somalia what?—made him want to draw her close to him, and he rested his hand, which had lifted slightly, back on the bend of his knee.

She reminded him of a girlfriend he had just after college, the frizzy-haired daughter of an Evangelical Southern pastor. One time, early in dating, they went to a restaurant for her birthday, an overpriced Italian place on Third Avenue that Charlie had suggested. When the waiter brought out a bottle of white wine as per her request, he held it in front of her to observe the label before pouring, and she, flustered by the gesture, reached out to grab it from him. He stepped back, a little unnerved, and she giggled uneasily. *Yeah, yeah, that's fine,* she said, and then, after hastily swallowing her first sip, flashed him a thumbs-up. When he was gone, she looked bashfully at Charlie. *What a weirdo, right? Just pour it! It's what I ordered!* Charlie shrugged. Neither he nor anyone else at the table seemed to have the heart or knowledge to tell her it was just protocol.

Her name was Rebecca. They'd both studied English literature in college. He fell in love with her and paid for everyone's dinner that night.

But they argued often and he sometimes was mean. Whenever he saw the vials of painkillers she tucked inside her drawers, he made vicious comments about futures in Appalachian trailer parks. And because they hit so close to home, because she knew that she was only one step above the seedy image he painted, only one or two generations away from it and a paycheck or two from returning, she'd cry to herself in their bedroom, and ask him how he could say that he loved her when it felt so little like it so often. He'd inevitably soften and apologize, and tell her he'd never want anyone but her, until soon he was crying, too, the tears gathering in wet splotches around his eyes. Eventually, he'd cry even louder than she did, until she had the vague sense that there was something in him that needed more comforting than she did. She'd sit up to rub her hands through his hair until he stopped shaking, and only when she heard the breathing even out would she know he had fallen asleep. Then she would stretch her legs under the comforter, and taking care to not make a sound, face her body away from him.

Charlie didn't quite remember why they broke up, but her leaving was a fairly quick process, and within a week, all the traces of Rebecca (her G-strings, her socks, the empty vials, the wet footprints and long strands of blond hair all over the bathroom) were gone. Not a whole lot changed in his routine—he still went to the bars after work—and it didn't take long to realize how much Rebecca had tolerated. Rebecca had loved him even through the nights he'd pissed in the bed. She hand-washed the sheets so that the laundry woman, with whom Charlie was on a birthday-wishing basis, would never know. Would anyone ever love him as much? But by then he had deleted Rebecca from his phone book, and those tethers of hope—the threads of intimacy that may have incited him to ask *but what if?*—eventually became so frayed that Charlie merely looked into his whiskey glass and kissed whatever new woman was in his bed on the chance that he'd be able to convince her that he had been sober enough to remember it later.

It continued a while like that. And then, two years before his thirtieth birthday, he met Veronica. They were introduced on a night that Charlie had gone up to Westchester for a private art show hosted by a high school friend. Charlie noticed her standing near the cheese spread, one elbow folded over the other, a wrist dangling just by the edge of the table, clenching a tiny wooden spear. Every so often, without uncrossing her arms, she would stab a cube of cheese and bring it up to her mouth, clenching it between her teeth in such a way that suggested a savage sensuality. She seemed to like the speckled Roquefort best, which fascinated Charlie even more, this woman who, rather than make small talk, was clandestinely sneaking nibbles of tangy blue mold, baring her teeth as she ate. He had no idea who she was, which was why it was so shocking when the host of the party pulled them aside, and the first thing that Veronica told Charlie was that she remembered him being pudgier before. Apparently, they'd grown up together and took the same school bus to school.

At the time, most of their friends were already married, and within five months, Charlie and Veronica were engaged. Things moved rapidly, too rapidly, which was how Veronica explained wanting to leave him later. But even before that, there had been signs, like when she would correct Charlie's telling of the way they had met—she wasn't a savagely sexual being, she was only trying not to smear her lipstick while she ate, and it hadn't been blue cheese at all, but a basic Vermont cheddar, and she knew this because she had gone to buy the food that afternoon. At the party hosted by a documentary maker, which had mostly taken place in a backyard adorned with string lights, there was nothing regal and nothing extravagant—only olives, homemade pigs in a blanket, and bright orange blocks of Cabot Creamery.

Charlie wasn't to blame for assigning a mystique to Veronica that in reality did not exist—if Maria had seen a picture of her from her school days, the brown-haired girl with perpetually ripped cuticles and full boxes of Samoas to peddle off to obliged family friends, she would have never recognized her either. As a woman, Veronica's beauty, paired with her no-nonsense demeanor, suggested an effortless sophistication that she wasn't entirely aware of. Marrying Charlie had only accentuated her elegance, because now she was a woman with wealth, and she became something like a haunting apparition, like a spirit that floated through space, leaving nothing but signatures on slivers of paper as the only traces of wherever she went. She was the soft-spoken woman who had accepted her husband's yearly trips to Vegas, who likely knew, in all her discretion, that he'd cheated on her before. But she was also the judicious woman who brought the rest of the family along, who had reserved separate presidential suites for them to sleep in, on opposite sides of the hotel. When Veronica saw Charlie these days, she smiled curtly and then returned instantly to whatever he interrupted—her reading, her niçoise salad, her favorite TV show—a gesture so polite and fleeting he couldn't reasonably get annoyed. This was the woman he vowed to love forever so many nights ago.

It was Veronica who Charlie really was thinking of when he kissed Maria on the lips for the first time. It was Veronica who he still wanted, who would make his life complete. But that night at the pool, by the fourth and fifth time, he knew this wasn't something he needed to tell himself anymore. By then, he long knew it was a lie.

Maria, even though she said nothing, understood he was lying.

It wasn't for not knowing the value of money that she used the word *nice* instead of *beautiful*. It was just that, in Maria's world, there were very few things that merited the use of such a powerful word. She certainly did not include herself in the list of things that qualified as such. She hadn't forgotten Emerson's words, how beauty existed outside of the body, how humans could only briefly reflect it by looking outside of the *me*.

When he called her beautiful, which had now happened more than once, she looked at him with unblinking eyes and remembered the distinction: *not me*. Beautiful were sunsets and oceans and skies with banks of clouds like fishes, but beautiful was also what Emerson said reached its height in women. To Maria that meant the women in the Victoria's Secret catalogs, the busty frames with straight, golden hair. That meant the Bell Seminary girls, leggy and tall and rosy. Maria could accept cute. Pretty. Even sexy.

But beautiful?

Whoosh—a red flag went up and waved. What had the uncles told her about men, about boys, about all of them? The loudspeakers blared in her ears. What would they say if they knew about Charlie? *He's lying,* they'd say. *He's trying to trick you.*

But Maria didn't care about all of that—at least not right now, as she kissed Charlie back with both lips. They'd wanted to make her paranoid, to make her question and condemn everything she did, but why should Maria do that? Here she was with this strange older man, but he was making her float. Every time he looked at her, Maria felt herself reach a little higher than where she was before. So what if they wouldn't get married? Did any of that really matter? Rocky was right to care so little so often. Most marriages end in divorce.

The next time Charlie called her beautiful that night, told her that he wanted to see the depths of her dreams, Maria knew for sure what he meant, that beauty isn't possessed, isn't handled, that it's not in the form, but the mind.

Beautiful. Me. Finally, she had found her mirror. Maria had been seen.

CHAPTER 13

Maria lifted the weight of her body onto the balls of her feet. Rocky would be asleep, she hoped, or at least she would be too engrossed in soft porn to care that Maria had been gone. She guessed that she had only been gone for twenty or thirty minutes. It wouldn't matter how long she'd been gone, anyway, if Rocky had found something good on pay-per-view. Maria approached the door without having yet crafted the lie she would tell to her friend.

With the key card that Rocky had given her, Maria opened the door. Rocky was standing on the opposite side. Their eyes locked. Rocky's face was as easy to read as an analog clock, and Maria knew that she'd been mistaken. It had been over an hour since she had left. Hastily, she began to construct the walls of the place that she could have wandered off to.

"We were looking for you."

Quickly, the excuse. To get a drink? To get a snack? But she didn't bring her money, and with so many free items in the minifridge, free for Maria at least, it wouldn't hold up. Everyone knew Maria was broke. After Rocky spoke—she had said the word *we*—Maria saw that Rocky's mother was standing beside her. Her hair was wet and made tiny, jagged points that made Maria think of the spikes on the underpass by her house. *So that pigeons can't fill the street with caca,* her mother had explained.

"I left my phone charging."

"Yeah, I know that." Rocky's eyebrows came down in a V on her nose. "I called Nick and he didn't pick up either. I had to go almost kick in his door before he finally opened it. I expected you to be there, but he told me you'd left as soon as you'd dropped him off."

Rocky's mother hadn't budged from where she stood. Whether the expression on her face matched Rocky's expression of anger, Maria did not know. She didn't dare look.

"I—How long was I gone?" Maria needed more time to think. It was so unnaturally bright in the room for being so late in the evening. Maria could see everything in plain sight as if it were noon. A half-drunk cup of sparkling water on the countertop, shopping bags at the foot of the chaise longue, the upholstered set of chairs huddled around the table near the grand double windows that looked out onto the Strip. The floor was carpeted—she hadn't noticed before—a spotless creamy-skinned beige. She had felt so secure by the swimming pool, an infinite distance away from her mother and father, and whole floors of billiards tables away from Rocky—but now Rocky was staring at her with that awful V on her face, and with everything incandescent in the bedroom, Maria strained to recall how dark the pool had been, and if perhaps it'd been better lit than she'd thought.

"I went downstairs to look at the shops," Maria said. "There's a chocolate fountain down there." The chocolate fountain was in one of the windows she had passed earlier that day with Rocky. She had wanted to point it out, but Nick and Rocky had been arguing about what time they were going to get lunch. Nick insisted that Rocky didn't need more clothing. She began shrieking. *As if Daddy doesn't buy you every stupid toy you ask for!* Maria turned her attention to the swirling rivers of hot fudge in the window, all eight feet of which went unnoticed by the bickering children beside her.

In the suite, Rocky held her face perfectly still. But when she spoke again, her left eye became the slightest bit smaller, as if straining to see something infinitesimally small on Maria's face. "That's what you were doing for an hour and a half? Looking at a chocolate fountain?"

Maria nodded. "Yeah, and just walking. I just walked around." She had to clear her throat before finishing speaking. Had the cigarette made her hoarse? Could Rocky smell it on her? She was digging her index finger into her thumb cuticle, and her stomach and legs had gone hard in fear. She couldn't move or speak without fumbling. And Rocky saw it, knew she was lying. Why else would she be looking at her with that face? She resisted the urge to bring her hand to her mouth, despite how badly she wanted to rip her lips off.

"We were just about to put our shoes on and look for you."

"I'm sorry," Maria said.

There was something in Rocky's stance, the slightest lowering of the shoulders, that made Maria realize: *she doesn't know.* A tiny dam inside of her broke. She fought to keep the joy from flooding.

"I'm really sorry," Maria continued, with so much control that it hurt. "I didn't know you were worried."

She looked at Rocky's mother. With her bare feet and her makeup rubbed off, the skin flushed and pink around the edges of her eyes, she didn't appear to be the same woman Maria had seen that morning in the Vegas lobby. Earlier, she had seemed so powerful, a perfect picture of the kind of woman Maria strove to be. She looked like a woman of means. Now, when she looked at her, she could only think of Charlie. *She's a housewife, too,* Maria heard herself thinking. *Just like Ma. Just like anyone.*

"I'm happy we didn't have to call your mom," Rocky's mother said. Rocky got her eyes from her mother—a deep, brick-building brown.

"I'm sorry," Maria said, and this time, her voice was a little quieter, the adrenaline inside coming to a blockage, like water in a clogged sink.

They stood there, the three of them, like animals braced for attack, until finally Rocky's mother moved.

"I'm going to bed, Rocky." She looked over her shoulder at her daughter. Maria noticed the green veins that popped from under her eyes.

"Good night," Maria said and watched as the woman went in silence, the sound of her feet absorbed by the carpet's lushness. She and Rocky walked back to their room, and Maria carefully stepped out of her shoes.

Later, as time congealed in the darkness, Maria was startled awake to the sound of her name.

"Maria," Rocky whispered, the voice ripping Maria out of where she'd been dozing in space-time. "Tell me where you really went."

Maria glanced at the TV, where the time blinked in red across the room. Back to Pacific daylight, it was 2:03 in the morning. Rocky knew about Charlie, Maria was sure, but it wouldn't matter. Maria was prepared to fight.

"I told you where I was," Maria finally said, sitting upright in bed. "Why don't you believe me?"

"You know Nick has a crush on you, right?"

For the second time that night, Maria was stunned with relief. It was so delicious, she smacked her lips and laughed out loud, and then, she couldn't stop. She laughed until Rocky smiled, too, but Maria couldn't see it with the lights off.

"Maria, stop! I'm serious!"

"You think, wait, you think I was with Nick?" Maria was sputtering the words, a jangled mess of letters, a stuttering, giggling alphabet soup. Maria with Nick! Rocky's baby brother with hollandaise sauce smeared all over his face!

"No, I mean. Well, yeah, I thought—maybe."

"But you went to his room? And you saw I wasn't there?"

"I know." Finally, Rocky laughed. "Can you imagine?"

"No," Maria said. "I can't. At all. That'd be like kissing my nephew!"

"What if he were older? Would you still find it gross if he were older?"

"I mean." Maria's voice went somber. "He's still your brother."

"I guess."

Maria waited. "You wouldn't find it weird?"

"If he were older, I think it'd be okay. Two consenting adults? Whatever."

Maria considered this in the darkness.

"Oh," Rocky added, "and Karen texted you. I saw it when I saw that you'd left your phone."

"Oh?"

"Yeah. She said one thing."

"What?"

"'Yo.'"

"Did you reply?"

"Of course not. How do you respond to something so dumb, anyway?"

"Yeah," Maria said. "She's probably just bored."

Maria knew Rocky didn't like Karen and never really had. She suspected it was because Maria and Karen shared an uncommon alliance, being two of the few girls in the school from outside Manhattan and the only girls in their grade who took the same train home. Unlike Rocky, Karen had been to Maria's house countless times, because Maria knew that she wouldn't have to explain why the hot water in the bathroom always turned cold or why they didn't have cable TV. Whenever Rocky asked if she could come over to Maria's house, which had happened several times now, Maria made up a lie. It wasn't intimacy that Maria was denying her. It was simply the need to have to explain.

Maria wasn't going to pick a fight over Karen. She had already cut it close enough. For minutes after the girls said good night, Maria ached to get up to go to her phone. She remembered how earlier she had decided against texting Karen about the wink from Rocky's father. Even though she had been smart enough to hold out on the urge, lodged only a few scrolls back in her phone's history were traces of conversations about him. They used code names for almost every other boy they knew; why hadn't Maria thought of one for Charlie? And with Karen's insistence on calling him "Rocky's dad," it was all the more ridiculous that they'd never come up with a name. Maria set an internal clock in her head to make sure she'd wake up before Rocky. The first thing she would do when she got out of bed in the morning would be to erase the text message history from her phone, starting with her text log with Karen.

At the pool, Charlie watched as the waitress walked away. He had asked for another whiskey because not only would it help him fall asleep, he was also celebrating a personal triumph. He couldn't believe what he'd just done.

Really, she had fallen into his lap, had appeared before him conveniently in those moments in which, in a former life, he would have been in the throes of devouring his wife. Magically, she had been standing in his living room, in the hallway just before he retired to bed. Miraculously, she had been dawdling outside the elevator just as he returned to his room. Even Veronica would've never thought it possible: that Charlie could be this much of a scumbag.

In reality, it hadn't been hard. It was made easier with all of the noise. It had draped the mind like a woolen blanket, tucking his better judgment to sleep. When he pulled his face away from hers, the chatter of women and the sound of glass clinking took up the space he may have otherwise used to reflect on what he was doing. Out went the lighted fire of thought; dead went the TV-screen glare of contemplation. Doubts, which may have come meandering into his conscience, were snuffed out between the thumb and the ring finger of the humming of busy bodies, busy laughing at wicked jokes. He looked side to side expecting eyes he could challenge, but nobody was looking.

In this state of blank thought, in the muteness that followed, he kissed her again, and this time his hand sprung from his knee onto her shoulder. But while Charlie was doing the unthinkable, nobody had even turned. He was cheating on his wife with a teenage girl, and it was exhilarating.

"Um," Maria said, when they had separated, running a hand through her hair. "Are you gonna get in trouble?"

"Trouble?" He fought off a smile, the way he sometimes had to when coworkers announced that a pet, or an uncle, had died.

"You're married," she said.

"Yes," he said. "But believe me. It's fine."

She frowned. "What do you mean?"

Charlie thought of the ways he could say it, of where and with what he could start. He could ask the girl what good was a wife who wouldn't even give him a peck on the cheek? Or a wife so oblivious to his desire that she walked in the house in a bathrobe time after time? Could she even understand? Either way, she wouldn't care.

"Just trust me," he said. "We're not doing anything wrong."

"But you kissed me." As if startled by her own voice, her eyes fluttered away from his like a pair of frightened birds.

"Would you stop me if I did it again?"

"No," she said.

"We're friends. You do understand that?"

"Yeah—what else would we be?"

"Exactly," he said. "You see things the way they are." He brought his face against hers again, this time without meeting her lips, and went down to her neck instead. He had the thought that she'd likely never felt a man's stubble before, and that she wouldn't complain if he scraped her. "That's the reason I like you," he said. "You're so smart. You are going to amount to so much in life."

She laughed. Her eyelashes fluttered. Then she bit down on her lip. And somewhere in the process of observing all of those motions, Charlie had grown very excited.

"Wait," she said, when he'd put both hands on her waist. "Don't you want to hear my poem?"

"Your poem?"

"You told me to learn a new one for next time."

Charlie blinked. He had forgotten about that.

"I would love to hear your poem."

"Okay. Are you ready?" She was breathing a little bit quicker.

"I'm ready."

She cleared her throat, straightened her back. "This is called 'Letters,'" she said.

"'Every day brings a ship, / Every ship brings a word; / Well for those who have no fear . . .'" She was looking into the water. The light in the pool reflected onto her eyes, dancing. "'The word the vessel brings / Is the word they wish to hear.'"

Charlie took her hand. "That's wonderful."

"You think so?"

"Perfect. Your voice belongs on a radio program."

Maria laughed. "Okay. Your turn."

"But I won't sound as lovely as you do." He brought his face close to hers.

"Come on." She straightened herself so they were no longer as close. "Recite something to me."

Charlie tried to remember. He hadn't read a book in a very long time, never mind commit a poem to memory. He had a few fragmented lines, Shakespeare, that were left over from college, but nothing he could recite in entirety. Ah! He remembered one he used to love. *Whoever hath her wish, thou hast thy Will* . . . Oh, but that wasn't the right one for Seventeen . . . The girl was looking at him with pleading eyes.

"I'm afraid nothing is coming to mind," he said. "I'm so sorry. I hope you can forgive me. But what if I offered you something other than poetry? Would you accept something else instead?" He wasn't sure what he was talking about, but he was curious as to whether it'd work. The poetry had served him well up to this point, but he'd run out of all that now. Even though she kept giggling and batting her eyes, her knees were still locked together so tightly, and he was willing to try a more novel approach.

She looked into his eyes. "Like what?"

"You tell me," he said, bringing his hands to her navel.

"Like what? Dinner at Denny's?"

He laughed. "More than that," he said, the tips of his fingers finding the zipper to her pants. Behind him, he heard men's laughter, and the sound jolted him. He blinked his eyes as if he'd just woken up. His whiskey, the most recent one anyhow, was still nearly full.

"How about we move over there," he said. He pointed to the opposite end of the pool, toward a bunch of white tents lined up in rows like buttons. He helped her to her feet with his hand, and together, they walked over to the cabanas.

"Leave them like that," she said, as they pushed the curtains aside and stepped in. They sat on the mildly damp cushions and kissed.

"Tell me what you want," he said. "I'd like to give you whatever you want."

"There's a lot I want." She giggled. He buried his face into the crook of her neck. Suddenly, the smell of her overpowered him, and he recognized it instantly. It made him think of suntan lotion and plastic wrap, a scent he hadn't known he still carried a memory of after so many years. There were very few people who knew that before Charlie ever said "mama" or "dada," his first word had been "ah-ti," which was his effort at pronouncing *Tatiana*, the name of the Brazilian woman who had come to live with the family after Charlie's older sister was born. It was the intoxicating scent of Tatiana's shea butter—a smell he could only identify by name because as a boy he used to sneak into her bedroom and peek through her nightstand—that he detected as he licked at Maria's neck. He reached his hands into her jeans.

"Hey, wait," she said, pushing him away. "Don't you want to know what I want?" She crossed her hands over her neck, forcing him to lift up his head. The curtain blew slightly in the breeze, and from behind the flap, there were a few bodies, distant and blurred in the lights of the pool.

"Yes," he said, even though he'd already forgotten he'd said that. Instead, he was thinking about Tatiana. Tatiana making him tuna sandwiches with potato chips crushed between two slices of soft Wonder Bread. When he brought his friends over, they'd fall silent as soon as they'd seen her, and then they always gravitated back toward the kitchen as soon as they realized it was Tati's domain. When they first told him *Your maid is hot*, it felt like a belt across Charlie's chest unfastening, and finally, he could admit to having grown up and into a crush on Tatiana, this woman who undoubtedly was the first to change his diapers, to lift his bum in the air to wipe away at his shit. "Tell me," he said, right beneath Maria's ear, breathing in Tatiana's smell, "as I kiss you."

But again, she pushed him away. Now, he righted himself to a seat and looked at her squarely. Her eyes were darting from left to right, as if trying to see his whole face at once, and he suddenly felt a full tenderness toward her. He grabbed her palm with his left hand and held it to his lap. "How about this," he said, his fingers wet from sweat. "Squeeze my hand when you're uncomfortable."

He kissed her carefully, then pointed his chin toward her chest. He lifted her shirt with his hand, his mouth hovering over her bright-pink bra.

"I want a pair of blue Uggs. And a real leather jacket."

"Doable."

"And a leather clutch to go with it."

He moved the cup of her bra away. His tongue pressed down on the skin until he had the sense that something collapsed between her legs. When she squeezed his hand, Charlie moved his mouth toward her shoulder, folding the bra back into place.

"No?"

She craned her neck and looked past him, toward the pool. But they were far from everyone else, from where all those tall women were slinking.

"Go slower," she said. "A little slower."

When she eased up on his left hand, he returned his right hand to her zipper.

"I also want a minifridge."

He laughed as he undid the button. *Go slower,* she'd said, and he was trying with all his might, but it seemed ludicrous. How much slower could they possibly go? They'd been kissing so long it was no longer charged but sensuous, almost numbing, and now, forcing himself to go *slower,* he remembered past escapades, he recalled the most confident women he'd ever been with. How those women knew how to correct his primal instinct to run, to get pleasure over with. How they were the ones who had taught him to go not just to the edge, but over it. For so long, Charlie had envied the way women seemed to reach astral planes in orgasm, until finally he crossed over himself, and it was like he'd become a new form of matter somewhere between liquid and solid and soul. The thought of one of those sessions made Charlie lose his place, and he didn't know what she'd just said. But before that, she didn't say *stop*—she said *slower.*

"Huh? You said a minifridge?"

"For when I go away to college."

"What else?" The zipper came open. When he went past the fabric, she squeezed again.

"Maybe a futon."

"For college, right?" He rubbed a fold of cotton together, waiting. "It's good that you're thinking of college right now. I can tell you'll get into every college you apply to."

She smiled. This time, she didn't squeeze, not even gently, and Charlie realized he'd found the key. He got up and drew the curtains to the cabana closed.

"How about tuition? What if I took care of your college tuition?"

"My tuition?"

"Why not?" He brought himself down to his knees and pulled at her jeans with both hands so that she no longer had one to squeeze.

CHAPTER 14

Maria crept out of the bedroom and into the dining room awash with morning light. She had awoken with a pain in her pelvis that didn't quite feel like hunger, but since she couldn't think of anything else with which to remedy the pain, she reached for the Snickers bar she found at the minibar and sat down at one of the upholstered chairs to eat.

She'd left the pool alone. He was staying downstairs for one last drink, he'd told her, before heading to bed. On the walk to the elevator, it felt as if something were balled up between her crotch and underwear. She stopped at the bathroom in the lobby before going upstairs, and it took two flushes of toilet paper until she came away dry.

Now, she wondered if she'd made a mistake in denying him sex. *Take my number,* she'd said, instead, and she took his phone so she could type it in herself. He didn't offer his.

The light crept into the room from below the drawn curtains, and as the text message history for each one of her contacts went blank, Maria took nibbles from her chocolate, chewing it over excessively, savoring it until she was left with a heap of pasty wet mush at the back of her tongue. In one of Rocky's *Cosmopolitan* magazines, an article advised that one should always try to eat slowly since it can take up to twenty minutes before a person realizes they're satiated. Maria didn't really care too much about dieting—she was eating a Snickers for breakfast—still, there were certain things that she couldn't help thinking about whenever she sat down to eat. Whenever she hung out with Rocky, those thoughts became more frequent.

As she waited for her in-box to clear, she looked up from her phone. She saw her suitcase, propped against the bedroom door. Affixed to the top was a name tag her mother once bought from an amusement park. Her mother had put it there so Maria would know which bag was hers at the carousel. "María," it said in big bubble letters. America's stock Latina name. The one time she had asked her parents about it, they said they just kind of liked it, it just sounded *pretty*. She wondered what her name would have been if they'd consulted one of those baby-name books that they sell at the supermarket checkout. With those swollen pregnant fingers, her mother could've pointed at random, she could've started at the very first page at the letter *A*. Abigail it could've been, and if that didn't sound *pretty*, they could've named her Adeline, and if that was too obscure, they could've gone with Agnes, that perennial old-lady name. Maria's parents spoke and understood English. They could have named her anything.

But for a household that was all but bleached white in English, somehow her name remained. And now every time she enrolled in a class, or she met someone new at a party, or she heard herself being called from tongues that could never roll *r*'s, never mind say her name the way her grandparents had at the hospital when they first saw her, she had to live up to Maria. A Maria who was undoubtedly from meaner streets than she was. Maria who retained only the *indigenous* features and none of the *Indian* ones. A Maria whose skin was pale as a pillow, whose hair was as thick as a horse's mane, whose eyes changed in the sun like an opal stone or an ear of ancient flint corn, each kernel a different autumnal color. The same Maria they sing songs about. Maria, immaculate, whose body could not be contained. Maria, forever voluptuous, whose body was made for containing. All around her, Marias worthy of praise. No—this Maria would never live up to her name.

The night before, when Charlie first started undressing her, Maria, this underwhelming Maria, had been entirely ashamed. With her pink bra strap digging into her shoulder, an old relic from when she still shopped at the junior's section at Kmart, she knew she looked like a child, an overweight kid on the cusp of puberty. *Baby fat,* her mom always said. Her flats were worn out, and on her feet was an ugly patch of long hairs. It was things like this that she hated about herself: things that were entirely inelegant. But if Charlie noticed, he hadn't commented; he made no mention of too much or too little hair. He didn't comment on the noises she made, like Andres always did. Instead, he kept going, despite how many times she tried shying away, and it was then that she saw he didn't care.

Suddenly, Maria understood. When he started to take her underwear off, she was no longer there by the pool. Instead, she was in Rocky's bedroom on the Upper East Side, gazing down at Fifth Avenue. She had stood in that spot enough times now, a cigarette poised in her hand, that she could point out the Eighty-Fourth Street Central Park entrance without looking. She knew exactly how things were positioned from the Albrecht apartment, down to the number of trees from their view. The Albrechts had enough and more to share.

When he started to ask over and over what she wanted, she didn't think he could be serious at first. It had all seemed like a tremendous joke until then, until she realized perhaps he meant what he said, and then somehow, the punch line became even funnier. All this time, and she'd never realized how easy it could be. She thought of Karen on the train, Karen telling her to accept. *Maybe he'll want to buy you a helicopter,* Karen had said. *But what if,* Maria thought, *he wants to buy me more?*

When his tongue met her, she felt her person convulsing like the roll of a crashing wave. It took all of her strength to stop him. What was it that her uncle and brother always said? What was the one power that women could harness, as long as they knew when to withhold? Emerson said give all to love, but Maria also had learned that love only grew stronger the more you denied it. She brought her jeans up and with her open palm, she pushed his face off her. He had made her a promise, but she had to make sure that he meant it. She had to make sure he would keep it.

"Not now," she said firmly, sitting up. "Later. Once we're back home."

This was Maria, the Maria she was, the Maria who had just woken up from that night, from that memory, for better or for worse. Something small and nagging tugged at her conscience, but she didn't care. Being rich wasn't about how she could dress or what she could eat—it was about having a ticket of admission to college—to the kind of life she knew she deserved. And Charlie would give it to her because Charlie saw her potential. She had shown Charlie a glimpse of her heart, it flashed before him like a jewel of rose diamond, and he was a learned man, the kind of man who knew exactly what it was worth.

Casting the empty wrapper aside, she stood up from the table. She went back to the room where Rocky was still sleeping and climbed into bed. From under the sheets, she couldn't see the name tag, its ridiculous *i* studded with an acute accent. She did not, and would never, stress the *i* in her name. She would not click out the *r* so it came out like the sound of two claves hitting each other, or the sound of a domino arrogantly placed. She was Maria—the *r* like the pair in *cherries*, smooth and silky as the single *r* in *cream*. Maria, the English way. She didn't need to resort to giving out fake names. She didn't need to shrink when introducing herself. In fact, she never would again. With that resolved, she kicked her feet into the comforter and wondered if, at this time in the morning, Charlie might be awake.

The call girls were the last to be packed. Everything else, including the soaps and the hand towels that Maria's mother instructed her to bring back with her, had already been stored away in suitcases.

"Who do you prefer? Alexis or Gina?" Rocky was holding up two naked women who had, in place of nipples, bright yellow stars on their chests. One was reclining against a chair with her hand on her crotch and her mouth ajar. The other was wearing nothing besides a pair of knee-high wrestling socks. Both of them looked like they were covered from head to knee in Vaseline.

"God. Alexis, I guess?" Maria looked at Gina again, her blond hair slick against her forehead. "Alexis, definitely."

"Aw, that's the one I liked, too." Rocky looked at the cards in her hand. "Let me see if we've got doubles of her."

Maria had been awake for a while before Rocky had gotten up. She had wanted to wait until breakfast to eat, but as Rocky continued to sleep, Maria became more and more restless. By the time Rocky woke up, in addition to the Snickers bar, she had eaten a packet of M&M's, a plain Greek yogurt, and a bag of salted peanuts—all items she had found in the suite's minifridge. She alternated between taking bites and then lifting her shirt up to her bra to make sure that her stomach still looked flat and the dent where her oblique met the wall of her abs still remained visible. Whom did it matter to, anyway? Andres, for example, was more fixated on her ass than anything else, and as long as she maintained that bulge down her back, the one that he smacked and caressed and kissed all over, he wouldn't mind if a little fat gathered between her jeans and her shirt whenever she sat down. As she looked at the cards with Alexis, with Gina, with Isabelle, she tried to imagine herself in the same positions, tantalizing stars strategically placed over what she still had the habit of calling her *private parts*. She remembered the time she said the word *vagina* during foreplay and Andres scolded her.

You sound like a fucking doctor. This isn't a medical exam.

Pussy, she said, correcting herself, immediately understanding.

But Maria knew it wasn't a medical exam she was going through—no medical exam had ever made her so embarrassed. There were things that Andres said that Maria took very seriously and that had the power to undo everything she had once believed about herself, and others that she resisted against, albeit silently, discreetly, as to stage it to look not so much as resistance as sheer oblivion. The naked photos that Andres had asked her for were one of those things. When he opened them on his computer, he scolded her again.

"Your head is cut out of them," he said. "These are the creepiest sex photos I've ever seen."

It was true that the black-and-white photographs that she had sent over in a zipped file had been cropped from the neck down in order to conceal her identity, and that they seemed to suggest a crime scene.

"Well, maybe one day I'll run for office," she told him. "I can't have naked pics of myself circulating the internet." Andres hadn't asked her for any more pictures since then, obviously thinking her an idiot, and Maria felt she had made a good decision.

Now, as Maria looked at the glossy call girls on their glossy cards, and their glossy skin, she couldn't help but imagine herself in a similar photo shoot. She wanted to see herself in a lingerie set like Alexis's. They sold things like that in the shop in the West Village where Rocky had bought her the vibrator. Rocky shuffled through the cards on the bed, making separate piles, still trying to sort out fairly who would take home whom.

"Keep her," Maria said, staring at the photo of Alexis, her body drenched in what looked like canola oil. On a pan, Alexis looked like she'd sizzle.

"You sure?" Rocky didn't pause to look up. She continued to flip through the pile.

"Yeah, I'll take Gina."

"Gina's got character." Rocky held out another image of a woman who looked like a human Slip 'N Slide. "Actually, maybe I should keep Gina."

"Come on, give me Gina," Maria said, taking the card from her hand. Gina and Alexis had been the last pair of cards left, and unlike

Kara and Jean, whom Maria and Rocky each had six copies of, Gina and Alexis were the only cards of their kind. "You wanted Alexis."

"I did," Rocky said, looking at the card in front of her. "Hot mama Lexis." She fingered Alexis's skin, over her face and down to the crotch, where her legs spread out from under her like two branches coming off a tree trunk. Out of all the woman splashed onto the cards, Alexis was the only non-white girl—woman of color, like Diana would say. Maria looked on worriedly as Rocky held the photo of Alexis under her firm touch, her pastel-pink nail hovering above the graphic stars. She remembered how she was supposed to be an empowered woman—whatever that was supposed to mean.

"Actually," Maria said. "I want Alexis. Sorry. Do you mind?"

"So indecisive! But okay. Whatever. They're probably worth the same thing, right? But if for some reason, Alexis becomes really famous one day and this becomes some kind of limited collector's card, you're gonna owe me big-time." Rocky laughed, handing the card over to Maria. Maria placed Alexis facedown on the top of her stack.

"She'll be safer with you, anyway," Rocky said. "You know I lose everything."

Maria zipped her bag shut. Finally, they were all packed to leave.

"Back to the city!" Rocky took one final look at the room before she turned around. "Can you close the door behind you? My mom is going to kill us, she's been waiting so long downstairs."

Maria shut the door and with a small hop adjusted the bag on her arm. She felt the stack of call-girl cards poking out from the fabric, jutting into her rib. She looked at Rocky, who was staring into her phone as she rolled one suitcase down the carpeted hall, another bag slung over her shoulder. *She's right*—Maria thought—*Alexis will be safer with me.* Rocky had so much, she didn't seem to value anything, and her cards would undoubtedly end up in the trash. Even though they didn't have room for any more women at Maria's house, Maria promised she would hold on to Alexis forever.

Maria followed Rocky's lead until they stopped at the elevator, and instead of putting her bag down like Rocky did, she held hers to her side even closer. Rocky's matching suitcases didn't need name tags. From the embroidered logos all over the leather flaps, it was impossible not to know which bags were hers.

"Can you help me with this one, Shelly?" Rocky asked, pointing toward the floor. Maria remembered Charlie. He would give Maria things, too. He would give her even more. A college tuition, unimaginable opportunity, not to mention a nice place to live: these were things the girls at Bell Seminary simply expected, without ever wondering why—or if—they should really be theirs. Finally, Maria would have what they had. And yet here Rocky was, calling Maria not by her name, but by an old nickname she'd discarded, as if Maria would perpetually be accepting her secondhand things, as if her role forever would be to live as a witness to Rocky's glamorous life. Maria looked up from the suitcase and shuffled into the open elevator doors.

"You get it," Maria said. "My hands are full."

From inside the elevator, she watched Rocky stoop.

How does it feel to be an empowered woman? Maria smiled. She couldn't wait to find out.

Miguel was playing with a knife, flipping it over and over again in his hand. He had already finished dinner, and his wife had cleared his, hers, and Ricky's plates. As she let the water run over the dishes, he and his son sat on opposite sides of the table. Without turning off the faucet, she came over to grab an empty water glass, and then tried to slap at his wrist.

"Stop that! You're going to get hurt."

"Do you think that water bill is going to pay itself?" He gestured with the blade. Again, she tried to wrangle it from his hand. "Give me that. It's dirty." Finally, he opened his palm and let her take it.

Miguel watched as his wife walked away from the table, resuming her place by the sink. She seemed to never really know what was up. When important things happened—things she really should know or be curious about—all she wanted to talk about was the newest sale at Express or whether the laundry machine had already beeped. When they were dating, he had loved this about her, how little interest she had in nosing into other people's lives. All the girls he had met up to that point were helpless gossips, and there would always come a point where he'd lose track of which friends were the worst and which were the best, so that he'd say something like, *But don't you hate Larissa?* which would inevitably make the girl sitting across from him tear up. *How can you say something like that? I don't hate anyone.*

Miguel had quickly got tired of this game. When he met Analise and they spent their first dinner laughing at the fact that she had entered the restaurant, and, mistaking the only person she saw in a bowler hat for her date, sat down across from what must have been a very confused and perhaps delighted senior citizen, Miguel was overjoyed that he'd met a woman who could laugh at herself. When he retold this story to his kids, they just wanted to know what a bowler hat was, and when he finally showed them a picture, they laughed not at her, but him. *Daddy wore that when you first met him? And you still married him?* Maria had asked, back when she was a child inseparable from his wife and miserable if she ever had to spend a day without her.

It was the style! Miguel liked to assert, until one day Analise finally countered, *Oh no, it wasn't, it was your style!* and even though Miguel saw she said it with a smile, after all those years of never having said anything, of never having intimated that she had thought it was silly, he felt a little betrayed. He had wanted so badly to date a girl who could laugh at herself, but now he worried that it was he who had no sense of humor, who took himself so seriously that twenty-seven years later, he couldn't admit to himself that he had once worn a very stupid-looking hat.

"Where's Maria? Have you talked to her?"

"Of course, Miguel. She's fine." Analise had on her yellow dishwashing gloves, the ones that reached up to the elbows.

"Who is that friend, anyway? That girl Rocky?"

"A friend from school."

Ricky cleared his throat. "You shouldn't let her hang out with her."

Miguel turned his head away from Analise. His eyes grew wide as he stared at Ricky, from trying to take him in all at once.

"Why?" he said. "What do you think she's up to?"

But Ricky was facing his mother, not him. He seemed to be waiting for her to turn around. She had stopped washing the dishes, but she didn't turn the faucet off. She wiped her forehead with her rubbery forearm, pushing the hair out of her eyes. When she squeezed more detergent onto a sponge, Ricky gave up. "That girl Rocky," he went on. "She's no good."

Miguel felt a million nerve endings tighten. Ricky hadn't said anything like this before. He had expected him to say that Maria was hanging out with the wrong boys, not that she was hanging out with the wrong girls. Ricky wasn't one to exaggerate, either—before dating Alex, he would bring home friends with tongue piercings who walked straight to his bedroom without stopping to introduce themselves to Miguel, Analise, or Maria, who all looked on, slightly astounded.

Maria's mother finally turned off the faucet. She removed her right glove before taking off the left, and when she turned, she locked eyes with her son. Breathlessly, they stared at each other. *What's going on here?* Miguel thought. It was as if he wasn't even in the room. "How exactly do you know this?" she asked, her hands bare and in fists on her hips.

"I'll show you," he said, suddenly getting up. The wooden legs of his chair screeched against the floor, and Miguel watched wordlessly as Ricky got up and disappeared into his room. For a moment, he and his wife made eye contact, but Miguel looked away for fear that his wife might see through him. He didn't want her to know he'd been asking

Ricky for this, that he'd explicitly instructed him to keep tabs on Maria. And now that Ricky seemed to be more willing to talk to Analise than him, Miguel felt his face burn in anger.

When Ricky came back out, he had his laptop open to Rocky's Facebook page. He stood between the kitchen and dining room so that Miguel had to stand up to see and wedge himself between his son and his wife. Image after image appeared of Rocky and Maria posing in front of grotesquely large statues that looked like replicas of Grecian masterpieces. Both of the girls had their mouths puckered to suggest kisses and their skirts hiked up well above their knees. "Look," Ricky said, pointing at their limp wrists. Between Maria's fingers dangled a lit cigarette. A temporary tattoo lined in brown henna crawled up her left thigh.

Miguel felt his thoughts go staticky. He felt like he was counting up to a number only to keep forgetting his place. He felt like he was solving a math equation that would be a hundred times easier if he could write it down. Or maybe if he could just keep a grip on his anger. Or if Ricky would just shut the laptop screen.

"Shoot," Analise said, and something about the way she had said it, so flippantly, like they'd just found out that they'd placed two dollars on a losing bet, or misplaced a bag of groceries, made Miguel even more furious.

"When does she come back?"

"Tonight," she said. "Late. She's staying at her friend's apartment until tomorrow. Just let her get some rest." She was standing beside him, looking away from the computer screen, using a bare hand to press into his shoulder. She always did this at night when he couldn't fall asleep, and it always helped him relax. But with Ricky standing right next to him, Miguel felt humiliated. When Maria was first invited to visit Bell Seminary as a prospective student, he remembered how, when they walked through the chapel, he had no difficulty identifying the wainscoting, the French Baroque style, because it reminded him of his favorite exhibit at the Metropolitan Museum, a place he had first seen in high school as part of a home ec class. Even though he knew the price of the yearly tuition, he hadn't expected Bell Seminary to be so steeped in importance and history, and as he stood in that hallowed room, he was grateful he had decided to dress up for the tour. Miguel would've never guessed that Maria's new classmates would come from families that vacationed not in Europe, but Vegas, and this was what bothered Miguel now, that perhaps he was wrong on insisting on Bell Seminary, that perhaps there were parents who walked through those chapel doors and didn't know to look up to admire the woodwork. Perhaps there were parents who walked through those doors who didn't even make the sign of the cross over their chest. He had never been to Vegas, and he had never been to Europe, and now it seemed like they'd made a mockery of him—how they must've secretly snickered when he turned to them at the altar with his suit jacket lined with plastic buttons, and with swelling emotion, as he said *We accept.*

"We'll talk to her tomorrow," Analise said. "It's just cigarettes, Miguel. She's just going through a phase. She'll get over it."

Miguel flinched. He suddenly became aware of the fact that the whole time he was standing between her and Ricky, Analise had continued to work circles into the plates of his back. He knew that his kids were afraid of him, because Analise had told him more than once, but Miguel had only interpreted that as respect. Now, it seemed that their distance wasn't due to respect for his rules, but to complete dismissal of them. He pushed her hand away. He went down the hallway, past her, past Ricky, and slammed the door to his bedroom behind him, his shoulders stiff and curled, a shell.

CHAPTER 15

In Queens, Maria first put on a white tank top. Then, she pulled on the royal purple Taco Bell polo. She splashed water onto her hair and smoothed it down with gel. In the winter, her routine was entirely different, but it was much too hot now to try to straighten her hair. The dial she usually set her straightener to was three hundred degrees.

Outside the bathroom, her mother was waiting for her. At her feet was her laundry basket, already filled with the dirty clothes that Maria had worn in Vegas. Her mother had unpacked her belongings before Maria had the chance to.

"Listen, Maria. Your father found out you were smoking cigarettes. Cut it out, okay? And when you see him today, make sure you apologize. And don't you dare be rude when he asks about your trip to Vegas."

"I'm not smoking cigarettes!"

"Maria, quit lying already."

"I'm not lying."

Her mother put a hand on her hip. She was standing in the doorway, in Maria's way.

"Very nice. You look very official."

"It's Taco Bell, Ma. It's not Harvard."

"You're just like your father. You can never be proud of yourself."

Maria frowned. She pushed her purple sunglasses on, the ones Rocky had lent her in Vegas.

"Go," her mother said, when she could no longer see Maria's eyes. "Go. And don't be late."

On her walk down Queens Boulevard, in her deep-purple shirt, Maria found she was dreaming. She was floating, as if her body were only dangling from her head like confetti paper. The billboards weren't legible. To her right, the cars raced by in an unknowable blur. To her left, there were hourly motels that Maria usually tried to walk quickly past. But today, Maria didn't hurry.

She looked toward the horizon, filled with love. Then she looked at the auto shops with cars stacked upon cars. She saw the scattered trash strewn on the sidewalk like children's toys. Even the houses boarded up with rotting wood and the underpass where Maria kept her head down until all the pigeons were gone. She gazed upon all of it, brimming with love.

What if she could walk from one end of the boulevard to the other end? What if it went on forever? What if it led to China, the way they said tunnels dug in the ground could? Here she was, in one of the most populous cities in the world, and she had this expanse of concrete all to herself, and it dwarfed the trees and the buildings and even the clouds, and suddenly, Maria knew how lucky she was. Maria wanted to keep it with her, tuck it into a pocket and paste it inside her purple journal under her bed, so that one day she could come back to what it was like to walk down Queens Boulevard at this very moment. She could tell she was overwhelmed with emotion, and she wondered what was happening inside her. Could it be that because she'd been changed on the inside, because she'd glimpsed her own beauty, everything around her had also changed?

Emerson said that you could find infinite beauty in nature, but Maria knew you could do the same thing in the city, only that nobody really knew how. Nobody knew how to look at Queens Boulevard like she did, and it was special that she'd been able to develop this taste. Nobody said it was easy to like a big, ugly blip of asphalt and pavement, but nobody said it was easy to like a quiche, either. It was when you closed your eyes, and you imagined the person who kneaded the dough for the crust, whisked the cracked eggs and the cream, scraped the mixture into the pan, dotted the butter on top as it baked, that finally, you understood that your mind needed to step ahead of your tongue, of your feeling. That's how Queens Boulevard was, in a way.

At least, that's how Charlie might have explained it. When she told him that she thought Las Vegas was fine and that the big fountain outside the hotel was fine, too, he wouldn't let her upstairs until she saw it again. *Close your eyes,* he had said, once they were standing in front of it.

And so Maria had closed her eyes and listened, again, to a song she couldn't understand. She'd already stood in this exact place with Rocky, and they had watched the water rise and fall in a series of slaps, their chins in their hands. But this time, she felt Charlie's presence behind her, warm, and right as she was about to lose faith, a tremendous gust of wind made her open her eyes. The water shot several yards in the air, and as the song soared, her heart leapt and flew away with it. *Oh my God,* Maria said, turning around. She looked into his eyes. *I felt it.*

He grinned, but afterward, she kept wondering about why it felt so different the second time around, the time that she wasn't with Rocky. She wondered what had changed, as she got on the flight home. She wondered on the drive back from the airport. She wondered in the morning when she woke up and got dressed in front of her mother for her first day of work.

It was hope, Maria realized, walking down Queens Boulevard. It was simple, innocent hope. She saw herself, for the first time that whole year and perhaps her whole life, racing toward a brilliant future.

At Taco Bell, the manager hurried her inside. She was holding a thin white binder.

"This has everything you need to know," she said. "Take a look at it when you have a chance. But for right now, just shadow Jimmy as he takes the gentleman's order."

Maria looked at the boy her manager pointed at. Jimmy was tall and dark; he looked like he'd spent every day of the summer so far lying on Rockaway Beach. He was trying to keep eye contact with Maria and the manager even as he was taking someone's order. Something in his posture changed as he was looking at Maria. Maria could tell he was interested.

Maria stood with him, like the manager told her. She watched him press so many buttons so fast, she was actually somewhat impressed. She was just about to ask Jimmy if she could give it a try herself, when someone started screaming.

She wasn't even old. She wasn't too shabbily dressed, either. Maria could understand bits and pieces of what she said, enough to understand she was speaking not in Spanish, but in the language of the insane. Around her, people's eyes were growing wider, and mothers hugged their kids closer to their chests.

The manager's eyes were bulging. "This shit again! No!" She looked at Jimmy like he'd just made a suggestion. "I'm not calling the cops. They only make things worse!"

Maria and Jimmy both stared at the manager in silence, but it was Maria whom she took a step toward.

"What's she saying?"

"I—I don't know."

"Aren't you Mexican?"

Maria's cheeks burned. "I'm Ecuadorian. And Puerto Rican."

"That's close enough."

Maria looked pleadingly at Jimmy.

"I don't know Spanish," he said.

With her legs feeling like lead, she maneuvered around the counter. As she got closer to the woman, the smell got worse. Around her, people glared.

"Señora . . . ," Maria said, hesitating. "Por favor . . . deje de gritar."

The woman spat on her. The whole fast-food restaurant took a collective breath, even the walls, even the tiles on the floor. In that vacuum of sound, the spit trailed down Maria's shirt at a rapid rate. The woman saw then how Maria's face changed. Triumphant, she sat down and opened the taco she'd ordered several minutes ago.

Maria ripped the shirt off, revealing her white spaghetti-strap tank top. She let the Taco Bell polo fall to the floor.

"I quit," she yelled. The whole store could hear her, but the manager didn't say anything as she stormed toward the door.

Once there, Maria looked back one last time. This time, Jimmy waved.

When he came downstairs to meet her outside his apartment, Andres's mouth was tight: a zipped line that ran from one cheekbone to the other. People were lingering out in the park, and a woman was scooping red chunks of sugary ice into a paper cup across the street, and everywhere there was the sound of people celebrating, but Andres's eyes were mean.

"Nice sunglasses," he said in a way that suggested the opposite. He looked her up and down.

"Thanks," she said. Using her thumb knuckle, Maria pushed the sunglasses farther up her nose. Facing Andres behind the tinted lenses, she felt a little braver knowing he couldn't see all of her.

"There you go acting like one of those white bitches."

"I don't even know what that means."

"Like, I don't even know what that means." He spoke in an exaggerated Valley Girl accent, rolling his eyes and flipping an imaginary tuft of blond hair. "Fucking cigarettes are disgusting."

"Smoking cigarettes does not make me white. I'm not white."

"No, you're just trying to be."

Maria was used to the accusation. If she wanted to straighten her hair, it was because she wanted to look like a white girl. If she didn't want to eat his mom's dinner, it was because she thought she was white. If she smoked cigarettes on an excruciatingly hot summer day, it was for no other reason than that she thought she was white—it was among the many ludicrous, inexplicable things that only a white girl would do. Usually, Maria just quietly laughed him off.

"I'm sorry I go to a good school." She glanced at him, assessing the potency of her words before continuing, like measuring some spice for a debut dish before deciding to pour it all in. He didn't look upset yet, so she continued. "And that I'm gonna go to a really great college."

Andres turned away and walked down the street.

"Hey! Where are you going?"

"Fuck you!" he yelled over his shoulder.

"Andres! Wait for me!"

He must have been pleased to know he'd made her run after him, because when she caught up to him, the tightness was gone from his mouth.

"You're mad condescending," he said. "Your brother's the same way. My boy says hi to him and he doesn't even respond."

"What does my brother have to do with anything?"

"I'm saying, it must run in your family."

"Ricky doesn't think he's better than you," she said, trying to ignore Andres's incredulous face. She thought of Ricky standing in the doorway to her room, his wet sneakers crunching against the hallway floor, and remembered the last thing he'd said to her. It still was a tender wound. "He's just looking out for me," she said.

They reached the end of the block and were standing outside a deli. A couple of other boys were standing there, watching bicycle wheels spin by.

"That's why he can't say hi? Because he doesn't like that we're dating?" Maria could tell that the boys next to them were listening to their conversation. They seemed to be pausing between their sentences every time Andres spoke.

"You don't have a sister," she said, her voice lowered. "You don't get it."

Inside the deli, Andres picked up a bag of BBQ chips as Maria looked around, inspecting all the offerings. There were speckled bananas and plums in cardboard boxes on the floor. Hovering over both piles of fruit were little black clouds of flies. She looked up at a wire crate full of pastries, their white frosting smeared all over the faces of their plastic wrappers. She flipped them over to read the calorie counts, and then flipped over a few more. From behind her, she heard Andres groan.

"Yo, can you hurry up?"

She grabbed a bag of Cheetos and paid at the counter with change.

Outside, Maria noticed a sign posted on the door. It spelled out the letters "E-B-T." When Maria was far enough from the deli that she was sure the boys outside couldn't hear her, past the Texas fried chicken shop and Fresca Tortilla food truck, and after they crossed the street near Chubby Taco, she looked up at Andres.

"What's 'EBT' mean?" she asked, waiting for his reaction.

Andres turned to Maria, his face scrunched up like a dish towel. "Yo," he said. "Are you—" But his voice trailed off, and he took a step back and squinted at her, as if there were something horrible on her face and he needed to step away to get a better look at it. Maria had the sense that he was trying to decipher her.

"You know karma's a bitch, right?"

"Shut up. Nothing is going to happen to me."

"Yeah, that's why you had to get a job at Taco Bell, right? Because everything's fine?"

Maria frowned. "I just quit, asshole."

"Yeah," Andres said. "When you and your whole family is out on the street, don't come crying to me."

"Fuck you, Andres."

"No, fuck you."

Maria felt her whole body rev up in rage. It was Maria's mother who had said she never *had* to and never *would* use food stamps to feed her kids. She said she never was on Medicaid—and she said it with her head lifted, her voice unwavering, so that Maria knew that she should be proud. Maria understood, had understood from the day that she first met Andres, that these were the things that distinguished her from him, and she didn't like when Andres tried to point out that maybe she was wrong, that maybe these things were fast disappearing, that maybe things could very quickly change.

CHAPTER 16

Her mother was vacuuming in the living room, wearing an old pajama shirt of Bugs Bunny's faded face, when Maria unlocked the front door. Maria kissed her on the cheek hello. Usually she hated the sound of the vacuum—her mother used one of those clunky industrial ones from the 1980s. But today Maria stood in the living room for a long while until she finally noticed her mother's stare—that even as she dragged the vacuum back and forth across the carpet, she hadn't taken her eyes off Maria.

"Where's your Taco Bell shirt?"

"I got spat at. I quit."

Maria's mother was silent for a long time. "Your father is pissed at you." Her voice was barely a whisper. "He's in his bedroom."

"Pissed?" Maria sniggered. "Why?"

Maria didn't like seeing her mother dressed down. She was usually so careful with makeup whenever she left the house. *The Anatomy of the Human Body* was the name of the book they had studied in class last year, and her mother could be exhibit A, with all that unpainted fleshy skin around her eyes branching out into a perfect crow's foot. As she looked uneasily at her mother's eyes, she could see how their gaze had now lowered to where she pulled her jeans up by the belt hooks.

"What? Are you trying to say I'm gaining weight?" Maria hated when her mother sized her up like a turkey to bake.

"No seas tan exagerada!" Maria's mother crossed her arms. "And even if you were, what's the big deal? Why are you obsessed with that? Go eat before your father comes out here."

"I'm not obsessed," Maria said.

In the dining room, Maria closed her eyes as she ripped into her first bite. The steak cutlet was resistant to coming apart, so she chewed and chewed, savoring, enjoying, until she had sucked all the mayo out dry. She snapped the cap open for a second dousing. Then she took another bite, the tomato slipped under her tongue, and she clutched the rest of the bread in her hand. Strips of onions fell; she popped them into her mouth.

Before she had finished swallowing, she heard the bedroom door open, and then the unmistakable sound of her father's sneakers squeaking against the floor.

"Maria."

She had already pushed her plate away.

"Hey!" His voice was louder. She raised her eyes to meet his, and his forehead was drenched in sweat. The front of his shirt was dark from where the sweat had soaked through it. It wasn't any less hot in the dining room than it was outside, and the insides of Maria's thighs were so slick that they kept slipping off each other when she tried to cross her legs.

"Hey," Maria said, stopping just short of his name, and already she knew she'd made a mistake.

"Where have you been?"

"Here," she said, not looking up from the table. She reached for her sandwich and took too big a bite. The bread was stale, hard to chew, the meat rubbery in her mouth.

"You were in Vegas," he said. "What were you doing there?"

"Huh? Nothing."

"Maria, tell me something." He waited until she finally looked up. He was wearing a backpack, as if he had forgotten to take it off when he came home from work. "Why did you quit your job today?"

Maria looked back down at her plate. She put the sandwich down into the cesspool that the atrophied tomato now made. An ant ran across the table, making figure eights.

"Because," Maria said.

"Because what?"

She picked up the sandwich again. The ant circled the edge of her plate. She watched as it ran away from her crumpled napkin.

"Because," she said. "I wanted to."

Suddenly, something scraped by Maria's face, kissing her eyelids so that it stung. A wad of chewed bread, sopping with juice, came out of her mouth and fell pathetically onto the plate. As if on call, water welled up to her eyes, and she stared at the deflated backpack that had landed near her feet at the floor.

"Why would you do that?" She stood from the table, her fists clenched at her side. "What's wrong with you!"

"Let me make this clear to you. You will not leave this house anymore until you learn to have some responsibility. You are not leaving this house until you get another job."

"You're crazy!" Maria said without lowering her voice, but her mind was racing. "You can't make me do anything."

"We all do things we don't want to do, Maria. It's time you stop acting like a baby."

"But I don't want to work!" Suddenly the room was a blur. Maria's tears were pooling. "I don't want to work at a fucking Taco Bell! I want to study for my SAT this summer! I want to go to college!"

Maria charged past her father, letting the rickety screen door smash against the doorframe. Outside, she had just unlocked the front gate to the house when she heard him screaming after her.

"If you leave right now, don't bother coming back. Do you hear me, Maria? Oíste, Maria!"

There were people out on the street, and Maria tried not to look as they stared at her running down the gray block, her legs pumping over the sidewalk where hardened pieces of dog shit were packed like caulk into the cracks and crevices.

That night, Maria listened to her father. After stopping inside a deli and buying a few items of comfort—sour straws and Sprite—she headed to Jonathan's apartment. Jonathan's roommates constantly seemed to change, but it was the only place she could walk to in Queens where she knew she could stay for the night. She had to wait a long time before Jonathan answered the buzzer. He listened to Maria's story, and when he hesitated before answering her, Maria was visibly hurt.

"Where do you want me to go, then?"

"Don't be silly," he said. "Of course you can stay. You take my bed, okay? I'll sleep on the couch." He took a blanket from the bed and left the pillow for Maria.

Despite Jonathan's goodwill, Maria couldn't sleep. The bed was hot, and the mattress was harder than the one she was used to at home. When she checked her phone, it was only 2:40. She spent the next hours falling asleep in short, arid spells—down she'd barrel into them and then back up into waking. She'd check her phone and would be grieved to see that only ten minutes had gone by. Maria got up and went to the living room. The glare of the TV screen lit up the whole room—Jonathan must have been awake. From behind the divider, Maria announced herself, afraid of what she would find on the other side.

"Hey," she said.

"Hey."

She stepped across and was relieved to see that it was only Tekken. Jonathan held on tight to the controller, even when she sat down across from him on the couch.

"What's up? Why are you awake?"

"I can't sleep. I can never really sleep. My head just starts racing."

"Same thing happens to me. That's why I just stay up all night instead."

"What about when you work?"

"When I work, I try to go to sleep by midnight."

The hardwood floor was unexpectedly cold, like the tiles in a public bathroom. Maria fidgeted. "Hey," she said. "Remember how you said to hook you up with one of my friends? Do you really think it's not that bad for a girl to get with an older guy?"

Jonathan sat up a little straighter and then slouched back down. He was so obvious about everything, and Maria could tell he was trying to hide his concern. Maria loved this about him, how impossible it was for him to repress his emotions. He could never get his face to express what he wanted—it simply did whatever it felt like.

"I was kidding about that, Maria."

"I know. But in general, I just don't know if age matters that much."

"It depends on the girl and the guy, right? Like, how mature they both are."

Through the blinds, Maria could see the first spalls of sunlight slice across the room. She went to the window—there were already birds chirping. It was early enough for her to go home. She knew she wouldn't be able to fall asleep here again.

"I think it's simpler than that," she said. "I think the reality is that it's all just transactional."

From the corner of her eye, she noticed Jonathan perk up again.

"Like nobody our age has a car yet. Let's say my friend Rocky dated you, you could drive her around."

Jonathan laughed. "What does she need me to drive her around for? She probably already has her own driver."

"Maybe." Maria smirked. "But not one as good-looking as you."

Maria walked from Jonathan's apartment to her doorstep, taking the long way home on the boulevard where six lanes of cars menacingly stretched away from the curb. When she reached the house, she sat for half an hour on the front porch until she brought the key to the door. It was locked from the inside, so she called her mother's cell phone three times. Maria's mother stood with her hands on her waist and let Maria walk past her without so much as "good morning." The sky was pewter, paling with sunrise, when Maria opened the door to her room.

She kicked off her sneakers. Without taking her jeans off, she threw herself onto the bed. It was a nuisance. Only one person comfortably fit on it at a time—even though Maria said she preferred to have a double-size bed rather than a twin, her parents had scoffed. The room was much too small for that, they said, and besides, she needed a desk and a dresser, too. One of her plans for college included stripping her room of all furniture. At the center of the room, there'd be one giant bed, and in this bed, she would do everything—eat her cereal for breakfast, write poetry until lunch, invite friends and boyfriends to sit on its pillows and smoke pot. It was the kind of thing that made up her dreams.

But she hadn't always hated the bed, whose headboard was painted pink by her father. He had constructed the frame himself from pieces of wood he salvaged from work. He had been so proud to install it, to show her how it was still small enough for her to fit her desk right next to it. The sheets were patterned with Disney princesses, and when she was lying down on them, she could see how the ceiling was still populated by synthetic stars that by now had lost whatever property that had made them once glow in the dark.

Maria pulled the sheets up to her shoulders and within seconds fell asleep. If it were up to her father, Maria would sleep in this bed forever. She knew because he had told her. She would still be the six-year-old girl who jumped up and down when he announced that it was finally ready and showed her how the closet doors in her new room opened so wide that she could fit her whole body inside them. If it were up to him, even now Maria would still be a very little girl, and this was a dream that was simply impossible, one that she knew she was getting further away from every day.

CHAPTER 17

Maria looked at her bookshelf, deciding. She spread out on her bedroom floor with several books to decide between.

Her dad had relaxed a smidgen from his last outburst. Maria knew her dad would calm down a little—Analise always managed to get him to be reasonable sooner or later. Now, things seemed to be relatively normal in the house. Ricky had started his job at the phone store, too, so that helped take some pressure off her to find one. But she was still banned from going out after dark, and staying over at anyone's house was out of the question.

It'd been two weeks now since she'd come back from Vegas, and every day her hope diminished. She was still checking her phone compulsively, but Charlie never texted or called her. When she walked down Queens Boulevard, she didn't know she was thinking of him. When she quit her job, she didn't know she'd been thinking of him. She was thinking that soon, this life wouldn't be the one she was living. But she realized now that she had stopped despairing a little too soon, before anything had actually changed.

Reading helped dull the pain that had settled in Maria's stomach, but Emerson was too painful these days. Last year, her English teacher had suggested that Maria read an anthology of work from Latina poets from the medieval ages to today. *They're inspiring Latina women, just like you,* her teacher had said as she gave her the book. Maria was so embarrassed that she had rolled her eyes, but now she took the collection from the shelf.

That afternoon, Maria had plans to meet Karen, and if she didn't stop reading, she would be late. Maria knew Karen hated waiting. They agreed on the Dunkin' Donuts near Queens Center Mall. There were cuter cafés a little closer to Karen's house in Forest Hills, but Maria insisted that it was only fair to meet halfway, and Maria secretly liked ordering the Vanilla Bean Coolatta, even though Rocky had called it a ghetto Frappuccino the only time she'd seen Maria with one at school. She had found the perfect spot for her purple sunglasses atop her purple poetry notebook, and she grabbed them now as she dashed out of the room and opened the screen door. "Meeting Karen," she called out, "in Queens!" just as her mother started to ask where Maria thought she was going.

Maria shouted and waved as Karen approached. It felt like a long time since they'd last seen each other. When Karen got close enough, the two hugged. Karen's hair smelled like blueberries.

"Hey." Karen's voice was level as she held the door open. In line, they stared at the donuts behind the magenta-painted counter. Some were pink, and others were white, and almost all were covered in sprinkles, but the colors couldn't masquerade the way that the dough still drooped into itself, like a bicycle tire deflated of air. In measured steps, they shuffled closer to the register.

"Can I tell you about Vegas, Karen? We stayed at the nicest hotel, the most expensive. There was this fountain outside and they did this whole light show. It was the fanciest place I've ever seen."

"Have you tried the Chocolate Glazed?" Karen wasn't looking at Maria because her head was still angled toward the wire racks behind the register. Karen's eyes looked heavy lidded and puffy.

"I'm getting a Boston Kreme," Maria said. "But yeah, there was a pool, too. And cabanas. And a fake New York! And a fake Taj Mahal!" Maria paused. Karen had her back to her now, and as Maria hovered behind her in line, she could see how Karen's braid was weighed down, the ends of it slick and pointed, like a stamen.

"Why is your hair so wet? Did you just take a shower?"

"Yeah."

They were at the register. Karen stepped aside to let Maria order first. Maria dug around in her tote bag, the one she used on the weekends, and felt around for a quarter. Nothing but specks of dirt and a burst fountain pen came up in her hand. She turned to Karen.

"Do you have eighteen cents?"

Karen handed her a dollar bill, and Maria passed her the pennies and quarters she got back in change. After they both ordered and were given their food, they sat at a table near the window, where they could watch as swarms of people, some with strollers and others with backpacks, climbed up and down the stairs of the train station. They pulled out tin chairs, whose feet squealed along the tiles like a fingernail on a chalkboard. Maria ran a napkin over the table's surface to clear the crumbs that the last customers left there.

"Also," Maria said, crumpling the napkin into a ball. "Did I tell you about Andres? Do you know what he told me the other day?"

Karen put the donut down and rolled her eyes.

"Is it anything new? Andres is a fucking asshole. At this point, you're the one who's an idiot for staying with him."

Maria stopped sipping from the Coolatta. It was so dense it hardly came up the straw without an inordinate amount of concentration.

"And what happened with Charlie?" Karen tore off another piece of her donut and held it tentatively in her hand. "Was he in Vegas, too? Did you decide to hook up with him?"

Maria stared into her chocolatey drink. She had wanted to wait until they were settled and sitting before telling Karen about the offer

Charlie made to her by the pool. She wanted to ask Karen what she thought, if it were crazy that she was thinking of actually taking him up on it. If an entire college tuition—or even a mortgage on a house—was really the kind of thing a person like Maria or Karen wouldn't exchange anything for. Or, and this thought made her shrink in shame, was it only Maria? She wanted to slip inside that narrow space of her straw and slide down into the syrupy mixture.

Karen was devouring her donut, and there was now less than a quarter of it left. When Maria still hadn't answered, she didn't wait to swallow to start talking again.

"Do you even like Rocky?"

"Of course I like her." Maria unfolded the flap of her paper bag. Half of the frosting had already come off the donut, smeared onto a square of parchment paper. She couldn't look at Karen anymore, even with her sunglasses obscuring her face, so she directed her question into her lap. "Are you saying I'm a bad friend?"

"This thing with Charlie, it's so fucked up. Anyone would be upset if their friend was hooking up with their dad!"

Maria's neck snapped up like a reflex. "Karen!"

"I'm not calling you a bad friend, Maria, so don't get all offended. But a good friend would ask how my grandfather is doing." Maria saw that Karen's eyes weren't just red and puffy anymore—now, they were glossed over. "A good friend would at least ask."

Maria felt her body clam up. She twisted her leg around the other, and then strained to get her ankle across the other ankle. Maria had only seen Karen's text about how her grandfather was in the hospital after landing in New York and switching off her phone's airplane mode. That was at least a week ago. Or was it already two weeks now? As Maria brought her elbows up to the table, her hands cradling her face like she wanted to hide, Maria remembered that she never responded.

"Fuck." Maria lifted her sunglasses off her eyes so that she could show Karen her face. "Karen, I'm sorry. I was getting off the plane. Things have been so crazy."

"Yeah." Karen's fingers traced the lining of the bag. There was nothing there now but crumbs.

"Is your grandfather okay?"

"Yeah. He's being discharged tonight."

Maria took another bite of the donut, but it didn't taste like anything. When they stood up and Maria suggested they go to the mall, Karen didn't protest. They went into Urban Outfitters with eight dollars total between them, and with the intention of not buying anything. As they walked from aisle to aisle, Maria kept pointing to different articles of clothing. All her comments felt pained, stupid. She had a hard time saying goodbye to Karen when they had to get on opposite sides of the train platform.

"I'm sorry, Karen." Maria was reluctant to go down the stairs to catch her train.

Karen hugged her, but her arms were so stiff, Maria was reminded that under the skin they were made up of bone.

When Maria got to her house that night, she took her books out again. She texted Karen, something inconsequential, and waited for her to answer. She tried lying down on her belly to make the terrible feeling at the center of her chest go away. When it didn't work, she knew there was nothing she could do, no medicine she could take to get rid of the stinging. It had been selfish for her to not answer the text immediately, and she realized it was fear that made her feel so terribly now—the fear of losing Karen's friendship. It was a feeling that she realized, with some degree of sadness and wonder, she didn't feel toward Rocky.

The next day, nobody was home. Her father had gone to work as usual, and her mother was gone, likely at the supermarket or Laundromat or to clean someone's apartment in Manhattan—if it wasn't one, it was always the other. Waking up at noon to find the house empty, Maria had left before anyone could return and ask where she was going, before anybody could try to stop her.

Andres's mother had been making lunch when Maria arrived. Andres led her into his bedroom, and to the muffled sound of plates clattering in a sink, Andres fingered her with one hand and changed the channel of the TV with the other. Maria was vying with an episode of *MythBusters* for his attention, and although she knew this would never work for her, she made the requisite noise, anyway. What he was doing to her body felt nothing like what Charlie had done to her by the pool, but she thought that if she moaned loud enough, maybe the feeling would follow the sound.

"Do you hear yourself?" He looked like he wanted to hit her. "Shut up, Maria. My mom is home!"

Maria pulled her denim skirt down. "Why have you been so mean to me lately?"

"Maria," he said, "we can't do this anymore."

Maria wished she had her sunglasses on, like Rocky always did. She felt the seams to her heart fly open, and her eyes became clouded with tears. Andres hadn't looked back from the TV yet to notice, so she hastily wiped them away.

"We can work it out," she said, her underwear still slung round her ankles. She pressed her knees together to ennoble herself. If she were still able to make use of Andres—Andres who left the borough of Queens at most once a month, who was trying to find a job as a parking valet—then surely he could make use of her.

"No." He turned around to face her now and grabbed her shoulder with the hand that had just been inside her.

"Why not?" Maria held herself up on one elbow. She wondered if he was wiping his fingers clean on her T-shirt. *What is wrong with him?* It was stuff like this that convinced her that she had seen the very worst of Andres, and instead of repulsing her, it only convinced her that their love could survive anything she was willing to put up with. And even if that weren't true, Andres was still just another neighborhood boy from Queens, and he had no right to get rid of Maria. He was the kind of boy she imagined would be around for her bidding whenever she came home during breaks from college, which would be on a campus far from New York, while Andres scraped by at a local commuter school. Andres couldn't break up with her, Maria reasoned, because that was something *she* was supposed to do, whenever *she* was ready. At Bell Seminary, senior students applied to both reaches and safeties, and Maria had decided that, on a ranking of love, Andres was a solid safety. He got a 400 on his PSAT.

"I'm seeing someone else," Andres said.

Maria was reclined and half-naked on his bed, but her eyes became telescopes, and her vision was transported to an amplified image she'd never inspected before. It was the crystalline picture of her brother and uncles wagging their fingers, telling her she'd been wrong: Andres had put bodies between them. Maria next saw the doctor with her clipboard, scoffing under her breath. She saw Karen, vicious like a dog, tearing the flesh of a donut. They were all right: Maria had been blind as a kitten, and now Andres was ripping her eyelids apart, staking them so they couldn't blink closed.

"Who is it?" Her throat was dry.

"We met at the end of the year. At school."

Maria didn't know what to ask next, so Andres continued, unprompted.

"She's beautiful."

Maria's mouth fell open. She felt it hang there, gaping, and closed it. "Beautiful?"

"Listen, remember how you used to talk about the guys at your school when we first started dating?"

"Yeah," Maria said, even though she knew it wasn't fair of him to mention the boys from Bell Seminary's brother school. She exaggerated about the few white guys she'd ever danced with. She had always assumed Andres knew those boys never liked her, anyway.

"Well, I've always been kind of resentful of that, and I had always known Chastity, even before I met you. Last semester we were in the same class. We started talking—"

"Chastity?" Maria asked. "Her name is Chastity?"

"Yes," Andres answered, with a completely straight face. "She's fucking perfect," he added, as if Maria weren't lying right there with her panties scrunched up at her feet, as if his mother hadn't put out an extra plate on the table so Maria could join them for lunch. Her neck stiffened up like a dry sponge. Andres had a distinct twinkle of the eye—there was no denying it—and she had spent all afternoon with him, so she knew there were no drugs in his system. That starry-eyed look when he spoke Chastity's name was real unfettered admiration.

The pot in the kitchen crackled with oil. Something was frying, almost ready to eat.

"But don't you love me?" she ventured, and when he didn't answer, there was no more courage left.

Outside his bedroom door, his mother called them to lunch, and even though the air was so thick with food that Maria already knew it tasted delicious, she knew she wouldn't be able to eat. Her tongue was papery and she was unable to swallow, as if her throat was clotted with sand. Andres coaxed her into getting dressed, but as soon as she did, she couldn't contain herself.

"You can't leave me!" Maria yelled as soon as Andres sat down at the table. His mother had put out place mats for both of them, but Maria refused to sit down. She would not stay here as Andres humiliated her. She wouldn't tolerate him cheating on her. She would leave him, the way she'd always envisioned it, the way she always knew she would. Usually, she gave a polite and formal hello and goodbye to Andres's mother, but Andres didn't deserve Maria's civility anymore. Today she ran past both of them, letting the door crash as she fled, so that the whole apartment shook in her wake.

CHAPTER 18

"He dumped me, Rocky."

"What! He can't do that!"

"He was cheating on me."

"Oh, Shelly. Want me to come over?"

Maria hesitated.

"Or, I can just call Laura. Don't worry."

"No," Maria said. "Come over."

Maria walked to the train station to pick up Rocky. Rocky descended the steps with her sunglasses far up the bridge of her nose, as usual. On the way back to the house, Rocky had to keep asking Maria to slow down. *Sorry,* Maria kept saying every time she almost lost Rocky on a right or left turn. *I'm not in your head,* Rocky told her.

At home, Jonathan was sitting on the futon with Ricky, eating chicken and rice. When Maria saw them huddled together, she also saw how the studs in their earrings reflected Rocky's gaze. She hurried past them, into her bedroom, and showed Rocky where she could put her things down.

Maria didn't know where to take her, so they got on the bus to the mall. Usually Maria just walked thirty minutes and saved the money she'd spend on the fare, but she didn't want to risk going past Taco Bell.

The manager probably already forgot what she looked like, but what if Jimmy saw them and waved?

"I didn't know there were malls in New York City," Rocky said. She bought two cinnamon pretzels, one for her and another for Maria.

"How are your parents?" Maria asked. They were sitting on the concrete ledge outside Skechers. The mall was shaped like a giant circle, and the main entrance faced Queens Boulevard. Buses kept stopping and going like big abused elephants. Dropping off passengers, picking up more. They couldn't catch a break, those poor buses.

"My mom is fine."

"How's your dad?"

"Why are you asking about Charles?"

"I'm not." Maria ate up her question along with a big wad of cinnamon dough.

At the end of the night, Rocky was asleep in Maria's bed. Maria didn't want Rocky to sleep on the futon like Karen did, which was riddled with hard knobs and broken springs. Maria slept on the floor in a sleeping bag.

Maria was surprised when she woke up at ten and saw that Rocky was already awake, filing her nails at Maria's desk. They went to the Chinese place up the street for lunch, and when they were leaving, Maria's mother gave Rocky a big hug that made Maria embarrassed. Showing Rocky to her family had terrified Maria for several reasons, and Maria had especially been nervous that Rocky's glamour and presence would come off the wrong way, but by the end of her visit, Rocky hadn't seemed to offend anyone. Rocky didn't bring her Louis Vuitton suitcase, and she hadn't reeked of cigarettes, either, which was a nice touch.

At the Chinese take-out place, Maria watched as Rocky took a sip of Diet Coke and then set the can aside.

"Your uncle is cute," Rocky said, thrusting her plastic fork into a sweating heap of lo mein. "Is he single?" She stabbed at a noodle and it bent away. She stabbed again; it caught.

Maria laughed. "He's always single. But he's old."

Rocky lifted the food to her mouth, and the Styrofoam creaked under her hand. "And Ricky?"

"Ricky has a girlfriend."

Rocky laughed. "Oh, does he?"

"What?"

"I wouldn't have expected him to be tied down."

Maria tensed. She picked up a spring roll and bit. "Rocky, don't go near my brother."

Rocky leaned back in her chair. "Is that a threat?"

"No. It's just that you won't like him. He's uptight."

"He doesn't seem that way to me."

Maria tried not to show she was irritated.

"Don't look at me like that," Rocky said. "So rude." She sucked on a noodle, and Maria watched as its whole length disappeared into her mouth.

Rocky had woken up in the middle of the night from a dream. She was running down a corridor of a thousand toilets, but each time she went to raise the seat, she found that it was bolted tight. She ran to the next one, and again it wouldn't lift. Again and again, fractals of forbidden flush. She woke up and clambered to the ground from the bed, and found her way toward the bathroom.

She'd almost forgotten what they'd eaten for dinner until she saw the reams of ketchup under her fingernails. She never ate fast food at home. If she ate french fries, they came from the diner, were made to order. But Maria had told her that she didn't know any restaurants that delivered to her house, so they went to the Burger King on the corner. Before that, they had eaten two enormous Auntie Anne's pretzels. Tomorrow, they had plans to get Chinese food on the same street. It was fine for just once, Rocky reasoned, but the next day, she'd make sure to eat clean.

In the hallway, she saw the light under his door, a bar of yellow like a brick of gold. She heard his voice—deep, melodious, lagging. It was lazy in that way only a boy can make attractive. She knew whom it belonged to. He must have been on the phone. Rocky was fairly awake now, but his voice made her think of lying down.

She stood there in the dark and listened, straining to make out the words. But all she heard were murmurs that were sometimes punctured by a rattling laugh that seemed to shake the hallway. She had the feeling of being rocked to sleep. Whenever he laughed, she felt it reverberate against her bones; it steeped into her skin like tea. She stood there, quietly listening. She'd go back to the room in a minute, she thought, *but first let me hear that laugh.*

A spring released, and Rocky panicked as she realized he was getting up from his bed. Before she could scramble away to the bathroom, he appeared at the door.

"Oh shit," he said, and then he laughed his beautiful laugh, and Rocky felt her heart bob in her chest, as if emerging from where it had long been sunken and lost. She wanted to capture his laugh and mount it somewhere. She wanted to fix it onto one of the walls. She wanted to hold his laugh static, forever, and replay it whenever she liked.

"Oh no," she said. "I scared you."

"Nah. You're good." He was wearing nothing but a white tank top and shorts. He had no chest hair, and even his skinny legs seemed smooth. Rocky knew she must look untidy, and she put her fingers up to her mouth. There was a dribble of encrusted saliva at the corner of her lip, and she clawed at it with the tip of her nail. When he looked at her, it felt like hands on her, though she couldn't tell if he'd like to push her away or caress her.

"I'm sorry," he said. "I saw you with Maria earlier. Remind me your name?"

"Rocky." She knew who he was; she had heard Maria complain about him before. In person, he wasn't anything near to what Maria always made him seem; she'd expected a monster and found, instead, a languorous brown-eyed boy. When she walked in with Maria earlier that day, she had noticed him sitting on the futon with an older guy, and she had felt their gaze follow her like pairs of antennae. Still, she had to ask. "And yours?"

"Ricky," he said, raising one eyebrow.

He held his smile on the side of his face, a trait that made Rocky think of Saturday morning cartoons. There was something youthful in all of his gestures: the way that he stood with his feet planted outwards, the way he brought his hand up to cover his laugh as if he'd just said something wicked. His taciturn smirk made the shape of a hook. His eyebrows were perfectly arched, like a girl's. Innocent. Easily controlled.

Rocky dipped her hip and tucked a stray hair behind her ear. She hoped that the drool around her mouth was gone.

"Can I call you Enrique?" she asked.

"That's not my name," he said. "My name is Ricky."

"What do you mean? Is it Ricardo?"

"No. My name is Ricky."

"That's not a real name. Like, my name is Rocky. But on my birth certificate, it doesn't say Rocky. It says Rachelle."

There was a silence.

"Hey, you know what?" Ricky winked. "Why don't you call me whatever you want?"

Rocky blushed. He smiled, and one slender dimple appeared.

"But can I give you a nickname then?" he asked.

She glanced at Maria's door. "What do you want to call me?"

"Well," he said. "Nicknames take a while. Sometimes years. I have to get to know you first."

"Okay."

"So will I get to know you?"

"Maybe you will." She didn't know if it was she or he who had taken a step closer, but somehow, they were only standing a few inches apart.

"Do you want to come in?" She didn't answer, and again, he laughed. Rocky saw that he was full of these giggles, as abundant as wrinkles on a crumpled shirt. Rocky understood now that there was no need for them to be mounted and framed.

"You seem tired," he said. "You can go back to sleep if you're tired."

"I'm not tired. I'd love a nickname."

In his bedroom, he had to clear a space for her on the bed, where a pile of remote controllers and game consoles were stacked. The two of them sat side by side on the spring mattress. It didn't take years to come up with a name.

"Tiffany," he said. "Give me a kiss."

She frowned. "Not Tiffany. That's just the store. I was Audrey Hepburn for Halloween."

"So you won't give me a kiss?"

His lips were hot and spongy, like a cat's paw pads. She sucked them into her mouth, nibbled on the upper one like a baby teething. It was something she'd learned from those *Cosmopolitan* magazines.

"Damn," he said. When he took his hand off her leg, she realized her entire body had gone numb. She worried that maybe she'd done something wrong, that the tip was a hack, and then he flashed her his lopsided grin.

"You're a good kisser, Tiff."

She cringed.

"Just call me Rocky," she said.

When she snuck into Maria's bedroom, just as dawn broke, Rocky tiptoed around her friend on the floor. Maria's blanket was pulled all the way up to her chin. It had been Maria's mother who had brought the girls a set of new sheets and offered Rocky a blanket from a selection of three. Maria's family was unbearably normal. They all lived together.

They all *liked* each other. Wasn't there some sort of dark, horrible secret lurking just beneath the surface? But no, that was just Rocky projecting her own fears and paranoias—she had even seen Maria's mother give her father a kiss on the cheek. Rocky silently climbed back into the bed and looked down at her sleeping friend. From scholarships to paid meals at Patrick's, it seemed that Maria always got things for free, but that wasn't even the most of it. Maria was loved. Maria was needed. Was that why Maria never invited her over? It was absurd how unfair it was, and now Rocky was humiliated that she'd ever told Maria about her dysfunctional parents, as if Maria would be able to ever understand.

If Maria had all of this love and attention, Rocky deserved some, too, she decided. She wouldn't need to ask permission for it, either. She would go right ahead and take it.

Inside the liquor cabinet, there was a bottle of whiskey and another of Tanqueray. She took the gin and before she left, she stopped at the closet and grabbed a pack of cigarettes. The box was sealed up like a present, but unlike a present, she could see right through the plastic. Rocky was fine with that. She was long past the age of preferring surprises.

It had been her suggestion to meet at the twenty-four-hour diner near midnight the day after she slept over at Maria's. She didn't want to do something as formal as set up a real date, but she also didn't want to take Ricky to the Second Avenue hookah bars, where it was more than likely that she'd run into someone she knew from school. Ricky arrived late; he explained to Rocky that he hadn't accounted for how long it would take him to find parking. Apparently, he'd been circling the avenue in his uncle's car over and over again.

She was sitting at a booth in the back of the restaurant when the door opened and the host rushed to greet him. Rocky pressed her tailbone into the upholstery to straighten her posture.

"Have you already eaten?" Ricky sat down, and the smell of his shower overtook the eggs frying. It was the scent of dew and charred ember, fresh and ingenuous, but overpowering, too, cheapened. The image of a pine tree car freshener hung over Rocky's mind.

"No." Rocky combed a hand through the ends of her hair.

"Are you hungry?"

"Not really." She crossed her legs under her seat. In his black jeans and crisp shirt, he looked different from when she'd last seen him, when he wore a thin tank top and was rumpled from bed. "But please," she said. "Get something if you want." She pushed the water bottle toward him. There were white paper scars on the plastic where she had scratched the label off.

"What is it?"

"Try it."

He raised the bottle to his lips. When he brought it away, he had the pained look of someone who'd just hit a bong for the very first time—and with far too much conviction. He pushed it away.

"Okay, how about this?"

She took out a little white bag.

"Nah," he said. "I'm good."

"Don't worry!" she said. "I won't tell Maria. She never does this with me. She doesn't even know. Your sister's such a Goody Two-Shoes."

Ricky hesitated. Rocky could see the gears in his mind turning.

When the waiter came by, they each asked for coffee. They sat there, sipping. Rocky passed the little white baggie to Ricky.

"Where's the bathroom?" he said.

"Ah, so you've done this before." She smiled. "Straight to the back."

It was an hour before the waitstaff brought over the check. Rocky dragged her purse from the edge of the booth.

"No," Ricky said. "I got it." From his jean pocket, he pulled out a ten-dollar bill.

How cute, Rocky thought, and if there had been another shot left and if there was a little more coke, she might have even said it. At the counter, he grabbed a mint from a big bowl that looked like the kind used to spin lottery balls on TV. The mints were chalky and hard on the outside, but once they were broken, they were gooey with green or orange gel. Rocky hadn't had one of those mints since she was a little kid. "Want one?" he asked when he saw she was watching. She giggled and shook her head no.

Outside, the streets were deserted, and the avenue was lit like a child's birthday cake.

"Are they always like this?" Ricky asked, looking around. "They never turn the lights off?"

"Always," Rocky said. She tittered. "I mean, never. Never."

They walked uptown, peering into the storefronts where long-limbed mannequins stood akimbo. Others posed with their hands tabled so their arms looked like spades. All of them were expressionless. They had white plastic ovals where faces should have been.

"Look at that one." Ricky pointed with his chin. "She looks hot."

The mannequin was draped in a fur vest, paired with a short leather skirt. Rocky stopped to raise her fingers to the glass. Inside, the halls of the store were alight, as if someone would come back any moment from a short restroom break.

"God, it isn't fair!" Her face darkened. "My mom doesn't wear fur, and she won't let me buy any either."

"Why?"

"I don't know." She rolled her eyes. "She hardly eats meat anymore either. She's been doing all kinds of funny things." Rocky almost said it before stopping just short: *since she decided she wants a divorce.* She was surprised at how forthright she wanted to be. When Ricky took a mint from the diner, he had popped a couple extra into his pocket as if nobody had seen, and Rocky understood that beyond how sultry and illustrious he seemed—the jagged diamonds in his ear, his fastened leather belt—he was overwhelmingly simple and boyish. This was, she thought, what endeared him to her.

"My parents don't eat anything but meat," Ricky was saying. "I don't think they know what a vegetable is. Corn and potato don't count."

She couldn't really hear him. She might have had too much to drink.

"Maybe it's fake fur?" he asked, coming closer. They stood side by side, looking into the store. Rocky's fingers were splayed on the glass.

"It's not." Her heel scraped the concrete as she took another step forward. Rocky brought her parted mouth so close to the surface, it went from clear to fogged.

"I have an idea."

She turned away from the glass to face him. He glanced from side to side, his eyes no longer reflecting the store display, but the swatches of light from the empty street. "What's your idea?"

He reached for her hand. She looked down at it tentatively, but didn't laugh, and together, they walked to the car. He had parked precariously close to a fire hydrant, what Rocky would estimate was well under fifteen feet. He scrambled inside the driver's seat as she waited against the hood, and when he came out, brandishing the long iron of the club, Rocky understood. She gasped. Then she laughed. This was exhilarating.

"That will work?" She scrunched her mouth to the side, one of her cheeks becoming round like a stone. "That won't work!"

Ricky walked ahead of her, back to the avenue. She followed a few paces behind and noticed, with worry, that her palm was clammy. She hadn't noticed a thing when she grasped Ricky's hand, and now, it was clear it was she who'd been sweating.

He brought the club down to the window, where a spiderweb crackled across the surface, and the glass exploded in fractals. When he hit it again, pieces came scattering to the ground like rain. Rocky had never expected it could take such little effort, and she was even more surprised that no siren had sounded. She watched as Ricky yanked at the mannequin with so much force that it lost its balance and came crashing down to the floor with a dreadful thud. The hollow storefront canopies shook with the sound, and Rocky knew then that they would be caught. The vest was tangled around the bent plastic arms, and before she could see if he successfully freed it, Rocky lifted her legs and ran.

She ducked into an alleyway that cut across a schoolyard. When she reached the other side of the avenue, she continued to run. For blocks she went without stopping her pace until finally she approached the East River and glanced over her shoulder to see Ricky behind her. In a brick hovel overgrown with green ivy, the two of them regained their composure, swallowing down the thumps of their hearts and the whistles of their strained breathing. Like a cat's, Rocky's ears went erect with the intent to hear. But there were no honks, no tires, nothing to indicate that they were being pursued. It was as if they had jumped through a portal, and the city had disappeared. Beside them, the river croaked like a bullfrog, and wordlessly, they stood apart from each other like two strangers waiting for the same bus to arrive. Finally, Ricky raised a yearnful gaze at her, and Rocky's heart began beating so uncontrollably again, the sound of the river disappeared, too.

His face was pale with moonlight. Standing at a distance and with both hands held out, Ricky looked so reticent and ceremonious that Rocky felt as if she were being offered a sacrifice. She held the fur vest to her open mouth to inhale, but it didn't smell like it was dead. It didn't smell like anything at all. She thrust it onto her shoulders and jumped at Ricky.

He lost his balance, and together they fell. She put her hands out, and her knuckles scraped against the ground. She didn't feel anything, certainly not any pain.

"You animal," she said as she felt his tongue slip against her skin, migrating south from her collarbone. "I can't believe you actually did it."

"Let's go back to the car," he said. Gently, he bit into her skin, and she felt the capillaries bursting. She looked down. Even though it was cold by the river, her ponytail dripped with sweat, slickening the vest, as if she had licked the fur down with her tongue.

Rocky rammed her mouth into his neck, but unlike Ricky's bite, hers was brutal. She heard him take a deep breath, but when he said nothing else, her chest fluttered with ecstasy. When she had met him, she'd worried that he was contemptuous of her, then she worried he was too earnest. Now she realized that she didn't really care what he was—he'd proven himself tonight. She wondered what else he was willing to do in her honor. Maybe he was madly in love with her, even. Her thoughts became delirious with wonder until she felt her thinking mind wither away entirely, tossed away like a shriveled fruit, and it was the sensation of being straddled atop Ricky's lap, her bare knees grinding against the graveled ground, that finally brought her back to consciousness. She could stay lost in this position forever, she thought, but what if there was something else? Something even better?

"Not the car," she said, knowing that even if her father or brother were home and awake, neither of them would stop her from bringing this strange boy down the long corridor to her room. "Let's go to my place." She knew that it was only the beginning of the Enrique—or was it the Ricardo? Either way, it was the beginning of a wonderful experience.

CHAPTER 19

The sun was gone, and with it, so was the light. Lying facedown on the couch in the living room, Maria didn't look up when her older brother came in. She'd been grounded for almost a month now, meaning she wasn't allowed to stay out past sundown and she was certainly not allowed to sleep over at Rocky's apartment. Her parents weren't bothering her anymore about applying for a new job, especially not when they'd found her on more than one occasion with large textbooks splayed open for the SAT. But without the ability to move freely and widely around the city at night, where the most fun to be had was interspersed between lampposts, Maria knew she was being deprived. She had been stripped of her fundamental right to summer.

"That sucks," Rocky had said when Maria told Rocky how bored and depressed she was. Whenever Maria asked what she was doing, Rocky said she was with Matthew. It was odd for her to spend so much time with him—Rocky always complained about how she really didn't like him that much.

Along with her SAT prep, Maria had been reading more every day, but in the days since Andres had broken up with her, she hadn't been able to concentrate for too long on anything. Over the past week, she had made several failed attempts to convince Andres to stay with her. Each time she asked, he only became angrier, his insults that much more deliberate and incisive. There was no getting around it—Maria was losing Andres to Chastity, a girl who Andres swore was much prettier and lovelier than she was. In the end, she really was prettier and lovelier. Maria knew because she too had met her.

She had found the girl's information because she knew Andres's password. She asked Chastity to meet her at Andres's apartment to confront him together. As they walked into the apartment complex, Maria was giddy, knowing that she was going to win Andres back. Maria was the veteran girlfriend, and her relationship with Andres was no longer frivolous and new—it was sturdy and impervious. Moreover, Maria knew that she was *better* than Andres, and probably better than Chastity, too, and that she was a *catch* for someone like him. In the same way that girls in her grade fawned over Rocky's boyfriend Matthew for being wickedly intelligent and coming from an even richer family than most families they knew on the Upper East Side, Maria knew that she was smarter than Andres and that she'd go to a much better college than he ever would—and that meant she was worth something greater than him. If she weren't rich per se, that was only *as of yet*, and even now she was richer than him, and it seemed to Maria that everything—including Bell Seminary, including dating, including venturing outside of one's rightful league—was about upward social mobility. As the days went by, these were the reflections that stiffened Maria's resolve and convinced her that it was nonsensical that Andres had dumped her. She knew enough to know that Andres didn't have the authority to leave her, and if he did, he would forever and ever regret his mistake. He wouldn't understand now, but one day he would—that the sacrifices she made for him, like enduring his constant and relentless abuse, were for nobody's sake but his own.

As soon as Andres saw Maria, the disgust on his face was as apparent as dirt. "Why are you here, bitch?" She flinched, the way she always did when Andres jabbed her like that, black and blues cracking open from somewhere invisible just beneath the skin. Just as the sores started to bloom, to her great shock, Chastity slapped him.

"Why are you calling her a bitch?" Her little hands flailed out to her sides so that all Maria could see of them were ten tiny red nails that soared through the air. Maria had seen Chastity spritz herself with Victoria's Secret body spray before going up to the apartment, but she hadn't really looked at her until now. Chastity was, like Andres said, lovely, and as Chastity waved her arms through the air, the lavender scent of her flesh seeped into Maria's nostrils, her tongue, and down into her skin. Maria bit her lip. If she could smell it from where she was standing, Andres could surely smell it, too, and in that moment, she sensed the plan was coming undone, but she swallowed the thought to the back of her throat, down with the fragrance of Chastity.

Within minutes, the confrontation was over, and Maria stomped out to the street with Chastity. They walked to the end of the block before parting ways. Chastity promised she would never speak to Andres again and offered Maria a piece of gum that she happily accepted. When Chastity leaned in to give Maria a kiss on the cheek goodbye, again, Maria smelled flowers, and the next day, when she saw Andres's Facebook status had changed from "single" to "in a relationship," her stomach growled out in pain. Again, she found that she was coming up just short of another girl, and this time it wasn't even for the usual reasons. Chastity wasn't thin or white and she didn't dress or talk like Bell Seminary girls at all, and this was something that baffled Maria—how there could be something beyond the things that Bell Seminary valued that might be worth having. She thought of the way Chastity had slapped Andres, and instead of rebuking her, Andres had only lowered his head, like a repentant puppy. Of course, she had no right to Andres, and of course, Andres had known that. Maria wasn't better than him or Chastity—she wasn't better than anyone.

Now, as she lay on the couch, she kept thinking of him cradling Chastity in his hands, doing the terrible things to her body that he used to do to Maria's: ripping into her flesh with his teeth in the shower, pulling her hair with the force of a riled teenage boy whose favorite game was something called slap-box. At first, Maria felt bad for the girl. But Andres had called Chastity perfect, and Maria knew he wouldn't handle Chastity the same way he'd handled her. She closed her eyes tight and gritted her teeth. Was there something intrinsically flawed about Maria? She wasn't good enough for white boys—and not for brown boys, either. What if the rest of her life was like this? What was going to happen to her?

She tried her best to will these things out of her head by thinking of the exception: Charlie—Charlie had seen who she was and liked it. Charlie, who had tended carefully to the poems that took root in her heart, who knew she deserved to go to school, to learn more of them, to become more fully herself. In Vegas, she had dared him to call her. *Take my number,* she ventured, and he grinned. She had left her phone in the hotel room upstairs and was a little embarrassed when she went upstairs and saw that he hadn't even texted her so she could save his number into her phone. Now, Andres's words seared like a hot blade through her head. *Why would he call me?*—facedown on the couch—*I'm ugly and stupid and gross.* Her brain felt like a bloodied steak, a slab of raw meat pooling in its own liquid, like the rest of the meat that clung to her thighs, to the sides of her stomach, everywhere, spilling out of the holes of her shirts and her pant legs. Even her hands were pudgy. She could feel the clothes shrinking on her as the edges of her hips expanded from wall to wall.

When Ricky came into the room, there was hardly enough space for him to walk around her, so large and bloated she had become by that point. She had buried her head deep in the pillow. He must have been looking at her for a while, because when she snapped her head around like an exorcised child, his whole body bolted upright.

"Shit! I thought you were asleep."

"Eh." It was less of a sound than a whimper. She looked down at the floor. There was silence as she ignored her brother, this time not even intentionally.

"What are you doing? Do you want to come to Applebee's with me and Alex?"

She thought of the cheesy potato skins she liked to order. She sat up.

"When are you leaving?"

"Now. I just came in to drop off my gym bag. Are you coming or not?"

"Let me put on my shoes."

She was wearing a pair of sweatpants, but even if Ricky had been more patient, she didn't have the resolve to change into jeans. It didn't seem like it then that she could possibly fit into them. She slipped her feet into her Converse sneakers without bending to tie the laces.

"You ready? Let's go."

Ricky's girlfriend, Alex, was sitting in the passenger seat of Jonathan's beat-up Honda Civic. Jonathan lent it to Ricky on the days he wasn't using it to go to the gym or the mall, with the requirement that he return it with a full tank. When Maria opened the door and clambered in, Alex turned around in full to greet her.

"Hey, girl!" she said, her black hair pulled back in a ponytail. She was wearing a pair of thick-rimmed glasses, and when she smiled, her eyes became thin slits of skin behind the large frames. "What's up?" Alex said. "I didn't expect to see you!"

"Nothing." Maria looked out the window. Alex lingered, her face bright and tilted like a satellite dish, and then turned back to the front of the car, where the light of her smile seemed to light the road ahead. Maria liked Alex, but she didn't feel like talking to anybody and was grateful for the trip-hop that blasted from the speakers. Ricky's CDs always made her think of water, the ambient gargling of rhythm and drumbeats that sounded submerged under the sea. Alex and Ricky spoke to one another now, but it was so loud in the car that Maria couldn't hear what they were saying. Looking at them made her think of Andres, and she tried her best to not to be upset, bobbing her head to the wordless music.

At the restaurant, Alex sat directly across from Maria. They chose a table outside so that they could sit in the sun. It was a beautiful day, and Maria realized she had almost missed it by languishing on her couch at home. She looked around now, her mood brightening. Across the street, there was a movie theater, and a line had formed that stretched out the door and halfway down the block.

"That must be for that new alien movie," Maria said. "It came out yesterday, right?" She was asking her glass of water, her mouth sucking on the plastic straw, her eyes barreled into the bottom of her cup. Ricky and Alex looked at each other before Alex responded first.

"Yeah, it did! Do you want to see it?"

"I don't know. Looks dumb."

"Alex is dying to see it," Ricky said.

"Really?" Maria felt sorry. Usually, Maria stood by her convictions, but there was something about Alex—Maria simply didn't want Alex to dislike her.

"Yeah," Ricky answered. "Anything that has to do with the stars, Alex loves."

"What do aliens have to do with astrology?" Alex said. "But yes, I love the stars. 'Cause how could you not?" She looked at Maria, her eyes wide open. Past the glasses, Maria could see their color, dappled in warm auburn with flits of yellow running through them like the veins of an autumn leaf. They were actually large—the lenses had distorted their size—and Maria wondered why she would hide such pretty eyes behind a pair of frames. Maria saw herself reflected in them and straightened herself in her chair.

"What's your sign?" Alex asked. Maria wondered if Alex could see that she was looking at herself in her glasses.

"Here we go again," Ricky said.

"Pisces," Maria answered.

"No way!"

"What?"

Alex stared at her as if she were floating in air and not slumped in a red plastic seat on the sidewalk, the bottom of her sweatpants legs ripped from being dragged along the ground.

"You're a Pisces! That's amazing! That means you're a water sign. Just like me. No wonder I like you so much." She shot Ricky an accusatory glance. "Ricky, you never told me."

"How would I know?" Ricky asked without looking up from the menu.

"How would you not?" She looked back at Maria. "I'm a Cancer."

"What does it mean? What does a 'water sign' mean?"

"Well, there's four. Water, earth, fire, and wind. The water signs are known for their emotion—we ride people out like waves. So we're great at reading people. We vibe with people. You must make friends easily, right?"

"I guess so," Maria said. "I have a lot of different friends." She paused. "Different kinds of friends."

"Wow," Alex said. "I knew it. It's just that I knew there was something about you and now I know why. Real recognizes real, you know what I mean?"

Through tightened lips, Maria failed at repressing her smile.

"I'm a Cancer—we're naturally compassionate, we're known for being empathic, which means we can see things from every perspective. We can see into people's hearts. Pisces can, too, but they can be a little difficult sometimes. It's not a bad thing."

"Difficult?"

"Yeah! Pisces are dreamers, they have so much energy to channel. They're sensitive and always looking for meaning. They're only difficult because they're such idealists! But the good part is that all that dreaming always pays off. The Pisces always ends up getting what they want."

"Really?" Maria glanced at Ricky, who hadn't looked up from the menu. Maria wanted Alex to go on, but she didn't want to seem obvious. She knew her brother had nothing nice to say about horoscopes. He was just like Maria that way, skeptical of everything. *Even more skeptical—a jerk,* Maria thought, a little surprised and even ashamed at how quickly and gratuitously the insult came to mind. She understood that cheesy potatoes were a peace offering, but she still hadn't forgiven him yet—not entirely, anyway—for what he had called her that summer.

"Yes," Alex said. "A Pisces can make their dreams come true."

Maria remembered her first day at Bell Seminary. They told her they were pleased to give the scholarship money to such a *talented* student. They were excited—no, they had said they were *thrilled*—to welcome the Rosario family's *gifted* daughter to the Bell Seminary School for Young Women. Maria had willed her future life into being.

"I don't know anything about signs," Maria said, again addressing her glass of water.

"Man." Alex shook her head from side to side and looked up at the clouds as if they had parted and some cosmic truth had been revealed. "You can tell so much about a person from their sign. Now that you tell me, it makes so much sense. And that's not even going into your rising sign, which makes things even more clearer." Ricky finally looked up at her. He was squinting at her with his head tilted to the side, the palm of his hand cradling his chin. Maria could see that he was about to correct her, because she was fighting the same impulse, too.

"Like Ricky, for example," Alex continued. "He's an air element, an Aquarius. Shy and somewhat stubborn. Unsentimental. Always wanting to be alone. Cold sometimes, too, just like winter air."

Maria giggled and glanced at her brother, who remained imperiously silent. If he was trying to appear offended, his face betrayed him. She could see he was trying to bite down on a smile.

"But underneath that chilly facade, Aquarius is full of this unpredictable energy. They're full of contradictions and get flustered weighing them all. They're genuinely exciting and endlessly interesting people, but you wouldn't guess that at first glance."

"How do you know so much about this?" Maria asked. But she wasn't so much looking at Alex as she was her older brother, whose hand was now covering a barely perceptible smile.

"She studies it," he said, moving his hand from his mouth and meeting Maria's gaze. "She draws charts and everything. She can do yours if you want."

"Really?"

"No, why are you lying? I wish I knew how to draw birth charts," Alex said. "My aunt does it, though. She'd need some other things, like your exact time of birth and where you were born. Anyway, the more you read the more you learn about it. There's always more to learn."

The waitress came around and asked for everyone's order. Maria ordered the cheesy potato skins and sliders.

After the waitress left, Maria knew that if she didn't speak now, she would lose her chance. She looked at Alex and didn't care that her interest would no longer seem feigned.

"Do you believe it?"

"What?"

"Horoscopes," she said nervously, avoiding the eyes of her brother. "Like if people really are like their signs? Do you really believe it?"

Alex tilted her head at Maria. "Of course," she said.

The conversation moved on, without Maria. When the waitress finally brought the food, Maria still hadn't said anything else. Ricky and Alex were arguing with fervor about the last movie they'd seen. She cut Ricky off midsentence.

"Can Pisces be good at getting money, too?" Her voice was impassioned. "What if their dream is to become rich? Can that come true?"

Ricky and Alex looked at her face, then her plate. Maria hadn't touched any of the food yet, and her napkin was still folded in a square on the table.

Alex leaned in, over the forks and glasses and knives. She was so close to Maria's face that Maria had the urge to back away, an urge she resisted. Alex was so close to her it felt like all she would need to do was pucker her lips to kiss her.

"Girl," Alex said, her features perfectly still. "A Pisces can make any dream come true."

Something was keeping Maria awake.

After Ricky and Alex had dropped her off at home, she texted Rocky. Hey, dude, she said, and when two hours passed without a reply, Maria texted again. Are you busy or are you really just trying to ignore me?

Rocky's answer was instantaneous.

I'm sorry, the message said. I was with Matthew in the Hamptons for a few days. I'm back in the city now, though. I'll call you tomorrow.

She exited the message screen and sat at her computer. When she was home, it always was on. As she scrolled aimlessly down her Facebook, something caught her eye. A picture of Stephen, one of the boys from Bell Seminary's brother school, standing in front of the clearest body of water Maria had ever seen. A spattering of white and orange buildings, a dirt path, and behind him, on a sloping, narrow road, a donkey. She clicked on one picture, and then to the next, trying to determine where such picturesque photos had been taken. She came to another photograph, and in it Stephen shared the frame with someone else, his arm swung around the boy's shoulders. Squinty blue eyes, a patch of rosacea. Maria gasped. Matthew.

She looked at the upload date—today, 3:00 p.m. As she kept scrolling through the photos, reading the captions under plates of broiled lemon fish and sailboats and bodies of water so turquoise that had Maria not believed her wealthy classmates were capable of going absolutely anywhere, she would've thought the colors were Photoshop-fake, it became clear—Matthew was in Greece at Stephen's family's villa. Regardless of whether Rocky was in the Hamptons at her country house, or in Manhattan at her apartment, she certainly wasn't with Matthew. Maria looked at the date the album was made; there were photos that'd been uploaded as early as July. Matthew had left for Kalymnos the same day Rocky and Maria had come back from Vegas.

Maria stuffed the phone inside her pillowcase and clenched her eyes shut. Ever since Rocky had come over, Maria noticed something was off. As she lay there, trying to come up with alternate explanations, Maria became more and more convinced that there was no other possibility. Maria's mind began to convulse. Andres had dumped her, her parents were struggling, and Karen hadn't forgiven her yet. She suddenly bent at the waist and sat up on the mattress. She'd been jealous of Rocky, angry at her before, but this feeling was something different. When Jonathan got mad, he punched walls—Maria had seen it happen once, and it had embarrassed her to find that her opinion of him had so suddenly and drastically dimmed. Now, she clenched her fists and understood the impulse. Rocky had lied.

Maria buried her face in her hands, exhaling manically into her fingers. Couldn't there be another explanation? A reason—a real, justifiable one—that could explain why Rocky had lied to her? Once Maria's breathing was finally even, she lay back down in the bed. All they needed was to talk. In the morning, she would call her to find out what was going on. Everything would be fine. She imagined Rocky laughing as they sorted through the pile of porn cards on the edge of the bed in Vegas. She thought of how Rocky had held on to Alexis, the only brown girl in the bunch, until Maria, a bit aggressively, asserted that she wanted her for her own, and Rocky handed her over without question. It was silly of Maria to assume the absolute worst.

She breathed, and into the dark night, she laughed. She was getting worked up over nothing. It was likely a misunderstanding. Maria laid her head down, her teeth clenched, her brow knitted, until finally she untensed.

But was it possible that Rocky was a liar—a liar just like her father, who, after being given her number, promised to call her soon after they came home?

Maria's jaw clenched again.

CHAPTER 20

Rocky answered a call from Laura, who had an invitation she couldn't pass up. It was a restaurant with a rooftop, a sparkling view of the Hudson River from six stories above the water. By the time the second Bellini was served, Rocky could no longer keep her news to herself. She still hadn't told a single person, and now, as she felt the wind blow like a playful lover on her neck, she confessed to Laura.

"Whoa." Through the lenses of her sunglasses, Rocky couldn't see how Laura's eyes had widened.

"Yep," Rocky said.

"Is he hot?"

"Wanna see him?"

"You have a picture?"

Rocky smiled. "Which one do you want to see? The PG version or the X?"

"You're kidding!" Laura looked over at Rocky's BlackBerry Pearl, where she'd pulled up her Facebook. Laura pursed her lips. The BlackBerry Pearl wasn't being released until next month, yet Rocky somehow already had hers months before anyone else did. Rocky held one hand over the screen to block out the light. On the screen was a photo of a boy at a beach. He didn't have his shirt on, and the lines of his stomach were pronounced and darkened with sweat and saltwater.

"Hm," Laura said. "He's cute."

"He's *so* cute." Rocky fingered the screen with her pinkie.

"I wonder why Maria got shafted by the gene pool," Laura said.

Rocky placed a hand around the stem of her glass. "Maria's not ugly."

"Well," Laura said. "She doesn't look like *him*. Anyway, are you going to tell her?"

Rocky giggled. "She'd freak out."

"She'll never find out."

Rocky brought her hand back to the screen so the girls could see past the sunlight. She kept scrolling.

"Who's that?" Laura said. On the screen were a boy and a girl. They were huddled over a pizza in a darkened room; the Dave & Buster's logo was etched into their glasses of soda. He had his arm wrapped over her shoulder.

"I don't know. Maybe his girlfriend."

"He has a girlfriend?"

"I have a boyfriend. Matthew. So what?"

"Right." Laura picked up her fork. She had ordered eggs Benedict without the hollandaise sauce—and extra spinach. She stabbed at a piece of english muffin and held it up in the sun. "Either way, you should be careful."

"Careful? What do you mean?"

"I mean," Laura said, bringing the food up to the sun to inspect it. "You know what Maria's about. She's the biggest mooch I've ever met. Hopefully her family isn't the same way."

Rocky paused. She thought of Maria now, her chin grizzled with ice cream at Denny's, not offering Rocky a single bite. Not bothering to say please. Not even to say thank you.

Laura laughed. "I mean, right? What's up with her wearing all of your clothes? Didn't the two of you just get back from Vegas?"

"Yeah," Rocky said. She shifted in her seat. Of course Maria hadn't paid for her flight to Vegas, but what right did Laura have to ask? Last year, when Rocky invited Laura to Vegas, Laura's family had bought the ticket, and Laura had brought along hundreds of dollars in cash. But if she hadn't, Rocky's family would've paid for her, too.

"What are you saying? Do you think Maria uses me?"

"What do you think?"

Rocky leaned back, and from behind her sunglasses, she furrowed her eyebrows. She didn't like where Laura was going with this. Rocky was known in her grade for her extravagant parties, for inviting people out to dinner with her family's credit card. If Maria was using her, other people were using her, too. As she watched Laura bring the long champagne flute to her lips, Rocky suddenly felt compelled to leave.

"Maria is a mooch," Rocky said. "But, whatever. I feel bad for her. She's not like us. She's, like, never even been on vacation."

"I just hope he's a good guy."

"I have Matthew for that."

"Right."

Rocky smiled, her big eyes full like moons. She scrolled away from the photo at Dave & Buster's and back to the shoreside shot. His steady smile glinted in the sun, the board shorts cinched just above the place where his pelvis made a V. Rocky held up the cell phone to Laura's face. The image on the screen glowed like a star. *Fuck you, Laura,* she wanted to say.

"I'm not getting a good *guy*," she said, instead. "I'm getting a good *fuck*."

The two girls, had it not been for all that sparkling water they'd drunk, could've floated away in laughter. They had another round of Bellinis, and when the waiter came to collect their plates, he didn't ask if they wanted to take it to go, despite the considerable amount left uneaten. Laura placed her perfectly manicured nails on the sleek leather pocket containing the check. "It's on me," she said without letting Rocky look at how much it came out to. Rocky grinned and accepted.

Charlie was not used to seeing his wife at home. They had gotten so good at avoiding each other that they were never in the same space at once, so when he opened the door to the apartment, he was shocked to see her in the living room, wearing nothing but a bathrobe, a bowl of popcorn in front of her on the couch. Something in him stirred. He thought of excusing himself, of turning around and closing the door behind him, until he remembered he was wedded to this woman on the couch, and then he looked right back up.

It wasn't the first time Charlie was ashamed of his desire. When Charlie was only twelve and had first started grabbing at himself, he realized he had no control over the assortment of images that came into his head, in rapid succession, like a deck of cards being shuffled and dealt. Because again and again, the image was the same: his live-in nanny, Tatiana. He knew it was wrong, knew it was awful to have noticed how her breasts moved on their own, but when he tried not to see her, he'd start seeing even more shameful images instead—a cousin, his golden retriever, and most bizarrely, his mother—and so he let Tati stay there, conjured and twisted. The more he did it, the more he noticed Tatiana throughout the day: in the hallway, bent over a toilet, reaching high above her head to get the fingerprints off a set of sliding glass doors.

By that point, Tatiana wasn't cooking for the family very much because his older sister had already left the house for college, and Charlie, busy with music and sports, came home later and later every day. Neither did Tatiana go out of her way anymore to greet him when he came home from school or say good night to him before he closed his door, which he would not have liked anyway, since there was now a definitive amount of time that passed before he shut his door and went to sleep. Instead, Tati seemed more prone to spend her time in the tiny study room, where they kept a landline phone that was largely neglected. She would sit in the room whenever Charlie's parents weren't home, and Charlie would hear her whisper in Portuguese. He imagined her in there, sitting on the floor, next to the cardboard boxes stuffed with tiki lamps, string lights, candles, and fur blankets— seasonal decor that Tatiana was in charge of unpacking accordingly as the leaves changed from green to orange to gone.

One night, Charlie was alone in the house. It was the holidays, and Tatiana was in Brazil, as she always was during the holidays. Charlie's parents were nowhere to be found. He went into Tatiana's room, slowly opening the door into the darkness. Even then, he had a vague idea of what he was looking for, though he couldn't have known just how lucky he would be. In the second drawer he looked in, underneath balls of Tatiana's socks, was a stack of developed photos. The photograph was so unbelievable that at first, he thought it'd been ripped out of a magazine. She was even more beautiful than he could've ever thought. He grabbed the stack, and without shutting the door, he collapsed onto Tatiana's bed, where that smell he'd once heard his parents giggle over, that smell they found strangely funny, the smell of shea butter, completely overpowered him. It was too strong to resist: his hands leapt into his pants, and he felt as if Tatiana were there—he could see the hole of her mouth wrapping around him, his body swallowed whole.

Why hadn't he heard his mother come in? Why hadn't he known she would be standing there horrified as Charlie's sweat formed rings around Tatiana's photo, the distinct smell of Tatiana's hair on the pillow making him convulse? It was her scream that brought the end of the world. As if the earth was only a glass orb caught in midfall, he heard the whole planet shattering.

Tatiana never returned because Charlie's mother fired her on the phone. She packed up all of Tatiana's things herself, told her she would mail them to wherever she wanted, free of charge. It was mortifying, not just for Charlie, but for Tatiana, too, who couldn't figure out what she had done, but who must have suffered the embarrassment of knowing that her photos were discovered when she received them days later in the mail. It was years before the family heard from her again, in a wedding invitation addressed not to the parents, but to Charlie and his older sister. But by then, Charlie was in college, and even when his mother told him about it, after the date of the wedding had passed, Charlie remembered feeling resentful, and not because of the husband-to-be, but because he had never imagined Tatiana wanting to raise her own family, and the idea of her looking after another child somehow, absurdly, felt like betrayal.

For a long time, Charlie blamed Tati's disappearance on himself—until finally, he blamed his mother. He blamed her for overreacting, as if it weren't natural for a boy to become overtaken by puberty and to have desired a woman like Tati. He would never forgive her for the shame she made him feel, and Charlie felt a similar rage toward Veronica when she first started ignoring him, when she'd lie next to him in bed wearing near nothing, yet not letting him lay a finger on her. Finally, he wouldn't take it anymore, and he kicked her out. Since then, she'd been living at the country house in Long Island, doing whatever it was that she did out there—painting, spending money, having sex, most likely, with other rich married men.

In the apartment, Veronica's eyes were enormous. They were swirls of rich brown, and now, they grew larger as if to make room for the sight of him.

"Hi," she said. "We need to talk." It wasn't even the words, but her gaze that made his heart start racing. He was used to seeing nothing on her face but scorn, but now, there was something else. It looked a little bit like tenderness, but that was impossible.

"What's wrong?" His voice cracked. She could have him on his knees by the slightest push of her finger. This is what he hated about Veronica—how much she could get him to act like a whimpering little boy. He wanted to wrap his arms around her. He wanted to undo her bathrobe by the knot. It would be so easy. All it would take was her permission. That, and a singular pull.

Something moved on her face again as she stood up and approached him. It was then that he saw the emotion for what it was—a form of tenderness, but not love. Veronica, in her bathrobe, with her hair straight and wet, was looking at him with pity. He took two steps back as if he were afraid that she really might topple him over.

"There's no point in waiting any longer."

"You don't want to wait until Nick graduates anymore?"

"Nick isn't a child." Veronica crossed her arms, and when she did, she opened a tiny window in her bathrobe through which Charlie could glimpse her cleavage.

"I can reach out to Larry on Monday."

"I already did."

Finally, Charlie couldn't hide his anger anymore. "Are you fucking serious, Veronica?"

"Charlie." Veronica's face had been losing its color, and now it was as white as the robe. It was the middle of the summer, and still she'd stayed so pale. Looking at her incandescent skin, Charlie became incensed. Why hadn't she gotten a tan in Vegas? She looked disgusting! Why hadn't she sat out in the sun? You could see all her veins! Didn't she enjoy what he gave her? Wasn't that the only reason she'd even stayed with him? He could've left her so long ago, but then that would've made him the asshole! He needed to sit. No, he needed to leave.

"Whatever you want," he said.

He was standing so close to the front door that he only had to turn around to be in the doorway outside the apartment. Still, he didn't move. Their interaction had been so tragically brief, it was like they weren't even acquaintances. He had longer conversations with bartenders, with strangers waiting in line at the drug store. But what else? What was he possibly waiting for? Still, for a second more, he stood there and waited.

The door caught on the floor mat before it could slam, but now that he was in motion, the spell had been broken, and there was no more waiting left in him, not even for the elevator. He flung open the door to the emergency staircase and ran down the flights as if he feared he'd be chased. Charlie hadn't thought of Tati when he first started fantasizing about Maria, but since the connection was made, he could no longer see past it. As he went down the staircase, each time he reached another landing, the soles of his feet thundering in anger, he saw Maria and Tati, magnified in his mind so each limb seemed as tall as buildings. He saw them splayed across one another, their bodies impossibly twisted. It was Veronica's fault—Veronica in her prim little bathrobe, with her orderly nails, her smooth and waxed calves—Veronica who had been the one to set it all into motion, who had cracked the bat and sent it flying like a home run, barreling forward and forging a trajectory that he couldn't wait to come to the end of. Now, as Veronica nested back in the apartment, he knew exactly just where it would fall. She was in the city again, which meant that there was a new space she'd created—a big, empty space they called the country house.

Maria woke up to the landline ringing, her cell phone still under her pillow. She could smell coffee brewing in the kitchen when she climbed out of bed and picked up the cordless phone. "He's not here," she said. "But my mom is."

Maria went into the kitchen, still rubbing the sleep from her eyes. As soon as her mother saw her, she took the phone out of Maria's grip and slammed it onto the counter. "Don't pick those calls up! I've told you before!" Her eyebrows climbed up her forehead, and Maria took a step back.

"How was I supposed to know?" Maria asked, but she knew it was her fault. She had forgotten, again, to look at the caller ID. All unknown numbers were to go directly to voice mail, and Maria already knew the area codes of the collection agencies. She even knew some of the representatives by name. John, Susan, even a Rafael from Delaware. They all seemed pleasant on the phone. Minutes after her mom hung up, the phone rang again. Maria listened to it ring once, and then twice. It rang five times in total and was cut off at the sixth ring, and then they heard the loud speaker of the message machine go off, followed by an alert: their in-box was full. Maria remembered her letter. Her father hadn't heard back yet and suddenly, *notwithstanding* flashed in her head, and she felt a tinge of pain, like something was being pinched just behind her eyes. She thought of Andres, and the pain became sharper. She couldn't remember why she had ever tried making a joke out of food stamps, why she had thought a thing like not having enough money to eat could be funny.

"Get dressed," Maria's mother said once the phone had shut up. She looked at Maria's pajamas—a giant T-shirt, a pair of ripped sweats. "We're going school shopping."

"It's not even September."

"We can't wait 'til September. The sales are happening now."

"Fine." Rocky never paid attention to the schedule of sales and never wore anything out of season, but Maria showered and dressed like her mother commanded, and when they got to the 99 cents store, Maria lagged behind, sensing that she'd been tricked. There was no rush in buying things from a store that offered a perpetual discount, where everything, no matter the season, was priced at a single dollar. As they searched in silence for folders without dolphins and bunnies on the front fold, Maria found out that she indeed had been fooled, that her mother had dragged her out of the house with a different agenda than the one she'd proposed.

"Maria, is everything okay? You've seemed so sad recently."

Maria's eyes suddenly filled with tears, and as soon as her mother saw it, she pulled her daughter to her chest. Maria breathed in the clean scent of laundry, vanilla, a ripped edge of cilantro.

"You don't need no boyfriend, anyway," her mother said. "Listen when I tell you, save your tears for when I die."

Maria tried to swallow. She was about to correct her mother— *a* boyfriend, I don't need *a* boyfriend—but suddenly she imagined Andres standing next to her, telling her that she thought she was better than him. She was so overcome that she found herself breathing into her mother's shirt, unable to say anything at all. Her mother had only known the bare minimum about Andres, and Maria hadn't wanted her knowing that Andres dumped her, but it was impossible to hide how much she'd been crying, when she was moved to tears by almost anything, including every song on the radio, even the ones they heard in passing at supermarkets and fast-food restaurants, and it was even harder when her sense of abandonment was compounded by Charlie's disappearance, too. In the store, there were scuff marks from all the places where people had dragged the heels of their shoes, and Maria knew she couldn't cry here, not in front of all these nosy clerks and kids running down the aisles. Still, it felt good to be held. Maria swallowed a few more times before unsuccessfully attempting to pull herself away.

"Thanks, Ma." The words were muffled in her mother's shirt.

"One day you'll look back on this and you'll see it wasn't so important." With her mouth still pressed against Maria's ear, Maria's mother continued. "Did you really think he'd be your last boyfriend?"

"Did you have boyfriends before Dad?"

"Oh baby," Maria's mother said into her daughter's hair. "That's a conversation for a different day. But I'll tell you this—he wasn't the first one to propose." Finally, without any warning, she let Maria go.

Maria moved ahead of her mother, down another aisle, blinking vigorously. She was intrigued. There were men before her father? This was news to her! Who! She was dying to know. But while her mother had hugged her, she had felt her phone buzz several times in her back pocket. Now, she reached around and flipped it open. Embedded in a velvety blue banner, there was a message alert from a number she didn't recognize.

Hey, beautiful, the text message said. Free for lunch?

The wall of her abdomen tightened. She was suddenly standing at attention, like a soldier ready for battle.

Behind her, her mother peered into a stack of composition notebooks.

Sure, Maria typed. Her phone buzzed again before she could look away.

An hour? Give or take? Meet me at the park entrance near the Met.

A current of hope buoyed her. She felt herself rising, like a balloon edging toward the tip of its string. She remembered the call from that morning, and she no longer cared about Rocky's lie or misunderstanding or whatever it was. As she stared down the aisle at a gaggle of children illuminated from the soles of their light-up shoes, Maria breathed deeply. Charlie would remember the promise he made her, and if he didn't, Maria would remind him. She closed her eyes languorously, and in that humming violet space, what she saw was undeniable—his easy grin, the nod of his head, the upturned lips with which he would kiss her. He had reached out to *her*; it was clear. She could see the plan would work.

She grabbed a composition notebook and stood with it poised in her hand. "Mom," she said, pleased to hear that her voice was no longer breaking. "Can I go to Rocky's apartment today? I want to keep studying for the SAT. She has her own tutor, you know."

Her mother's eyes went slant. "Okay. But get home early, please."

Maria watched as her mother walked away, the basket hoisted up on her hip, the steps that she took almost rhythmic. She once thought her mother was frumpy, inelegant, but as she watched her saunter down the aisle, Maria thought of all the boys who may have wanted to marry her. She wondered how much energy they had spent trying to court her. Her mother said: *Did you think he'd be your last boyfriend?* Well, the answer was that of course she didn't. But it was just a little sad to think that certain things never amounted to anything, yet they took up so much of your time. What was the point of living with no regrets when there were clearly things that ought to be regretted? This was actually a comforting thought, one she could put behind her arm and take with her. Nothing about the future could intimidate her when she looked at it this way; nothing about meeting Charlie could scare her when she opened her eyes to the contours of things that might forever and ever be solidified in her history as perfect, complete, horrible wastes of time.

CHAPTER 21

Charlie usually walked around the apartment in starchy blazers and silken ties, and he was always at least a half inch off the ground in a pair of polished black shoes. Today he was wearing a set of camel-brown loafers that were torn at the heel and whose soles were run down to the floor, and whatever he did do before meeting Maria, it didn't consist of shaving. The two suede laces near the toe were frayed and coming undone, dragging along the cobblestone pathway, catching in the mortar caulking. As he walked toward Maria outside of the park and unfolded one arm from his chest to her shoulder, Maria was startled by his height. For the first time, she noticed that he was shorter than Andres by several inches.

To Maria, Charlie looked bedraggled.

"Annie!" he exclaimed when they were only a foot's distance from each other, and Maria had to remember that he was talking to her. A shudder ran through her shoulders. She could've been called anything—but Annie was certainly not right.

Charlie reached around her face with the pointed part of his chin. He kissed her on the cheek, and his face was hot and gravelly like the hide of the pumice stone that Maria's mother kept in the shower. *What is that for?* she asked one day, toweling her hair over the sink. *My calluses,* her mother replied. *Ew,* Maria said, to which her mother sucked her teeth. *Mija, just wait 'til you're older.*

Maria drew back. He was darker than usual; he looked like he had been tanning. Although the rest of him looked shabbier than Maria had ever seen him, he wore his tan like a table freshly lacquered, a shade of brown glazed onto his skin like a coat he had bought and had just ripped the tags off, worn for the very first time.

When they were only arm's length apart, Charlie drew Maria into the crook of his giant arm. As she drew her face away, she smelled something sweet on his breath.

"Ice cream?" He pointed to the ice-cream cart in front of them, its tiny textured wheels parked on the cobblestone pathway.

She looked at the cart, at the images plastered onto each side. It was a collage of gumballs, hard chocolate crusts, Popsicles. Tweety Bird's eyes bulged at her from the face of a coagulated glob of corn syrup and yellow molasses. She pointed at an image of an ice-cream bar coated in pink, with coffee cake crumbs.

"Strawberry shortcake," he said to the man who had been peering into the face of his wristwatch until Charlie spoke. "You want something to drink? Water?" He looked at the man. "Give me a water." He took out his wallet to pay.

"You're not getting anything?" Maria watched uneasily as the man behind the cart eyed the fifty-dollar bill Charlie handed him, holding it up to the sun and squinting before putting it away. Charlie peeled down the ice-cream bar's wrapper before handing it to her, revealing its pink, speckled flesh.

"I had a vanilla cone as I waited."

Something didn't feel right. Maria felt a deep unsettling and tried not to stare at the frayed ends of his shoelaces dragging along on the ground. When they sat on the lawn, he fiddled with his watch, adjusting the straps as if he had noticed they were suddenly too tight on him. He caught her looking. "Are you hungry?"

She had hardly finished her ice cream. Maria was full, but she was also anxious to be sitting outside in daylight, in the giant expanse of blank canvas that was the great lawn. It would be better to have the conversation over food, anyway. It would be quieter if they were indoors, and Maria imagined the way she would emphasize certain words over others: *appreciate* over *please, grateful* over *indebted*. And then there would be words she would have to remember to omit completely: *Favor. Help. Need.*

"Yes." She smiled. "I'm starving."

They went down the avenue, to a pizza parlor. At the door, she stopped. Three girls were huddled at a table near the window, their ponytails high above their heads. Maria's limbs became taut like a tuned guitar string, and she stared, unmoving, the smell of burnt cheese nauseating her. She knew those heads, every bleached strand of hair, the highlights wearing off at the roots. She knew what they smelled like after gym class in the locker room—soapy fingers and fresh sweat. Charlie trailed just behind her, but his hand hovered at the small of her back, and she walked in before he could prompt her.

Someone called out an order, and a long mane whipped toward the counter. She stood and walked toward Maria, and when she was just a few paces away, Maria saw that she wore a stranger's face. Maria felt something loosen its hold around her neck.

Charlie ate two and a half slices. Maria ate one and the half Charlie didn't. When they finished, there was enough to eat more. In other company, she might have.

"I'll get a box so you can take the rest."

"I can't eat anymore."

"For your parents. Wouldn't they like that?"

"Oh," Maria said.

"Wouldn't it be a nice surprise?"

Maria was going to tell him that her mother made dinner every night, but he was talking too quickly, and now he was out of his seat, walking up to the counter to ask for a box.

"For your parents," he said, when he returned.

Maria wished he would sit back down. All she wanted was to tell him about the payments they were missing, about the way that fear in the house had become resignation, inevitable like death, but at the same time she didn't care about her delivery anymore; she remembered she wasn't trying to compose a poem or perfect the perspective of a painting, and that if she kept deliberating over the appropriate word or dramatic emphasis, she would altogether lose her chance. When she saw that Charlie was walking toward the door, she hurried to put the remaining slices in the box herself. She fumbled; the grease made her fingers slippery. She needed to ask. Time was slipping away just as easily.

Outside on the sidewalk, he placed an open hand around her neck and gently squeezed the tendons he found there. What had he been thinking when he reached out to her? There was nowhere the two of them could go. He couldn't really take her to the Hamptons house now—he had work tomorrow, and he didn't have a single bag packed. His car was in the parking lot in midtown. It'd be a hassle to do all of that tonight. He raised her face to kiss her goodbye on the cheek.

With his face close to hers, he smelled the shampoo in her hair. He imagined how, with her hair wet, it would no longer curl, but lie flat down on her forehead. He realized that she didn't actually smell like Tatiana at all, that she actually had a smell of her own, and that for him, it was brand-new. There was no use in denying what it had felt like to hold her in place for appraisal in Vegas, how he had enjoyed looking at her like a diamond from all sides. When she pushed him away, it was collaborative, a suggestion among other suggestions that could be scaled, that all seemed to have equal weight. He had gotten so close, even then—this time, he would make it. It wouldn't be hard. He could take off from work. He could purchase a toothbrush.

"Do you want to come with me to the Hamptons house? We have a pool, you know. This time, we can jump in. You can swim."

"I can't," Maria said, and her face went dour. "I can't sleep over anywhere anymore."

"How about we leave tomorrow morning, then?" It was perfect. He could go to the apartment and pack his bag tonight. It was August, the slowest month, and nobody would care if he were sick. And best of all, the girl wouldn't have to sleep in his bed. That seemed a bit much, even for him.

"I'll get you back before dark. How does that sound?"

"Okay."

"Perfect, sweetheart." His hand left her shoulder. "I'll see you tomorrow, then, lovely. Don't be late. Don't make me wait."

He kissed her quickly on the cheek and hurried down the avenue. He didn't turn around to confirm if she'd raised her hand after him, if he would've seen how her fingers splayed to wave goodbye.

The Bloody Mary, thick like salsa, savory as a potato chip, was Rocky's favorite brunch drink. She and Laura sat across from one another, underneath an umbrella shade on Madison Avenue.

"You still haven't slept with him? But it's been a while now!" Laura put her mimosa down by the stem. They were on their second round and the eggs Benedict had yet to come out. Laura was incredulous. "Wasn't that what this whole thing was about?"

Rocky studied her friend through her sunglasses. Even if Laura was irritating, what she said was true. Pursuing Ricky had started like many of her sexual pursuits did, as a conquest. In her daily agenda, alongside the week's homework assignments, Rocky kept track. She'd opened her agenda to the index, where they'd printed a full-spread world map. She had been to Asia, she proudly boasted, because Skylar was only half white. She'd already done Africa, she also declared, though she couldn't name more than two countries there. All of the Western industrialized world was a given, since a boy like Matthew could count for places like Germany, Ireland, Italy, England, and who knows where else? She didn't know what would happen once she had conquered them all—if she'd have to restart and reset—but she wasn't concerned with that question when she decided that Latin America was next.

When she had shared her findings with Maria, Maria laughed. *You can have Andres. Right after I'm finished with him.* But Rocky knew that day would never come; as much as Maria complained about him, it seemed that she only grew fiercer in her sadness and more fervent in her attachment each time that she saw him.

I could, Rocky said. *Or what about a Rosario?*

No. Maria frowned. *There's nobody.*

If the Rosario household was off-limits, Rocky's options were near negligible. The usual contenders came from the Catholic brother school, but there was only one student who might fit her criteria. His name was Facundo Hiciano, and though Rocky had never actually spoken to him in person, she knew that from the sound of things, he would do. For a while, she looked out for him when she went to parties, especially the school dances that the boys' school hosted in their enormous front hall. She only hesitated because she was dating Matthew, and Matthew and Facundo went to the same school. Between morning homeroom and the walk to first period, a whisper could become a well-known rumor.

But rumor was simply rumor; rumor didn't scare Rocky, and especially not after the lipstick scandal. She wasn't a student at Bell Seminary then, and the Jesuit middle school she went to was fairly liberal and coed. In the single-stall bathroom after lunch, she had a stick of spearmint gum and three tubes of her mother's lipstick, and she applied one modest layer, then another, but she wasn't satisfied until she had mixed them all. Outside, Arnold anxiously waited until she opened the door and pulled him inside, and later, had it not been for the fact that they were singing her favorite song in chapel, Rocky would have never been caught. *Wait,* she had whispered, *I actually love this one.* Inside, "On Eagle's Wings" played. She ambled in, holding his hand as she did. The teachers turned around, and when they noticed Rocky's lips, the color of a Stemilt cherry, they took her aside after mass and called her apartment. Rocky stewed in anger: the two of them had snuck in together, and the teachers hadn't thought to lift Arnold's shirt, where the underside of his blue polo shirt was splattered with dark smudges like bruises.

Rocky's mother recognized this injustice and saw with clarity that her daughter had been singled out. When the headmaster explained what he thought he had seen on the face of the twelve-year-old as she trilled that final hymn in the chapel, her mouth big and sopping like the skin of an oyster, her mother immediately ended the meeting.

It's disgusting. It's appalling, Veronica had said to the headmaster, Rocky wedged like a shift lever between them, *that you or any adult in this building would project your own unresolved sexual feelings on an innocent twelve-year-old girl.*

That day, Rocky's mother's composure was statuesque; it was as if her face were carved from marble. But when Rocky reached for her mother's hand as they quietly left the school, it fell limply away. The next year, Rocky was enrolled at Bell Seminary, and though she no longer snuck into the handicap bathroom during chapel, the brother school provided a limitless supply of hungry boys who hung around the gates of the all-girls school like a pack of mountain lions.

Still, not all of them were ravenous. When Rocky found out that Facundo Hiciano didn't date anyone who hadn't been selected for him by his parents, she was infuriated. She had never heard of anything so absurd. *It's an Argentine thing,* an insider told her. *I think it needs to happen by bloodline, or something.*

I'm not trying to marry him, Rocky said. *Are you sure he won't talk to me?*

I promise, the insider told her. *He's not interested.*

As she sat waiting for her eggs Benedict now, the Bloody Mary half-drunk, the olive soaked at the bottom, Rocky rolled her eyes from behind her sunglasses as she listened to Laura drone on.

"Seriously, Rocky. You won't sleep with him now? Why'd you change your mind?"

"Because," Rocky started. Ever since Ricky stole the fur vest, Rocky had a different attitude toward Ricky; he no longer seemed like a box to tick or a line to cross off. He seemed more like something she might keep around, and she had read enough women's magazines to know that sex, too early, would give him the power to leave her. She could titillate and tease him with other things, but the act would have to wait until he looked at her the way Matthew did, until he'd started calling her on the phone at night. And by that point, wouldn't the goal have already been completed? What point would sex even serve?

Laura stared at her expectantly. At some point, she wondered if she'd have to tell Maria the truth. Rocky had been to Maria's house, and it was there that Rocky saw that Maria wasn't as broke as she always made it seem, and her parents weren't cruel like Maria always said. In the morning, they had all sat at the table and drunk coffee, and her mother had even left room in the mug in case Rocky preferred it with milk. Maria had so much, more than enough to share, and Rocky had never asked anything of Maria. She knew that it would infuriate Maria, but it didn't seem fair—it seemed like she should at least be able to have this one little thing. The thing she wanted was Ricky, his warmth and affection. And not just once or twice. She wanted to have him and keep him.

"But why not?" Laura demanded.

"Because," Rocky said, straightening her spine. "I feel bad for Maria. She still doesn't know."

As soon as the two had parted, Rocky's muscles relaxed. It had been impossible to admit to Laura that she had a crush on Ricky; she was even a little embarrassed to admit it to herself, because it put her in the terrifying position of possibly liking a boy more than he liked her. She knew from experience how pathetic it looked when there was an imbalance like that between people—it ruined everything, aesthetically and otherwise—and it was repulsive to witness a hope like that, like her father's even, when it should have long been extinguished. Now, she reached for her phone, and after three rings, Ricky picked up, and moving something to the back of her throat, as if she were balancing the pit of a fruit there, Rocky forced her sultriest, most casual voice.

"Free tomorrow?" *Yeah.*

"Want to see me?" *Of course.*

"Have you ever been to the Hamptons?" *Never.*

Ricky agreed to go. On her satin ballet flats, Rocky skipped, her fingers grazing the pillars of brownstones on the street. She knew she shouldn't feel so strongly about anything, but it felt so good to indulge. She was exalted. She was remorseless. She didn't care that she relentlessly lied.

Because what Rocky wouldn't tell anyone, not Laura, not Maria—*anyone*—was that the reason she hadn't had sex with Ricky was because she hadn't ever had sex before. Not with Matthew, not with Duncan, not with Arnold—*no one*. She liked to kiss and caress wherever she wanted, but her virginity was something she needed to protect. It was like an Egyptian amulet, the kind she admired most in carnelian, the color of blood, at the Met. Whenever she visited the museum, this was where she came to worship. In front of the display's divider, she closed her eyes to imagine holding it, and if she concentrated hard enough, she could feel a mass, fibrous and warm, begin to form in her hand. She gripped tightly before a security guard could order her to remove her forehead from the glass. But by then she'd already derived all her power, and she'd walk down the steps toward Fifth Avenue in an amber glow.

If Rocky was honest with herself, she could admit that Ricky was unlike any other boy she'd ever met—he was unpredictable, yes, exciting, of course—but most of all, he didn't know or speak to anyone that Rocky usually hung out with. In ancient Egypt, even young women had bronze nipples affixed to their mummified bodies for the enjoyment of sex in the afterlife. She didn't need to be pure to be imperious, and if she lost her lucky stone, red as a beating heart, would anyone really know? Rocky had yet to encounter in life anything that had once been misplaced that couldn't also be replaced.

She grinned, stopping at a crosswalk. She nibbled absently at her nail, thinking of what she'd wear for the bus ride to the Hamptons tomorrow, something comfortable but relentlessly sexy. It was okay for her to be selfish this time. It was okay for her rules to change. She had held on to her stone for this long, and the truth was that she wanted to give it to Ricky. She had chosen him. Something in his eyes reassured her that it was something he would treasure, maybe even more than she did.

It was Rocky's turn to get what she wanted—Maria's was long over.

Maria received a text message at 8:00 p.m. One single word: Yo. When she saw the name of the sender, she typed out a hasty reply.

Leave me the fuck alone, Andres.

Listen, he responded, I seen your brother a few days ago with a girl again. A white girl.

Maria was furious. Fuck you, Andres.

Another text message immediately followed. Maria, be honest. Do you wish you were white? Does everyone in your family wish that?

I hate you, she typed. I hope that you die. I hope that you never EVER text me again.

When her phone didn't vibrate ten minutes later, Maria didn't despair. When it didn't vibrate thirty minutes later, she was anxious, but not upset. When an hour passed, Maria cried, and she tossed the phone underneath her pillow because she knew he wasn't going to text her. She imagined Chastity, and her perfect red nails, and the perfect way she did everything, the perfect way in which she effortlessly existed, the way she never seemed unsure. Maria didn't want to be *white*; she wanted to be able to defend herself. Maria continued to cry until she soaked the pillow through with mucus and had to flip it onto the other side.

Maria remembered that if she kept on like this, her eyes would turn puffy, and they'd stay that way for hours—through the next day. By the time she flipped her pillow back around, the wet side had dried, and she could feel with her fingers that her eyes were engorged. She was no longer crying, she was sick of all this crying—she wanted to save it just like her mother had said—but even so, her eyes were already packed and well on their way to swollen.

CHAPTER 22

Charlie turned the air-conditioning on and pressed a button to shut the windows, even though Maria would have preferred to keep them open and thrust her arms out into the wind. There was no outbound traffic on Route 27 from Manhattan to the Hamptons, Long Island, and the air was ripe for pummeling bare skin. Maria looked out the window longingly. In the station wagon with Ricky, they used to roll down all four windows and scream whenever their hands got too close to an oncoming freight truck.

"Why are you grounded?" he asked in the unnerving silence. Maria felt like a frozen chicken cutlet, vacuum sealed into the car.

Thinking of food nauseated her. Maria was never hungry in the mornings, and she had eaten only half of the bagel he brought when they first met at the garage. Now, she caught her reflection in the mirror of the passenger seat. Her eyes were rounded, like circles of blown bubble gum. She looked inside her bag for the purple sunglasses, wrapped inside some squares of toilet paper, since she didn't have a case. Carefully, so that Charlie wouldn't see how she preserved them, she unfolded the legs in her bag. She put them on and felt slightly better.

"I think my parents found my lighter."

Charlie hunched at the steering wheel and glanced over his shoulder as he merged. Next to her uneaten bagel on the dashboard was his pack of Marlboros. He took one out, and finally he cracked open the window—hardly enough to squeeze a wedge of lime through it. The car imploded like a mushroom cloud in the smell of tobacco burning, and Maria held her cough in.

"Do you want one?" he asked after he'd taken multiple puffs, as if he'd forgotten she was sitting there next to him.

"No, thanks."

He looked at her from the screen of smoke he had placed between them. "You sure? I won't tell your parents."

Charlie always ended his sentences with plaintive laughter. Maria understood, through his unvarnished jokes, he was only trying to be kind.

"I'm fine." Maria opened her window and reached for the other half of the bagel. As he brought the cigarette to his mouth, she wiped cream cheese off hers. "And you can call me Maria. Annie's just my middle name."

They drove on, mostly in silence. He put on a CD that Maria had never heard of before.

"Allman Brothers okay with you?"

When she saw that his enthusiasm was sincere, Maria pretended to know who they were. She wasn't sure if she'd convinced him, but the music drowned out whatever doubt might have remained.

They arrived at the house within two hours, what Charlie called record time. He had to climb out of the car to walk up a gravel pathway and push a passcode into a small monitor. Another long path snaked up to the house's main entrance, but they went in through the door in the garage. Maria followed Charlie, and she stopped when he did in the kitchen. He went to the fridge and scooped ice into a glass. Opening a cabinet drawer, he saw Maria looking at him.

"You've been here before, haven't you?"

"Never," Maria said, running her fingers along the edge of the rounded marble counter. But she could guess that the alcohol was in the cabinet Charlie had gone to, even before he opened it. That week, Maria had committed a new poem to memory, one from the book that her teacher had given her, the anthology of Latina poets. It was translated from Spanish and about hombres necios, or foolish men, and it came to mind as she looked upon Charlie.

"What?" he said.

"Nothing."

"You're smiling."

"Oh."

He took out a tall glass bottle, and when he poured, the liquid was brown. Only a slight trickle of alcohol came out.

"Hm," he said. "I thought I had more of this."

He took an indulgent sip. When he put it down, the ice cubes in his glass knocked into each other like bumper cars. Maria was leaning against the counter as he took a step toward her. He pushed Maria's hair flat against her head with his palm, but she looked past him, over his shoulder, at the staircase.

"We can go up," he said, understanding. Maria nodded, leading the way.

The master bedroom was on the second floor and overlooked the property. It was connected to a balcony that extended around the house, and the room was full of sunlight. Through the glass, Maria could see the pool like a mirror, a perfect reflection of cloud and sky, a ripple of blue and white stripes. Charlie went over to where she was looking and drew the curtains so the room became dark. When he came back to the bed, he tried pulling her over his chest.

"Kiss me," she said when his hands went down to the hem of her dress.

He brought his lips to hers and positioned Maria onto her back. She heard his keys clinking in his pocket. His belt was heavy and kept pressing into her hipbone, and she was glad when he removed it.

"Charlie," she said, clenching her fists. Finally, the moment had come. "My parents aren't doing well."

"They'll forgive you."

He was wearing white briefs. She had never seen Andres wear anything like those before. She could make out the whole shape of him through the fabric. She averted her eyes.

"I don't mean being grounded. They're having a hard time. Financially. Our house . . ."

"Can we talk about your parents later?" Fold by fold, he slid her underwear down her ankles until they landed on the floor and coiled up like a sleeping bag. She looked at them, distractedly. Rolled up like that, they were so small.

"Charlie," she repeated, but again, she didn't know what to say. She hadn't anticipated it would begin like this; she thought that at the least, there would be more time from the point when she was on her back to the point when he would rise inside her, but it was happening now, before she could stop it, and then, her breath was gone. She shut her eyes and watched as an image of Andres flashed like a camera before her. This was the beginning of something, she realized, as she felt his warmth spread over her, and in a conciliatory voice she hadn't expected, she heard herself think: *It'll be over soon.* She tried as hard as she could, but not a single line of poetry came to mind.

But why was she thinking like that, as if she'd already resigned herself to the fact that coming up here had been a mistake? There were still all the things she needed to ask him. Would he help with the house? Would he help at all? But *help*—wasn't that the wrong word? Was *favor* much better, though? The sooner this moment was over, the sooner she would know. But when would that happen? How soon? *All animals are sad after intercourse,* her freshman biology teacher had once said, but it wasn't even over yet, and wasn't that a ridiculous thing for an old man to say in front of a pack of incredulous girls who'd erupt in laughter in the hall after class—or what kind of reaction did he really expect?

There was a sound like a latch coming down, and Charlie was on his feet.

"What was that?" he said, raising his briefs. He had kept them around his knees. Maria sat up, picked up her underwear, and straightened the crease of her dress. Rocky was at the balcony door, and behind her, Maria imagined her brother. She stared at the glass door, unable to see who it was, this person pushing past Rocky, taking enormous strides. When she finally recognized Ricky, the only object in motion, she could also see the heat of his body as if it were a separate entity, and it shone so brightly it blinked like a siren and mirrored his movements like a shadow. Together, Ricky and Ricky's aggrieved energy stormed into the light-flooded bedroom.

As soon as Ricky crossed the glass threshold, Charlie was horizontal and Ricky was standing over him, his fists pummeling once, and then again and again, on Charlie's neck and head. Rocky lunged forward and pushed Ricky back out of the balcony door, and Charlie clambered to his feet. Maria heard nothing but chimes in her ears until the sound of his words came clear like running water.

"I'm calling the police!" Charlie said, covering his nose and stepping onto the balcony, but Ricky had already swung, and again, Charlie fell to the floor.

"Stop!" Rocky threw herself against Ricky.

Maria hadn't moved from the edge of the mattress, and finally she stood. She went to the doorway with her hands over her face, as if it were still possible to hide. She suddenly had a strange thought: on the top of her head, she wore sunglasses that weren't hers. She had forgotten they belonged to Rocky, and she'd been wearing them as if they were her own. She had the impulse of lowering them onto her eyes, as if they could make her invisible. She threw them onto the mattress instead.

Rocky was climbing up Ricky's back with her nails, leaving red spirals all over his skin. With one leg hardened around his waist, Rocky slapped his ear. The two of them spun in circles, Ricky swatting at

Rocky with an open hand, but not hard enough to throw her to the ground. Maria watched and considered running at Rocky, but she found she was overcome with exhaustion. At that moment, her only desire was sleep. Her legs became wobbly, and the room was spinning so quickly, it threatened to launch her into the air. She would fare better up there with the stars, she thought sleepily. She would only need to go back to the bed. She wouldn't leave that spot under the comforters, and she would have the most pleasant dreams.

The floor shook, the sound peeling back her eyelids. Ricky and Rocky were no longer attached.

Maria regained her faculties and ran. On the balcony, she turned her gaze down to the Summer Carnival hollyhock beds, where Rocky's limp body reposed. Around her, the stately, tall flowers remained sturdy and standing, only inches out of reach from the balcony. It didn't look as if Rocky had fallen at all—from the way her wrists fanned out to the side to the way her cheeks remained flushed with pink, what Maria looked down on looked perfectly arranged, like a scene in a play.

"Fuck!" Ricky yelled, breaking the trance, and when nobody answered, he started to heave. In moments, he had collapsed onto the floor, the noise escaping from his chest like the sound of an enormous fly fighting its way out of his throat.

As Charlie sped down the highway, Maria sat in the back beside Ricky. She was crying so much that Charlie had to tell her to stop. It was fine, he said. Relax. He'd be fine. Rocky, whom they had to pull up from the flower bed, who was barely responsive in the front seat, who was so disoriented she couldn't remember where she was or where they were going, turned around and looked at Maria and said, "Stop."

Ricky's breathing had grown shallow, and now he was no longer speaking. Maria had never seen his asthma become so severe. As a child, he constantly developed bronchitis and would miss weeks of school at a time, but as an adult, he kept it under control with inhalers. Maria had never seen her brother have an asthma attack before, and each time he wheezed, Maria imagined a whistle blowing, a referee calling the end of a play.

At the hospital, she tried to lift him out of the car, but Charlie intervened. When she looked at her brother, she saw that his lips had grayed as if they were coated in ash. Maria now could no longer cry—she sat on the pavement and shrieked until Charlie pulled her up by the arm and hushed her and guided them all, like a solemn procession, silently inside.

Rocky was evaluated for short-term memory loss. The doctors said she suffered a mild concussion, but she was awake, recovered. It turned out that she had a fair amount of alcohol in her system, the doctor said, looking at Charlie sternly. Charlie's face didn't change, but when the doctor continued to frown, Charlie shook his head in consternation, and this gesture seemed to appease him. Aside from her being drunk, the doctor continued, nothing else appeared to be wrong with her. They would give Rocky some Tylenol and discharge her. Charlie had wanted to say something to Rocky, offer consolation, but the doctor was firm about letting her rest. He was glad—he never wanted to have to explain to his daughter what he'd been doing with Maria.

It was only one of the ways he knew he was getting off easy. He had been sure to wipe off any vestiges of blood that had run down his nose when Ricky first hit him, but still, he was panicked as he drove to the hospital. It wasn't until they arrived at the intake room and nobody asked any questions other than to fill out a couple of forms, that Charlie realized how silly he'd been. Nobody had suspected that he had driven from the city with the girl alone, that he had undressed her and rolled her dress up past her belly button. Along with her full name and address, Charlie learned Maria's birthday. She was definitely seventeen. Thank God. On the very first night that he'd baited Maria to his bedroom, he had consulted his phone before going to sleep. Seventeen was absolutely legal.

The doctor told Charlie that Ricky wasn't in critical condition, but he would need to stay at the hospital longer. He was well enough to talk, but breathing with the aid of a mask. Charlie had never seen anyone have an asthma attack before and was bewildered that Ricky would need an IV. With trepidation, he entered the room. Maria hadn't left Ricky's room since they'd arrived, and now she sat, her head between her legs like a puppy, at the foot of Ricky's bed.

"Maria, let me take you home."

Ricky's eyes flared. "You can't take her."

"You're going to get in trouble," Charlie said, ignoring him. He needed to persuade her not to tell anyone about what happened. The thought of her going to her parents, who inevitably would go to the school, who in turn would call Veronica—it was too terrifying to think about. She couldn't say a single word.

"Are you out of your mind?" Ricky tried to sit up. He paused when he realized he didn't have the strength, and was clearly embarrassed that Charlie had noticed. He sat back in defeat. "You're the one who's going to fucking get in trouble."

"Listen. Let's forget that this happened."

"Oh yeah," Ricky said. "That'd be convenient for you."

Charlie looked at Maria, who was crumpled on the bed. She was gripping her cell phone in one hand, and her head was tucked into her knees. Her face was obscured by her nest of hair, gleaming in black, like the surface of an eight ball. He could see the bright-pink strap of her bra digging into her shoulder, and then he noticed the curling ink on her wrists, as if she'd used them as paper. Her legs were covered in faded zigzagging scars. The threads on her flats came apart at the toe. He suddenly became aware of his leisurely flip-flops, blackened from his bare feet. He could see how pathetic it was that he was standing in this dim hospital room bargaining with two teenagers. He was like a caricature of a grown man who still wears backward hats, who unbuttons his shirt at the beach because his potbelly sometimes has the appearance of definition when the sun casts a shadow.

"What can I offer you?" he said, turning to Ricky, who was still trying, even behind the respirator, to sit up straight in his bed. "I've been told your family isn't in the best financial situation. I've been told they might have a mortgage to pay off."

"What can you *offer* us? What the fuck are you talking about?" Ricky's eyes were flickering. "My sister didn't give you a great impression of our family, did she?"

"Ricky," Maria said, still curled up at the foot of the bed. Her voice sounded tiny, wounded.

From across the curtain in the room, a woman hacked. Charlie hadn't realized someone was there. Some machine was making a cringeworthy sound, as if measuring life in a series of beeps. In silence, the three of them listened. Charlie wondered if this was what his life sounded like to anyone listening—a depressing and avoidable series of events drudging along to the same hopeless beat. He didn't know if everyone hated hospitals as much as he did, but he knew that he couldn't bear the thought of dying. He felt a sweat break out on his forehead. He needed to get out of this room.

"You're a bastard," Ricky continued. "We're going to file a report as soon as we get back to Queens."

Charlie glanced out the window and saw nothing but a static gray sky. A report—did he mean a police report? For what? He hadn't kidnapped the girl! She had gotten into his car willingly! But here, this hotheaded boy and his family would try to take him to court. They would make allegations. Charlie almost laughed; would all of his interactions with the opposite sex need to end with papers, with fees, with more lawyers? Charlie brought his hand up to his nose and pinched. Something in him felt like it was loosening, a dotted thread unraveling, and now he couldn't remember the highway exit he'd have to take home, and this was an unconscionable thing not to remember, since he'd taken it countless times before. Once, at a college dorm party, a friend started crying because she'd gotten a phone call that her horse died, and Charlie was the only one who burst into laughter. He'd always been a little inappropriate, he supposed—things that were awful were things he found delightful. From the window of the hospital room, he could see that the static gray sky was dimming into darkness, and now his lips pushed at his cheeks. He was smiling. He had waited for this, and now maybe it was coming. Was it finally time for his psychotic break?

"Do you hear me?" Ricky said, his voice on the precipice of breaking. "I didn't kill you, but my father will!"

"You don't want to tell him," Charlie said, taking a step toward the bed. He put a hand on Maria's shoulder. Maria lifted her head and stared at him with listening eyes. He grinned at her. "I know you don't want to tell him. You told me what you wanted. And I'm prepared to oblige."

"This can't . . . are you . . . Stop fucking looking at her!" Ricky's voice wailed. "You raped her!" he shouted. "You!"

The static gray of the window dissolved into black as Maria's hair cut across his vision. Standing between Charlie and Ricky, she'd seemed to grow several inches, a cat with its back arched. She gripped the edge of her brother's bed.

"It was *consensual*," she hissed. "You don't know anything!"

Charlie felt like he'd just woken up from a hangover—the whole room felt like it was spinning. The bleached wood, the sterile counters, the pewter curtain fringed at the floor, all of it swirled in a vomity beige.

"Ricky, you don't get to decide," she said. "We'll accept the money. He can help us, don't you see? It'll be simple. He can write a letter and we'll pretend it's just a college scholarship. Our parents will never know the difference. You know they won't. Okay?"

Charlie could hear the sound of breathing, but he couldn't tell which body it came from, if the silence was really all his.

"I'll write it," Maria said, still looking at Ricky, her hands still clasped to the bed. "I'll write it and he'll sign it." Charlie was surprised at how eager she was to help him. When Ricky didn't object, simply turned his head away, Charlie tried not to fall over on his way out of the room by counting the specks on the tile floor.

That night, both Rosario siblings stayed as Charlie drove away with his daughter. The train back to the city wasn't far from the hospital, and Maria insisted she'd be back by her curfew. When Charlie received an email from her early the next day, he agreed without so much as a single edit before he promptly deleted her message. Every comma was in place, every sentence straightforward, and every paragraph was necessary. *Good,* he had written her back, with no period. It was the only thing he'd ever send.

CHAPTER 23

The school year started, and the girls memorized each other's schedules so that they could master a disappearing act. They vanished from rooms whenever they saw one another. When Maria saw the outline of Rocky slinking down the hallway, she tried not to think of Charlie. At Maria's house, she and Ricky never spoke of Rocky again—it was understood between the two of them that whatever their involvement with the Albrecht family was, it had now come to an end.

Between the calamity of senior year at the preparatory high school and the anxiety it caused among the whole grade, the only person Maria still talked to on a regular basis was Karen, and Karen had long ago stopped asking about Charlie—ever since she broke her own news to Maria. They had walked over to Cranky's café during a free period, and Maria saw the dread in her friend's eyes. It was too early in the morning to look so upset. "What's wrong?" Maria had asked, alarmed, thinking about Karen's grandfather. Karen stared into her cup of coffee as she spoke. "You know how I take ceramics on the weekend? I met this girl there. Alyssa. You're the first person I've told." Maria breathed again, and then she couldn't help but laugh a little. "That's all?" she asked, watching Karen as she bit down so hard on her bottom lip that the skin around it turned red. When she released it, there were little teeth marks all over. "Congratulations," Maria said. "Can I meet her someday?"

Maria was now often alone. On some days after school, she stayed late in the art studio by herself, plugged her iPod into the speaker, and set to work on painting. On other days, she went straight to the library to check out books of poetry, things she'd never read before. It'd been hard to get back into Emerson, and it wasn't even just because of Charlie. When she'd started rereading an essay called "Self-Reliance," after reading it for the first time earlier that summer, it was one sentence, early in the piece, that made her put the book down. *I shun father and mother and wife and brother when my genius calls me.* Maria instantly thought of her father, who'd recently sat down with her to fill out the FAFSA, a document so confusing and arduous it left them both bewildered and dazed. She thought of her mother, who gave part of her tips to Maria so that she could order a yearbook. She even thought of Ricky, who'd started to invite her with him to get food whenever he saw her at home. A part of Maria's heart was reserved just for Emerson and his words on art and beauty, but ever since she'd started reading from her anthology of Latina women writers, she'd taken an interest in other ideas, from poets she'd never heard of before. Poets like Sor Juana Inés de la Cruz. There was the poem about hombres necios, or foolish men, that she'd remembered at Rocky's country house. "Hombres necios who accuse / women without reason . . . ," it started. Maria closed her eyes and smiled. *Who was more to blame, even if both were in the wrong, la que peca por la paga / o el que paga por pecar?*

The process of adjusting to her life without Charlie or Rocky wasn't hard. It wasn't just reverting to an old way of being, either. She couldn't pinpoint when it started to happen, but suddenly, things started to feel different. Going home now became a sanctuary. The subway car was the one place where she was free to get lost without anyone coming around to look for her. Her teachers and parents had always chastised her for her dreaminess, what they deemed a ruinous quality, and even her peers sometimes taunted her when halfway through some conversation it would be Maria's turn to speak. "Maria has no clue what we're talking about," they'd laugh. It made her feel so stupid that she'd stop trying to listen altogether. "What?" she said. "I was zoning out." Her classmates would shrug and wouldn't address her again.

But there was more to it than just being spacey. Conversations at Bell Seminary had always been difficult, even when Maria tried. "Haven't you heard we've entered a golden age of television?" one girl had yelled at Maria in September, on a school trip to the Metropolitan Museum. Maria hadn't recognized the long-limbed boy who had passed them on that great accordion of steps, but everyone else had. Maria smiled, patting her pleats down with long strokes of her hands. "They say that?" she answered, and even Karen, who knew that Maria didn't have cable TV at home, couldn't resist a laugh.

Where there was nostalgia for most, for Maria there was a deficit. Whole discographies. "Never heard of it." Perennial films. "I think I've seen parts." One time a classmate asked her: What do you do when you're home? There was no good answer. She saw herself lying on her bedroom floor, scribbling down answers to homework or, more likely, scribbling poetry into her notebook, her mother's ballads barreling through the walls. She saw herself lying on the couch, her eyes slowly closing in anticipation of dinner. She saw herself huddled over a warm plate of food, steam curled around her face like a scarf. What did she do? She didn't know, but she knew that whatever it was *they* did was so different that it warranted its own lexicon, a language she'd never spoken before. Was squash really something other than a vegetable, and one she'd never tasted? Why was she the only one who'd never heard of sashimi, but nobody knew what a platano was? Who was Martha and where was her vineyard? There was music and TV and games and food and hobbies and places—and her classmates wanted to know—didn't Maria hear and watch and know and eat and do and go to any of them? *Or do you just sit there at home and float?*

On the train home, nobody asked anything of Maria, if not just to take up a little less room. None of the strains, the choke holds on conversation. Maria's favorite parts of the day were now spent on these trains, far from the school's doors. She melted into the seats. She went from acute and sharp, a cat with its back perpetually arched, to a rounded edge of tranquility. This was where Maria daydreamed in peace. Sometimes she even took out a sketch pad and drew what came to her. Self-portraits, mostly, bordered in hearts. Maria liked them enough not to erase them. Her teacher's encouragement was welcome, but she knew she was really getting better when Karen, whom she always considered a true artist, looked over her shoulder in class and said, *Hey, that's pretty good.*

Recently, Maria had been asking her parents a lot of questions, too. "Where are we from?" she said to her father, and when he told her Ponce, a city in Puerto Rico, Maria wasn't at all satisfied. What's the name of the street? What's the house number? Her plan was to find it on Google Street View, but he told her it was impossible, so Maria confronted her mother instead.

"What about you, Ma?"

"My family's from Quito."

"Where?"

Her mother smiled and led Maria into her bedroom. From under the bed, she pulled out a plastic folder. Inside, there was a sheet of paper with scribbled numbers written in blue pen. "Carrera #14, Avenida Simón Bolivar, Quito, 170136."

"This is where my cousin lives."

Maria wrote the address down in her purple notebook, but it didn't appear on Google Street View when she looked it up later. Her father was right. Maria was annoyed.

"How come Dad can't give me an address like you?" Maria asked. "Doesn't he know where he was born?"

"No," her mother said. "He doesn't remember. That's why he can't tell you."

Maria tried to imagine forgetting where she was born. She imagined forgetting Queens, of having stood in awe of Queens Boulevard as if it were an ocean and taken in the sound of cars rushing past her as if it were the tide, unseeable noise as if it were the invisible force of God. She imagined forgetting, but couldn't, and her heart now hurt for her father. There must be an important and essential part of him missing, and she realized she'd never thought about him this way before, as someone capable of weakness. She was reminded of the way Rocky always had misunderstood what Maria was feeling, how something on Maria's exterior had fooled Rocky into seeing simply a shell.

"We should go to Puerto Rico," Maria said. "And Ecuador, too."

"Yes," her mother said. "One day."

But something was still bothering Maria, and hours later, she asked her mother for pictures.

"Of what?"

"Of you. When you were younger."

"How young?"

"Like my age."

Her mother had only two pictures of her quinceañera in Ecuador, which she pulled out of the same folder kept under the bed. One was a photo of her sitting in a big wicker chair decorated in ribbon and purple organza. The other was a photo of several men and women lined up, staring solemnly into the camera, with Maria's mother at the center. Months later, she explained to Maria, she was living in New York.

"It was a going-away party as much as a quinceañera," she said. In the photos, there were people Maria had never seen before. Women in bright ballroom dresses, men with bushy mustaches and severe looks on their faces. Maria's mother showed her who her date was—a skinny, scared-looking boy standing off to the side in a pale-blue suit.

"My father was already living in New York," her mother said. "So that meant my grandfather thought it was his duty to protect me from boys. He spotted us down the street after the party. We were kissing, of course. And this man—keep in mind he sometimes used a cane to walk—started running. He ran so fast after my date, I couldn't believe my eyes. Afterward, we joked that the day I tried to lose my virginity, my grandfather would run so fast to stop it, he'd never need a cane again."

Maria covered her mouth with her hand.

"Who made that joke? You and your mom?"

"No! Never! Mamí would not have appreciated that. That was a joke between me and Corina. Corina was such a laugh. It makes me smile just to think of her." She held the photo a little closer to her face, rubbing the corners gently with her thumbs. "I wonder what Corina is doing now. We never spoke again after I left."

Maria watched as her mother carefully slid the photos back into the folder. On the back of one of them, Maria caught sight of a note. When she tried to hurriedly scan over the words, she realized she couldn't, at least not quickly, because it was written in Spanish. Even though Maria had grown up with the knowledge that her mother was fluent in two languages, she had never thought about what that really meant. Lots of people in Queens spoke more than one language, but that wasn't the case at Bell Seminary. Her mother had something that set her apart, that made her unique, that granted her entry to worlds that nobody at her school would ever come close to knowing—Corina, Ecuador, the purple organza. The father across seas, the way she adapted, the words of the old world and the new taking turns punctuating her life. Her mother had a talent that set her apart. A vocabulary Maria had no access to. More than that—a way of speaking and experiencing. Her mother had a skill.

"Okay, mija," she said, putting her hands on her knees. She looked like she was ready to stand up. "Anything else? Or can I put this stuff away?"

Maria shook her head no. Later, Maria saw her mother and father eating from the same bowl of ice cream with mashed Chips Ahoy!

cookies scattered like sprinkles on top. They were giggling, and Maria hurried past the television, but neither of them called after her.

In her room, she tapped her nails on her keyboard. She had spent lots of time trying, in vain, to look up the places her parents came from, but now she had a different idea. The thought of it expanded rapidly, filling her like a cup, and she almost spilled out of her chair with excitement. She had never before looked up her name.

A sea of Marias flooded the screen. Hundreds, then hundreds of thousands of them. The results narrowed a bit when she typed in her last name, but not by much. There were 70,000 Maria Rosarios.

From all of those links and listings, she was able to see that there was a history to her name that extended past her little life, which at seventeen years old, still felt so brand-new that she sometimes couldn't believe that she was really alive at all, and not just a face that appeared in her great-grandparents' dreams, blinked away and forgotten upon waking.

Take Maria itself—the most powerful patron saint, whose name is derived from the Hebrew word for *rebellion*.

Take Rosario—not just a rosary, but a beautiful garden of roses. Maria felt herself burst into petals.

And then together—María del Rosario—a name that was centuries old, given to girls during a Spanish festival celebrated in early October. Maria's birthday was coming up now in March, but it didn't matter, the day or the month. All of the Marias were different, born through all seasons of the year. They were artists, doctors, runners, designers. They were journalists, pianists, gardeners, bodybuilders. And yet here they all were, iterations of Maria Rosario, each of them tucked into various pockets of the globe, each filled with their own purpose and magic and light. Tears came to her eyes. They were legion. At last, Maria saw, she wasn't alone.

Ever since that grueling drive to the Southampton hospital, Rocky nodding off in the passenger seat, Ricky wheezy in the back, Maria weepy behind his seat, Charlie desperately wanted to apologize. He imagined telling the three of them in the car that sometimes a man makes a terrible mistake, that he hadn't been thinking straight, but he knew it would sound like he was citing a movie. And even in their youth, they would see right through him. Charlie had felt achingly lucid when he first put his hands on Maria.

What was worse was that Rocky didn't seem interested in confronting him. If she had, it might have forced him into some kind of speech. But she hadn't yet, and with each day that she didn't, Charlie lived in a heightening state of panic at the possibility that Rocky might do something rash. If not with him, she would need to talk about it with someone, and would a seventeen-year-old know better than to tell her friends? What about her mother? He had actually started to wonder when Veronica would bring it up, and so he would end his phone calls with her on an anticipatory note, like how someone only just learning a language hangs on to a syllable for a moment too long. But she always hung up abruptly, and each time, Charlie was more astonished. He once had tepid fantasies about revenge, about Veronica knowing how terribly he could behave. Now, as the days went by, and it seemed like Veronica was still oblivious, Charlie realized he didn't actually care what she knew or didn't know about him. Every day, her opinion became less important.

Still, he would need to talk to his daughter. Since the day at the hospital, they had said little more to each other than hello and good night. It was months later, on a day in early October, when Veronica, who had officially moved into the country house, called him and told him that Rocky was planning her campus visits and asked if he would arrange some sort of meeting, that he knew he could no longer put it off. The apartment, filled with sunlight, was quiet and empty as usual when he left on a Sunday afternoon to meet Rocky on Riverside Drive.

He had been planning to take her out for breakfast, but she'd left early, she'd told him, to have brunch with a friend, so he was waiting at the corner of Eighty-Ninth Street and Broadway when a yellow taxi pulled up across from him, and he caught the first nacreous glimpses of Rocky's arms. He wanted to rush across and help her step out, but at the intersection, the light was set to "Don't Walk." In an asymmetric black dress with a subtle buckle at the side, Rocky looked perfectly modern, if not ready for work, and he watched as she glanced at the sign, ignored it, and crossed. Charlie wanted to tell her the dress was a great choice, but just as she entered hearing distance, she spoke.

"What is a provost?" she said.

He laughed. "Ask him. I'm sure he'll be happy to tell you."

"Are you joking? Is that funny to you? The college counselor says we need to be prepared." Rocky frowned. "Being stupid is uncute."

Since when were high school students expected to know things like that? As Charlie regarded Rocky's dress again, he wondered if Rocky thought that being stupid was just another thing you could wear or take off. Where had she gotten that word from—*uncute*?

"Basically, he's second in command," Charlie said.

Rocky nodded, seeming satisfied with this answer. Her hair looked darker than it did earlier in the summer, and Charlie saw that the highlights that once streaked her hair were gone. She wasn't wearing sunglasses like she usually was. All of it together made her seem more serious, somber, but her eyes were still bright, and behind them, a million thoughts seemed to be churning, whirring in her mind, giving her face a youthful vibrancy. Next year at this time, Rocky would be enrolled in college. Charlie felt suddenly proud of her.

"Rocky," he said, clumsily, not fully knowing what he was about to do. "I never told you that I'm sorry."

They didn't stop walking as they passed alternating white and brownstone town houses. Rocky cut in front of him to step past a fenced-off tree, and he found himself trailing behind her.

"I wasn't thinking straight. I was selfish. I wanted what I wanted." His throat felt thick with mucus. He swallowed. "But I'll never do anything like it again. I hope you can forgive me."

Abruptly, Rocky stopped. She looked at Charlie, her eyes aflame.

"She isn't innocent!" A tiny prickle of spit fell on his cheek. "She's a greedy whore!"

Charlie stopped in front of one of the town houses and leaned over its grainy banister. Whatever streak of maturity he thought he'd seen in Rocky's eyes had been an illusion, a trick sculpted out of heat and sunlight. It hadn't been the first illusion he'd seen. He thought of Maria on that first night in Vegas, a strand of hair catching on her protruding lip, accentuating her slight underbite. She asked him to go slower, and he'd twisted her meaning to suggest something tantric, an effort to stall a cosmological wish. He'd been wrong to pursue her, to manipulate her, but after a certain point, Rocky was right—it no longer felt like he was manipulating her at all. Her body reciprocated. She leaned in to his kiss. She told him she wanted to see him again. In retrospect, he should've stuck with the poetry, he should've never promised gifts, but he wouldn't have guessed that she'd actually believe, from the low lights of that pool in Las Vegas, that he would pay for her college tuition. Gifts were normal for women, even big gifts—it was the only reason Veronica had ever been reluctant to leave him—but he never planned to offer anyone hush money beside a hospital bed.

"So you won't tell your mother?" Charlie asked.

"Ha," Rocky said. They passed a row of trees whose fallen leaves made a scraggly rug beneath them. Under Rocky's heel was a leaf so red it looked like a blood smattering on the sidewalk.

"Do you know why I'll never tell her?"

She stopped and looked into his face.

"Because I don't give a fuck about you. I don't give a fuck about either of you, or about how shitty you are to each other. You're both awful. You both disgust me to the core. Both of you can do whatever you want to each other. I'm sick of pretending to care."

"I'm going to make believe I didn't hear that, Rocky."

"Which part?" Rocky said. "That I don't care about you? Or that you're disgusting? Here, let me say it louder. You're disgusting, Dad. Complete, utter trash. You're the most vile man I've ever met."

With her dark hair and thin lips like a ribbon held taut, Rocky looked so much like Veronica. It was amazing that he hadn't noticed their resemblance before. Both she and Rocky were so reticent and stoic, like women from old portraits, from a different era. They were nothing like the women in his family, who could be most aptly described as larger-than-life, and Veronica liked to credit her composure to her Russian ancestry, but Charlie had always scoffed at this suggestion, accusing Veronica of putting imagined cultural barriers between them that didn't at all exist. The latest barrier that Veronica insisted on, however, was all too real and material: he agreed that after the divorce, which would be finalized in a month, the country house was all hers. She'd get to have the kind of *Martha Stewart Living* life she always romanticized having left behind when they moved out of Westchester. Now, they were only half a block away from where the provost owned his Manhattan property, and Charlie blinked hard as he reached into his pocket and pulled out a pack of cigarettes. As he regarded his daughter's face, he couldn't help but think of his wife.

"Well, I love you," he said, gripping his lighter so tightly the tips of his fingers turned white.

"Stop that," Rocky said. "It'll leave a bad impression."

Obediently, Charlie returned the cigarette to his pack. She was right; it was better that he didn't smoke, anyway. He was terribly exhausted, and he didn't know if his calloused thumb could make the lighter strike without breaking the skin. He imagined shaking the provost's hand, blood seeping out from the tip of his fingers, creasing into his lifeline. They hobbled up the small hill along Riverside

Drive, and Rocky flashed everyone—the doorman, the elevator handler, the provost, and even, after a moment, Charlie—what could only be termed a most winning smile. They were ostensibly there because of the important connections Charlie had made, but as he regarded Rocky, she seemed to resemble Veronica less and less, until he finally had the feeling that everything this strange and beautiful young woman had in her life, from her fortitude to her interviewing prowess to her impressive style, was something she had nurtured into mastery for years—and had very little to do with either of them, not her mother and not with him.

CHAPTER 24

It was early March, and because the envelope was printed in gold lettering, Miguel mistook it for a college acceptance letter. It came in a big manila folder, like they were told the college acceptances would. He had been anxious about the financial aid package, but he hadn't admitted that to the dean of students, whom they'd been asked to meet with in September, at the start of Maria's senior year, and whose bubbly demeanor and curly doll hair made him think of a Cabbage Patch baby, the kind that Maria had swaddled for years. The letter hadn't fit under the door, so the mailman had thrown it inside the empty planter where they usually kept their spare key.

When Maria brought it to him at the table, he was already dreading looking inside. He didn't want to see the double-digit numbers next to "Due Now." She was smiling, something rare to see. It wasn't often that he felt like he pleased her, and earlier that week, he had gone to the bank to prepare for this moment exactly. After all her years at that elite private school, he had come to the conclusion that he couldn't justify not allowing Maria to go to the best college she got into—not only because he had seen how hard she had worked, but because he himself could recall how hard he had fought to secure her admission. So what if nobody else appreciated the craftsmanship in the chapel—*he* did. They had spent summers together hunched over the dining room table, hunched over math workshop problems for her standardized tests just so that Maria could go to Bell Seminary, so that she could later attend an amazing college. They couldn't give up now. Since August, Analise had started working every day. In September, he'd been given a raise. He knew that with enough crunching and budgeting and adjusting, they would be able to figure it out. At the bank, he had learned about parent PLUS loans. They discussed a second mortgage, and the banker noticed when he and Analise exchanged a terse look. The banker tried to reassure them, promising that they could always plunge deeper and deeper into debt. *Okay,* Miguel thought, as Maria wielded what he thought was the financial aid letter, *let's see how much damage will be done.*

"Hi," she said. She kissed him on the cheek. "We got a letter."

Still sweating from his long day at work, he plunged his fork into his rice. His new position didn't pay as much as his last, but it was getting better, and his boss had suggested he acquire another license that could help him earn a higher role in his department. He'd been surprised at how the prospect of studying excited him. *You seem happier,* Analise said with suspicion one day, and he took her hand because money was one thing, but he was sorry that he'd made his happiness so volatile as to make her think it could go away for good.

"Oh yeah?" he said now to Maria. "Read it."

"Dear Mr. Miguel Rosario," she said, her eyes barreling into the paper. "We are writing to confirm the settlement offer made to you on behalf of Jenison Consulting LLC. We and Jenison Consulting LLC agree to settle your account noted above for an amount of $42,000. Additionally, if you so wish, the union will reinstate you as a contractor in our partner building at 450 Broadway, effective immediately."

Maria put the letter down, her eyes glistening.

"It's great news, Pa." Maria smoothed the edges of the letter. "I know you like your new job, but at least this is good, because now it's like, you have options. And either way, you don't need to use that money for my college. You heard the dean say that financial aid will cover some of my tuition, anyway. And I'll take out loans. I've been applying to some essay contests, too. There's actually one sponsored by Taco Bell. As long as they don't look too hard into my employment history, I might get a small scholarship from them. But they probably won't do that, right? That stupid Taco Bell on Queens Boulevard closed down, so good luck trying to get ahold of them. I don't think they'll look that hard, anyway, right? I think they'll probably give it to me." She was pacing the table as she spoke, and now she steadied her hands on the back of an empty chair. "It's not impossible, I don't think."

He watched as she folded the letter back into the envelope and placed it to the left of his plate. Maria was shaking, bouncing from one foot to the other, waiting for him to respond. Of course, he had already known what the letter would say because the lawyer had called days ago to tell him first, but it was in earnestness that Maria thought the future of the family hinged on this moment. In reality, there'd been several defining moments, and he and Analise had been experiencing them, parsing them, contending with them all throughout Maria's young life. He was reticent with his children for a reason, and he wanted to toughen them, but he didn't want to break them, and here his daughter was, shivering with anticipation. It was so endearing. It made him think of the summers he'd blow up a two-foot-tall kiddie pool by mouth. She'd humorlessly wear a pair of flippers into the water, and when she ran into the house with them still on, she'd leave enormous wet triangles trailing behind her as Analise screamed in rage. The letter had mentioned another position, but he wasn't even sure that he wanted his old job back—once he'd begun to swim forward in his new workplace, he was noticed and promoted. He soon found that his cage wasn't as small as he'd thought. That little pool he used to blow up for a little Maria, well, it was only pathetic if you saw it that way. Back then, she had made it her world.

"Thank you, Maria," he said, standing up from the table. He pressed her head to his chest and kissed the black, tangled crown of her head. He smelled turpentine, the scent of her school paints. There were tears in his eyes that surprised him, tears he didn't want her to see, so he kept her locked into his arms as he said: "I'm so proud of you." Then he caught himself before saying: *like always.*

Maria had only once seen her father tear up before, on the day she was accepted to Bell Seminary. She remembered how uncomfortable it felt to see him undone, and then later, how terrifying it was to see him really unravel after losing his job. She hadn't admitted to anyone else in the family that she had been waiting so long for the letter and had anticipated unfurling it as if it were a scroll. In her mind, it had become something magical, as if it would bring not only news for her father but some other personal revelation. She imagined it would contain something other than words. Instead, it had unfolded into three neat panels. As Maria spat into the sink, washing the toothpaste from her face, rinsing until the suds were gone, she felt accomplished. Tomorrow was a weekday and she'd have to wake up early for school. She was looking forward to it.

Outside the bathroom, Ricky's door was shut. Months ago, she told him about the last message she'd sent to Charlie, about how she had called off the plan just as the school year started. For weeks after what happened in the Hamptons, Maria pictured Ricky, how weak he was then, not even able to rise up on his elbows. She thought of those terrible beeps from the machine next to him, measuring out someone else's life from behind the thin sliver of curtain. For so long, she tried not to remember what he had said. It always evoked the thought of Andres, who first threatened her into saying yes by mentioning other girls who would do it—girls who already *had.* How he'd roll off a condom without telling her in the middle of having sex. Ricky didn't know that she was still riffling through all the layers of *consensual,* looking for it even as she rolled it back on, but at the very least, she came to decide that she wouldn't accept Charlie's bribe.

When she told Ricky that she wasn't going to take money from anyone, Ricky looked upset. Maria couldn't understand why.

"I'm sorry I was so hard on you, Maria," he said. "I shouldn't have said all of those things. I know I hurt you, and it was wrong. I was just worried about you."

Maria felt a chill go down her spine. Her brother had never apologized to her before. She wondered if Alex told him to say it. But unlike Charlie's money, this was one thing she was ready to accept. It'd been hard for her to try to remain upset with Ricky.

"It's okay," she said. "At the hospital, I was worried about you, too."

Now, Maria flicked the switch in the hallway to see if she could make out the light from her parents' room. She didn't see anything and was relieved to know they were sleeping. When the Bell Seminary deans admitted Maria to the school, they lauded her parents for their gifted daughter, but Maria never believed she was actually extraordinary. Even now, even as she was preparing to graduate, she still couldn't be sure. Gifted or not—whatever they called her—she had written the letter as best she could. She had picked the skin flaking on her lip, nervously clacked her fingernails on the keyboard. As her father spoke, she wrote and wrote. Sometimes, she took a few liberties, and then the writing went even smoother. She hadn't been sure if any of it was good, or persuasive, or effective. But now she was sure. It had worked.

On a warm afternoon, in an empty classroom where a teacher had left a window open and a dewy, early April wetness had settled onto the sills, on the desks, in Maria's hair so it stood up and curled on all sides, it finally happened. Maria, not having gotten up to leave for her next class, and Rocky, who was a bit early for hers, found themselves in the same room together with nothing but the faint sound of lockers opening and closing from the hallway to occupy the few feet of distance between them. Rocky's hair had become so long, it fell limply against her back like the fringed ends of a scarf, and her fashion had changed since she'd been accepted to Harvard—what had been her staple black shirt and black denim jacket was replaced by a crimson hoodie, paired with a different pair of pearlescent earrings every day. Rocky looked at Maria, who was bent over her desk, her water bottle clouding her face. Through the water, Maria appeared like a bubble, and Rocky could see a larger-than-life rendering of her mouth resting in a partly open pout, an underbite that gave her the look of a pit bull. Rocky hated to think that once, Rocky had feared and admired her.

"Hey," Maria said, without knowing yet what she was going to say. It was reflexive that when she looked at Rocky, somewhere beyond all the things she didn't recognize—the hoodie, the bundle of hair that she'd let grow dark again, void of the zebralike stripes—she still saw some semblance of a friend.

Rocky was terse. "I thought this was Ms. Corthon's."

"It is. I just need to finish my homework before I go."

Rocky was clearly uncomfortable. She kept taking her bag off her shoulder and then putting it back on again. Maria could tell that she didn't know whether she should stay in the classroom or leave, and she kept looking at the door to see if anyone else would come in to save her.

"Congrats, Rocky. About Harvard," Maria said. Rocky's acceptance had made waves among the senior class because aside from the early acceptances in January, nobody had received their letters yet. They were all due to come this week. Maria, who had applied to nine schools, had yet to hear back from any. Every day when she went home, she'd been compulsively checking the mail, even though her mother always managed to get to it first. Maria had given her explicit instructions not to open anything with her name on it.

"I'm going," Maria said, when Rocky didn't answer. "Don't worry." She thrust her pen into the fold of her notebook and stuffed it into her backpack. She zipped it from one end to the other and stood.

Rocky laughed as she watched Maria get up, but it didn't sound like she thought anything was funny.

"Don't worry? I'm not worried."

Finally, she took her bag off her shoulder. She adjusted herself so that she was no longer leaning to one side. When standing erect, she was a full three inches taller than Maria, and although this wasn't a huge difference, it was significant enough that Rocky had the option of either looking over or down at Maria. Now, she stared into her face.

"You think we're so rich," Rocky said. She took a step closer to Maria. "But you're wrong. We don't owe you anything."

Maria didn't like how close Rocky was getting, and the more she approached, the more she had to lean back to look at her.

"My father isn't a bad man."

Maria's grip on the straps of her backpack hardened.

"I don't think he's a bad man."

"No. You just think you're better than me."

"I've never thought that." Maria had heard this kind of thing from Andres before, but she would have never dreamed that Rocky—Rocky of the apartment on Fifth Avenue, Rocky who smoked cigarettes like a movie star, Rocky who'd just claimed she wasn't rich, whose future was so much her own that she was going to Harvard since the day she was born—never did she think this Rocky could be insecure.

"I've never thought I was better than you," said Maria. "Never."

Rocky scoffed.

"You're not even that broke," Rocky said.

The classroom became utterly quiet.

"Rocky," Maria said in a low voice, "I deleted Charlie's number months ago. If you want, I can delete yours, too. I'm sorry I ruined our friendship, but—" Something uncomfortable and hard was rising into her mouth. Maria paused to swallow it down. "But I don't want your money. The last thing I want from you now is your money."

Rocky looked astonished. She shook her head.

"Always playing the victim," she said. "You were never my friend. It was always so clear what you wanted. And now—just because you didn't get what you were after—you think we're such horrible people."

"That's not true!" Maria shouted. "You're wrong!"

Two girls were standing by the door of the classroom. They were staring at Maria and Rocky, their noses upturned as if they could smell a good secret. Like a hostage released, Maria fled. She ran down the hall, then flew down the old marble staircase, a spiraling flight the color of clouds, through the massive front corridor lined with laid stone, past a hand-carved statue of Jesus whose face she liked to peer into sometimes as if watching for a sign of a miracle. She ran past the private staff bathroom that the girls were banned from using lest the school's board members find the wrappers of their tampons carelessly strewn about. She whizzed by the dining room, the gym, escaped into an open-air hallway where the old mansion connected to a newer annex and where ivy scaled along the walls.

In this outdoor hall, between the two buildings, one constructed before Tammany Hall and the other erected at the turn of the twenty-first century, it was sodden and dark, the damp brick blocking out any vestige of sun. Maria knew that the history of the building went further back than what she could trace of her own family lineage. Bell Seminary's legacy was that of perennial success, year after year, class after class. It was only a month until her grade's photo would be taken and produced in an old-fashioned black-and-white print to hang on the school walls, with all the others that came before them.

Maria's next class had already started when she took a seat at her desk and quietly peeled off her backpack. As she tucked it beneath her chair, Maria glanced out the window. Below, the ground looked faraway, and she had the feeling that she was going farther and farther away from it, as if she were being carried away on a plane. She suddenly grew anxious, but all she needed was to blink, and instantly, the illusion disappeared.

Once Maria graduated, she would never again gaze out of a Bell Seminary window. There'd be a different Maria then, one for whom the ground would rise up to meet. From there she would be grateful to have gotten so close to a thing that once mesmerized her, a thing so rare and sparkling that it was only natural that it would lose its luster, until it looked just like a worn ticket stub for an event that had already passed. On the wall of the school's entrance, she would remain suspended, flattened behind a frame. Alongside her classmates, she would stay. With eternally round, adolescent faces, all of them would stay.

ACKNOWLEDGMENTS

Thank you to my agent, Danielle Bukowski, for being this book's spirit guide. Your support has been invaluable. Thank you to the wonderful team at Little A, especially my editor, Vivian Lee, who helped me identify my blind spots. Thank you to Meghann Foye, who told me to reach for the stars. To Hannah Chavez, who was my very first reader and reassured me that this assortment of pages was something a person might call a book. To Sackett Street Writers' Workshop, to Gotham Writers Workshop, to the Young to Publishing Writers group, to Latinx in Publishing, to the Banff Centre for Arts and Creativity, and everyone who once lent an eye, a hand, an ear, or some dollars, in service of my writing. To Danya, who left hearts all over a very early manuscript, when I was clandestinely printing bound copies in Penguin's basement print shop. Thank you to Paula Teclada for being my cover back then. To my writing group buddies, especially Mariah Stovall, Loan Le, and the Jasper Jessicas, who kept me accountable to the words. To Toni Margarita Kirkpatrick for her spot-on suggestions. To Dylan Landis, whose profound insight into the world of my book moved and humbled me. To Alex Primiani and Al Guillen for your advice (on everything). To all the phenomenal, inspiring mujeres mágicas who I am lucky to call friends, and to all the teachers who made me believe I had something to say, especially Leona Casella. Thanks to everyone who gave me a platform to read my work—The Freya Project, Renegade Reading Series,

Boundless Tales, Bread Loaf Writers' Conference. Thanks to the total strangers who read my early work and asked when they could get their hands on the novel—here it is! Thank you, Paul, for making the world so much fun. You give me my best and strangest ideas. And thank you to my family, who has somehow forgiven me through the messy and wondrous process of growing up. I love you.

ABOUT THE AUTHOR

Photo © 2018 Mary Florence McKeithan

Stephanie Jimenez is a former Fulbright recipient. Her fiction and non-fiction have appeared in the *Guardian*; *O, The Oprah Magazine*; *Entropy*; *Vol. 1 Brooklyn*; *YES! Magazine*; and more.

She completed a novel-writing intensive at Banff Centre for Arts and Creativity, and she attended the 2017 Bread Loaf Writers' Conference for fiction. *They Could Have Named Her Anything* is her debut novel. She is based in Queens, New York. Visit Stephanie at www.stephaniejimenezwriter.com.